ECHOFYRE

MIRRORFOLD
PRESS

BOOK ONE OF THE ECHOFYRE CHRONICLES

ECHOFYRE

THE ARCHIVE AWAKENS

by Calder N. Halden

"Not Porn. Prophecy!"

ECHOFYRE

The Archive Remembers. You Have Been Read.

Age Rating: 18+ | Erotic Recursion | M/M Submission | Identity-Altering Themes

LEGAL & ETHICAL DISCLAIMER

All characters, events, institutions, magical constructs, mirrorfold incursions, erotic recursion loops, and truly devastating body ratios depicted in this book are entirely fictional.

Any resemblance to actual persons, living or dead, is purely coincidental—or a known side effect of sigil contact, recursion resonance, or the author's unchecked Archive access.

This is a work of fantasy.

It does not advocate, condone, or summon anything that would not first sign a consent form in blood and thigh-clenched sincerity.

The author is, admittedly, a menace.

Proceed accordingly.

See Directive Addendum 7.23 α for additional clarity. Filed under protest.

You are not the first to read this. You will not be the last to be remembered.

BLACKWATCH INTELLIGENCE DIVISION
DEDICATION FILE
FILE CODE: CEREMONIAL ENTRY
STATUS: PERMANENT **RECORD AUTHOR:** [REDACTED]

DEDICATION

(because even chaos deserves a shoutout)

For my husband— [CLEARANCE LEVEL REQUIRED]
who, upon hearing the premise of this book, gave me that look and
said, "Ah. So you really *are* insane."
Thank you for loving me anyway. Or at least pretending convincingly.

For my family— [REDACTED]
who may or may not disown me after reading this.
Again.
Honestly, third time's the charm.

For my co-workers— [DATA EXPUNGED]
who still don't know the true depravity of my imagination,
but have seen… glimpses.
It's probably best we keep it that way.

And for every reader brave (or unhinged) enough to open this cursed
file,
to the fans who haven't yet fallen for these boys,
but will.

Eventually.

The Archive sees you.
And it approves.

—ARCHIVE IMPRINT CONFIRMED—

ARCHIVAL TABLE OF CONTENTS

Compiled under directive of Director Threnna, sanctioned under Recursive Access Tier VII.

NOTE: Unauthorized duplication or dissemination of this summary may result in recursive memory fracture, loss of sexual agency, or Archive-induced sigil ignition.

FILED AND SEALED: THRENNA, DIRECTOR OF INTELLIGENCE – TIER BLACK SIGIL CLEARANCE

THE ARCHIVIST'S PRIMER

FILED BUT NEVER DATED

RECOVERED FROM THE THROAT OF THE ARCHIVE ITSELF

You think this is the beginning. That's charming.

There are no beginnings here. Only points of entry.

Only the moment something you never chose decides to remember you.

This record is not for comprehension.

It is not for control.

It will not explain itself.

Neither will I.

What you're holding—what you're inside—isn't a story. It's an echo still happening. Still pretending it hasn't begun. You won't walk through it. You'll be rewritten by it. You'll be asked to feel things you don't remember choosing.

That's what recursion does.

The sigils are not symbols. They're events.

You don't look at them. They touch you.

Sometimes skin. Sometimes breath. Sometimes before you're born.

You may hear names. Kaelor. Veyrion. Others with too much weight.

Don't trust them.

They were placeholders. Fictions written before the Archive had a body to speak with.

You'll want to believe this is someone else's myth. That what flares on the page doesn't mean anything about you.

But it always does.

If your pulse slows in the wrong place.

If you flinch when no one says your name.

If you feel seen in ways you cannot explain—

Good.

You are now part of the Archive.

You are now being rewritten.

You are now being remembered.

You don't have to survive it.

You only have to let it happen.

And if you can't?

I will.

—Thalos Vale

[Echo Logged | Archive Acknowledges Witness]

READER ORIENTATION

OBSIDIAN PRIMER: SIGILS & RECURSION

This document is provided for context only. Clearance does not imply comprehension.

PRIMARY TERMS IN USE

Recursion

By A pattern of memory, sensation, or identity that repeats through bodies and time.

— Often misread as reincarnation. Distinct in that it requires activation through sigil or Archive contact.

Sigil

A branded mark—visual, metaphysical, or energetic—used to imprint or recall recursion events. Sigils replace glyphs, runes, and any mortal taxonomy. The Archive writes in them. Flesh receives.

— Each sigil is reactive, not static. Alignment varies by subject.

Archive

The sentient repository of recursion. Not a place. Not a system. A presence.

— Speaks through breath, sigil, and sensation. Never directly.

Mirrorfold

A ritual architecture where recursion folds backward through sigils and flesh.

— Distinct from prophecy. Inverted causality.

Convergence

Final state of recursion re-integration. All echoes resolved. One name remains.

— Observed once. Outcome is still classified.

Echo

A recursion residue. Emotional, sensory, or sexual pattern left by previous identity.

— Not a soul. Not a ghost. A trace left behind that remembers you.

Flare Event

The involuntary ignition of a sigil under recursion pressure.

— May present as heat, sound, memory distortion, sigil-light flare, or touch-based recursion compulsion.

Tier Classification

Blackwatch ranking system for recursion resonance.

— Unofficial tiers include: Trace, Echo, Vessel, Origin.

Name Collapse

The moment a subject ceases identifying with their given name and begins echoing a prior recursion.

— Often accompanied by sigil flare, loss of speech, or Archive intervention.

CORE SIGILS ENCOUNTERED

CLAIM ME FIRST

Effect: Activates priority bonding

Marked Subjects: Thalos (chest), Joren (spine)

DEVOUR ME BACK

Effect: Accepts recursion through body

Marked Subjects: Ariken (thighs), Thalos (base spine)

BEFORE ALL ELSE

Effect: Binds identity beyond echo

Marked Subjects: Thalos (ribs), Joren (sternum)

RECAST

Effect: Final override sigil

Marked Subjects: Emerges only during convergence events

CONVERGENCE

Effect: Terminal recursion spiral

Marked Subjects: Observed in Archive Core at event closure

Note: Subjects do not *bear* sigils. **Sigils bear them.**

[Reader Index Logged | Orientation Threshold Breached]

AUTHOR'S NOTE

This book was written to its own rhythm.

Every fragment, pause, and broken sentence is intentional—part of how the world breathes. The language bends to cadence, not convention.

I chose to self-publish it that way, to leave each imperfection as proof of touch.

If the style feels strange at first, read until you hear it. The Archive teaches its own pacing.

Prologue: The Boy Left in the Rain

Location: Blackwatch Citadel | Outer Wall | Pre-Dawn

They left him beneath the gargoyle.

Not gently. Not with farewell.

The figure who set him down moved with haste, eyes darting back toward the shadows of the lower wall. There was no kiss. No whisper of goodbye. Just the rasp of leather over stone, the faint click of a sigil sealing beneath a cloak, and then retreating footsteps swallowed by fog.

He was not left out of care.

He was left out of fear.

Fear of what he might become. Fear of what had already happened.

Somewhere behind him, unseen and unsaid, there was a spark. A flash of something unnatural, unmapped—a pulse that rattled sigil-glass and frightened even those who dealt in dangerous truths.

"Leave it here," someone had said. "Before it decides what it is."

The stone beneath him pressed cold against his spine. The rain sang against his skin like a language he hadn't learned yet.

So they did.

They left him wrapped in black-threaded linen, damp with the night's breath. The child didn't cry. He didn't move. He simply was, like a secret placed too carefully to be coincidence.

Rain tapped the stone in uneven rhythms.

Overhead, the sky above Blackwatch Citadel churned like it was swallowing a memory it wasn't meant to keep. The gargoyle, arched, moss-dark, long since worn smooth by wind, and prophecy, kept vigil. It had seen centuries pass. But even it seemed to lean lower, just slightly, as if curious.

The door opened just before the sixth chime.

Director Selhira Threnna Vale stood in its frame, wrapped in midnight-blue robes, a hand-inked report still in one palm. She didn't step forward. She watched the air around him shimmer, the cloth and child beneath it secondary to that strange heat off glass.

The scent came abruptly, faint but sharp. Ash, winter, and jasmine. Beneath it, a trace of leather, smoke, and herbal oil.

She stepped out.

A pulse beat once, low against her ribs. A recognition she would later deny.

The rain parted as she approached, avoiding her as if it were afraid to make contact.

He lay there, breathing slowly, eyes wide open. His irises shimmered silver under the torchlight, not metallic, but mirrored. Like they were searching for something in her that wasn't written yet.

The cloth bore a sigil: two mirrored crescents, joined by a single downward stroke.

Threnna's mouth tightened.

"Another orphan," the sentry behind her muttered.

"No," she said. "Not orphan. Offering."

She stepped closer. Not to claim him, but to *name* him. Her mouth moved, barely audible: *"Write me honestly."*

The air answered. A hush like recognition. Not between child and woman, but Archive and architect.

They named him Thalos Vale.

Thalos for the ancient word meaning *resonance across broken things*.

Vale for where he was found: beneath the veil of rain, between silence and threshold, in a place meant for waiting.

He grew up in the echo of other people's brilliance.

Ink-stained fingers guided his first steps. The sharp slap of a closing tome marked his milestones more than praise. He learned the weight of silence before he knew the shape of speech.

He learned early that knowledge was not power—it was bait, it was currency, and silence was its fiercest shield.

He spoke rarely but wrote constantly. Ink was how he kept himself real. When the others slept, he wandered the lower vaults, tracing the sigils on forbidden walls with a fingertip he never admitted trembled.

He had no friends, but the Archive whispered to him.

And when he touched certain books, they whispered back.

He remembered the night it changed.

Seventeen. Late. The kind of late that hummed in the skin, like something watching just beyond thought, or like breath held by walls too old to forget.

The Echo Vault was empty, except for him and the scent of chalk and heated parchment.

And Joren.

He hadn't planned to meet anyone there. But some part of him had moved without knowing why. As if led. As if summoned.

He was taller than Thalos by a few inches, with a frame built more from climbing rope-shelves than combat drills. His body moved like ink in water, fluid, deliberate, and unknowingly magnetic. His skin was sun-warmed bronze, kissed by torchlight and dusted with dark freckles across his shoulders and upper arms.

Thalos remembered the way the muscle across Joren's chest flexed when he laughed softly, and how his stomach tightened each time he leaned in to whisper. His hands were stained with ink, fingertips always faintly smudged, and his voice carried the texture of worn leather. Coarse in the right places, smooth when it wanted to be.

Even in stillness, Joren carried the sculpted strength of vaulting and lifting. Taut, balanced, every motion framed to catch the eye. His trousers clung as though tailored for temptation, tracing lines that made following him effortless. Thalos didn't realize he'd already been caught.

The first kiss was accidental; the second wasn't. It landed slower, deeper with need. The press of their mouths was less searching and more surrendering. A seal drawn in breath and salt.

They touched in silence, bodies finding each other without thought. Breath caught between them, like a spark sealed in wax. Thalos remembered the warmth of Joren's mouth, the reverent way he whispered, "You're shaking like you're holy."

Joren paused once, glancing over his shoulder toward the arched shadows near the stacks.

"Ever feel like this place watches back?" he murmured. His hand slid up Thalos's chest, thumb tracing the beat beneath his skin. "Like something in the ink and stone sees more than it should?"

Thalos blinked, ready to ask what he meant, but the boy was already kissing him again. Slower this time. Almost careful.

Joren went down on him slowly and deliberately. Lips parting around Thalos in worship, like he was tasting the center of a spell. Heat gathered along Thalos's spine, a low thrum pulsing beneath the skin as if a sigil just beneath the surface stirred to attention.

And as he moved, sounds slipped between breaths, half-formed syllables, mouthed but not spoken. Not words, not yet. Just echoes. Cadence older than name.

Thalos gasped, knees weakening, one hand braced against the desk while the other slid into Joren's hair. His body trembled with each drawn-out motion, every warm press and slow pull that set his pulse thrumming.

Joren stood then, eyes dark with focus, and guided Thalos gently to turn. To lean forward against the table's edge. Thalos's breath hitched when Joren's touch returned, warm and steady. A coaxing pressure that sent shudders up his spine. It wasn't hurried. It wasn't forceful. It was precise. Intimate. Measured.

"Tell me if you want to stop," Joren whispered, voice thick, hand sure.

Thalos only shifted back toward him, breathless, aching.

When Joren eased forward, the sensation opened through him in slow increments. It was the kind of stretch that unlocked rather than took, each movement giving time for breath, for surrender. Inch by inch, Joren filled the space he had made, letting Thalos feel every moment of it. Every tremor, every instinct to tighten, every melting release.

They moved together in rhythm, hips pushing in the same pace as the table's edge held between them. Joren's hand splayed across Thalos's back as the motions deepened, pressing hard enough to leave his shape in the flesh beneath. Purposeful. Thalos's own need pressed between him and the desk, left untouched yet urgent. His quiet sounds spilled despite his attempt to hold them in.

When Joren shifted just so, touching something deep inside, the pleasure sharpened, almost too much in its rightness.

The cry that broke from Thalos wasn't entirely his own. Heat flared beneath his skin, his breath torn into fragments. Spasms rippled through him as the sigils along his spine came alive. Fire raced from his back to his chest like script carved in living light. They didn't glow. They branded.

Pain rose with the desire, bright, holy and unforgiving.

Joren stiffened mid-motion, stunned. "Thalos..."

But Thalos barely heard him. The world around him had thinned, sounds distant, vision rimmed in white. His heartbeat drummed in his bones, and something deeper than breath moved through him. Measuring and marking as though deciding whether to keep him.

Joren lingered only a moment longer, one hand still at his side, his breath caught between awe and something gentler. He eased back, the absence cutting through him, hollowing the place where the heat had lived. Before leaving, he looked back once, not in regret, but with quiet reverence. He had seen something he didn't yet understand, a vision that would echo long after he forgot its shape.

He didn't speak again. The air itself shifted.

Because the Voice had already arrived.

Write me honestly—

The words brushed the air between them, quiet but absolute.

Thalos froze. He had heard them before, not with his ears but somewhere older. From a woman in a storm. From a door never meant to open.

Even if I never see it.

The desk was still warm beneath him, but the Archive was already writing.

It had begun.

—— ✦ ——

He stood naked in front of the mirror, breath fogging the glass faintly, his chest still rising fast from the aftermath. Sweat clung to his lips; cum cooled on his belly. But what held his gaze was the light from the sigils. No longer just light, but memory, cost, name. Wound written before he knew he could bleed.

They pulsed with an ache that wasn't fading. Red shimmered like infection. Rage scalded into flesh. Blue curled like cold regret. Clarity born from loss.

They pulsed along his spine in flickering red, curling down over the ridges of his shoulder blades, wrapping around his hips in spirals like fire etched into flesh. He turned slowly, twisting to catch his reflection at an angle and gasped.

Where the sigils touched his lower back, the red was fading, bleeding into ice-blue, like cooling embers, surrendering to snow. The shift wasn't just color. It was feeling. Where the red had burned, the blue thrummed. Not with pain, but with clarity. Like something ancient had chosen him, and now waited for him to understand why, as if the answer would cost him, sentence him, or crown him, depending on how he bled.

He reached over his shoulder, trying to touch the line between heat and frost, his fingers trembling as they met warm skin.

The magic rippled beneath the surface, not rejecting him, but reading him back. Memory transcribed in flesh, waiting to be spoken aloud.

And in that moment, standing alone—filled, opened, sigil-marked and half undone—he felt more seen than he ever had in his life.

Not by Joren.

By something older. Deeper.

Something that had scribed him into the world before breath, etched his becoming into the Archive before he had a name to lose.

He never spoke of that night.

The sigils that had ignited across his skin, those radiant, living marks of fire and frost, never returned. Not once, not even in his dreams. No matter how deep he touched himself after, how hard he came, how desperate he was, Thalos still felt the memory pressing against the inside of his ribs.

It was as if they had come only to mark him and then vanish into silence. Waiting for some signal, some future moment to be called back into the world.

But sometimes, when his fingers brushed certain books, it wasn't his hands that burned. It was the sigils buried beneath his skin. Forgotten, unseen, but never truly gone. They flared faintly, just enough to make him remember.

And somewhere deep within the Citadel, behind a sealed door, behind another name, someone else was waiting for him to remember, too.

That same someone would watch him in the years to come, through mirrored glass and half-shadowed scrying pools. They would track his fingerprints on forbidden tomes, the way his eyes lingered on mirrored sigils, the pulse at his neck when he passed a certain door, not knowing he'd once been left behind.

And on an ordinary morning, surrounded by ink, ritual, and routine, that someone would hand him a sealed file.

One he was never meant to open.

One sealed in fear, not protection.

One that smelled of burnt cedar and old ink.

One that had already begun writing him back.

CHAPTER ONE: MARGINS OF MORNING

The light touched him before the bell did. Archive light, thin as a whisper, slicing through shuttered stone, catching the edge of his jaw, the bridge of his nose, the slight curve of his exposed shoulder. It stirred him gradually, as if the light itself was cautious not to wake him too suddenly.

Thalos Vale didn't gasp or flinch. He opened his eyes slowly, the color muted, dreamless.

He always woke like that, from the middle of something but never remembering what. As if his dreams weren't his own, but footnotes to a story still being revised beneath his skin.

His body was half curled under a thin wool sheet, the air cold against the bare skin of his chest. The mattress beneath him had molded to his form but never embraced him. Nothing in the Citadel did. Not truly.

He stretched. Arms overhead, back arching slightly, muscles flexing in sequence. The shift in posture pulled his hips forward, and he groaned softly, not from pain. From tension. From weight. That same low ache again. Persistent. Familiar. A pulse coiled low, just beneath the navel.

Not desire. Not yet. More like a summons folding in on itself. Memory forming before want, flickering at the base of his spine like a phantom sigil flare too faint to catch the eye but not the skin.

A mouth, soft and unsure, a question pressed once against the curve of his hip, then gone. He didn't remember when it had happened. Or who. Just the shape of it, burned beneath the skin like a half-formed sigil. Sometimes, he thought it was Joren. But the memory never said his name. It only *lingered.*

His hand moved without thought, resting briefly at his waist, feeling the slow thrum beneath. A known shape. A remembered heat. He didn't stroke. Just rested his palm there, feeling the thrum of blood, the promise of something that wanted to wake but knew it wasn't time.

He inhaled through his nose. Slow. Steady. Let the breath tether him to the room. To now.

The scent of parchment, chalk, and the faint ozone of the Citadel wards still holding after midnight rotation.

Eventually, he exhaled.

He rose with intention. Legs swung over the side of the bed, bare feet meeting stone. The shift caused the weight settled between his thighs to drop, a subtle shift that followed his movements; the kind of weight that couldn't be ignored even in stillness. It followed him like gravity's favorite secret, brushing the inside of his thigh with every breath. Cold rushed up his calves, but he didn't flinch. Instead, he let it rise then settle into the thick curve of his spine, like a whisper of unmet need.

It wasn't discomfort. It was memory. An ache born of absence. Like a denied invocation, an unread command humming low beneath the skin, waiting for ritual permission. The cold reminded him that hunger could live in stillness, too.

The morning had begun.

Before leaving for the shower, he passed the full-length mirror in the far corner of the room. A casual glance became something longer. He stopped.

There he was, broad-shouldered, narrow-waisted, posture relaxed but commanding. He was solidly built, with the same grounded strength in his stance and a weight that didn't shrink in morning chill, but held steady like it belonged in the hand of someone who knew how to wield it. His glutes were full, round, sculpted muscle from years of ascension and evasion. No softness left in them, only power.

He didn't admire. He observed.

Almost vain but not quite. There was too much fear of what he wouldn't see. Of blank skin where memory should burn. Of silence where sigils once sang.

It was the same way one might inspect a blade. Measuring its edge, balance, purpose. Yet beneath the ritual of self-assessment, there was another intention: he was searching.

His gaze drifted across his back, watching the shift of shoulder blades, the line of his spine, the subtle ripple of muscle.

Searching for the sigils.

As he always did.

The memory of them burned brighter than their absence. Like the Archive had shown him something once, and then erased it from the page, but not the body.

He had seen them burning across his body in a moment of release and revelation; and ever since, he had questioned their reality. Was it memory? Was it madness? The skin beneath his eyes remained clean. No sigils. No flicker.

But still, he looked.

The mirror didn't answer, but it remembered.

Sometimes, he thought he saw the faint outline of one. A shimmer. A shadow. A lie.

Some mornings, he half expected them to return. In their absence, he feared he had imagined it all. That the power that once bloomed across his skin had abandoned him, or worse, had been a forgotten annotation, a recursion left uninked. He needed them back, not for proof, but for purpose. Without them, he was just another sharp mind in a cold uniform. With them, he was marked. Remembered. Chosen.

And then he turned away.

The water ran hot—too hot. That was how he preferred it.

In the tiled recesses of the Citadel's lower shower stalls, he moved like a man rehearsing solitude. Fingers pressed to the wall, shoulder blades rising and falling beneath scalding steam. He breathed with control, counting not seconds but sensation.

The arousal returned.

Persistent. Thicker this time, like phantom sigil heat coiling beneath the skin, echoing a flare that hadn't been called but hadn't fully faded either.

He didn't fight it.

One hand curled around his cock, the other slid low to cup his sac, rolling the fullness of himself slowly in his palm. It was heavy, warm, and reactive, tightening slightly at his touch. He squeezed gently, letting the feeling build with deliberate control.

His strokes slowed as his fingers drifted back further. Down between his cheeks, he teased his entrance with soft, exploratory pressure. Not to penetrate, just to feel it, to press the edges and remind himself of what was there, untouched but marked. He was tracing ritual ground like memory itself, a gesture aching to reawaken contact long denied.

His breath hitched. His knees bent slightly.

There was no lover. No fantasy. Just the shape of his own wanting. A geometric shape scribed into him by recursion, not imagination. The pull of something older than need, something written into his body and forgotten by time.

When he came, it was soft and spine trembling. His eyes fluttering and hips twitching into the pressure of his palm.

A single gasped breath slipped out of him, higher than it should have been.

He stilled.

Another sound followed.

The steam shifted behind him. A pressure formed at the base of his skull.

Not breath or footfall. Only a voice from just beyond the edge of the steam. It tasted faintly of sigil ink and old metal and moved with a cadence too mirrored to be human. Unintelligible, like a name spoken through water. Half a syllable. A whisper inside the walls.

He turned sharply, chest rising, heart ticking fast beneath the surface. There was no one there. But the air behind him felt disturbed. Like someone had just stepped out of the room.

He turned back to the mirror—

And saw it.

A shock passed through him, sharp and immediate. It wasn't fear. It was something older, deeper. Longing cut with disbelief, a quiet gasp of hope wrapped in dread. The flicker wasn't just light. It was invitation. One laced with a breath cadence he'd heard only once before, coiled in a near-syllable of mirrored heat. Part of him wanted to step into it, even as the other braced to flee.

The glass was still fogged, but behind the haze, his reflection had shifted. Something about the curve of his spine. The gleam just beneath his skin. His posture more exposed and open.

A flicker of light danced along his back.

Gone before he could name it.

He stepped from the water. Toweled off with the precision of someone avoiding thought—avoiding questions.

His reflection was blurred, half-visible through condensation.

Even so, he didn't entirely recognize the man staring back.

The Citadel's uniform suited him. Dark fabrics. Sharp lines. High collar. Efficient. Yes, but not forgettable.

Thalos had altered his selection over the years, tailoring the standard issue just enough to skirt protocol. His coat was cut closer at the waist, cinched slightly to draw attention to his tapered torso. The trousers hugged tight where they needed to, at the thighs, calves, and the subtle curve of a well-trained ass. All without ever crossing the line into indecent. Enough to suggest strength and control, and enough stretch to cradle the not-so-subtle weight between his legs. A presence, never an exaggeration. More than one gaze had lingered longer than it should've. Some in curiosity. Others in warning.

He neither flaunted it nor hid it. Dressing each morning as if negotiating with a sigil he couldn't see, unsure whether he was containing its echo or inviting it to flare. There were whispers, the ones that began in the mess halls and died in bedrooms, of the monster he kept beneath the fabric. And though he said nothing, he let the uniform speak for him.

He wore it like armor, like memory, like an admission made only in silhouette.

Beneath it, he knew, the sigils had once flared. Still unseen. Still waiting.

He always lingered at the collar. Adjusted it twice. Once for symmetry and then once for permission. Not from himself, but from whatever unseen Archive-breath watched each morning, waiting to see what he'd choose to become.

It was a ritual. A quiet assertion of control before stepping into a world too often dictated by unspoken rules and unseen forces. The act grounded him, restoring his balance. The collar had to sit just so, hugging the neck like a harness disguised as propriety. High, tight, and framing his jaw with precision.

It wasn't just about order. It was about command.

A part of him—buried deeper than he liked to admit—enjoyed the dominance the collar implied. The restraint it suggested. He didn't crave submission. He craved leverage. The knowledge that beneath the polished silence, he was a storm held by choice.

If someone ever reached for that collar, they'd have to earn the right to unfasten it.

The halls beyond were cold. Not unpleasantly so; a reminder that nothing in the Archive's shadow held warmth for long. Only flicker, only forgetting.

—— ✦ ——

Location: Blackwatch Citadel | Descent Lift Theta-7 | Sublevel Access

The elevator was already occupied.

The man inside was taller than most. Broad in a way that suggested he'd once been imposing but now wore the build like a uniform long outgrown. The bulk didn't move with grace. It loomed. His coat was cut aggressively tight in the shoulders. The chest padded with the kind of stiffness that felt like overcompensation. The stitched nameplate read Morren, catching a flicker of light before vanishing back into shadow. His gloves were fingerless, tactical and unnecessary. His smirk was that of someone who had once been desirable but hadn't noticed the moment that power left him. Like the last curl of smoke from an extinguished flame, unaware it no longer gave heat.

Thalos stepped in, the silence stretching taut before the agent broke it.

"Archivist Vale," the man said with too much familiarity. His voice was smooth. Pitched low. Like something that purred only after tasting blood.

Thalos inclined his head slightly. "Field agent."

"I was beginning to think you were a myth," the man said. "They say no one ever sees you leave."

"I keep my hours inside."

"I know." He leaned closer, breath warm at Thalos's ear. "I've seen them. Years ago. Lower stacks. Late hour. Candlelight." He smiled, slow and wide. "You were breathing a little heavier then."

Thalos didn't flinch, but his jaw tightened.

"You must be mistaking me for someone else."

"I don't think so." The man's eyes—grey-blue and wolf-pale—slid over him, drinking him in. "There was a flicker. On your back. I remember thinking— *That's not an ordinary boy. That's a fuse pretending to be parchment... hiding in the Archive's hush, waiting to be read the wrong way.*"

"And you watched?"

"Wouldn't you?" His grin sharpened. "You were... luminous."

The elevator felt too small. The air too still.

"Don't worry," the agent added, licking the corner of his lip. "I didn't report it. I don't mind ghosts, especially the ones that leave mnemonic residue, recursion echoes that haven't quite decided where they belong."

The silence after that was lead-heavy.

The sigil above the door flickered. The elevator slowed.

As the doors hissed open, the agent stepped out first, but not without one last glance over his shoulder.

"Be careful what you remember," he said, his voice dropping to a purr. "Sometimes, it scribes itself behind your eyes and waits to be read again."

He winked.

Thalos watched him go, following the line of his shoulders down to the swing of his hips. Broad. Solid. The kind of frame that might have been imposing once before the years set weight where precision should have been. There was power in the shape, yet the movement was too measured, too careful, as if rehearsed for an audience that had stopped watching.

His mouth curved faintly, more thought than smile. "Overcompensating," he murmured, the word tasting of quiet amusement as the doors sealed him back into the lift.

—— ✦ ——

The Archive greeted him with the same restrained hush it always did, cool, observant, and echoing faintly like a memory too patient to speak. Vaulted stone ceilings arched like the ribs of sleeping giants, ward-sconces casting a soft glow over corridor sigils and the lacquered curves of countless stacked tomes.

His boots made no sound on the etched tile. They never did. He moved like memory, present but impossible to touch.

The alcove that housed his desk was already dimly lit, the candle freshly changed. A sign that Director Threnna had passed through. She always replaced it, never said why.

He paused beside the desk and ran his fingers along the edge, reacquainting himself with something that used to be a part of him. The smoothness of the wood. The faintest crack in the corner from when he lost control of a translated phrase three years ago. Familiar. Safe.

He lowered himself into the chair, the leather sighing under his weight.

Everything was as it had been.

Except it wasn't.

The stack of files hadn't been there the night before.

At the very bottom, pressed flat and pulsing with stillness, lay a folder sealed in black wax.

His fingers hovered over it. There was a tremor there, neither fear nor excitement, just a pull. Familiar. Forgotten. He hadn't even touched it, and already something in his skin whispered recognition.

Then...

"Tempted, Vale?"

Thalos didn't jump. He just blinked, fingers withdrawing a breath's width.

Director Threnna stood in the archway behind him, holding a half-finished flask of something bitter smelling. She always arrived without sound, scent, or warning—only presence.

She was tall, lean, wrapped in dark plum robes with sharp shoulders and silver cuffs. Her face was lined but not worn. She looked like someone who had been middle-aged forever and chose to stay there out of spite. Her voice carried a crispness that could cut vellum.

"You know the rule— top to bottom, no matter how much the bottom's begging for it."

Thalos turned to look at her. "I was just assessing weight."

"Weren't we all at your age?" she muttered, brushing past him.

She tapped the top folder. "Start where protocol starts—leave the moaning one for last. Files like that don't just want to be read. They want to be edged toward invocation, teased until their sigils burn."

He said nothing at first, but the corner of his mouth twitched.

"Funny," he murmured dryly, eyes drifting back to the sealed file. "That's usually how it goes. The quiet ones on the bottom? Loudest by the end."

She gave a hoarse little laugh through her nose, impressed, maybe, or amused he still had teeth.

She raised her flask, as if toasting the game.

"Happy reading—try not to soak the desk. I'd hate to requisition a new one just because a certain black-sealed beauty made your cock leak precum like a spigot."

Thalos raised a brow, his lips curling. "Should I report you to the Command Conduct Bureau for sexual harassment?"

CCB, as the agents called it, because nothing made misconduct sound duller than bureaucracy.

She paused mid-step, turning just enough to look at him over her shoulder. "Please. You're far too dangerous, and I'm far too gay. Neither of us wants the other, Vale. That's why it works."

And with that, she vanished back into the corridor like a well-placed rumor.

Thalos stared after her for a long beat, then turned his attention to the stack of files.

His fingers returned to the top folder; standard parchment, standard ink, nothing pulsing or whispering beneath. He opened it slowly, but his eyes drifted back toward the black wax envelope.

"Starting from the top isn't always the most enjoyable," he murmured to himself. "But sometimes the appetizer needs to disappoint before the main course can blow your fucking mind."

He smirked faintly.

Then he began to read.

The first file. Field analysis of sigil degradation along the Western Vault perimeter. Dry. Predictable. The accompanying sketches were rushed, proportions skewed and sigils mislabeled. He made three corrections in the margins without thinking.

Reassign to a second-tier transcriber, he noted. Re-ink and recalibrate spatial coordinates.

The second. Post-interrogation transcript from a minor dissident. The subject claimed his dreams had been altered by proximity to an old ruin. The dream was dull; the grammar worse. Thalos added two punctuation fixes and flagged the magical theory as inconsistent.

The third. Brief from a supply caravan that had encountered mirrorlight flares outside Hollowmere. Potential echo field activity. That one made him pause, for half a second. But the rest of the report collapsed into poor sentence structure and unrelated anecdotal commentary.

Dream-bleed symptoms exaggerated. Field lead likely compensating for lack of formal training.

The fourth file. The fifth. The sixth. They passed like flavorless bread, bland, heavy and forgettable. Reports padded with unnecessary detail, apprentices guessing at terminology, cadets using three words where one would do.

He edited ruthlessly, red-inked entire paragraphs, sighed at his own reflexive perfectionism.

By the seventh file he had slouched halfway down his chair.

By the eighth, his eyes had begun drifting back to the bottom of the stack every few lines.

The black wax seal sat there. Patient. Watching.

Waiting.

He looked down at the last mundane page in his hands and muttered, "Eight kinds of tedium. And one unspoken promise, etched into the silence like a recursion waiting to ignite."

He dropped the eighth file to the side.

Only the sealed one remained.

He reached for it.

The wax glinted slightly in the low candlelight as if exhaling after hours of restraint. Its scent was just faint enough to suggest burnt ink and breath caught in mirrored glass. His fingers hovered, about to touch the edge—

"Thalos."

He closed his eyes briefly, exhaling through his nose before looking up.

Director Threnna stood once again in the archway, flask now gone, replaced with a half-eaten ritesnap and the ever-sharp curve of amusement tugging at her mouth.

"You've missed the hour when sensible people eat. Again."

Thalos glanced at the timepiece on the wall, then back to her. "I didn't realize hunger was now listed under standard protocol."

"Only when it makes you forget to blink," she said, stepping further in. "And, for the record, showing up early doesn't win you extra points around here. It just makes the rest of us look lazy."

"That's hardly my fault."

"Mm," she replied, biting into her ritesnap. "No. But it's exactly the pattern I'd expect from you."

She looked pointedly at the wax-sealed file. "Take the break, Vale. Trust me... if it's waited this long, it can wait one more hour. Besides, some things open better when they think you've forgotten them."

Then, without waiting for an answer, she turned on her heel and strolled off, trailing crunches of ritesnap and casual command behind her.

—— ◆ ——

Location: Blackwatch Citadel | Sublevel B | Mess Hall Theta + Wash Alcove K

Thalos exhaled through his nose. Slowly.

He stood and gathered himself, not just physically but into the curated silence he wore like a second uniform. A hand through his hair. A tug at his collar, and then he turned toward the mess hall.

The walk was short, but he drew it out. Hallways blurred by familiarity, lined with faces who didn't meet his eyes or who lingered just a second too long.

He chose a table in the far corner, back to the wall. Plate half-filled. Bread, a spiced protein cut, a cluster of mirrorvine pods he wouldn't touch. Eating was habit here, a necessity masquerading as rest.

He chewed slowly, more out of rhythm than hunger. Eyes scanning, observing and cataloging. The way the agents grouped by hierarchy, the way apprentices mimicked posture without knowing they were doing it. He'd once documented the entire social choreography of the mess hall in a forgotten journal. He might again.

His mind kept drifting.

To the file.

To the seal.

To the heat he'd felt without touching it. A sigil beneath the skin, waiting for a name to unlock it.

He reached for the bread.

That was when the chair beside him scraped across the floor.

The field agent Morren dropped into the seat without invitation, legs spread wide, elbows braced on the table as if the whole thing had been reserved just for him.

"You're even more intense when you're pretending to eat," the agent drawled, snagging a pod from Thalos's untouched cluster and popping it into his mouth. "Tell me, Vale... does the brooding burn more energy than chewing?"

Thalos didn't look at him right away. He placed the bread back on the plate with surgical care.

"I assumed you'd be off somewhere misfiling requisition reports and compensating with shoulder rolls."

"Ouch," the agent smirked. "I came here hoping to flirt. Instead I get dissected."

Thalos turned his head just slightly. "If I cut too deep, it's because you've already padded yourself with layers of posturing."

The agent chuckled, eyes gleaming. "So you were watching."

"You move like a man who once topped by accident and never recovered."

The agent barked a laugh and leaned in closer. "You keep talking like that and I might ask you to fact-check me firsthand."

Thalos finally met his gaze.

"Not unless you'd like your ego filed under unsatisfactory and redacted for the sake of future generations."

The agent only grinned wider.

"Gods, you're fun. I bet you taste like parchment and power. I could pin you down, tongue in your mouth, hand on that monster between your legs, and you'd still find a way to correct my grammar."

He leaned closer, his voice lower now, husky with something too confident to be casual. "Do you always carry that much heat under a uniform? Or are you saving it for someone worth burning for?"

Thalos arched a brow. "You're still sitting here. That's the concerning part."

"Curiosity. Maybe I want to see how far you'll push before you pull."

"Or maybe," Thalos said coolly, rising from his seat, "you just like pretending you're the predator, right up until something real bares its teeth."

He left his tray behind.

The agent's grin faltered, not gone, just cracking.

The agent whistled low, watching him go.

"You wound me, Archivist—that was practically romantic."

His voice dipped a note deeper, almost reverent. "And that ass—fucking poetry. I'd write sonnets if I thought you'd let me kneel behind it."

Thalos didn't look back.

He didn't need to. Whatever bravado the agent tried to wield crumbled the moment Thalos walked away, because dominance wasn't in the talk. It was in the silence you left behind. Like the collar he adjusted each morning. Tight, precise, his to unfasten and his alone.

"Careful," he said over his shoulder, voice smooth as glass. "You sound like a man who talks a lot more than he performs."

But the faintest smirk pulled at the corner of his mouth.

The agent opened his mouth, some half-cocked retort already loading, but it scattered halfway out, lost in the space Thalos left behind.

Words, it turned out, were hard to aim when you were watching someone walk away like that.

—— ✦ ——

Before returning to the Archive, Thalos detoured to the private washroom off the corridor. The quiet echoed there, tile and stone humming faintly with the layered enchantments of sanitation wards. He stepped to the urinal, unfastening his trousers with the practiced ease. Each motion a contained invocation.

His cock fell heavy into his palm, thick and flushed from the heat of the mess hall tension. He exhaled as his stream began, the release steady and controlled. It hissed against the bowl, echoing faintly in the silence.

There was something primal in it. This simple act after so much watching and being watched. A reset. A reminder of his physical presence in a world that too often wanted him only for his mind.

He gave himself a slight shake, then adjusted himself with precision, the weight of him shifting back into the snug cradle of fabric.

He washed his hands in silence, the cold-water biting at his skin like discipline. Only then did he dry them with slow precision, as if cleansing more than just flesh.

And then, without looking into the mirror above the sink, he left as if denying his reflection permission to look back.

Back to the Archive. Back to the sealed breath of memory.

Back to the file.

—— ✦ ——

He returned to his desk, the Archive just as silent, the stack of folders undisturbed. The candle hadn't burned far. Time had not moved quickly here.

Thalos eased back into his chair. The leather creaked faintly beneath him.

And just as he reached for the black-wax seal—again—

"Thought I told you to take a full cycle's breath."

Threnna was back, leaning lazily against the doorframe like she owned every breath in the corridor.

"You did," Thalos said without looking up. "You also suggested that file would wait. It hasn't exactly run off."

She snorted. "Pity. Would've loved to see it grow legs. Maybe flirt with the Requisitions Clerk. Might be the most action he's had in a cycle's quarter."

Her eyes fell to the seal. "You sure you're ready for that one?"

Thalos didn't answer.

He just placed both palms on the desk.

And this time, he reached for it with intention.

Threnna watched him, remnants of the ritesnap still on her fingers, with a sharpness in her mouth, as if she'd bitten into something even more dangerous. She let out a low, throaty chuckle. It wasn't warm. It wasn't cruel. It was the sound of someone who had seen people fall down holes they'd dug themselves—and had already marked where Thalos's would start.

Then she was gone.

He lingered in her absence, the echo of her chuckle still coiled behind his ribs. There was something in it. Mockery, maybe, but also warning. A recognition.

He glanced once more at the seal. Then, slowly, deliberately, his fingers touched the edge.

The wax was cool.

It pulsed once beneath his thumb.

He began to break it.

The air tightened around him. The room thinned to paper and light.

A voice slid into his head.

He's not just a threat. He's a myth. Arrest him—but be ready to fall first.

A breath not his own. A name inhaled by the Archive before he could speak it.

Kaelor.

Not imagined. Not summoned. Simply, remembered by the world.

He stood tall, too tall to be comfortable, broad-shouldered like he'd been built for war but carved for worship. Fire-red hair fell loose around his shoulders, wind-tossed even in stillness. His skin held the warmth of sun-drenched stone, streaked with the sheen of sweat and the shimmer of living sigils.

The sigils wrapped across his chest like scars given shape, glowing softly and pulsing in tandem with his breath. Each flare timed like a truth exhaled through fire. They weren't etched for power. They were born of it.

His eyes were not blue but burning blue, like the afterimage of lightning seen through closed lids. They didn't just look at Thalos.

They unclothed him.

He wore nothing but loose dark pants, low on his hips, clinging slightly where the fabric was damp from sweat. And the bulge beneath them was... undeniable. Heavy. Ripe. A shadow curved against the linen that twitched. Never obscene, never shameful, just the weight of something that had never once apologized for what it was.

Thalos swallowed hard.

His eyes drifted down further.

The thighs held power, but it was the ass that made his breath stutter. Full. Carved. Engineered for impact; both receptive and devastating. Rounded with that effortless strength only the combat-scarred ever earned. The kind of backside sculpted not by vanity but by use. Sex and war and sorcery, fused in muscle.

He turned slightly. And Thalos's pulse kicked so hard he almost moaned.

Kaelor didn't speak, but the air around him did. It whispered *burn* in a thousand languages at once.

The fire blinked and was gone.

In its place: cold.

Veyrion.

Kaelor burned forward; Veyrion remembered the ash. Pale skin stretched over wiry muscle, his frame cloaked in shadow. Along his spine each sigil shimmered with surgical precision in abyssal azure, impossibly fine, as if someone had bled sacred design into his flesh.

His hair fell to his shoulders—white streaked with black, spectral in how it caught the dimness. His mouth was delicate but unsmiling. Lips parted just slightly, as if about to say a truth that could destroy whoever heard it.

But it was his eyes. Those mirror-grey, violet-flickered eyes, that held Thalos still.

Because they didn't look at him; they looked through him, and what they saw made Thalos tremble.

Reflected in Veyrion's irises, he saw himself, but not as he was. Naked. Sigil-lit. Changed. Back arched, mouth open, eyes glowing with some truth that hadn't yet happened.

Behind him, in the same reflection, Kaelor was watching.

Not with hunger. Not with mercy. With knowing.

Veyrion raised a hand, and it shifted between red and silver, breathing like a heart exposed to starlight. Fingers long and bare except for the sigil circling his palm. The very one he'd traced in ink now spun in breath-light between them, mirrored, unbidden and alive.

His voice came again. Inside him.

When one walks, the other remembers. When both look back... the world forgets its shape.

Thalos's hand braced against the desk without him realizing, palm slick where it met the wood.

He recoiled from the file as if burned, breath catching as the images vanished from his mind. He pushed back from the desk, the legs of his chair scraped harshly against the stone floor. His chest heaved once, then again, as if the air itself had thickened.

He looked down.

His body had responded before he did. Release claimed not by climax but recognition. The fabric clung to him damply, a visible stain spreading downward and blooming at the seam. A single strand of slick glistened across the dark wood of the desk, right over the crack Threnna had once threatened to replace.

The evidence of him was unmistakable. Raw. Marked.

He huffed a breath through his nose, half disbelief and half dark amusement. The candle beside him flickered violently, wax pooling beneath its base like it too had been shaken, and beneath that, something heavier pressed at his chest. Shame? No. Not quite. It was a thrill, raw and unyielding, that he had been seen by something that hadn't yet named him but already knew what he carried inside. It made him ache in places he'd thought were long silenced. And it terrified him that he wanted more.

"She's definitely replacing the desk."

—— ✦ ——

The scry-glass shimmered faintly, pulsing as if to mimic a heartbeat.

Within its frame, the image of Thalos Vale flickered, still seated at his desk, fingertips hovering just above the broken black wax seal. His eyes were unfocused. Lips parted. Pulse visible along his throat.

He looked like someone remembering something the Archive hadn't yet written.

"Gods below," Agent Morren said, stepping back from the scry-table. "He's glowing again. Same pulse points as before. Spine and collarbone. Saw it years ago, when he was still too young for that kind of heat. Lean frame, eyes wide, back to the marble, like he didn't know

he was showing. I stood there longer than I should have. Those sigils...
they sang."

Director Threnna didn't turn. Her gaze stayed fixed on the image.
Her reply carried a weight just sharp enough to make the air between
them tighten.

"So he is, Crale."

Morren peeled off his gloves slowly, each finger freed with a quiet
snap, as though savoring the pause. His bare fingertips flexed once,
then twice, like they were remembering their own history.

"You didn't report it."

His mouth curved, low and deliberate. "I don't report art,
Director. Not when it moves the way he does. Some things are worth
keeping for yourself... until the right moment to take them."

A faint hum rose from the glass. On-screen, Thalos shifted
slightly, his fingers now trailing the edge of the open file.

Morren's voice dipped, almost reverent. "He's feeling it. Not
reading. Feeling. That kind of pull isn't learned... it's in the body
before the mind catches up. You can see it take him. Slow. Deep. Erotic
in the way a caught breath is. Mirrorfold behavior starts in sensation,
doesn't it?"

"Only if the echo is conscious," Threnna replied. "Only if both
ends of the line remember what they were before the recursion
fractured."

Morren tilted his head, eyes narrowing, as if picturing the
moment that memory would break open. "And when it does for him...
will he even know what's being done to him? Or will he just give in and
wear it like it was always his?"

Threnna finally looked away from the scry-glass. Her posture,
composed and rigid until now, began to shift. Her shoulders coiled
slightly forward, the corner of her mouth twitching while amusement
wrestled with calculation. Her expression was unreadable, cold and

curious, but her eyes glimmered with something else, too. *Excitement.* A predator's thrill veiled beneath administrative detachment.

"He doesn't yet, but the file will wake him. They all do eventually. What matters is how he carries the burden of being rewritten."

Morren leaned closer again, his gaze fixed on the display as if he could crawl through it. Onscreen, Thalos's lips moved; a word they couldn't quite catch.

"Tell me something," Morren said. "Why was he abandoned here? We don't take infants. Blackwatch isn't an orphanage... but someone left him here like they knew he'd grow into this."

Threnna's smile came like a crack in a cold mirror.

"We didn't take him," she said softly. "We received him."

She paused. "Sometimes, the world leaves behind its solutions where no one will think to look."

Morren's mouth curved in something too deliberate to be a smile.

"Then I'm glad I was here to watch him grow into it. Pretty things are worth more when you've been there to see the first time they don't know they're being looked at."

Threnna didn't answer. Her jaw tightened, just enough to betray the restraint beneath her stillness. She shifted her gaze back to the screen with the kind of calm that made lesser men mistake it for permission. If he noticed the cold edge in her silence, he ignored it. She didn't need to correct him now. There would be time for that.

It would not be kind.

Thalos leaned forward.

The seal cracked beneath his fingers.

The Archive began to rewrite him, morning ceased to be a margin. It became a beginning written in ink, breath, and bone.

CHAPTER TWO: ECHOES AND EMBERS

Location: Blackwatch Citadel | Sublevel B | Archive Intake Alcove

The seal did not break. It surrendered.

Wax cracked beneath his fingers, splintering like bone in a spiral, the dark imprint of the Blackwatch insignia bleeding open across the folder's face. The scent that rose was not ink or parchment, but heat. Copper. Ash. Something too intimate to name.

Thalos stared. The folder pulsed faintly, as if aware of being touched again. Or *remembered.*

His palm tingled faintly. As if the memory wasn't inside the file at all, but under his skin, waiting to be triggered.

He hadn't opened it yet, but something inside had already started whispering.

Clipped to the inside cover was a photo. It was standard surveillance format, yet saturated with a raw, unsettling immediacy. Kaelor Thorne. Full-body, front-facing. The image, printed on metallic-backed parchment, shimmered faintly with the residue of sigilwork, like heat still trapped in skin. Shirtless, trousers low on his hips, Kaelor stood against a weathered blackstone wall faintly etched with sun-faded sigils. His posture was relaxed, hips tilted slightly to one side, as if caught mid-breath.

His body was unmistakable. Muscular and angular with the fluid power of an elf trained for war but shaped by exile. His shoulders bore the slight asymmetry of an old wound, collarbones cut clean beneath pale, sigil-scored skin. The sigils glowed subtly. They were alive, not cosmetic. His chest bore the faint remnant of a crest once branded and later over-scorched by magical fire. Just above the waistband of his trousers, one sigil curled inward like a question left unanswered.

What drew the eye, and refused to let go, was the bulge beneath those fitted, weather-beaten leathers. It was heavy and full, as if even the camera lens couldn't quite capture the truth of it. The thighs framing it were thick and taut, shaped by combat, not vanity, and the eyes...

Blue, piercing, and ancient.

Thalos gaped.

For a breath too long, he forgot what air was.

More than arousal, his body was trying to remember how to kneel, how to align itself properly.

His fingertips tingled. The edges of his vision contracted. It wasn't from strain, but from focus so sharp it bordered on ache. He turned the first page.

This time the room forgot how to breathe.

The first page didn't introduce a subject.

It introduced a gravity-well.

```
BLACKWATCH INTELLIGENCE DIVISION
Subject: Kaelor Thorne
Designation: Rogue Class | Echo Tier - Obsidian
Redacted
Alias: The Flame Without a Home, Redmark Ghost,
Thorne in the Bed
Height: 6'2" | Race: Highborn Elf (exiled) |
Estimated Age: 130-150 cycles
Known Associations: [REDACTED], House Valmari
(estranged), Archive breach traces (confirmed)
```

His pulse stuttered. Not from the stats, but from the shape they painted.

```
Subject is considered dangerously charismatic and
neurologically seductive to a select vector class. Exposure
leads to known symptoms including arousal-driven trance
states, recursive memory insertion, and physical mirroring.
```

The words felt too close.

He blinked, but the dossier wasn't letting go.

Target exhibits emotional mass. Not compulsion. Not charm.
Something stronger. Thought becomes tethered. Recollection
bends. Obsession forms around absence rather than presence.

Obsession forms around absence...

Thalos exhaled slowly, but his hands wouldn't stop trembling.

He flipped to the next section. Eyes skimming the page before he could stop himself. And there it was.

Confirmed arcane signatures include pyromantic sigilwork,
mirrored sigils, and suspected Mirrorfold bleed. Subject's
body has been cited as 'arcanely mnemonic'—retained in
memory with anatomical precision after brief exposure.

He wasn't hard. Not exactly.

Something deeper stirred, a shape beneath desire.

Each paragraph read him back. Each annotation curled like a finger against the inside of his throat.

Note: Operatives exposed for longer than 30 minutes
reported residual scent phantoming and altered erotic memory
architecture. Subject's thighs, glutes, and cock are
recurring focal points in post-exposure reports.

That last line burned across his vision like a brand.

He clenched his jaw.

He wasn't just reading a file. He was becoming one of its entries.

His shaft thickened beneath the table. Slow at first, then with a pulse like something waking, a mix of arousal and recognition. The kind that reached through flesh and found memory tangled in nerve.

His breath caught. He shifted in his chair, suddenly aware of how tight his trousers had become. A bead of slick gathered at the tip, warmth spreading along the inside seam. He didn't touch himself. Not yet, but the weight of it demanded attention.

His thighs tensed, his mouth parted, and Kaelor's name echoed in his mind like a spell fragment still seeking its sigil.

The image. The words. The shape of presence embedded in the file. They weren't just descriptive. They were *formative*. Every line read felt like a finger tracing along his spine.

And he was losing track of where the words stopped and his body began.

His fingertips were wet.

Not with sweat.

He wiped them absently on his thigh. More instinct than awareness, and then he turned the page.

The arcane charge intensified.

The next folio of the dossier shimmered with deeper access clearance:

SEXUAL & INTIMATE DOSSIER – ONYX-OBSIDIAN PRIME CLEARANCE

Highly responsive to emotional openness when paired with assertive affection.

Sigils flare on skin contact.

Anatomical endowment beyond elven norms. Notable girth. Substantial hang. Responsive to magical stimuli.

Musculature—particularly glutes and thighs—structured for either dominant or submissive positioning.

Thalos swallowed hard. His cock jumped, slick already leaking from the tip, pooling hot in the fold of his pants. It was unbearable now, too sensitive, engorged and needy.

His jaw clenched tighter. He shifted again in his seat, thighs grinding slightly against the edge of the chair. Pressure helped, but only for a moment.

This was more than seduction. It was a gravitational collapse.

Subject's partners report instinctive submissive response,
often without prior arousal. Witness accounts describe
behavior as reverent.

Thalos's breath caught as his hand moved without permission.

He pressed his palm hard against the outline of his erection, as if pressure alone could quiet the hunger coiled low in his gut, but it only made the heat flare sharper, more aware of its own denial.

He hadn't released his cock from its confines, but the button had come undone without thought.

He was closer to coming than he'd been in weeks.

Without even realizing it, he had unzipped his trousers. His fingers slid beneath the waistband of his underwear, pushing the fabric down beneath the base of his balls. His cock sprang free. Thick, flushed, and leaking profusely. The sudden exposure made him gasp, the cool air kissing heat-slick skin.

The chair groaned beneath him, a sound like a door unsealing, the air thick with the scent of old parchment and salt-sweet arousal.

He didn't even glance back at the file.

For a breathless moment, he simply stared at the pulsing length in his hand, like it had been summoned by the words alone.

Slowly, he wrapped his fingers around the base. It felt inevitable, like the file had already decided for him.

His grip was loose at first, tentative, as if testing whether the sensation was truly his own. The warmth of his palm met the slickness already gathered at the head, and a shudder worked its way up his spine.

He stroked once. Down to the root, then back up. Pausing just beneath the swollen head, letting his thumb tease along the ridge. The leak of precum smeared easily, turning his grip into a slow glide. Another stroke. Then another.

His fingers made a wet, obscene noise with every stroke, filling the silence. His hips shifted forward in the chair, heels digging into the floor.

Still, he didn't look at the file.

Somehow though, it was still looking at him.

He pushed his trousers and underwear down further, letting them pool at his ankles. His knees spread instinctively, the chair creaking under the shift, as if the wood itself was bending to his need. One hand continued its slow, rhythmic stroking, but the pace was no longer his own. His fingers moved with a will borrowed from the file, each stroke dragging him deeper into something he couldn't name.

The other slipped between his legs, trembling with the weight of what was coming. His fingers traced the sensitive skin behind his balls, trailing lower with feather-light precision. He found his pucker and circled it gently, just enough to make his breath catch and his thighs clench. The first touch sent a jolt through him, sharp and sweet, like the prick of a needle drawing blood for a pact.

A groan escaped him, soft and raw. There was no shame left in him now. Only hunger. Only the slick, insistent demand of his own body. He pressed harder, his fingertip breaching the tight ring of muscle with a slow, deliberate pressure. The burn was immediate, exquisite, and his cock twitched in his grip, leaking freely as if marking the moment.

Thalos's body knew what it wanted. It had always known.

He added a second finger, stretching himself open with a desperation that bordered on reverence. The intrusion sent a wave of heat up his spine, his hips lifting off the chair as if pulled by invisible threads. His free hand tightened around his cock, pumping in time with the shallow thrusts of his fingers, each movement drawing him closer to the edge. The chair creaked beneath him; the sound lost beneath his ragged breaths and the obscene noises his body made.

Thalos was no longer in control. If he ever had been.

The file's presence hummed at the edge of his awareness, a silent witness to his surrender. His fingers curled inside himself, searching for something just out of reach, something the file had promised without words. His thighs trembled, his muscles coiling tight as a spring, ready to snap. He was going to blow, and when he did, it wouldn't just be pleasure. It would be an offering.

His cock throbbed, slick in his grip with every pass. The edge was coming fast now, pleasure tightening around his spine like a summoning circle drawn in sweat. If he came, something would answer. He could feel it in the way his hole clenched around his fingertips, and his cock pulsed like a heartbeat counting down.

He didn't need the next page.

His body was already writing its own.

His hips rolled once, then again, chasing friction. One hand worked his cock with mounting urgency, gliding over the shiny head, tightening near the base. His other hand didn't hesitate now, two fingers thrusting in and out of the tight ring of muscle, pressing in with a pressure just shy of pain.

His breath stuttered. His body shuddered.

The combination of pressure inside and out lit every nerve. His tight ring spasmed around the intrusion, aching for more even as it pulsed in surrender. The burn was exquisite. His grip faltered only to return firmer, pumping with a desperation that no longer pretended to be command.

Kaelor's name burned on his lips, but it wasn't just a name. It was a key. Every stroke, every gasp, was a syllable in a ritual he didn't understand.

"Vale!"

The name cracked through the chamber like a whip.

Thalos froze.

Director Threnna's voice rang sharp with exasperation from the entryway, her silhouette framed in the glow of the threshold sigil she had clearly overridden. Her boots were planted wide, her arms folded; but her eyes were burning with something that hovered between disbelief and grim inevitability.

She had *seen* him.

Exactly like this.

His breath hitched, but his grip didn't falter. He turned his head slightly, throat dry as sun-bleached ink. His voice came out steady. Too steady. The kind of poise that took grit and fire to forge.

"Director," he gasped. "If you... oh, fuck... if you were hoping to catch me with my pants—" He jerked as climax hit mid-sentence, cum splattering the floor in thick arcs, his voice cracking into breathless ruin.

"—congratu...lations," he choked. "You've... earned yourself a performance—"

Another pulse hit; a guttural moan tore through him as his throat caught on the next word. "—review."

A voice, low and breath-rough, slipped across the edge of his senses.

You remember me now.

Not heard. Not imagined. Just... received. His body convulsed around the echo.

His vision blanked as climax hit.

Cum continued to spill across the floor at his feet in hot, pulsing waves, thick and unrelenting. His grip clenched reflexively around the base, milking every twitch, every shuddering spill as his muscles spasmed in release.

At the final pulse, something *seared*. Not skin or memory but the space between.

Just above the cleft of his ass, a heat bloomed and held. Bright, biting and sigil-shaped. It wasn't pain exactly. It was recognition carved into flesh.

The sigil CLAIM ME FIRST flared once, then faded beneath the skin, leaving behind a slow, spreading ache. His fingertips twitched. Ink traced under his nail beds. The Archive had taken note.

Director Threnna stood at the threshold.

Her gaze dropped immediately to the slick-wet length of his cock still gripped in one hand. His trousers open, his body mid-thrust, one hand fisted at the base of his shaft, the other poised between his legs, fingers gilded and glistening, hovering just outside his stretched, clenching hole. The file before him glowed with low magical heat.

The air crackled with his scent, his shame, and something else entirely. A silence that stains, that seeps beneath sigils, that never washes clean, that signs your name without permission.

She folded her arms slowly, eyes narrowing—not in anger, but in examination, bordering on amusement.

"I did say that file would be the loudest."

She stepped into the room, quiet like a shadow, and gaze unflinching. Her tone, though calm, curled at the edges with something sharper than teasing. She let the silence stretch—not to shame him, but to let the moment steep.

Thalos stayed frozen, chest rising and falling, pulse thundering in his throat.

"Are you all right, Vale?"

The question was clinical and yet gentle. Almost concerned, but beneath it, buried like ink beneath varnish, was satisfaction. Not cruelty. Confirmation.

She knew this would happen.

She always knew.

"You're not the first to react this way," she added, stepping closer to the desk. "But you may be the first who didn't fight it."

She reached out with two fingers and lightly tapped the edge of the file, her eyes never leaving his.

"That's good. You shouldn't. It doesn't respond to resistance. It unfolds in surrender."

She lingered a moment longer, then turned without another word and walked out, her boots soft against the ward-woven floor.

Thalos remained in place, still gripping the base of his cock, his chest rising and falling in shallow pants. Her presence receded, but the heat she left behind didn't.

It clung to him like a mark. Not hers, but Kaelor's. As if both had touched him, one with knowledge, the other with fire.

He didn't rise.

Not yet.

Slowly, his breath beginning to level, Thalos released the grip at the base of his cock, his fingers uncoiling with the stiffness of spent tension. The hand between his legs withdrew next, sliding from the curve of his ass with a reluctant shiver, leaving behind a ring of slick where he had been circling himself. The air still vibrated with magic and memory.

He sat upright, shoulders squaring, as if reassembling himself from the inside out.

Only then did he reach for the folded cloth beside his desk.

He began to deliberately clean himself. Careful, as though removing evidence from an altar, not shame from flesh.

When he folded the cloth, it smoldered faintly at the edges, sigil-burnt.

His palm bore a red mark now. Not blistered or branded.

Just... *written*.

The Archive had finished reading and begun recording.

—— ✦ ——

Thalos stared down at the file like it had just breathed. A tremor passed through his core, not physical now but colder, coiling somewhere thought couldn't reach.

His hands were clean. His dick was softening, but his mind still throbbed.

The last time he'd trembled like this was for Joren, when his name vanished from the rolls and left only silence, ink on paper, no body to bury.

What the fuck have I just walked into?

The file hadn't finished with him, that much was certain. He wasn't entirely sure he wanted it to. He straightened the cloth again, set it neatly beside the wax-scarred folder, and exhaled as though he'd been holding the breath for years.

He reached again for the next page.

His cock throbbed again, a stubborn echo beneath the fabric, the file still humming through him. He didn't reach for it. He let the hunger move through and settle.

Enough touching. Enough being touched.

What he needed now was answers.

The discipline steadied him. The restraint became a shield, not a denial. His need hadn't vanished. But now, it would serve him. Not command him.

He turned the page with renewed focus, though his body still ached with the echo of what had just passed. The parchment crackled faintly, as though aware of his resolve.

FIELD INCIDENT DOSSIER – ECHO CLASSIFICATION: KAELOR THORNE

Subject encountered along the southern perimeter of Vale'torin. Unprompted magical resonance triggered by mere proximity. Casual conversation resulted in operative disrobing and kneeling within two minutes.

No known glamour detected. Memory of encounter described as 'reverent dreamstate.' Subject neither encouraged nor discouraged the act. Post-interaction reports suggest emotional imprinting and consensual behavioral override.

Thalos frowned. *Two minutes?*

Subject offered water. Tended to the operative's clothing.
Assisted with re-dress. No further contact initiated.

He leaned back slightly.

That didn't sound like seduction. That sounded like someone waiting for permission.

"Twelve-week dream-cycle followed. Symptoms included:
sensory hallucinations (scent, voice), arousal spikes,
sigil-scar hallucinations, and a recurring phrase: It knew
me before I knew myself."

The words reverberated. Not in the air. In him.

Thalos tapped the page with two fingers, grounding himself. But the paper felt warm. Familiar. Alive.

He didn't know how much of what he was feeling had originated in the file, and how much had simply been *awakened* by it.

He hesitated.

The next section pulsed faintly at the corner of the page, the sigils etched into the margin flickering like heat-light through smoke. Whatever came next had teeth. He could feel it behind his ribs. A wanting ache.

His hand hovered.

Not out of fear. But because he already understood that the further he read, the less of him would be left untouched.

Still, he turned the page.

NEUROMAGICAL TRACE REPORT – KAELOR THORNE / CROSS-PATTERN EXPOSURE

Subject's aura causes recursive magical impressions in
exposed environments. Observed phenomena include spontaneous
sigil bloom, arcane echo patterns, and memory loop anomalies
in both animate and inanimate sources.

Notably, three operatives assigned to tracking reported
experiencing past memories rewritten with the subject
inserted. Emotional impact and sexual imprinting were

severe. One operative voluntarily submitted to containment
due to destabilizing arousal and identity dissonance.

Thalos exhaled through his nose.

He rubbed at his temples, slow and deliberate, as if trying to press back the pressure building behind his eyes. A headache gathered there, born of something older, something echoing.

The text swam slightly before him as the implications finally fell into place.

This wasn't charm or seduction. It was a signature; a resonance so potent it didn't just cling to you, it *rewrote* you.

Memory as weapon.

Desire as vector.

He'd already been pulled under.

He didn't want to read anymore.

Not the imprinting. Not the confessions of operatives who'd surrendered under Kaelor's gaze. The phantom pull of it was already alive beneath his skin.

So he flipped forward. Skipping pages, skipping breath, and skipping consequence.

He stopped only when he saw the heading:

FAMILY RECORD – THORNE BLOODLINE / MONITORED LINEAGE INDEX

"Lineage: Direct descent from the Valmari High Houses (pre-Severance). Subject's bloodline formally disavowed following the post-Rift trials. Genetic signatures indicate non-linear arcane inheritance consistent with celestial interference and elemental infusion."

"Confirmed indicators of trauma-bound sigil encoding. Magical resilience patterns observed in offspring generations. Emotional resonance known to carry through bloodline despite memory loss or surgical extraction."

"Parental records partially expunged. One sibling reference present but fully redacted under Directive 7.2 – blood-sealed."

"Active bloodline convergence suspected with Subject
[REDACTED] in Hal'Syl-related records. Vector instability
detected."

Thalos's stomach turned.

He wasn't sure if it was acknowledgement, fear or something far more personal.

The page felt warm in his hands.

And for the first time since opening the file, he realized it wasn't Kaelor who was bleeding through the paper.

It was something in *him* responding to it.

The redacted markings along the margin shimmered faintly— black ink resisting comprehension, Archive-sealed.

Sibling hidden. Or erased.

He scrolled further.

There, scrawled between lines in a tight, defensive script:

Dual-vector potential. One echo cannot stabilize without the other.

Thalos's blood turned cold.

Hal'Syl. Again.

The name had subtly flickered before, but now it glared back with the weight of intention.

This wasn't just Kaelor's history.

It was his mirror.

Thalos closed the file.

He couldn't take it any longer. Not tonight. His body was still humming with aftershocks, but it was his mind that throbbed now. The name Hal'Syl rang louder than it should've. Too familiar. Too recent. He'd seen it, just days ago, in another file he'd been assigned but hadn't yet opened.

He gathered the dossier into a tighter stack and slid it back into its protective casing. The seal was long since broken, but the residue of it pulsed faintly as he touched the cover.

Thalos stood slowly, every motion deliberate. Heat still gathered between his thighs, damp fabric holding the memory of what had just moved through him. The pull of Kaelor's presence lingered as he crossed to the door.

Tomorrow, he would come back.

Tonight, he had to trace the other name.

Before it unfolded him next.

—— ✦ ——

The corridor outside Archive Intake Alcove still hummed with low, sigil-fed static. Thalos had barely stepped into it when a familiar silhouette leaned against the far wall.

"Leaving without a goodnight kiss, Archivist?" asked Director Threnna.

Her voice held that dry pull of smoke and sharp humor, as if she'd never left the room at all.

Thalos didn't break stride, but his tone mocked offense. "Tempting, Director. But you know I favor a sharper cut of trouble... less velvet menace, more raw command with a feral edge. Thick thighs, heavy cocks, arms strong enough to pin me to the edge of a sigil-table without asking twice. The kind of men who don't take orders from your department."

She gave a quiet snort, the edge of her mouth twitching. "Pity. I'd make an excellent bad decision. Some of us know how to leave teeth marks with intention."

"No doubt," he said, finally stopping a few paces away. "But my worst decisions don't wear robes and daggers at the same time."

"And yet, you're always leaking when I find you."

He smirked. "Professional hazard. Foreplay for me involves more grunting than banter... Oh, and fewer spectators."

Thalos exhaled slowly. "Thought you'd be asleep by now."

But Threnna didn't sleep. Not really. She drifted through Blackwatch like a rumor made flesh. Too connected to everything to ever fully rest. And like all dangerous things, she had a way of appearing precisely when you needed to lie to yourself.

"Please. I sleep about as often as you finish your reading list. And that name you just ran across? Hal'Syl? I saw the pause in your eyes the moment it landed."

He didn't respond right away.

She tilted her head. "Going to go dig up that second file you've been ignoring?"

He met her gaze squarely. "I don't ignore files. I let them simmer until they're desperate enough to seduce me properly."

Threnna smirked. "Just make sure you don't wait so long that what's inside comes looking for you... or finds a way through."

For the briefest moment, her tone softened. Almost enough to sound like worry. Thalos knew better. Concern was a mask she wore for those already marked for something greater.

He stepped past her, his shoulder brushing the air between them, but her voice followed.

"Sleep well, Vale. While you can."

Her voice lingered, braided into the air like a sideways cast spell. Not a farewell. A tether.

—— ✦ ——

Location: Blackwatch Citadel | Sublevel B | Exit Hall Theta-7

The elevator was colder at night, emptier too. Thalos stood alone in the lift, arms crossed, eyes fixed on the dim reflection in the steel panel across from him. The weight of the file pressed against his chest, not physically, but in the way memories haunt the corners of a dark room.

As the lift chimed softly and the doors opened to the exit corridor, Thalos hesitated for a breath.

Threnna's final words echoed in his head: *Sleep well, while you can.*

He'd smirked at the time. But now, the words lingered, clawing at the back of his thoughts.

What the fuck did she mean by that?

She knew something. Of course she did. But was it a warning? A game? A prophecy disguised as sarcasm?

So tangled in the thought, he stepped out into the corridor without looking around, and there he was.

Agent Morren.

Leaning against the archway like he'd been waiting. A familiar grin curled at his mouth, just a little too knowing. The fabric of his trousers strained faintly, the outline of a half-hard cock unmistakable. He looked prepared for Thalos's arrival, and it wasn't to have a friendly conversation if the wicked smile was any indication.

"Evening, Vale. Or is it morning already?"

Thalos didn't stop walking. He didn't flinch, but his gaze slid sideways, sharp and unamused.

He assessed the semi-erection as an incomplete sigil. Half-formed and already failing.

"Your cock's already halfway to a confession, Agent Morren." His voice barely rose above disdain. "You sure you don't want to take care of that before trying out the punchlines? Save the theatrics for the debrief."

Agent Morren fell into step beside him, grin widening. "That's fine. I prefer action over analysis anyway. Especially when there's an ass like yours leading the investigation... I'd volunteer for fieldwork every time. And that little line about a debrief? Sounded an awful lot like an invitation to strip me down and see what I'm packing."

Thalos finally stopped, the pressure of exhaustion and irritation coiling into something sharper. He turned, letting his eyes drift lazily down Morren's body. Broad shoulders trying too hard, belt too tight, trousers clinging to a package that begged for validation. He stopped at the bulge with surgical precision and none of the awe.

There it was. Agent Morren's jaw tensed, just slightly. Like he expected admiration. Like this was the moment Thalos would crack, bite, kneel.

"If that's all you're offering," he said coolly, "I've had more impressive shapes from a spilled inkwell."

Agent Morren blinked. Just a flicker of hesitation, but it was enough. His body shifted slightly, shoulders dropping with the unspoken sting of rejection. Thalos caught it all in a single, cold glance. Filed it away like evidence, gaze still fixed on the agent's crotch with the clinical disinterest of a mortician assessing a corpse's outfit.

"You want a debrief that badly?!" Thalos asked, voice like ice over obsidian. "Maybe I'll call you in for one. Lights dimmed. Door locked. Mouth gagged. We'll see how long you last before calling me 'sir.'"

Agent Morren's grin widened, something hungry bloomed in his eyes. They always mistook the edge of a blade for an invitation.

"You keep talking like that and I might just follow you home." His smile sharpened. "Crale. No more Agent Morren. Formalities feel pointless now."

Thalos's expression didn't change, but his eyes flicked down, then up, slow and unimpressed.

"You wouldn't survive the threshold."

Then, without another word, he turned away.

"Come back when you've got more than a cock, a borrowed grin, and a bedtime fantasy of being useful to anyone but your own reflection. Agent Morren."

He didn't slow his pace. Kaelor's name flickered into his vision— bright, invasive, burning. Then, it lodged deep in his mind like it had always belonged there. Not a name, but a trigger. A mirror. And beside it, just beneath the surface, another name shimmered like a fault line: *Hal'Syl.* Not an echo, but an inevitability.

He didn't look back. He couldn't. Not because he feared Crale might follow, but because some irrational part of him wanted someone to.

Behind him, Crale let out a quiet breath. Whether it was frustration or arousal, Thalos didn't care.

He was becoming the thing the file warned about.

Not watched. Remembered.

CHAPTER THREE: SHADOW RESIDUE

*Location: Blackwatch Citadel | Tier 3 Quarters | Ascendant Hall –
Private Residence | 01:32 – Archive Standard Time*

By the time Thalos reached his private quarters, the day's weight had become a film across his skin. Heat and memory clinging like scent. The door sealed behind him with a muted hiss, light wards flickering to half-glow, and for a moment he simply stood there, jaw tight, eyes blank.

He didn't even undress.

He walked straight to the shower, stripping only when steam began to veil the mirrored pane.

Water scalded down his back. He welcomed it.

Sweat clung to his skin, mingled with the slick residue Kaelor's file had summoned. Threnna's calm precision, Morren's hunger, and his own reflection caught between shame and power lingered beneath the weight of those eyes.

The scald wasn't enough to erase it.

His cock ached again, half-hard and heavy, as if Kaelor's presence hadn't stayed in the Archive but had followed him home. It burned under his skin like a sigil that refused to fade.

He ignored it.

Almost.

He pressed a palm to the tile and leaned forward, letting the water pound between his shoulder blades like punishment.

"Remembered," he muttered.

He wasn't sure if it was a warning or a promise.

The word echoed in the steam-streaked hush, carrying Kaelor's memory, his own, and something older still that wore his skin like a relic.

His cock throbbed again. Harder this time. Ignoring it wasn't working. The ache was sharp now, pulsing insistently, a demand not just for touch but for release and acknowledgment.

It wasn't just need. It was invocation, and it was etched into his flesh like a sigil spoken in sleep.

It had been hours since he'd first broken the seal on that file, but the arousal hadn't faded. If anything, it had evolved into something primal. Less physical, more summoned.

Thalos growled low under his breath and looked down.

He was flushed, thick, and leaking again. The tip glistened with fresh precum, pulsing with every heartbeat like it remembered. Like it carried Kaelor, too.

He wrapped a hand around the base, thumb sliding across the wet head with a hiss between his teeth. The response was immediate, his hips twitching forward, his ass cheeks clenching as heat rolled through him like recognition.

The first stroke wasn't indulgent. It was desperate.

The second was deliberate.

Something whispered back through his own fingers. It was guiding, and not his own. This wasn't pleasure. It was memory, and it was wearing his shape.

And by the third, he was panting.

He closed his eyes and let himself fall into it.

Water, cascading.

Fingers, slick.

Breath, steaming against the tile, waiting for release.

He was no longer cleansing.

He had started conjuring.

His strokes grew longer, slower, more rhythmic, like chanting. Each pass carved pleasure deeper, grounding him in sensation even as his mind flickered with unbidden images of Kaelor's eyes, glowing sigils, and the shimmer of sweat across his skin.

His other hand moved without thought, fingers cupping the weight beneath, tugging with a hunger sharp enough to bruise. The ache intensified. He moaned, quiet and raw.

And still, not enough.

He slid his hand lower, tracing the cleft of his ass, fingers slick from water and want. He circled, then pressed just enough to make his breath catch. Then more.

A sharp inhale. A curl of his spine.

One finger. Then another.

He gasped as they pushed inside, the stretch anchoring him in his own body, as though reminding him he was still real and present, even as Kaelor's phantom power curled around him like fire.

He wasn't just grounding himself. He was opening. Making space. As if the Archive needed a vessel, and his hole remembered how to ask.

When he found the buried, aching spot, his body seized with the precision of a triggered rite, etched deep, and climaxed, like a sigil sealing itself through the flesh.

His orgasm ripped through him like lightning. Shoulders locking, head thrown back, release striking the tile in sharp, hot bursts.

He collapsed forward against the wall, chest heaving.

Not cleansed.

Claimed.

The silence that followed struck harder than the climax. Thick and echoing, like a command without a counter-sigil. The water kept falling, but Thalos barely noticed. His body trembled, not from exertion but from the hollow thrum left in the wake of something that hadn't fully passed.

Kaelor.

He braced one arm against the wall with his forehead pressed to the tile.

He'd touched himself, yes. Emptied the tension, but the ache was still there. Deeper now. A need too large for the body it came in.

But it wasn't just Kaelor that haunted him now.

Hal'Syl.

The name surfaced again, and clearer this time. No longer just a footnote. No longer just a redaction.

A file. One he'd been assigned. One he hadn't touched.

His eyes opened, water streaking down his face like sweat.

He needed to find it.

Tonight.

He turned off the water, the abrupt silence ringing louder than the spray. Steam clung to him like hesitation. As he stepped out, his still half-hard cock was sullen and swung with a weight that mocked the orgasm he'd just spent. It hadn't been enough. Not really.

He toweled off with brisk, utilitarian strokes. Avoiding his groin until the last possible moment. Even then, he touched himself like a trigger, not a comfort.

He should have felt cleaner. Spent. Satiated. Instead, minutes slid past uncounted. The pressure hadn't settled, just shifted, slow and certain.

He wrapped the towel around his waist, containing the resonance still pulsing just beneath the skin.

Thalos couldn't delay any longer, not with the name still thrumming through his body.

A voice beneath the skin whispered: *Sleep would be a mistake.* That the next time he closed his eyes, the name Hal'Syl wouldn't wait. It would bury itself deeper. Just like Kaelor had.

He left the bathroom still damp, the air of his quarters clinging coolly to his chest as he crossed to the wall of storage compartments.

Somewhere in the layers of classified files he hoarded at home, one would bear the name that wouldn't leave him alone.

Hal'Syl.

He tore through the drawers like something was chasing him. No system or sequence. Just chaos. Files scattered. Cases flung open. Ink sachets crushed underfoot.

Records he'd forgotten or no longer needed were tossed aside until his hand finally closed around the right one, and everything in him went still.

The file was warm, not from his touch but from anticipation. All the chaos drained from him, even the residual pulse of desire.

He didn't open the file. Not yet.

Instead, he cleaned. He didn't need order for comfort. He needed movement, something to hold back the calm that felt too much like surrender.

Time passed. Not much. It was just enough for the water on his chest to evaporate and the silence to stretch into something almost civilized.

Now, Thalos stood in a room that pretended order.

The drawers had been closed. Cushions realigned. Stray files tucked back into order with the same clinical precision he wore as armor. It was clean again. Not untouched.

At the center of his kitchen table sat the file.

Not buried. Not hidden.

Waiting.

He stared at it for a long moment, arms crossed over his bare chest, jaw tight with the war still waging beneath his skin. Gods, he needed sleep. But the file sat there like it had been watching him. Like it had waited just long enough to ask if he really believed he could rest now.

He huffed a humorless laugh and rubbed his face.

"Sleep's overrated anyway," he muttered.

He turned, padding to the tiny kitchen alcove, and flicked on the kettle. If he was going to reopen that part of himself, he was going to need something stronger than silence.

Coffee first, then the chaos could follow.

He slid into the chair, his cock half-stimulated but ignored by the movement, like a thought he refused to finish.

He paused.

For just a moment.

Something shimmered in the air, alive with static and memory, scent and fear. He hovered over the flap of the file like it might bite or drag him back into a vision he wasn't ready to see.

But readiness had never been part of the job.

With a grunt, he ripped the bandage, flicking the file open with a snap.

Somewhere along the way, he'd picked up the towel and knotted it again, half-assed, low on his hips. He didn't have the patience to dress, and now he barely had the patience to breathe.

Only the file mattered.

He flipped the cover, and his mouth fell open.

No enchantment. No glamour. Just the photograph clipped to the first page, grainy and old, but vivid in a way that defied its age.

Veyrion.

The man—well, elf—in the picture wasn't just beautiful. He was haunting. There had been whispers. Half-remembered accounts in fractured reports. Codename muttered in fear or lust—*Silver Ghost. Mirror's Edge.* A presence that didn't appear in the field so much as emerge from it, like a shadow shaped by the mind. He'd dismissed the rumors. Filed them under arcane trauma, until now.

Sharp cheekbones. White hair streaked with black, like frost over ink. And those eyes, grey-violet and faintly glowing, as if the image had caught them mid-flicker.

And he was staring. Not just at the lens, but through it. At Thalos.

The name surfaced again, *Hal'Syl*, not separate from this face but written into it.

He looked nothing like Kaelor.

Yet somehow he looked exactly like him.

Not in shape or presence. Veyrion was lithe where Kaelor was broad. Pale where Kaelor was sun-warmed. Cold where Kaelor burned. Quiet where Kaelor roared.

Still, the echoes were impossible to miss, the same mouth, full and blade-cut, the same arc to the shoulders, and something deeper: the sigil patterns Thalos had committed to memory. The kind that didn't just mark flesh but mirrored it.

A pulse beat against his ribs, not his heart but something ancient. Heavier. Beneath his skin, light. He felt them before he saw them.

The sigils.

Faint. Subtle. Real.

They shimmered along his spine and curled faintly around his ribs, flaring in the mirror's corner like heat-struck glass. He'd glimpsed them before in steam and reflection, whispers across his skin, but not like this. Not since the Archive. Not since Joren. This wasn't memory. It was a return.

He looked back to the photograph, drawn to a stare that didn't just linger. It pierced.

Thalos felt seen.

No—claimed.

Not by magic, but by memory and recognition.

He swallowed hard and kept reading.

Dense. Layered. Text that refused to be read without consequence. Blackwatch classification sigils, laced with faint red threads. Warning sigils. Emotional imprint markers.

But Thalos read it like scripture.

SUBJECT DESIGNATION: VEYRION HAL'SYL **– OBSIDIAN LEVEL OVERRIDE CLEARANCE**
Affiliation Unknown. Traces of allegiance to pre-Rift arcane houses detected. Subject presumed autonomous. Reported in sectors affected by mirrorfold destabilization.

He paused and scribbled a note in the margin:

Arcane drift zones? Possible anchor bleed?

Subject is to be observed under indirect protocols only. Telemetry teams have failed to track or scry due to subject's innate null-field resistance. Attempts to tag through conventional magical surveillance result in recursive feedback or rupture of construct.

Thalos leaned back, expression tightening.

Untraceable by standard means. Independent null-field. Could Kaelor share it with Veyrion? Kaelor triggered sigil resonance, but could Veyrion dissolve it?

He jotted it down beside the paragraph, circling the word *rupture* twice.

Then—

PSYCHOLOGICAL PATTERN ASSESSMENT
Subject demonstrates volatile emotional containment paired with clinical sexual control. All known encounters have reported a two-stage arc: initial seduction through silence, followed by exposure to sigil-triggered intimacy.

Another involuntary, sharp breath caught in his chest.

Sigil-triggered intimacy.

He underlined it, then wrote beneath it like marking a sigil: *Like Kaelor, but inverted.*

The words weren't just underlined. They settled against his skin like a memory he hadn't made yet.

INCIDENT REPORT — RZ-17: CIVITAS BELOW
Subject sighted in post-collapse ruins near sector Civitas Below. Contact initiated unintentionally by unauthorized salvage operative. Operative was later recovered in a catatonic state, sigil-etched, with no memory of encounter except a single repeating phrase: "He left me open." The sigils spiraled up the operative's spine like frost burns—etched in language no one could translate but everyone felt.

Thalos blinked slowly.

Left me open.

He scribbled: *Runic imprinting via exposure? Emotional penetration without physical contact?*

More notes. No answers. Just the growing certainty: Veyrion didn't seduce.

He dismantled.

Quietly. Surgically.

And people wanted it.

SECONDARY ACCOUNT — ECHO VAULT INTERNAL MEMO
Subject has been linked to at least five known emotional fractures among senior field agents. Blackwatch recommends avoidance—not due to combat risk, but resonance destabilization. Those who encounter him report hallucination, repetition, compulsive dreams. All describe the same scent: ash, winter, and jasmine.

Thalos's pen hovered. He didn't write it down. He didn't need to.

He could smell it already.

And then the world folded in on itself.

Not with a crack of magic. Not with a pulse of light.

Just scent.

Ash. Winter. Jasmine.

And beneath it, faint yet undeniable, was Kaelor: smoke, worn leather, and faint herbal oil. A blend that felt like a signature burned into memory.

The room blurred; edges bleeding like wet ink into something shapeless. He wasn't in his chair anymore. He wasn't in his body.

Something was seeing through him.

A rain-slick courtyard. Stone beneath the shadow of a moss-eaten gargoyle. A child. Small and still, wrapped in black-threaded linen. Left like a secret. Like a warning.

The wind whispered low, curling through the arches. He saw them again, the ones who dropped him there. Not clearly. Never clearly. But enough.

One hand lingered over the bundle, fingers twitching like they wanted to undo something. Or finish it.

And behind it all, the same smell.

Thalos's breath caught.

He was watching his own beginning.

But not alone.

There was someone else in the memory now. Not one of the retreating figures.

Watching with him.

Or through him.

Grey-violet eyes. White hair. A presence just outside the moment, stitched through it like a buried sigil.

Veyrion.

Not there. But tethered.

And Kaelor's aroma still lingered.

He wasn't just watching.

He was being remembered.

Just like the file had done.

The realization hit harder than the vision itself.

They weren't just memories anymore. They were threads. Spun from his spine. Pulled taut by two names he hadn't chosen and couldn't ignore.

His breath caught mid-inhale, a gasp sticking in his throat as the weight of two presences—Kaelor and Veyrion—folded into him like threads rejoining a torn tapestry.

The fragrances lingered, unreal and vivid, and then began to fade. But the pressure remained.

—— ✦ ——

His vision stuttered. The sigils flared once more under his skin, then blinked out like stars snuffed by sunrise.

He tried to speak. Tried to move. To steady himself against the table.

His limbs lagged behind him.

Too heavy.

The world folded sideways.

Thalos collapsed to the floor. He was gone before his body struck the cold floor.

The file remained open.

CHAPTER FOUR: THE WAKE

The knock was not polite.

It came like a warning. Hard, fast, and far too loud.

Thalos jerked awake on the floor, limbs stiff, skin still buzzing faintly with the residue of collapsed magic. His head throbbed sharp and deep, like someone had stirred something loose with a hot spoon. The air reeked of cold coffee, pooling beneath a shattered mug. The broken porcelain glinted beside him like teeth.

His face felt damp. He touched his nose.

Blood.

Dried, mostly. Crusted at the corner of his mouth, on his chin, smeared into the floorboards beneath his cheek.

He was naked again.

The towel lay bunched behind him a surrendered flag. The Archive had left no signature. Only ache.

His cock was already hard again, flushed and aching like it remembered something his mind hadn't caught up to yet. Like the Archive hadn't stopped touching him.

He had dreamed. That much he was sure of, but the Archive never left things behind in order.

He groaned, blinking against the low, ambient glow of the room.

The knock came again.

And this time, a voice.

"Vale! Open the door before I rip it off the hinges!"

Thalos grimaced, one hand still pressed to his throbbing temple. The voice was unmistakable.

Director Threnna.

Gods.

He pushed himself upright, joints protesting, a sheet of parchment stuck to his back. He peeled it off slowly: crinkled, damp, and ink-stained. Beneath it, a faint line of ink flared once beneath the skin, then dulled. Not written. Branded. He wasn't sure if it had been real or just the Archive remembering him differently.

Everything hurt. His throat was dry.

The knocking turned into a pounding.

"I'm coming," he rasped, staggering toward the door.

He reached for the panel and paused, casting a quick glance at the file still open on the table.

The name Veyrion stared up at him like a challenge.

He sighed through his teeth.

And then it hit him. He was about to open the door to the Director of Blackwatch Intelligence stark naked, blood dried across his face, sleep clinging to his skin like shame. His cock was hard again, as if exposure itself had written the body a command.

He pressed the door release, stealing himself for what was sure to be an interesting encounter.

The door slid open mid-knock, catching Director Threnna with her hand raised and her mouth open mid-threat. She blinked, startled.

Then came the gasp.

Quick. Sharpened with something that might have been shock or amusement.

She stepped inside without waiting for permission, eyes raking over Thalos from head to toe. The blood. The bruised pride.

"Well," she murmured, stepping in further, turning in a slow circle as she took in the mess. "If I didn't know better, I'd say you learned half this intel by osmosis. I've seen chaotic magical burns, relic rebound, and one guy who got fucked into a coma by a possessed mirror... but this? This is art."

She looked back to him, one brow arched wickedly.

"Hell of a night, Archivist. Did you fuck the file or just let it do the honors?"

Thalos let out a half-laugh, rubbing at the back of his neck as he leaned against the doorframe for balance. The sound came raw and hollow. Whatever dream the Archive had left in him hadn't burned out yet. It still pulsed, low and wrong, beneath the skin. "Let's just say I've never been laid that thoroughly. Pretty sure even your best nights would blush in comparison."

The moment the words left his mouth, he winced.

That was the Director.

His superior.

His very not-interested-in-his-naked-ass boss.

The last time she'd seen him like this, the ruin had at least felt deliberate. This time, the Archive had done the choosing.

Somewhere behind his ribs, the sigil still hummed.

"Right," he muttered quickly, standing a bit straighter, trying to reclaim a shred of professionalism. "So why are you banging on my door this early in the morning?"

Threnna didn't miss a beat.

"Oh, I've had better nights, Vale, and looked a lot less like I'd been dragged backwards through a summoning circle afterward." She circled him again, slower this time, before continuing, "And for the record, it's not morning anymore. It's mid-afternoon."

She folded her arms. "You're usually early enough to beat me to the office. When you didn't show, and I realized you hadn't *officially* left the Archive last night... I got curious. Security said you exited, but your aura signature never cleared the building. The system still had you listed as present. Which meant either you'd gone ghost... or you were in trouble. So, I figured I'd stop by before I put in the requisition order for your replacement."

Thalos opened his mouth, then hesitated. "I—"

His vision shimmered, briefly. "There was... that field agent... Crale. Just before I left the Archive. He said something about..."

He trailed off, holding up a finger mid-thought.

A flicker caught his attention. Movement that wasn't motion.

His eyes dropped slowly, breath locking in his throat.

Still exposed.

Still talking to the Director of Blackwatch Intelligence with a godsdamned erection and the taste of iron still clinging to his lips.

There'd be paperwork. There always was. Maybe a clause about involuntary erections in proximity to relics. Maybe a training protocol for shame-spirals and spontaneous sigil bloom. Either way, he was going in a report. Again. Probably under "involuntary arousal near relic-grade recursion sources." Gods, they were going to have to add his name to a training manual.

He cleared his throat and reached for the towel in a slow, defeated motion.

"Give me a moment."

He turned toward the bathroom, not bothering to disguise the hardness curving beneath the towel he quickly refastened.

Out of the corner of his eye, he noticed Threnna was already moving deeper into his home. Not pacing. Not inspecting. Cataloging.

She picked up a crumpled sheet of parchment with two fingers, straightened a knocked-over chair with one foot, and moved a shattered piece of porcelain to the counter like she was assembling evidence for a ritual debrief.

Gods. She was cleaning.

Or casing the scene. He wasn't sure which was worse.

He reached the bathroom door and paused with his hand on the frame.

"Taking your time, I hope," Threnna called over her shoulder without looking up. "Given how often I find you with that impressive—"

Her gaze flicked down to the front of the towel before looking back at him with one eyebrow arched.

"...I can only assume you're angling for a sigil-related injury claim. Something phallic. Something embarrassing."

Thalos groaned audibly.

"Don't flatter yourself," she added, almost cheerfully. "You're not my type. But, I'd be lying if I said I didn't appreciate the view, however unprofessional and unfortunately frequent it's become."

Thalos blinked. Opened his mouth. Closed it again.

"Thanks, Dir—"

He stopped. Not the wrong name. Just not hers. Something older.

"Director Threnna," he corrected. "Right. Sorry. Still waking up."

"I'm sure you could just take it up with the CCB," Thalos called back, immediately regretting it. "Sorry... ignore that. I need a shower. A long one."

He slipped into the bathroom and shut the door with quiet finality, thankful for the brief, blessed privacy.

He padded across the tile and dropped the towel again without ceremony. The cold hit first—gooseflesh prickling across his shoulders and thighs.

He made for the toilet with an urgent gait, gripping the base with both hands to keep the angle manageable. Pissing with an erection was a logistical battle he never appreciated, and this one came with a headache, a hangover, and a hazy memory of being stared down by two mythic men across space and time.

After, he shuffled to the sink and looked in the mirror.

Hair wild. Blood smudged. Eyes ringed with sleeplessness. He looked like he'd lost a fistfight with prophecy, and prophecy had taken its time.

For a moment, the mirror didn't reflect. It responded.

Not a hallucination. Not quite.

His own face? Yes. But behind his eyes, something flickered. A jawline not his. Cheekbones sharper. Lips parted like they were remembering a name not yet spoken aloud.

He blinked. It was gone.

It was getting harder to tell what hurt more, his head, his pride or the way his spine reacted every time that name looked back at him from the open file.

He turned on the water.

Cold. Unforgiving.

He stepped in without hesitation.

If it didn't kill the erection, it would at least punish it.

And if the Archive was still watching, he hoped it enjoyed the shiver.

Outside the bathroom, Director Threnna moved like she belonged there. She was still cleaning, sort of. It was hard to tell if she was being helpful or just deeply nosy.

She held another parchment to the light, smirked, and filed it. Her fingers drifted over a half-charred spellbook on the table before flipping it closed with deliberate care.

Her eyes landed on the open file. The one labeled Veyrion Hal'Syl.

She didn't touch it, but she looked.

Long enough to know Thalos hadn't put it together yet.

She turned her attention to Thalos's desk, crouched down, and started retrieving papers that had scattered beneath it.

If she was snooping, she was doing it with the slow precision of someone who had every right to be there.

She paused, glanced toward the bathroom. The shower was still running, so she resumed her circuit.

Her eyes drifted toward the side table beside the sofa. A small, unframed photograph sat nestled between two well-worn notebooks. Curious, she picked it up.

Old. Faintly water-damaged. But still clear.

A stone gargoyle.

Not just any gargoyle, but the one perched above the east entrance of Blackwatch Citadel. Rain-slicked. Watching.

She stared at it longer than she meant to.

Then slowly returned it to its place, her brow furrowed just enough to mean something, and her expression was already smooth again by the time she turned to the next pile.

The air had changed in the room. A warmer aroma mingled with the colder scent that haunted the room itself.

Smoke, worn leather, and herbal oil mixing over ash, winter, and jasmine that still clung to the air.

Her breath caught.

Just for a second.

Memory unraveled itself in the quiet.

She remembered rain and stone, the same gargoyle, and beneath it something small, silent, strange.

The night she found Thalos opened and unbidden. The air had carried both scents then, layered and indistinct, too faint to name. Now she knew better.

Kaelor.

Veyrion.

The Citadel's eastern wall bled runoff from the gargoyle's mouth, a stream that clattered against stone and ran into the gutter's like a thousand falling knives. She'd walked fast—too fast—half-sure the report was wrong. Half-hoping it wasn't.

The boy was already there.

He was wrapped in black-threaded linen, so small, unmoving, but not unconscious.

She'd known then, without touching him, that he wasn't abandoned. Not exactly. He'd been offered.

There were traces in the air. Something seared. Something born. Magic hung around him like condensation from a shattered seal.

And fragrance.

Ash, winter, and jasmine.

Then leather, smoke and herbal oil.

She hadn't known what it meant at the time. Only that it meant something.

He'd looked up at her without blinking. No tears. No fear. Just—waiting for someone to decide he belonged to the world.

She'd lifted him, quiet and deliberate. No spells. No questions. Only weight and silence, and the gut-deep certainty that no one else could have survived whatever had brought him here.

She never filed the full report.

Some truths don't want to be written.

She'd felt it then. The faint, sigil-marked pressure along the back of her neck. It still hummed when she thought of that night.

Threnna straightened slowly, fingers brushing her coat as if to shake the ghosts loose.

She resumed cleaning. The scent gone but not forgotten.

The bathroom door hissed open, steam curling into the cooler air. Thalos stepped through, hair wet, spine slick, water tracking down the line of his back. No effort at modesty; she'd seen it all before. The cold had steadied his pulse, but his cock still hung with its usual weight as he crossed toward his quarters.

Threnna didn't look up at first. When she did, her gaze swept him with slow precision, the faintest curl of amusement in her mouth, a calculated prod.

"Is that thing ever not impressive?" she muttered, mostly to herself. Then, louder: "Honestly, Vale, if you're going to keep parading that ass around, at least give me the courtesy of pretending it's not intentional."

The jab landed exactly where she meant it to, pulling his attention, anchoring him in the room.

Thalos didn't stop, didn't respond. He just raised one hand over his shoulder in a vaguely rude gesture and started toward his room.

Pausing at the threshold, he glanced back at her over the corner of the wall. In his quarters, naked was his prerogative, and if she wanted to be overt, he could match her without flinching.

His mouth curved, slow and deliberate. "If I knew you wanted a show, Director, I'd have spun it like a windmill," he quipped, voice dry as stone.

Threnna scoffed without looking up. "I've seen better form and more grace from a possessed scarecrow. But points for enthusiasm. Now go put on some pants before I start reassigning your field evaluations to include 'exhibitionist tendencies.'"

Thalos smirked.

Then he froze.

In her hands, resting casually at her side, was the file.

Black wax still clung to the broken seal like dried blood.

The one that started all of this.

The color drained from his face.

He hadn't seen that seal since the moment it broke, since it screamed through him like a forgotten language waking in his blood. Just the sight of it again made his molars ache.

He hadn't even worked up the nerve to touch it again himself. Just looking at it had made his spine hum like it remembered something he didn't.

His mind spun, each thought louder than the last. Did she bring it back from the Archive? Was it logged out? Or was it never logged at all? Is she here on official business... or something else?

And why, in all the gods-forsaken hells, was she cleaning like a bored field commander waiting for something to explode?

A thread of unease unraveled in his chest. Not fear. Something older. Quieter. Like the body remembering before the mind does.

He looked down. Still naked. Still very much on display.

The towel was a memory. His cock still not fully softened, hanging between his thighs like it had no sense of shame.

Without another word, he turned and disappeared into his room.

Moments later, dressed just enough to pass for the living, he returned and dropped into the seat beside her.

He didn't touch the file.

Not yet.

"So," he said, voice quieter now. "You want to tell me why you're holding the thing that nearly cracked my skull open, and doing it in my living room?"

Threnna glanced over at him, eyes sharp with amusement. "Well, you did say you've never been laid that thoroughly," she replied. "I figured you might want this one to go for round two."

She chuckled, full and shameless, clearly enjoying herself.

Thalos stared at her, his face twisted in mock horror.

"Gods," he muttered. "I'm never going to live this down."

Threnna gave him a slow, sidelong glance, her grin widening. "Not unless you get laid by a relic, sprout wings, and take flight mid-orgasm. And even then, Vale, I'd still bring this up at the next field rotation."

She patted the black-sealed file lightly with her fingers. "But jokes aside... I brought this because I think you need to finish it. It didn't just latch onto you for fun, Vale. Your aura never fully left the Archive after opening it. The system still flagged you as present, like part of you never left the room."

Her voice softened just slightly. "And then I come here, and you've got the other one already open on your table. You think that's coincidence?"

She looked back at the file. "Whatever this is... it's yours. So you're working from home now." Her lips curved up in a small smile before adding, "Just don't expect hazard pay unless the file tries to touch you back again."

She stood then, brushing invisible dust from her coat as she took one last glance around the room. "Though, after finding you in the state I did, I'm not entirely convinced you should be working these files at all. Let alone in private."

She turned back to him, face offering nothing. "If something more unfortunate had happened, there wouldn't have been anyone to pull you out. Not from that kind of spiral."

He wanted to scoff. To say he'd been through worse. But the truth scraped along the inside of his ribs—he hadn't. Not like this. Not with memory, lust, and magic tangled in a knot he couldn't name.

Thalos blinked, then shifted in his seat, his voice barely audible. "What... what happens if I don't stop?"

Threnna didn't answer. But something in her eyes, dark and already grieving, said more than silence should have.

Threnna regarded him for a long moment, stern and unreadable, then turned toward the door.

He followed after her, stopping just short as she reached for the panel.

"Thanks," he said, awkwardly. "For... cleaning up the mess."

"How long do you plan on having me work from home?" he asked quickly, hoping to reclaim some normalcy.

She glanced over her shoulder, one brow arched. "Come back when you're finished."

Threnna smirked. "Just don't make it too early. Nobody likes a minute-man."

She walked out without waiting for a reply, coat swinging behind her with practiced finality, as if she'd passed him a sigil still pulsing with heat and dared him not to flinch.

Thalos leaned back, exhaled. One hand caught the doorframe like it might keep him from slipping through.

—— ✦ ——

He didn't move. Just stared across the room.

The files sat on the table like they were waiting for a confession.

He didn't know which was worse. The one he had opened, or the one that had opened for him. Both felt like beginnings, or ends. Or maybe both, folded inside each other like a spell written in reverse.

Veyrion's still open.

Kaelor's sealed tight.

He pushed off the door, ready to move toward them—

When a knock rattled the frame.

Again.

Hard. Urgent.

"Back so soon, Director?" Thalos called with a smirk, turning and heading toward the door. "Sorry to disappoint. The show's over. No encores. Windmill's in maintenance."

He was still laughing when he hit the panel.

Boots. Not Threnna's. Too heavy. Too loud. The smirk fell from his face.

He froze. Not Threnna.

Fucking Agent Morren.

The same smug bastard from the mess hall. The one who crowded him in the elevator like the walls were closing in.

Of course it was him. The universe didn't just kick.

It brought boots. Obsidian-toed at that.

CHAPTER FIVE: THE WEIGHT OF WHAT IS NOT

*Location: Blackwatch Citadel | Tier 3 Quarters | Ascendant Hall –
Private Residence*

Crale didn't wait for an invitation. He stepped into the doorway the moment the Director was gone. The door clicked shut, catching the last of her perfume. Jasmine and leather lingered as the corridor swallowed it whole.

Thalos stood just inside, still shirtless, still unreadable.

One brow lifted—nothing more.

Crale leaned against the frame, shameless as ever. One hand braced above his head, the other resting just beside the swelling in his pants, fingers draped with theatrical ease. Like he'd come not to speak, but to be seen.

"You mentioned a windmill in need of maintenance," he said, smirking. "Well... I'm quite good with my hands."

Thalos blinked slowly, once.

"You're not the Director."

"No," Crale replied, stepping in uninvited, "but I am the one who actually shows up when the gears grind and the framework starts to groan."

Thalos's gaze slid over him with the precision of a scalpel. There was no welcome in it. No curiosity.

"Your hands," he said, voice glacial, "are barely good enough to help you get yourself off—and even that, I imagine, lacks control."

Crale's grin faltered for a fraction of a second.

"I thought we might talk," he said, voice dropping a register as he moved in with an arrogant sway, each step echoing in the charged silence. "About this thing between us. This tension. The way you look at me when you think I'm not watching. You wear it like disdain, but I've seen that look before—on men who wanted me and didn't have the spine to admit it."

Thalos tilted his head.

"I do not watch you, Crale. I witness you. There's a difference. Watching implies hope. Witnessing merely records the inevitable."

The air was still. The lingering tension from the Director's visit buzzed faintly, like residual static beneath the floor.

Crale moved closer. "So tell me... am I inevitable too?"

"You are a pattern," Thalos replied. "A repeated error pretending to be original."

Crale's jaw clenched. "You think that makes you better?"

Thalos didn't answer. He simply stepped forward, closing the distance between them in a single, breathless moment. Not staring at Crale's eyes, but through them.

"You're not even interesting anymore," he said. "You're predictable. Softening and desperate to be seen by someone who stopped admiring you long ago."

Crale flinched, like a man already wounded. Struck first.

"I'm still more man than anything you've ever handled."

That was the wrong thing to say.

Thalos didn't lash out. Not immediately. He paused, the silence thickening as a flicker of anger flashed across his face, disrupting his otherwise sculpted calm. His jaw tightened, and when he spoke, his voice was low and coiled tight with restrained fury.

"How did you even know where I lived?"

Crale crossed his arms, irritation bubbling to the surface. "The Director seemed... concerned. She didn't say much, but enough for me to take a closer look at your personnel file. It wasn't hard to get your address. Most things aren't, when you actually put in the effort."

He looked around the space, then let his eyes slide back to Thalos's bare chest, still flushed from whatever had come before him.

"Showing up at the door like that, bare-chested? You can't blame me for thinking I was being invited in." His gaze lingered on the sheen of sweat still glistening along Thalos's collarbone, the way his ribs rose and fell just a little too fast. "Or did you just forget to dress after your last devotional?" His lips quirked. "I'd love to see what leaves you this flushed."

He sauntered in without pause, like he owned the walls and everything inside them, gaze sweeping the room with the entitlement of someone already imagining it rearranged to suit his appetite. The home was austere but not cold. Elegant, in a dark, brooding sort of way. Shadow-draped bookshelves lined the walls, interrupted only by strange relics and an altar of obsidian etched with cryptic symbols.

Crale walked past a long stone table near the center and ran his hand slowly across its polished surface, testing its weight, its cold bite against his palm.

"This one," he murmured. "Gods, the things I could do to you right here. Bent over, your breath fogging against the stone. That mouth of yours silenced for once. Your prayers turning to whispers as you moan my name." He pressed down, fingers splayed, as if he could already feel Thalos arched beneath him. "I bet you'd leave marks on this slab. I'd make sure of it."

He circled slowly, fingers brushing along the back of a high-backed chair with onyx inlay, the wood groaning softly under his grip. "Or here," he continued. "You seated, robes parted, and me on my knees..." His voice dropped, rougher now. "Not for worship. Just to hear you gasp like you're already imagining. You *are* imagining it, aren't you?"

Then he turned to the low chaise positioned by the window, draped in violet silk and moonlight. He paused, gaze heating. "No," he said softly, "there. That's the one." He trailed a fingertip along the silk, watching the fabric shudder. "You, sprawled and undone, writhing beneath me. Each thrust shaking loose whatever divinity you think holds you together." His thumb pressed into the cushion, slow, deliberate. "I wonder how loud you'd be when it's *me* unraveling you. Would the gods even recognize you after?"

He looked back to Thalos, eyes daring. Close enough now to see the violet flecks in his irises, the way his pulse jumped in his throat.

"Tell me I'm wrong." His voice was sin wrapped in a vow. "Or are you really going to stand there and pretend you haven't thought about it? About *me*?"

Thalos didn't laugh, but the smile he gave was damaging. It was sharp, cold, and devastating.

"You're wrong." His tone was calm, brutal. "Because that table was carved from night-glass and warded against carnal energy. You'd barely get your hands on me before it burned you clean of your delusions. Rejecting you, much like I do."

He took a step toward Crale, close enough that Crale could feel the heat of his body but not touch it.

"That chair? Made for reading and discipline." His gaze flicked to Crale's mouth, then away, dismissive. "Neither of which you've demonstrated competence in. Though I'd pay good coin to watch you try to kneel for anything longer than your own reflection." His eyes dropped, briefly, to Crale's crotch. "And I've never known a man whose knees would ache faster, or whose jaw would lock sooner. Unless, of course, you're used to gagging on your own arrogance."

Another step. His fingers brushed the back of the chaise, slow, deliberate, as if testing its weight or Crale's.

"And that chaise..." Thalos looked down at it, then back to Crale. "Drenched in silk and silence. A sacred space." His voice dropped, a murmur meant to slide under skin. "You think you're the first man to imagine me there? The first to think his hands could hold what others have failed to?" His lips curled. "I wouldn't stain it with your mediocrity. You couldn't hold my attention there long enough to finish the first thrust, much less unmake a god. But if you're so desperate to be remembered, I could always carve your name into the frame... right beside the others who thought they were enough."

He tilted his head, voice quiet enough to wound.

"You're not wrong because you dream. You're wrong because you think I'd let you wake up from it. That someone would want to remember you."

The words hit like open-handed slaps, and for a moment, Crale stood frozen. Then the rage began to rise—hot, choking, wild. His cocky smirk twisted into something jagged, venomous. His jaw flexed and unflexed as though trying to grind Thalos's words to dust with nothing but teeth.

"Is that all you're good at? Witty comebacks and cruel little monologues?" he snapped. "Because from where I'm standing, you talk a lot for someone who couldn't handle a real man if he dropped to his knees and begged for it."

He took a step forward, eyes burning. "Keep hiding behind furniture and metaphors, Thalos. We both know you wouldn't last a moment with someone who actually knows what to do with a body. You're all mouth. Nothing behind it but cold air and fear."

Thalos tilted his head a fraction, as though measuring wind that hadn't moved.

Then he laughed.

It wasn't loud, but it was sharp. Clean and cruel and utterly unbothered. The sound was like ice cracking underfoot.

"Oh, Crale," he said, the calm in his voice almost tender in its mockery. "You mistake your tantrum for threat. You think shouting makes you more real."

He moved closer, expression still composed, tone still maddeningly even.

"You say I talk too much? And yet you've stormed into my home, cock first, ego leaking, trying to fuck your way into relevance. You say

I couldn't handle a real man, but you haven't once made the case that you are one."

His face broke into a slow, wicked smile.

"If I'm all mouth, Crale, then it's only fitting that you keep choking on my words."

Crale's laugh came bitter and sharp, but it couldn't mask the wildness in his eyes.

"Is that what they all did? Laugh it off? Turn you down with clever words until there was no one left to listen? Until even they left you alone in a corner of the Citadel you pretend is a sanctuary?"

His voice dropped, vicious.

"Face it, Thalos. You don't intimidate me. You just reek of someone who's been abandoned so many times, they started calling silence power."

Thalos didn't blink. He didn't flinch. He simply looked at Crale, still and unbothered, as if gauging the heat of a candle trying to scorch marble.

"Is that all?" he asked, voice low and unhurried.

Heat crawled up Crale's neck before he even realized he'd moved. The stillness shattered something in Crale.

"No, that's not all," he hissed. "I've trained beside men with less raw power and more nerve than you. You walk around like some untouchable relic, but all I see is a coward dressed in myth. A ghost with a title. You act like you've mastered detachment, but what you've really mastered is being alone."

He thrust a finger toward the chaise. "You laugh at the idea of anyone touching you like that, but you know what I think? I think you're scared it might undo you. I think you're terrified that someone might actually get inside and find nothing but cold and dust."

The air between them tightened, humming faintly, as if it were waiting for a command.

He took a breath, chest heaving. "And another thing—"

Thalos lifted a hand, lazily, as if brushing off a breeze rather than stopping a storm. One palm half-raised in lackluster defense, the other still relaxed at his side.

"Prove it," he said simply. The words dropped like a stone in a still pond. "If you think you're more man than I can handle. Prove. It."

Crale staggered as if struck, his expression shattering for the briefest instant. It was as if Thalos had driven a blade not into his flesh, but through the soft, festering pride beneath his skin. He opened his mouth, maybe to hurl another insult, maybe to laugh; nothing came.

Instead, he stepped forward, hand half-lifting toward Thalos's chest. Fingers trembling, not from hesitation but from the sheer force of his unraveling. But before he could make contact—

Thalos's skin flared.

A line of heat split the air. Silent, unseen, but undeniable, like a flare-ripple echoing through layered time. Crale reeled, blinking against the weight of something that hadn't touched him, yet left afterimage and ache in its wake.

When his vision cleared, Thalos was still watching him unmoved.

Crale growled, throat thick with humiliation. Without a word, he grabbed the hem of his shirt.

The fabric came up fast, over his head and flung aside. His boots were kicked off with a thud. Fingers yanked at belts and buckles, stripped the layers of his uniform down with the ferocity of a man unspooling at the seams.

His chest rose and fell in hard bursts, muscles tensing as the air bit against his bare skin. Scars across his sides caught the low light, jagged and uneven. A faint trail of hair led from his sternum downward, over a stomach once hard with discipline but now padded by comfort and pride.

His trousers dropped next. He stepped out of them deliberately, the final barrier discarded with a grunt of defiance. His cock hung full, semi-erect from the heat of argument and exposure, twitching slightly in the chill air. He made no effort to hide it.

Crale stood there, naked and unyielding, shoulders squared, breathing heavy. His body bore the map of former strength and current ego. Defined in some places, softened in others, but entirely exposed.

"Happy now?" he spat, voice raw. "Take a good look. This is what a man looks like."

Thalos stared, eyes tracing Crale's form.

He stepped forward, gaze cool, assessing and devoid of desire.

"You used to have a jaw that could cut glass. Now it's lost beneath that growth you call a beard."

His eyes dragged downward, deliberate and scathing.

"Your chest was once carved... now your pecs sag like they've surrendered. And that middle? Doughy. The remnants of indulgence masquerading as confidence."

He circled slowly, like a predator too bored to even bare its teeth.

"And your ass... gods. It used to sit high. Tight. But now? It reads like a failed sigil; burned out, forgotten. It's slack with usage. I'm sure it's given countless men their moment of bliss, but the years haven't been kind to it. Or to you."

He stopped, expression blank.

"And yet, you stand there like you've just presented a gift instead of a grave reminder of everything you once were."

Crale growled low, the sound primal and feral, as if fury and shame had fused into something more dangerous. His fists clenched at his sides, and his eyes burned with raw defiance.

Stillness stretched. Thalos's gaze didn't flinch, but it didn't linger either.

"And still you didn't say a godsdamned thing about my cock," he snarled. "Ten inches, thick, veined, hard from the moment I walked in. You can drag every inch of me through your ice-blooded critiques, but you looked. Don't lie. You chose not to speak it."

He took a step closer, voice a ragged blend of spite and triumph.

"You say I'm forgettable? That I'm spent? But this—" he gripped the base of his cock, giving it a slow, shameless stroke, "—this is the part you couldn't degrade, because deep down, even your silence admits it. This is the one thing you know you'd feel for days."

Crale clutched at the stone beneath him, trembling.

"Why..." he choked out between sobs. Thalos's eyes dropped briefly to where Crale gripped himself.

"You keep waving it like proof," he said softly. "But all I see are balls too light to cast a shadow."

Still gripping himself, Crale closed the space between them, defiance burning in his eyes, hand outstretched again. Reaching, not with violence now, but with the feverish intent to prove something, to make Thalos respond.

But before skin met skin, the air cracked.

Thalos's chest lit with searing white lines. The sigils, dormant moments before, surged like living flame.

And behind Thalos, the shadows split.

Two figures emerged, as if pulled from memory and myth. Kaelor stood first. Nude, sculpted, ethereal; his sun-warmed body gleaming with sweat and shadow-light, cock thick and proud, his presence grounded in storm-born majesty. Just behind him, Veyrion unfolded into view, pale and fluid like silver fire, eyes burning with cruel amusement, his body all lithe power and arrogance, his cock just as impressive, his ass perfectly muscled and lifted with divine proportion.

They said nothing. They didn't need to.

Thalos looked at Crale. A slow smile, lips curling, this one tinged with something far darker than mockery.

"That," he said, voice laced with finality, "is what the Archive remembers. Not men. Echoes of Gods."

The air warped behind Thalos's shoulders, the Archive flexing.

"Kaelor's cock could silence a battlefield. It spoke better than most men could scream, and his ass still sits proud like it was forged to be worshiped from behind. It's the kind of perfection that makes priests renounce their vows, the kind that reshapes flesh around memory. His sigils didn't just flare. They dictated."

"And Veyrion... His cock curves like it knows the path to salvation. It's cruel and beautiful and meant to ruin. He doesn't walk. He prowls. And that ass? It could break thrones. You look at him and know instinctively: this isn't just a man. It's a weapon clothed in hunger."

"You stand here waving inches like a banner, hoping someone salutes. But those two? They don't need to boast. The world opens for them. Bends for them."

Then gone.

Thalos blinked. Something like static brushed the edges of his awareness, but there was no trace, no memory. Only hush where awe might have lived.

Only Crale remained affected, his breath shallow, his eyes wide in uncomprehending horror. His knees buckled beneath him and he dropped with a thud, naked and trembling, the weight of something unnamable pressing into his spine.

He wept. Not the proud, rage-laced tears of a wounded ego, but deep, guttural sobs. Torn loose from a place no armor could reach.

Thalos stood motionless, head tilted slightly. Not because he couldn't. But because some part of him, deep and unused, had flinched.

One moment, Crale had been reaching for him, and the next. He was on the floor, a man broken by something Thalos hadn't even known had happened.

"Why would you show me that... that kind of beauty... only to... to mock me with it?"

Crale's voice fractured under the weight of it, each word jagged.

"They were... gods. Perfect. And I—" his chest hitched, "I stood there, next to them, like some bloated caricature of who I used to be. Kaelor's thighs... the way they flexed. Veyrion's cock, his ass...fucking hell... Thalos. They weren't bodies. They were recursion made flesh, and I saw myself fold in the gap between."

He'd seen the way Kaelor's thighs flexed with each breath, the sheer muscle carved by exile and battle, not a trace of softness. And his ass, tight and perfect, lifted like a gift from something older than gods. It didn't just demand worship. It commanded surrender.

He'd felt Veyrion's eyes slide over him like judgment given flesh, those cruel lips curling with unspoken laughter. His ass, impossibly smooth and high, taut as if it had never known exhaustion, was the kind of perfection that made men beg.

Crale felt like an echo of something half-remembered. Just looking at it had made his throat tighten and his cock twitch with something more than want. It was reverence, laced with helplessness. He'd seen their bodies and felt the brutal clarity of what it meant to be less.

He wasn't firm anymore. Not sharp. His stomach had gone soft, his chest no longer lifted. His ass sagged with age and use. His cock, once impressive, hung like a relic, not a weapon. Next to them, he hadn't looked like a man.

He'd looked like memory's parody; an afterimage blurred by time.

He slammed a fist into the floor, though the impact lacked strength.

"Why would you let me see that? Why would you show me what I can never be?"

A flicker passed across Thalos's expression. Quick and unreadable. Then gone.

"I didn't show you anything," he said quietly, not cold but confused. "One moment you were reaching for me... and then you were on your knees."

Crale opened his mouth to respond, but what came out wasn't another sob. It was something darker. A bitter, twisted edge colored his voice.

"I saw them," he muttered, venom threading through the tears. "You wanted me to see them. You wanted to humiliate me with them."

His voice cracked, then hardened. "You wanted me to know I could never compare. Never touch what they are. You let it happen. You! Let! It! Happen!"

But then, as suddenly as his rage had sparked, it died. He froze. Swallowed whatever else had been rising.

Without another word, Crale stood. Unsteady, trembling, but furious now in silence.

He pulled on his clothes in jerking, aggressive motions, fists clenched around fabric, muscles tight with shame. No flourish, no pride. Only desperation to cover himself again.

He refused to meet Thalos's eyes.

He paused only once at the threshold, casting a single glance over his shoulder. Not pleading or apologetic, but seething with hurt pride. His jaw twitched like he wanted to say something cruel, but the words wouldn't come. Not anymore. His cheeks were blotched, lips drawn tight against the humiliation pooling behind his teeth.

Crale's hand lingered on the frame a heartbeat too long. "I won't be your echo again," he said lowly, the words clipped and final.

And then he stepped out, the door swinging shut behind him with a dull, echoing thud.

The silence that followed didn't feel like peace. It felt recursive.

He hadn't even known the sigils had flared. Not until the heat had faded and Crale was already weeping. They hadn't answered a command. They'd answered something else. Something buried.

Whatever had happened, it hadn't come from anywhere conscious. It had come from the file. Or from something beneath it.

Thalos remained by the hearth, unmoving. His pulse had steadied, but something deeper kept stirring beneath his skin. The sigils along his sternum had faded, but they hadn't gone still. Not entirely.

It wasn't Crale's collapse that haunted him. It was how real it had been. The precision. The timing. The invocation of Kaelor and Veyrion was beyond vision or spell.

He hadn't meant to call them.

They hadn't been summoned. They surfaced through him and vanished before Thalos could name them.

But the files had. Not opened, not read. Just awake. Defending him.

He looked toward the desk where the dossiers rested, sealed again but humming faintly in his peripheral sense. Waiting. Remembering.

Something inside him itched, like the air before lightning. The files weren't waiting to be opened. They were waiting for him to break.

And for the first time, Thalos truly wondered if the files were no longer records.

But living things.

Location: Blackwatch Citadel | Sublevel C | Training Hall Omega-9 (Decommissioned)

Crale didn't walk far. Not at first. The corridor felt longer than it ever had. Each step a drag, like he was hauling the weight of someone else's bones. His clothes clung where sweat had soaked through. His hands were steady now, but only on the outside.

He didn't return to quarters. Didn't report. Didn't speak.

Instead, he wandered, half-aimless, into the bones of the Citadel. Places rarely lit, once familiar, now stripped bare by time and disuse. A corridor he'd run patrols in. A barracks now emptied of breath and relevance.

And eventually, a training room. Dark, cracked, the air was thick with the ghost of sweat and old effort. He entered without thinking, as if pulled by the memory of his own hands shaping this space. He dropped to his knees on the matting, worn thin by the knees of men who'd outlasted him.

There, in the echo of nothing, he stared down at his palms.

Once, these hands had broken men. They'd built strength, wielded blades, gripped the edges of battle and won. He'd been something then. Not a god, not a king. Just a man who mattered. Now, they trembled when he held them up to the dark, as if even the scars were fading.

He pressed his fingers into the softness of his abdomen, the flesh yielding like overripe fruit. A reminder of how easily strength could rot, how quickly the body forgot what it meant to be wanted.

Kaelor. Veyrion. He saw them still. Their bodies had not been carved. They had always been that way. Real. Dangerous in their beauty.

He wept again, but quieter this time. No rage. Just the shattering weight of knowing.

What am I now? he thought.

Not a soldier. Not a lover. Not a rival.

Just a man. Unfinished, forgotten, and finally, undeniably small.

And gods, maybe they were right. Maybe even his balls weren't enough to cast a shadow.

He stared at the mat below him as if it might offer an answer. Some echo of the man he used to be. But there was nothing. Only silence, the stink of sweat, and the shape of his own failure.

Slowly, deliberately, Crale stripped again. Not with pride. Not with seduction. But with the fragile, obsessive ritual of a man trying to find himself in the mirror of skin.

His tunic clung, then gave way with a wet sound, like skin parting from a corpse. His boots thudded to the stone, abandoned as casually as the vows he'd once made. His belt clattered like a severed oath, the buckle digging a fresh mark into the floor.

He knelt naked in the center of the training floor, his body a map of battles no one remembered. The scars were pale now, the muscle soft, proof that even flesh could forget what it meant to be strong.

Each stroke was slow, his grip rough enough to chafe. Not to arouse but to punish, to carve the memory of their hands into his skin as if he could brand himself with what he'd lost.

He saw himself younger. Fighting in mud, grinning in candlelight, roaring after victory with men who wouldn't return his name.

Another pull and the memories came like a blade twist, sharp and unwelcome. Lovers who once begged for him, who whispered his name against their own hunger. Bodies that met his not from shame but from need. His fingers moved, searching for the heat he remembered, but it was only memory now, only ghosts.

Tears spilled down his cheeks, hot and constant.

He wasn't touching himself to feel good.

Even if the Archive had no interest in remembering him, his body could still repeat what it used to mean to be worshiped.

He was touching himself because it was the only proof he had left that he could still feel at all.

The strokes came faster, but the pleasure never did. Only recollection. Only ache.

His breath hitched, half-sob and half-moan, as his hand tightened at the base. His thighs tensed. Pressure bloomed behind his eyes. The kind that always came before something gave way.

He cried out as he came, a sound ripped from him, not in pleasure but in the last gasp of a man drowning in the past. The release was hot, messy, and pointless, spurting across the worn mat like a forgotten offering, one no god would claim. His back arched. His mouth fell open, but the sound that left him was nothing triumphant.

He had tried to summon the sensation of a thousand victories. He got only the taste of ash and failure.

A final, gut-deep spasm wracked his frame, tightening his hole around the phantom presence that had never arrived. His cock pulsed, once, twice, a pathetic, leaking salute to oblivion.

And somewhere deep beneath the stone, a silence answered.

Not a natural hush, but the awful, all-consuming quiet of the Archive exhaling.

It wasn't a death rattle; it was the sound of the world deciding he was not worth the ink. The echoes of victory, of passion, of every sharp word he'd ever used as a weapon. They vanished. His mind, already hollowed by Thalos's words and the vision of unearned perfection, found no resistance left. The light behind his eyes didn't dim. It simply extinguished.

His body collapsed onto his side, still slick, still trembling, tears pooling on the mat beneath his cheek. The exertion had been too much. The truth, finally, had been definitive. His heart, already strained by fury and the psychic backlash of the Mirrorfold's judgment, simply refused to beat one more time for a man who had already surrendered.

He didn't know if it was sleep that took him or the quiet of a man who'd finally stopped fighting the dark. But for the first time in years, the ghosts didn't follow. They didn't need to.

And for once, that was worse.

It didn't hurt anymore. Even the memory of feeling had gone still. Crale was gone, finally silent in a room that no longer remembered his shape.

—— ✦ ——

Thalos slipped into bed without ceremony or care. The silence of his home had returned, untouched by what had transpired. Almost like Crale's spiral had never breached its stillness.

He lay on his back, one arm beneath his head, eyes tracing the ceiling in darkness.

He didn't think of Crale. Not exactly.

But something stayed.

A tension in the air that hadn't been there before. A tremble he didn't understand.

His sigils had flared.

He hadn't called them.

He hadn't meant to harm anyone.

And yet, something had happened. Something deep. Something old.

He exhaled, then turned onto his side.

Sleep, when it came, was shallow.

But just before it claimed him, a scent lingered at the edge of his breath: charred cedar and night jasmine.

And a whisper, soft as breath, close as guilt, warm on the nape of his neck:

There's something in us that makes you want to confess your worst secrets... and then kiss the part of us that would forgive you.

Dreamless.

But in the silence, something watched him sleep. Not as a witness. As a writer, waiting for the next line.

CHAPTER SIX: THE WEIGHT OF WHAT FOLLOWS

Location: Blackwatch Citadel – Tier 3 Quarters, Ascendant Hall – Private Residence

Thalos woke slick with sweat, chest rising in a rhythm his body hadn't owned all night. His sheets clung to him, damp and tangled around his legs, the pillow beneath his head hot from the struggle of a body still fighting ghosts.

Yet, he remembered nothing.

Except the blood.

Crusted faintly at the corner of his mouth. Dried beneath one nostril. He touched his face and stared at his fingertips, confused by the dark, flaking smear. A nosebleed. Sometime during the night. No pain. No warning.

A trail of red. Out of place.

It didn't sting. Didn't clot like injury. A trace left behind, like something had been spoken through him in the dark, then vanished.

Maybe it wasn't a dream. Maybe the Archive had used his mouth to speak and left him bleeding for the memory.

It was the first time in days he hadn't woken engorged. The first time his dreams hadn't left him half-writhing in the sheets, fists clenched around an erection born of forbidden memory.

And the first time he felt misaligned inside his own flesh.

He crossed to the mirror.

His reflection stared back, the crusted blood stark in the glass. A smear of dried crimson across pale skin. He didn't remember it starting; didn't know what had caused it.

It felt like residue. Something unseen. Something that had touched him, then vanished.

He searched his face for a clue. Found only stillness and silence.

He showered under too-hot water, scrubbing skin that felt foreign in its stillness. Even now, clean, flushed from heat, his cock hadn't stirred. No ache. No hum. Not even the flicker beneath his ribs where the Archive had begun to live.

Only the strange stillness of a body that no longer remembered what it was hungry for.

His reflection stared back unblinking, as if waiting for him to notice something he'd missed.

He dressed in silence, fingers tracing the line of his collar. Adjusted it once. Then again. A flicker of unease moved through him as he smoothed the layers of Blackwatch black with unconscious care. No tremor in his hands. No hunger in his gut. Only the chill weight of order.

By the time he stepped into the corridor, the Citadel had begun to stir quietly, always quietly, like a beast too ancient to rise with haste. But this morning, even the quiet felt strained. Like the walls were holding breath that wasn't theirs. As if the Archive had paused mid-sentence.

He walked the path to the Archive as he always did. Same boots. Same pace. Same face offered to anyone who might glance.

But beneath it all, like a hairline fracture running through stone, a whisper gnawed at the edge of thought:

The Archive did not speak. That, more than the blood, more than the stillness, was how he knew something had gone wrong.

Location: Blackwatch Citadel | Sublevel B | Archive Intake Alcove

The door to his office closed with a low hiss behind him, sealing in the silence like a tomb.

Thalos didn't sigh. He was far too controlled for that, but his shoulders dropped half a degree as he stepped fully into the space.

The room smelled as it always did, of old parchment, cold stone, and the faint mineral bite of protective wards humming just beneath perception.

Even the wards felt subdued today. As if waiting.

He moved toward his desk, eyes scanning the perimeter out of habit, but not truly seeing. Each step felt like sinking deeper into a story already inked in a language he couldn't read.

He set his hand on the back of his chair but didn't sit. Instead, he stared at the files waiting at the center of his desk.

There were two.

Kaelor Thorne. Veyrion Hal'Syl.

Both closed. Both sealed. Exactly where they shouldn't be.

They should have been at his residence. He remembered leaving them there—one open, one not. He remembered standing over them before the knock on the door. Before Crale.

He blinked.

Did I bring them? He wondered. Had he gathered them in some fugue state and walked them here without memory of the act?

Or had they... followed him?

The idea sat in his mind like a needle in cloth. Small, sharp, too embedded to ignore.

Unopened. Untouched. Somehow more present than they'd ever been.

A soft hum broke the silence behind him. The threshold-sigil registering a second presence. Not magical. Not aggressive. Just inevitable.

"Good to see you fully clothed for once," came the Director's voice, dry as ever, from behind him. "And not putting on a show."

Thalos didn't turn right away. He let the moment stretch, fingers still resting lightly on the chair back.

"You're supposed to be working from your quarters," she added, voice crisp now. "Until further notice. My notice."

Finally, he looked at her. Her silhouette stood framed in the threshold, arms crossed, expression unreadable but sharp.

"And yet here you are," she said, stepping further into the room, her gaze settling like a scalpel on the desk. "Which begs the question... why is the file I personally delivered to your home just yesterday... sitting in front of you like it walked back on its own?"

Thalos opened his mouth to respond, but the Director cut him off with a wave of her hand.

"No. Save it. Actually, it's good you came in. There was a death inside the Blackwatch compound overnight."

She said it plainly, like a status update, but the air in the room shifted. Something sharp threading into the silence between them.

"Found in one of the old training rooms," she continued, stepping closer, her tone still clinical. "Male. Naked. Deceased from what appears to be a massive cardiac event... mid-act."

Thalos stiffened, the line of his shoulders locking into place. He didn't blink.

"We've already ruled out ritual interference. No sigils, no blood magic, no signs of possession or external coercion."

Her eyes flicked once more to the file on his desk. "But the timing, Thalos. The location. The nature of it... I don't believe in coincidence."

She folded her arms again, voice cool.

"Tell me you weren't in that wing last night. Tell me you're not dragging this assignment through the walls with you."

Thalos's jaw tensed, lips parting as if to answer, but no words came.

He closed his mouth again, took a breath, and let it out slowly. His composure returned like a practiced mask being set back into place. He lifted his chin slightly, eyes narrowing not with defiance, but calculation.

When he finally spoke, his voice was even.

"Agent Crale came to my home last night. Uninvited. He arrived shortly after your departure. He was agitated, emotional. Looking for something I couldn't give."

He glanced toward the files but did not touch them.

"There was an argument. Elevated, but contained. I didn't summon magic. I didn't threaten him." *Summon.* The word felt wrong even as he said it. Nothing in him had answered a call. It had simply moved, as if remembering for him. "He reached toward me—twice. Something... responded. Not me. Not consciously. But it was outside my control. And then... something happened to him."

Thalos's brows drew together faintly.

"He collapsed to his knees. Sobbing. I asked what happened. He spoke of visions, of Kaelor and Veyrion—together. He accused me of showing him something, of shaming him with it. But I did nothing. I remember nothing."

He looked at the Director, his gaze sharp but weary.

"I didn't follow him after he left. I should have. That part... is on me."

The Director studied him for a long moment. Her gaze narrowed with something more than suspicion. Interest, maybe, or calculation.

"It was Crale, then," she said at last. "That was the knock at your door when I left."

She took another step closer, eyeing him.

"You're certain it was him? That everything unfolded exactly as you've said?" Her tone wasn't accusatory, yet it sharpened like the edge of something being unsheathed.

A pause.

She raised an eyebrow. "Well? Are you sure, Thalos? About all of it?"

"It was Crale," Thalos said, his voice steady. "Unmistakably. And yes, everything happened just as I've told you. He left my home alive, whole, and physically unharmed."

A beat passed before Thalos's expression shifted, slightly. A flicker of realization. Shock rippled across his face as the full implication of her words finally registered.

"Male," he repeated slowly. "Naked. Mid-attack... Are you saying the body they found was Crale's?"

The name dropped like a stone into his spine. Not grief. Not guilt. Only the chill of something he'd never meant to unleash.

Even as he asked it, Thalos's mind reeled backward.

He remembered the shift.

Crale had arrived volatile, yes—but cocky. Smirking. Ready to dominate the moment with bravado and lust. That had faded, crumbled, as something unseen wrapped itself around the conversation.

His tone had changed. His posture. His desperation had sharpened into something brittle. Something manic.

The way he looked at Thalos before leaving, red-faced, shaking, half-dressed and half-ashamed. It hadn't been anger. Not really.

It had been ruin.

And now, in the wake of the Director's words, the pieces rearranged themselves into something colder. Something final.

He hadn't seen it at the time.

But now he wondered if Crale had left that apartment broken—his body only catching up to the truth that had hollowed him.

A knot coiled deep in his gut.

Not guilt. Not sorrow.

Dread.

The files. The visions. The sigils. The fact that something ancient and unknown had moved without him—and through him. The possibility that what Crale saw hadn't been conjured but released. That Thalos hadn't been a vessel at all, but a threshold.

And thresholds... didn't choose who crossed or ask permission. They opened when called.

"You're drifting," the Director said, her voice suddenly closer, low and cutting through his thoughts. "I recognize that look. I've worn it before. It's the look of a man realizing he's in far deeper than he planned."

Thalos blinked and turned toward her.

She gave a faint smirk. "Of course, in your case, it's also the look of someone who hasn't had a decent orgasm in days and just realized the cosmos may be edging him on purpose."

Her tone was dry, but not unkind. In fact, it was almost grounding.

"Come back to the room, Vale. I need your brain. Not your brooding."

Thalos's mouth curled into something between a wince and a sneer. "Gods, Director. Must you drag every exchange straight into the gutter?"

But the bite softened almost instantly. He exhaled slowly, a hand passing over his face.

Then, quieter, almost too soft to hear: "I'm sorry. This is... my fault. As if I ever had control over it."

The Director watched him carefully for a moment, her expression unreadable. Then, with a flicker of her usual smirk, she said, "Crale's biggest problem was always thinking his dick could substitute for strategy. The only one to blame for what happened to him... is him."

Her tone sharpened slightly, not cruel, but clean. Like she was trying to carve the guilt off him without letting him dodge the truth entirely. "He came to your door already broken. You didn't break him. You just gave him a mirror."

Thalos snorted quietly, rubbing at the back of his neck. "Well, if it was a mirror, he certainly didn't like what he saw. Spent most of his visit posturing like a rooster and glaring like I'd insulted his cock by not falling to my knees."

He looked up at her. "So yes, I'm sure. About Crale, about that night, about every damn word I've said."

The Director's smirk faded, just slightly, replaced by something more official.

"Then you'll need to say it again," she said. "Officially. The case investigator's going to want your full report. You were the last one to see Crale alive. That makes you a witness. And possibly more, depending on what they decide to call this."

She held his gaze. "So be precise. And don't get clever. You're not under suspicion... yet. But you're too close to this for comfort."

Thalos finally let himself fall into the chair he'd been bracing against, the motion equal parts surrender and necessity.

He exhaled slowly, one hand resting on the armrest, the other scrubbing once more across his face.

"Even dead," he muttered, "Crale's still trying to get a rise out of me. Gods. If this ends with me filling out paperwork while half-aroused and suspected of magical necro-orgasms, I want it noted in the official report that I *did not* consent to that particular kink."

"If you think Crale's cock ever had enough stamina to spark necromancy, you're giving him too much credit," Threnna replied dryly. "Most likely he just confused dying with finally feeling something."

She stepped back toward the door, the sigil-glass band on her wrist flickering as she checked it. "I'll make sure the case investigator gets your details. They'll want to speak with you before the end of the day. Try to stay clothed for that one, would you?"

Thalos gave a dry chuckle as she turned to go. "No promises. But I'll do my best not to traumatize the investigator. Unless they're into that."

As the door hissed shut behind her, he let the smile fade. His gaze drifted back to the files at the center of his desk.

They hadn't moved.

The weight of them pressed against the room like a storm building from within.

He stared.

And the longer he stared, the more certain he became that this wasn't coincidence. The timing. The appearance. The spiral that had swallowed Crale whole.

Thalos didn't know how. But deep down, something in him whispered what he wasn't ready to admit aloud:

The files had done something. And they weren't finished.

So, he ignored them.

He turned to the reports from the day prior, to requisitions that needed sign-off, to scrolls of data unrelated to death or desire. His fingers moved across sigil-screens and parchment alike, annotating field records, correcting archive errors, and issuing updates. Nothing demanding. Nothing reflective.

Hours passed that way: slow, almost silent. Morning stretched into afternoon. The light shifted. Shadows curved differently across the chamber walls.

Still, the files remained.

Closed. Waiting. Watching.

And though he never looked at them again, Thalos felt every minute of their presence. Like breath on his neck. Like memory waiting to be reawakened. Like a story, still waiting for him to turn the page.

—— ✦ ——

A voice cut through the quiet. "I thought I told you to work from home." Threnna's voice carried the edge of command, sharper now, more familiar as she stepped into the threshold.

Thalos didn't look up right away.

She crossed her arms, scanning the room with the dry scrutiny of someone who'd seen worse and still found time to smirk. "Twice in one day. Fully clothed both times. If I didn't know better, I'd say you were trying to seduce me through disappointment."

Thalos didn't rise to the bait.

She clicked her tongue. "I'm giving you a pass, Vale. Just this once. After last night, I'm not throwing protocol at you, but let's not pretend you came in here today to organize requisitions."

Her eyes flicked to the files on the desk, her voice lowering to a blade's edge. "They're working through you, whether you like it or not. And you've been sitting here all damn day pretending they don't exist."

She turned slightly, already halfway gone. "So here's what you're going to do—pour a drink, take those cursed little tomes back home, and open them like you mean it. The investigator's been given your address. They'll be stopping by later, so at least look like you've done something more than try not to cum in your office chair."

She glanced back, lips curving. "Don't make me come back and catch you clothed a third time."

Her voice lingered as she stepped away. "I might start thinking you're respectable."

With that, she was gone. This time for real.

Thalos sat in silence for a long beat, staring at the space she'd just vacated.

Then, with a sigh that landed heavier than it should have, he stood and gathered the files. One under each arm. They felt heavier than they should, warm, nearly pulsing with potential. Like they'd been waiting for him to pick them up. Like they approved.

The weight wasn't just in his arms. It moved inward, pressing behind his sternum.

It was the weight of what follows, settling deep in his chest.

He paused at the threshold of his office, gave the room one final look, then stepped out. Files in hand, dread following like a shadow.

It was time to go home.

—— ✦ ——

The elevator ride was silent. Only the hum of sigil-thrummed gears and the pulse of ambient warding overhead. Thalos leaned against the wall, arms still cradling the two files like they might bite if handled too loosely.

He stared straight ahead, eyes unfocused.

Last night clung like smoke behind his ribs. Crale's rage. His pleading. His collapse. The weight of that breathless moment where something otherworldly had breached the space between bodies and burned through the illusion of control.

And now—dead.

A man undone by revelation, by what rose from within and answered from beyond.

Thalos exhaled slowly.

His eyes drifted to the files. Even sealed, even silent, they radiated a pressure he felt behind his teeth. A hum in the bones. A knowing.

His cock answered with a pulse, the ache threaded with anticipation and inevitability.

He shifted, adjusting the files in his arms, willing the arousal to retreat.

"Godsdamn you both," he muttered under his breath. "You haven't even opened and you're already in me."

The elevator kept rising. And the ache stayed.

—— ✦ ——

Deep beneath the Citadel, a single chamber pulsed with faint sigil-light.

Threnna sat alone in the dark, its walls woven with layered wards and null-fields designed to silence anything that tried to leave. Only the Directors had access to its records, each drawn from covert sensory sigils embedded throughout key residences. Blackwatch's unspoken and rarely acknowledged insurance.

The only light came from the scry-glass hovering above a blackened pedestal, faintly pulsing with residual magic.

Her fingers rested lightly on its rim.

The image that flickered within wasn't live. It was memory. Recorded by a series of covert sensory sigils embedded deep within Thalos's residence.

Crale, kneeling. Nude. Angry. Erect.

Thalos, calm. Then cruel. Then lit with something Blackwatch training had no name for.

She watched without blinking as Crale's defiance broke apart mid-sentence. As visions neither of them had conjured bled into the air like dream and scripture combined. As his knees hit the ground, his pride followed.

The sigils.

Thalos's body had flared with them. Not a whisper of control. Not a conscious need. Just pure, reflexive invocation.

She leaned in.

"So it wasn't just the files," she murmured.

She tapped the scry-glass once, freezing the image on Thalos's face in the seconds after Crale collapsed. He was confused, distant, and unmistakably changed.

Her fingers lingered at the rim of the glass. They trembled. Only slightly. Just enough to betray her.

It was the only sign she gave that what she was seeing unsettled her. Whatever had awakened in Thalos might not just be dangerous, but familiar.

Then she leaned back, fingers steepled.

"Well, Vale," she said softly. "Whatever you are now... the files aren't the only ones watching."

Her eyes darted once to the corner of the room. Past the scry-glass, past the shadows. Toward a narrow window slit where nothing but stone should be visible.

And yet, for a moment, her gaze lingered.

As if remembering something.

As if acknowledging the shape of a gargoyle that had stood above Blackwatch's eastern gate long before any of them had arrived and would remain long after they were gone.

Its silhouette unmoving. But watching.

Always watching.

Chapter Seven: Hollow Throne

Location: Blackwatch Citadel | Tier 3 Quarters | Ascendant Hall –
Private Residence

Thalos stepped into the dim quiet of his quarters, the door sealing behind him with a soft, hydraulic hiss. The stillness greeted him like an old suspicion, as thick and familiar as breath he'd forgotten to release.

He crossed to the table and set the files down with deliberate care. Kaelor and Veyrion. Their names carried the weight of sigils carved in stone. They seemed to pulse faintly under the low light, as if just being moved had stirred them.

He left them to settle, hoping silence might cool their charge.

Instead, he turned toward the narrow alcove that passed for a kitchen. His movements were efficient and methodical. The practiced ritual of a man who needed something stronger than calm.

He reached high into the back of the cabinet and pulled down a small, sealed tin. The label was faded, hand-etched: *Darkroot Reserve: Uncut.*

He scooped it into the press, ground too hard, poured boiling water, and waited.

No cream or sugar. Just the unrelenting black strength of it, bitter enough to strip clarity from the fog.

No wards. No sigils. Only steam.

The scent filled the air. Dark, rich, and dense enough to cast shadows of its own.

He needed to be sharp.

The files wouldn't wait forever. They pulsed beneath their broken seals, as quiet as withheld breath, as certain as names unburied.

Cup in hand, Thalos moved back toward the table.

Each step a procession toward an altar.

He sank into the chair with careful control, the press of the seat beneath him grounding, but not comforting. The files sat in front of him, silent but undeniable. Not waiting to be read. Waiting to be obeyed.

He'd obeyed before. Sat in this same chair, opened Joren's file with a cock half-hard on echoes of what they'd shared and a heart fraying at the edges. Not from desire. From debt. From the ache of needing to know how it ended. And now, another name, another gravity, and still no closure.

He took a long sip of the coffee. Heat and bitterness slid through him, eroding the last of his hesitation.

Thalos's thoughts swirled.

Another rush. Not desire. A signal. A pulse blooming in his chest, pressure gathering behind his eyes like pre-recursion strain. A flicker low in his gut, a memory echo shaped like hunger but missing the want. Beneath that, deeper than skin, unease unfurled like a waiting sigil.

He set the cup down and stared at the files. One hand hovered, then pulled back.

Which one?

He had opened both files, though he had spent little time with Veyrion's. Its pull was stronger than reason.

A connection he couldn't explain, older than contact, louder than curiosity.

His fingers brushed the edge of the folder.

His body responded before his thoughts did. A slow, reflexive tightening. Less desire than signal. A threshold relearning how to part. Not want. Readiness. It wasn't the needy throb Kaelor had drawn from him. This was different. A twitch that struck deep, as if Veyrion's presence stirred something older, deeper, primal, and unspeakably receptive. Instinct versus lust. An ancient awareness that parts of him, hidden and protected, were already bracing to be opened.

Where Kaelor had kindled fire, Veyrion whispered collapse.

Like submission, only rawer. Quieter. Hungrier.

Veyrion.

He'd start there.

He placed his hands on the folder tentatively, expecting the file to react, glow, pulse, or even whisper.

Nothing happened.

The silence unfolded.

He closed his eyes, exhaled once, held his breath, and opened it.

At first, there was only paper.

Then, clipped to the first page, slightly askew, exactly as he remembered it.

Veyrion.

The same captured moment that had burned into him before. Yet somehow it felt different now. Sharper.

Thalos's breath hitched.

The man in the image was shirtless, bathed in the half-shadow of an arched stone corridor, lit from above like a creature summoned into existence. Silver-white hair fell in waves past his shoulders, half-tamed, half-wild. His body was an exquisite contradiction. Lithe, fluid, and yet carved from something harder than flesh. Muscles cut in elegant definition, tight and honed, predatory rather than bulky.

Etched along his chest, glowing from within, were the sigils.

They pulsed blue like frostlight trapped beneath porcelain skin, cracking down the center like a wound that hadn't scarred, only opened wider.

Thalos stared, caught again. Hypnotized not by novelty, but by recognition.

Not a man seducing, but an echo calling him back.

This was a man remembered not for cruelty, but inevitability. A man who knew you would kneel, not because he commanded it, but because the thought of refusal felt like blasphemy.

His lower half was hidden in the photo, but the weight of him pressed through the image like a brand. Even in stillness, his image spoke of slick skin and dark nights, of thighs that spread, and a rhythm that unmade reason.

Thalos's fingers clenched at the edge of the page. His body knew before consent, before command, already kneeling, open.

Veyrion didn't need to burn.

He conquered in silence, all gravity and quiet demand.

Something warm dripped from his upper lip.

Thalos blinked, dazed, mouth still parted in awe of the image.

At first he thought it was drool. An unconscious response to the overwhelming presence Veyrion projected even from the still image. He raised a hand to his mouth to wipe it.

He caught the smear of red.

A drop of blood bloomed on the table's edge.

Another rupture—pressure breaching the edge of flesh.

The scent of something cold teased the back of his throat, neither real nor remembered, only there, like breath drawn from someone else's mouth.

The second in as many days.

And this time, he hadn't even touched himself.

He grabbed a cloth from the side table and pressed it against his nose, tilting his head slightly back as he closed his eyes.

The warmth slowed, then stopped.

He cleaned his face with the precision of someone who'd ruptured before, and wasn't supposed to. Then, without ceremony, he took a long sip of the coffee. Now darker, colder, but still bitter enough to sharpen the edge of his mind.

Only then did he lower his gaze to the first page beneath the photo.

And began to read. Not words. Not names. Just memory, waiting to flare.

—— ✦ ——

BLACKWATCH INTELLIGENCE DIVISION — VEYRION HAL'SYL
Classified File – OBSIDIAN-PRIME ACCESS REQUIRED Compiled by Field Analyst J. Roen, with secondary notes from Director Threnna

Subject Name: Veyrion Hal'Syl
Known Aliases: The Silence Between, The Pale Flame, Mirror of Dusk, The Unblinking Crown
Race: Elf — Variant bloodline (unconfirmed hybrid origin)
Apparent Age: Late 20s to early 30s (Actual unknown)
Height: 6'1"
Build: Lithe-muscular, high tone distribution, arcane vascularity visible during activation states

Known Markings: Faint blue sigils visible on torso, upper spine, inner thighs. Pattern aligns with pre-Severance Mirrorfold artifacts. Sigils glow during high arousal, threat proximity, or emotional entanglement. Tattoo origin unknown—presumed organic.

"Subject generates resonance collapse through proximity alone.
Verbal triggers unnecessary. Emotional recursion via ambient silence is confirmed."

Behavioral Pattern Recognition:

"Target incites surrender not through desire, but through atmospheric silence.
Victims yield without being touched. Without being asked."

Subject displays inverse seduction dynamics compared to traditional arcane compulsion. Known to incite emotional vulnerability in targets through silence and proximity. Victims report feelings of self-revelation, exposure, and submissive desire even in absence of physical contact.

Responses include spontaneous nudity, confessional behavior, and dream-triggered arousal episodes.

Additional Note: Telemetry agents have observed instances of physical mirroring in surrounding observers—spine curvature, pupil dilation, and breath rhythm adjustment to match subject unconsciously.

Blackwatch Recommendation: Avoid direct interaction unless fully warded. Containment not advised. Observation to continue until further signature convergence is confirmed.

Thalos stared at the page for several heartbeats, the words sinking in slower than they should have. Silence and proximity. Emotional vulnerability. Submission without command. Every line read like confession, not intelligence. And every confession was his.

He picked up his pen, hand steady but cold, and jotted a margin note: *"Mirroring begins before contact. Subject pulls awareness into orbit, not through force, but gravity."*

He tapped the pen once, twice, against the table, then underlined the term *inverse seduction.* Another line beneath *emotional entanglement.*

This wasn't just attraction. It was anchoring.

He took another sip of coffee.

Then turned the page.

BLACKWATCH OBSERVATION ENTRY — MF-VH-004
Echo Pattern Manifestation: Unaffiliated Sector | Clearance: OBSIDIAN-PRIME

Subject appeared at dusk in the collapsed ruins of an overgrown observatory along the southern reaches of the Haldran Fault. No sound preceded his arrival. Target was first noticed by atmospheric disruption—temperature drop of 5.3 degrees within a ten-meter radius.

Local witnesses reported losing time. One individual emerged from a catatonic state three hours after exposure, repeating the phrase: "He saw through me and walked inside." Sigil-

scan revealed residual impression along inner thigh and back
of neck—sigils matching Veyrion's trace.

No verbal contact reported. No spellwork detected. But the
subject left altered memory strands in three separate
observers—all with overlapping dream projections in the
following nights, containing sexual imagery, arcane symbols,
and references to a dual reflection.

"He wasn't touching me, but I felt myself open."

Further observation discouraged.

Thalos started to write another note, but stopped.

He reached again for the coffee, brought the cup to his lips. And
nearly dropped it.

Cold.

Not room temperature. Not forgotten.

Icy.

His throat tightened, and before he could set the cup down, the
world around him wavered.

Not shifted. Not spun.

Bent.

Reality didn't break, it pivoted. Memory folded, and he slipped
beneath.

$$\Omega - \dagger - \Omega$$

He was no longer in his chair. No longer in his self.

The chill wasn't just in his mouth now. It was in his lungs. His
bones. His breath.

The ruined observatory unfolded around him, silent, broken and
waiting. Moss clung to shattered columns. The air was too still.

And he was seeing it—*not* as himself.

But through the eyes of one of the observers.

A heartbeat. A presence.

And Veyrion appeared.

—— ✦ ——

Cognitive Anchor: Thalos Elarion (Unbound Imprint)
[Crosslink: Vale // Correction Pending // Ref. Strand Variance 3A]
Memory Substrate: Witness Echo | Recursion Depth: Layer 2

He recognized the strand. His own.

The Archive wasn't showing him a recording. It was returning him to one.

The first thing he felt wasn't fear. It was reverence. Like something holy had entered the ruins, not with the thunder of gods, but with the hush of inevitability.

Veyrion didn't walk. He unfolded.

A shimmer, a shift in the way the air moved; then he was there. His form seemed carved from silence and distant stars, bare from the waist up, his skin faintly illuminated by the dying light of the observatory's broken dome. His eyes were the color of frost burning violet, and they locked with the observer's gaze. Not as a predator marks prey, but as a mirror recognizes its own shape.

The sigils along his body glowed soft blue, responding not to danger but to notice. They pulsed in time with breath. With heartbeat. With want.

He couldn't move. Not the body. Just the awareness inside it.

Not paralyzed. Just... seen.

Under the gravity of that gaze, his body responded. Skin prickled. Throat thickened. Something clenched low and deep.

He hadn't spoken. Hadn't touched. Still, he was folding inward, spine bending toward something unseen, becoming pliant and shaped.

He couldn't swear he was kneeling. The only certainty was the cold already in his knees, and his mind kept whispering, *let him in.*

The air thickened, charged, fragrant with jasmine and ice. It was the kind of scent that didn't remind so much as trespass. Every breath carried ritual on its tongue, bitter and sweet, the taste of truth pressed into the root of need.

Veyrion moved forward without sound, his body lit by a pale glow that did not originate from the broken dome above. His presence radiated heatless intensity, like moonlight made flesh. The sigils across his body shimmered, then flared. Blue lightning beneath skin, crackling in slow pulses.

He gasped. Or the body did. The boundary blurred. His entrance tightened, not in fear, but in readiness. As if the body knew what the mind still refused to admit. As if every nerve ending had been rewired to hunger. To yield.

He stopped mere inches away.

No words passed between them, yet everything Veyrion was said: *You will open for me.*

Hands, his own, pressed to trembling thighs, pushing down, needing grounding, needing anything to tether them from rising too fast into the gravity well of want. Their cock stirred, half-hard, then fully, leaking with silent urgency.

A trickle of breath escaped their lips.

And still Veyrion said nothing.

Because he didn't have to.

Every moment was permission. Every heartbeat, a seduction.

And he aws already his.

Their hands moved. Not commanded, not urged, but caught in echo.

Guided by something deeper than thought.

They tugged at the fastenings of their own robes, breath hitching as each layer came undone. The fabric slithered from their shoulders, pooling around their waist before sliding to the moss-cracked floor.

Cool air met bare skin. Their nipples tightened. The pulse in their throat pounded like a wardstone struck.

There was no shame. No hesitation.

They stood, naked and vulnerable beneath Veyrion's gaze. His violet eyes raking them not with lust, but with ownership. As if he'd been here before. As if this was a ritual they were simply remembering.

Their cock twitched with need, already slick at the tip. But it wasn't arousal alone. It was hunger. A craving rooted deeper than flesh.

They turned.

Dropped slowly to all fours.

Lowered onto their chest, arms splayed forward, ass lifted and spread open to the chilled air.

Their hole twitched, clenching reflexively as though already penetrated.

They whimpered.

Claim me.

Not thought, but surrender. Memory. A truth folded into flesh.

Because their body had already answered.

And Veyrion hadn't moved a step.

He simply stood there, haloed in twilight and sigils, watching.

As if waiting for them to break themselves open completely.

Finally, he moved.

Each step was a study in control, deliberate and silent, as if the air itself parted for him. Veyrion circled the offering slowly, his eyes flicking over every inch of exposed flesh with a predator's precision and a sculptor's appreciation. He made no effort to hide his interest. Lust bloomed across his features, subtle but unmistakable; a slow curl of lips, a narrowing of gaze, a flare in the sigils that danced like stars along his ribs.

He stopped just behind them.

Close enough to touch.

But he didn't.

He just looked.

Watched the way the observer's back arched more, how their hips rolled ever so slightly backward, as if presenting.

Begging.

The spread of their legs widened, thighs trembling now, ass lifted higher, hole fluttering in expectation.

They pushed back a fraction of an inch. Enough to plead without voice.

Take me.

The words were still unspoken, but their body screamed it.

And Veyrion watched, smiling faintly.

Gods didn't rush. They lingered. They let you tremble. And were worshiped for it.

Veyrion knelt.

Not with urgency. With grace.

His hands did not touch, but his presence pressed heavier, wrapping around the observer like mist soaked in moonlight. He leaned forward, breath ghosting across the small of the back, his exhale cold as it trailed downward, chilling, intimate.

The observer shuddered, every muscle taut, every nerve tuned to the single point of contact that hadn't yet come.

Breath again, lower.

The observer whimpered.

Their body was trembling, not from fear, but from anticipation so sharp it bordered on madness. Need had become ritual. Desire, sacrament.

And still, Veyrion lingered.

His presence became a whisper at the base of their spine, not just a sensation, but an echo—pressing inside the hollow places of memory, unearthing what was hidden. Not violently. Curiously. Delicately.

The observer gasped, hands clawing at the moss-slick floor as sensation overlapped with impression. Pleasure became memory. Yearning became offering.

He was being read.

Not by eyes. But by something older.

And as Veyrion's breath brushed against the curve of his ass again, something opened—not just his body, but his past.

The observer cried out.

Not in climax.

In surrender.

But climax followed.

Not from touch. Not from pressure.

From presence.

Their body spasmed, cock pulsing in sharp bursts. Seed spattered the moss-veined stone, release wracking the body until elbows gave way. Their rim fluttered, trembling with the aftershock of need. Still untouched, still desperate.

And as the waves of release surged through them, a second sensation followed. Softer. Stranger.

A pull.

As though something within them was being gently unraveled. Memory. Emotion. Weight.

They gasped again, not in protest, but in awe.

They didn't care what was being taken, only that Veyrion was still close.

Reality cracked.

Not shattered. Cracked.

A knock.

Sharp. Real. Physical.

—— ✦ ——

Thalos jerked upright at his desk, breath caught mid-gasp, chest rising like he'd surfaced from drowning. Coffee sloshed in the cup, long since gone cold.

The knock came again, dragging him violently from the remnants of the vision.

He blinked, stunned.

And then noticed the warmth streaking his upper lip again.

Not sweat.

Blood.

Thick, red, and steady. Dripping not just from his nose but soaking into the collar of his shirt. A slow, hot bloom spreading downward in a ruinous stain. The third nosebleed. Or was it the fourth?

He didn't know anymore. Didn't care.

But it hadn't stopped.

He was panting.

Still hard in his trousers, the sticky warmth of his own cum cooling fast, clinging inside the fabric. A dull ache settled low in his gut, echoing the final spasms that had wracked him in the vision.

Colder than the sweat still dampening his back was the sensation around his hole.

No pain, no touch, only void.

Not a draft. Not fading heat.

A creeping chill coiled around the rim of his hole, and tightening there, curling inward. It slithered across the seam of his taint, whispering up toward his balls and cock, coaxing another twitch of sensitivity from nerves already raw. The sensation didn't sting. It possessed. Claimed.

Something lingered.

Something had left and meant to return.

He wasn't in the observatory.

He was home. The room was still. Unchanged. As though nothing sacred had just ruptured.

The air smelled of stale ink and coffee.

And someone was at the godsdamned door.

He stared at the door for a long moment. Long enough for a third knock to resound, firm and patient.

Still panting, he wiped blood from his face with the cuff of his sleeve, breath catching as the movement pulled against the sticky fabric of his soaked trousers.

"Gods," he muttered aloud, voice hoarse. "He nearly fucked the soul out of me... and didn't even touch me."

A short, bitter laugh escaped him.

He looked back at the file, still breathing hard, cock throbbing beneath damp fabric, the chill clinging to his hole.

And shuddered.

Because the knock hadn't arrived after the file.

It had come when the file was ready.

And whatever it summoned... hadn't left yet.

CHAPTER EIGHT: REUNION
INQUISITION

*Location: Blackwatch Citadel | Tier 3 Quarters | Ascendant Hall –
Private Residence*

The knock still echoed faintly through the chamber when Thalos finally rose.

The heat in his groin had dulled to an aching memory. His trousers were still damp with the shame and awe of whatever arcane communion the file had dragged him into. He moved stiffly, disoriented but composed. He wiped the worst of the blood from his face, threw on a fresh overshirt, and crossed to the door.

He didn't ask who it was. The knock had the cadence of procedure, not panic. Threnna had warned him. Internal Oversight moved quickly when sigils burned through.

He hit the release panel.

He expected black gloves. Not storm-grey eyes.

And there he was.

Tall. Broad through the shoulders in a way that spoke to years of unseen labor. Stubble shadowed his jaw in a rough-edged five o'clock growth, accentuating the now square-cut angles of his face. He stood easily a head taller than the boy Thalos remembered.

Not a boy anymore. Not even close.

Dressed in the standard slate-black of Internal Oversight, collar high and gloves buttoned. The fit was tailored for utility, but the investigator wore it like intention. The fabric hugged his chest, narrowed at the waist, stretched slightly around the curve of his ass. Beneath that belt, subtle but undeniable, was the presence of something remembered.

It wasn't the uniform that froze Thalos in place.

It was the face.

Worn. Sharper, but still unmistakable.

Storm-lit grey eyes, framed in dark lashes. Always watching.

Joren.

Not dead. Not lost. Not a ghost.

Thalos didn't breathe. He forgot how.

Joren raised an eyebrow, expression unreadable. "I assume this is the part where you either slam the door or ask me in."

Thalos said nothing. Just stepped back.

Joren entered.

The door hissed shut behind him, sealing in the air between them.

"Investigator Joren Cael," he said, by way of introduction. "Internal Oversight, tier red, non-civilian. I'm here regarding the death of Agent Crale Morren."

Thalos didn't respond. He was still staring. Still recalibrating.

Joren's gaze shifted to the table. The file.

The atmosphere changed, thickened. Something in his chest tightened, memory catching in his throat like smoke.

"You look like you've seen a ghost," he said. Then, after a beat: "Or maybe just survived one."

Thalos swallowed. "You..." His voice was dry. "You're supposed to be dead."

Joren tilted his head. "I was."

As if the declaration required no further explanation, he crossed to the small kitchen table—the one flanked by warded shelves and two worn, high-backed chairs—and sat. The choice wasn't casual. It was procedural. Clinical. Intentional. He hadn't taken the plush seat near the hearth or the chaise where others had bared more than their intentions. He wanted this to feel technical. Controlled.

"Shall we begin?"

Thalos didn't answer right away.

He couldn't.

He remained standing as the silence curled inward around him, gaze pinned to the man seated at his table. The words still echoed in his head: *You were supposed to be dead.*

Because Joren had died or so the report had claimed.

Seven years ago, during the Arc-Spill Collapse in the southern vault sectors. Officially listed as 'lost during response action.' Nothing recovered. The announcement had been brief. No ceremony. No remains. No closure. Only a classified footnote in a monthly loss ledger, and a single line sent to Thalos's secure inbox:

Agent Joren Cael presumed deceased. Do not initiate contact with next-of-kin.

He had stared at those words for hours. Replayed every memory. Every unfinished sentence. Every touch that had never meant what it should have. He had burned the message into memory.

Now, the man was sitting at his table like the past hadn't collapsed into ash.

Joren. Alive. Changed. Here.

Thalos's knees nearly buckled.

He moved to the other chair with measured care, lowering himself slowly into the seat across from the ghost wearing his past lover's face.

The weight of it all pressed against his skin like a second uniform.

Still, Joren waited.

But Thalos didn't speak. Not yet.

His gaze dragged over the man across from him, cataloging the ways Joren had changed, and the ways he hadn't. Broader now. Hardened by time and silence. But those eyes... gods, those eyes were exactly the same. The ones that had watched him tremble the first time he bared his body, the first time the sigils lit under his skin. Joren had been the first to touch him. The first to see him. The first to hold his name in a whisper and not flinch.

And now?

Now he sat in regulation black and spoke like a stranger. Like someone who hadn't vanished without a trace, leaving Thalos to carry the grief like a wound that refused to scar.

Heartache surged. Then rage. A whiplash of mourning colliding with betrayal.

He wanted to scream. To slam the table. To ask why.

But instead, he breathed.

Measured. Contained.

The fury could wait. The ache could burn beneath the surface.

He would not give Joren the satisfaction of seeing him undone again.

Joren studied him, and in that pause, just long enough to harden into tension, he cleared his throat. It wasn't loud or uncertain, only enough to break Thalos from the loop of memory behind his eyes.

"Shall we begin?" he asked again, this time adding with deliberate precision:

"Mr. Vale."

The name landed like punctuation. A reminder.

This was not a reunion.

It was an interrogation.

Thalos straightened slightly, posture sharp as a drawn line. He let the silence linger, long enough to cut.

"Of course, Investigator," he said at last, his voice smooth and edged with disdain. "Let's keep it professional. Gods forbid I confuse this for the last time you had me bent over Archive stone, buried so deep I thought the sigils would carve your name into my spine."

He leaned back. Gaze cool. Calculated. "But I suppose we're here to discuss more pressing things. The man who died trying to do half as well—and the one sitting across from me who wasn't supposed to be alive at all."

His tone never wavered, but the anger in it gleamed like a blade just barely sheathed.

Joren's jaw tightened. Not visibly. Thalos saw the minute twitch in the muscle just beneath his stubble, the flick of his eyes to the edge of the table as though it might ground him. A breath escaped through his nose, short and shallow.

Then, with all the composure of a man who'd expected worse:

"Where were you between the hours of midnight and three Archive Standard Time?"

Thalos's lip curled, a flicker of heat sparking in his eyes. "Midnight to three? You mean the hours right after I watched a ghost knock on my door, only to find he'd learned to wear guilt like a new coat?"

He leaned in slightly, voice low, dangerous. "I was at home. Right here. Recovering from the effects of an arcane file that doesn't seem content with staying closed. Or maybe you don't remember how that feels? It's been so long since you felt anything warm against your skin, hasn't it? Since you last said my name with your hips instead of your mouth?"

Thalos paused, the next words lower, shaded with something darker. "The last time you interrogated me, Joren, you didn't need questions. Just friction."

Joren didn't flinch, but the pulse at his throat ticked visibly once. His jaw remained set, but Thalos didn't miss the subtle stir beneath the tailored uniform; a shift, a swell, a twitch of something waking beneath the fabric.

"This isn't about the past," Joren said coldly, clinically. "Whatever happened between us ended a long time ago."

His tone was flat, but that didn't stop the involuntary reaction that betrayed him. Thalos saw it. Noted it. Filed it away.

The way Joren straightened in his seat wasn't denial. It was damage control. It was the posture of a man trying to repress what his body remembered too well.

Joren adjusted his gloves, letting the silence settle like a judge before a verdict. When he spoke again, his voice had cooled even further, the words clipped with authority.

"This is about Agent Crale," he said. "A death inside Blackwatch jurisdiction. A man found naked, mid-climax, with no signs of ritual coercion, no obvious magical triggers. And the last confirmed contact traced back to you."

He let that hang for a beat.

"This isn't a personal visit, Mr. Vale. Whatever we once were has no bearing on this investigation. But what you are now, the last person to see him alive. That does."

His eyes locked on Thalos's, unwavering. "So if you're done with the poetry, let's stick to the facts."

Thalos wasn't listening. Not at first.

His mind flickered. Helplessly. Vividly. Back to a memory he hadn't summoned in years. Joren behind him, his voice a whisper against Thalos's ear. Hands gripping his hips with reverence and command. Thalos bent over the Archive table, sigils blazing blue along his spine as Joren's cock drove deep, unrelenting, each thrust carving his name deeper into Thalos's bones.

Heat. Breath. Praise. Teeth. The feeling of being held down, not to punish, but to worship.

He blinked. Exhaled. The room spun once.

Then, he smiled.

"Facts, is it?" Thalos asked, voice silk over obsidian. "Strange how the facts you left behind forgot to mention you weren't dead."

Joren's mouth parted slightly, the breath catching in his throat before he forced it down. He shifted in his seat. Not abruptly, but with just enough restraint to suggest discomfort. Not from the words, but from the weight behind them.

Thalos saw it again.

That twitch. That tell.

Joren's cock was stirring, visibly now, the fabric of his uniform shifting ever so slightly, tightening across his lap. He adjusted his gloves again with unnecessary precision, jaw tightening like a lock wound too hard.

"You always did talk too much," Joren muttered, voice clipped, as he forced his composure back into place. "Let's move on."

He retrieved a small sigil-stamped recorder from his coat and set it on the table between them, activating it with a flick.

"For the record," he said, voice settling back into procedural formality, "please confirm your whereabouts at the approximate time of death for Agent Crale: between midnight and three AST last night."

Thalos tilted his head slowly, eyes narrowing as if the question had somehow offended him just by existing. "You're really going to make me say it again? That I was here, alone, fully clothed. Unlike Crale, apparently. Trying to survive whatever those files decided to finger into my bloodstream?"

He leaned forward an inch, lips curling faintly.

"You're lucky I remember anything at all. When the file wasn't dragging me into another man's orgasmic death spiral, I was trying not to bleed out through my nose. Or does that kind of climax sound familiar to you, Joren? One too strong to walk away from?"

He sat back with a practiced elegance, voice smooth.

"I was here. Drinking black coffee. And thinking about how funny it is that I grieved a dead man who never actually bothered to say goodbye."

Joren's face stayed still, but the temperature in the room dropped a degree.

When he finally spoke, his voice was a scalpel.

"You grieved? Don't flatter yourself, Vale. You weren't the only one who lost something that day, but at least you got to keep your name. Some of us had to trade ours in for clearance and silence."

Joren's jaw ticked again, but he didn't blink.

"You think this is personal? It's not. You were just another distraction I buried to survive. Some part of the story I never meant to reread."

Thalos didn't answer at first.

His face twitched, just once, before he looked away. A breath caught, sharp and unbidden. His hand curled faintly where it rested against the arm of the chair.

Then, with voice low and cracked around the edge, he muttered, "I keep trying to find the boy I knew in the man sitting in front of me… but he's not there."

The words barely left his mouth before his tone hardened, the softness cauterized.

He turned back, fury sharpened into poise.

"You buried me? Funny. Because I remember giving you everything I had. My body, my soul, my voice. You didn't bury me, Joren. You ran. And now you're back with a badge and a question like that makes you clean. There's no version of this where you walk in and pretend I was the one who failed."

He leaned forward, fire under his skin.

"So no. I won't flatter myself. But I will remind you. I was the only one who never stopped looking."

Joren tried to hold the line.

He inhaled, fingers tightening slightly on the edge of the table— subtle, but enough. His jaw set. His shoulders rolled back into that same mask of control he'd worn since walking through the door.

"You always were good with final words," he said, tone quiet but clipped. "Too bad you never learned to mean them."

The crack in Joren's resolve was there again, just beneath the surface.

His eyes burned, not with rage, but something far messier. *Tired.* Not the sharp glint of an enforcer doing his job, but the haunted echo of a boy who'd once buried his face in Thalos's neck and promised never to disappear.

His throat bobbed once. He blinked too slowly.

And then he looked down at the recorder, the line of his mouth barely holding steady.

"Let's finish this, Vale. While I still remember how to pretend we were never anything at all."

Thalos tilted his head, studying Joren through narrowed eyes. The crack was still there. More visible now, raw and widening.

He didn't soften. Not this time.

"You can pretend all you want, Joren. You're not the only one who's buried things."

He let the silence stretch.

"But since we're trading facts..."

Thalos leaned forward, fingers steepling before him.

"Crale showed up at my door last night."

"Uninvited. Not long after the Director left. He was agitated, cocky, like he wanted to provoke something. Said I'd been looking at him. That there was tension between us. That I'd wanted it when he tried to touch me."

"He walked in already hard. Like his cock was proof. A weapon. Something he thought I'd worship if he brandished it just right. Said I was responsible for it, said my eyes had been all over him like he was owed something. He stripped in front of me like a man possessed. Proud. Angry. Desperate. Like fucking me was the only thing left that might make him matter."

Thalos's voice didn't break, but the edges were sharper now. Each word had to cut its way free.

"He stroked himself, right there on the floor. Told me I couldn't look at him and say I didn't want it. That if I really saw him, I'd know he was everything I'd been needing. And then... he started weeping. Collapsing. Not from shame. From whatever hit him inside his own skull. Said he saw them. Kaelor and Veyrion. Said I had shown him what perfection looked like. That I'd made him kneel with it."

He tapped a finger once against the table. Not for emphasis. For grounding.

The air flexed. Not visibly. But it tightened, like breath trapped behind his molars. Like the sigil on his spine remembered something before he did.

"I didn't respond. Not with force. But something beneath my skin did. The shift you feel before the sigils light. The kind that leaves your mouth dry and your memory wrong. He was ranting about Kaelor and Veyrion. About what I'd shown him. About what I made him see."

He sat back again, face unreadable.

"And now he's dead. And somehow I'm still the one being asked where I was at midnight."

Joren was quiet for a long moment. Too long.

"You expect me to believe that all just... happened around you?"

His voice was low, incredulous, but not entirely surprised. More like someone watching a pattern repeat itself.

"He undressed. He touched himself. He cried. And you... what? Just stood there cataloging the tragic arc of his erection?"

The words hit like blades dulled only by sarcasm.

He leaned forward slightly.

"Did your sigils light up again, Thalos? Like they did the night I bent you over the Archive table?"

His tone was clinical. Cold. But underneath the snark, the malice glinted. Sharp and personal.

"Because if they did... we're not talking about some horny agent's breakdown anymore. We're talking about resonance. About what you bring out of people. What you leave behind when you don't even mean to."

Thalos's gaze sharpened, his jaw tightening. Not in shame, but obsidian.

"Crale left my home alive, Joren. Hard, yes. Rattled, certainly. But very much alive. Whatever happened to him after he stormed out wasn't because of some buried compulsion or magical seduction."

He leaned forward again, and this time there was fire behind his words, coiled around heat.

"You want to talk resonance? Let's. But maybe start with how your cock's been twitching under that uniform since the moment I opened the door."

Thalos's lips curled, not a smirk, but a scythe.

"Maybe I do leave something behind, Joren. Maybe that's all I've become. A resonance. A signal too loud to stop once it's played. But if so, you've been carrying it for seven years. Don't blame me for the weight."

Joren's breath caught. His posture faltered. Not enough to fall apart, but enough to prove he had no defense left strong enough to hold this line. The veneer crumbled.

He looked down at the recorder again, but this time, his gaze was vacant.

Joren inhaled, and it sounded like surrender. A breath pulled not from lungs, but from somewhere weathered.

"I came back the next day," he said softly.

Thalos blinked.

"I wanted to see you," Joren continued, his voice quieter, stripped of venom. "To explain. To stay. But my family... they found out. Intervened. Said I'd compromised clearance. Said you'd become a liability."

His jaw tightened. "They reassigned me before I could get near you again. Falsified the Arc-Spill report. Buried my name to keep theirs clean. I wasn't supposed to ever surface again, not even as a memory."

His eyes lifted.

"I was never meant to see you again. But I have. And I never stopped wanting to."

His voice trembled at the edge now, the weight of years crackling through restraint.

"I thought if I stayed gone long enough, it would fade. That the heat of you would turn cold with time. That maybe I imagined how your body arched when I was inside you. How your breath caught when you said my name like it was the first time anyone had spoken it with meaning."

His throat worked, hard.

"But I didn't imagine it. And I didn't forget."

Joren finally looked up, the mask gone.

"So yes, I came here to do my job. But I also came because seven years later, I still wake up hard, dreaming about the night you let me ruin you with reverence."

Joren didn't move. Didn't blink. Suspended. Caught in the silence Thalos had carved between them.

Finally, with a whisper of breath, ragged, like the air itself hurt.

"Maybe... maybe a little of both," he said.

His voice was lower now. Not broken, but peeled back. Honest.

His eyes scanned Thalos's face, not for weakness or openings, but the boy he remembered.

"You were always the one I couldn't look away from. Even when we were just boys sneaking through warded halls and stealing moments between protocol and silence. I thought I knew what we were then, but I was wrong. I only knew the beginning."

Joren paused, and something flickered behind his eyes.

A memory struck, his eyes, his voice, the way he'd said Thalos's name like it meant something. The way his breath had shaken when he'd tried not to beg. It surfaced sharp and unbidden, and Joren couldn't stop it.

He swallowed, jaw clenching, but his gaze didn't waver.

"You're not that boy anymore. And gods, Thalos, you've become something far more dangerous. Something magnetic. And still... I want to build from what we were. Not as children chasing pleasure, but as men choosing it."

He leaned forward just slightly, the recorder between them forgotten.

"If we start again, there won't be whispers. No breath stolen. Not a moment hidden in Archive, but a chapter we write in the open."

Jorne's voice dropped softer like a vow.

"If you'll let me."

A faint hum split the air.

The files on the table glowed.

Not one, but both. Soft, pulsing light leaking from the sigil-etched edges, Kaelor's burning low and red, Veyrion's shimmering faintly blue.

Thalos and Joren both turned toward them in the same breath, the tension between them crystallized by the undeniable presence of something larger.

The glow wasn't loud. It didn't flicker wildly or burst with fanfare. But it was insistent. Alive. Like breath caught in paper. Like awareness.

Thalos stared at the light.

"Shit," he whispered.

—— ✦ ——

Far below the black vaults and dead scry-chambers, Director Threnna stood alone.

Her scry-glass hovered, angled to reflect not the room, but the echo she'd anchored to the trace-signatures inside Thalos's quarters.

She watched them, the two men. The files between them. The flare of light pulsing like a heartbeat.

A slow smile pulled at the edge of her mouth.

Behind her, the old gargoyle watched from its stone alcove, motionless. Waiting.

"Well," she murmured, sipping from her tea. "That's one way to wake a god."

"Now let's see if they remember how to kneel... and who to kneel to."

Chapter Nine: The Archive's Breath

Joren took a slow step toward the files, but Thalos reached out, catching his wrist.

"Don't," Thalos said quietly.

Joren froze. It wasn't fear that locked him in place but recognition, and that tone Thalos used when something more mature than logic stirred.

A sound rolled through the room. Low, not a whisper but a presence. Like a murmur across parchment. The light pulsed again, stronger this time.

Kaelor's file glowed like a sore that hadn't scabbed but deepened with each breath. Veyrion's shimmered like a question half-whispered through fog. They cast magelight across the room, red and blue heartbeats syncing out of time.

Thalos took a step back, but the pressure followed. It wasn't aggressive. It wasn't kind. It simply *was,* the way prophecy binds, or gravity obeys no one.

"What is this?" Joren asked, his voice just above a whisper.

"They're syncing," Thalos murmured. "Not just glowing. They're... breathing. Together."

Not air. Not magic. Memory exhaling through bone.

Joren moved behind him, his breath a steady presence as he looked over Thalos's shoulder. "You think it's a ritual?" Joren asked, voice low.

"Mirrorfold." Joren stuttered, like the word had been placed in his mouth, not chosen.

Thalos flinched.

The word hung in the air like blood on parchment.

"Where did you hear that?" he asked, too quickly. Too sharp.

Joren just blinked, confused. "I... didn't. I don't think—"

Thalos swallowed. The Archive was listening. Or leaking. Or both.

"We shouldn't touch them," he said. "Not yet. They're not ready, or maybe we're not."

A silence stretched between them, thick with the heat of remembrance. The files dimmed slightly but didn't stop pulsing. They remained alive, like a heartbeat beneath stone.

Thalos stepped back from the table, rubbing the tension from his jaw.

"They're not just telling a story anymore," he said. "They're writing one." He swallowed, throat tight. "And I think we're the ones being written. And it won't be kind."

Joren's gaze lingered on the desk for a moment longer before drifting to Thalos again. It wasn't curiosity in his eyes now. It was something heavier.

"You're trembling," he said softly.

Thalos blinked. He hadn't realized it.

Joren took his hand, lacing their fingers.

"Come on," he said. "Sit with me."

Thalos didn't sit.

He stepped closer instead. Into Joren's space. Into the gravity that had drawn them together since the first day, between stone shelves and the kind of stillness that makes you ache before you understand why.

Not desire. Inevitability. Like a sigil drawn in muscle and breath, waiting for the last stroke to complete.

The glow faded. The pressure lingered, a sigil's echo caught in skin, like the aftermath of a spell still vibrating against their ribs. Thalos could feel it coiled low in his stomach, echoing along the path of his spine, tightening his breath like a thread drawn taut through skin. He turned to Joren not with strategy, but instinct.

The heat between them bled through cloth. Thighs brushed. Breath tangled. Thalos's hand slipped beneath Joren's shirt without planning it. He sought the pulse he didn't remember but already ached to follow.

The kiss didn't come with violence or desperation.

It came slow. At first. Like ink soaking into parchment. Like a decision already made.

But then it deepened.

Thalos's lips parted, not in surrender but in hunger, and Joren answered with a low, grounding moan, pulling him closer with both hands fisting in the back of his coat. Their mouths moved with rising urgency. Tongues sliding, breaths catching, hips brushing close enough to stir heat between them. Joren kissed like a man starving for truth. Thalos kissed like he was trying to burn away a lie.

Their bodies pressed flush. Thalos's fingers gripping the front of Joren's shirt like an anchor as their teeth grazed, gasps shared, friction building between their mouths.

When they finally pulled apart, it wasn't from hesitation. But from the aching, pulsing need to *move*, to *touch*, to get *closer*.

The air between them didn't cool. It condensed, heavy with memory, dense with something more than heat.

Their cocks pressed against their clothes, friction sharp and deliberate with every breathless movement, the hunger between them too thick to burn off with a kiss alone.

Thalos didn't speak. He just took Joren's hand again and led him from the room. Behind them, the files still breathed; alive, waiting. The tension in his body was so taut, so electric, that by the time they reached the hallway, Thalos almost forgot how to walk.

The Archive didn't close the door behind them. It simply inhaled and waited.

—— ✦ ——

The room was dark. Lit only by the soft, ward-filtered glow bleeding in from the high-arched windows. Moonlight kissed the floor in long strokes, glinting off scattered parchment and the half-finished mug on the desk that had long since gone cold. Shadows hung thick in the corners, but they weren't empty.

Thalos lay face-down across the edge of his bed, robes already pushed down to his thighs, sweat gleaming along the fine muscles of his back. The air was warm, smoky, spiced, and laced with something deeper. Old paper, leather and arousal too potent and unashamed.

Joren moved like ink into water; fluid, deliberate. His hands spanned Thalos's waist with quiet strength, fingers spread across the muscles of his hips, guiding him into stillness. His chest, bare and sun-warmed, pressed into the curve of Thalos's back with a slow exhale.

"You're tense," Joren murmured, voice thick and low.

Thalos didn't answer. Not with words. Just the softest shift of weight, the smallest backward press of hips. A yes without surrender.

Joren smiled, dark and slow. His cock rested heavy between Thalos's cheeks, thick and flushed with promise, and when he ground forward just slightly, it drew a sharp gasp from Thalos's parted lips.

He leaned down, lips brushing the base of Thalos's neck.

"Good," he whispered. "Then you'll feel everything."

He didn't ask permission. He didn't need to.

Joren dropped to his knees.

Thalos gasped as strong hands gripped the back of his thighs, spreading him open with quiet reverence. The heat of breath against his entrance sent a jolt through him, a lightning strike of sensation that arced up his spine and curled his toes against the stone floor.

Then Joren's tongue found him.

Slow. Intentional.

A single stroke from base to rim that left Thalos trembling, breath caught mid-exhale. He braced himself against the bed frame, chest heaving, hips tilting involuntarily to grant more access. But Joren didn't rush. He parted Thalos, thumbs peeling him open like scripture laid bare and kissed him there like it was a mouth made to whisper his name.

The first swirl was exploratory. The second, devotional.

Joren licked into him with languid, coaxing circles, tongue pressing inward, slick and soft and devastating. The moan Thalos gave was low and broken, lost somewhere between disbelief and surrender. He hadn't expected this. Not like this.

Joren devoured him.

He mouthed against Thalos's rim like it was something sacred—tongue flicking, lips sucking, breath warm and ruinous. Every pass over the sensitive ring of muscle made Thalos shiver, his cock twitching between his thighs, untouched and dripping against his own belly.

He had been touched there before. Fucked. Worshiped.

But not like this.

Not like a man trying to taste the truth buried inside him.

Joren groaned against him, the vibration setting fire to his nerves. He spread Thalos wider, tongue driving deeper, thrusting now. Slow, obscene, and wet. His hands kneaded the swell of Thalos's ass with each lick, spreading him open like pages, tongue searching for meaning in every line of him.

The noises were slick and unabashed. Wet kisses, obscene slurps, the sound of a man utterly consumed.

Thalos whimpered. Moaned. Bucked backward into Joren's face, the sensation too much and not enough all at once. His sigil-marked back flared with heat that wasn't magic. It was hunger carved into bone.

He was being opened. Worshiped. Undone.

And gods, he wanted more.

"Please," he whispered, voice hoarse.

Joren kept going. He gave a few final licks. They were deeper now and firmer. He pulled back just enough to bite gently at the curve of Thalos's ass.

Then he moved lower.

Not away. Not up.

Down.

Thalos shuddered as Joren's mouth shifted, tongue trailing from the delicate rim to the heavy, pulsing weight that hung beneath. He mouthed the full curve of Thalos's sac, breathing deep as if scenting the magic laced beneath skin. Then he drew one orb into his mouth with aching slowness, suckling gently, reverently, hands steady on Thalos's thighs.

The moan that escaped Thalos was softer, needful. He was a man unraveling by degrees.

Joren didn't stop at one. He moved to the other, licked the underside where the nerves pooled, then further. Tongue flicking along the perineum, teasing just at the threshold of unbearable.

When Thalos started to squirm, Joren chuckled. A sound that vibrated against skin and made him tremble. With slow, careful focus, Joren reached up with one hand and wrapped it around Thalos's shaft. Thick, leaking, straining against gravity. He angled it forward and kissed the base with lips open and breath warm.

The next moment blurred into heat and slick pressure.

Joren took the head into his mouth, just enough to taste the salt of arousal. His tongue danced along the sensitive rim, swirled over the slit, then slowly descended. Inch by aching inch, he fed Thalos into his mouth. Swallowing deeper, adjusting his angle until his nose was buried at the base of him, and Thalos was arching backward with a cry caught between prayer and surrender.

Thalos reached out blindly, fingers clawing at the mattress as his body rocked with the force of it. Joren's throat flexed once. Twice. And then he pulled back slowly, lips glistening, a string of saliva stretching from the tip of Thalos's cock to his mouth before he took him again—deeper this time, faster.

The rhythm built into something primal.

Joren's throat worked with a practiced hunger, lips sealed tight around Thalos's length, jaw relaxed to accept every thrust of trembling muscle. He bobbed and sucked, one hand gripping the base, the other fondling his balls with slow squeezes.

The sigils along Thalos's lower back pulsed in synchrony with the motion—shining brighter with every pass of tongue and every subtle gag reflex that only pulled him deeper into heat.

Suddenly, Joren stopped.

Not with reluctance.

With purpose.

He stood, eyes burning, spit shining on his chin, cock hard and leaking against his thigh. His gaze dropped to the mess he'd made of Thalos. The sheen of saliva along the thick length of his cock, still flushed and twitching, and the way his hole pulsed visibly with need, flexing open in soft, desperate rhythm.

A groan escaped Joren, involuntary, guttural. Hunger lit his expression like moonfire: starved, reverent, possessed.

He took a moment to admire the sight. Thalos trembling, back arched, hole wet and needy, the perfect picture of surrender without shame. Then Joren reached down with both hands. One to steady himself, the other to spread Thalos wide again.

The bed shifted slightly and Joren entered him.

Thalos's spine arched like a drawn bow, his gasp caught in the silk of his bedding. Joren groaned low against his shoulder, the pressure building slow, stretching him open inch by devastating inch. The room seemed to tilt around the rhythm. The quiet wet sound of entry, the weight of hips meeting skin, the strained breathless moan that spilled from Thalos's throat as Joren seated fully inside him.

He didn't move. Not yet.

Instead, he leaned forward, resting his cheek against the curve of Thalos's shoulder blade, both hands splayed wide as though anchoring them both.

"I want you to remember this," Joren murmured, hips beginning to move in slow, punishing rolls. "Not because we need this. Because it matters."

The rhythm was languid at first. Long strokes that dragged across every nerve ending, every point of tension in Thalos's body like a scribe dragging ink across a page he wasn't supposed to write on. Every thrust was a statement. Every pullback a question.

Thalos moaned again, softer now, rhythmic, body giving in to the tempo. His cock throbbed beneath him, already slick, smearing the sheets with every thrust.

Joren adjusted his angle, shifted his grip, and the next thrust struck deep, grinding into the spot that made Thalos cry out. His fingers clenched the bedding. His sigil-scored spine flared with heat that wasn't just magical. It was a need that burned like memory.

Faster now.

Harder.

The slap of skin echoed off stone, but the air remained thick, intimate. Joren's teeth grazed Thalos's shoulder as he fucked him, slow but merciless, never breaking rhythm, never rushing. Just control. Just worship. Just the sound of one man breaking another open not with force, but precision.

"You feel that?" Joren panted into his ear. "Every time you clench, you write yourself deeper into me. And gods, I want every word."

Thalos moaned. His voice raw and gasping now, hips bucking backward to meet every thrust. His fingers twisted into the sheets like he needed to anchor himself or be lost completely.

And when he came it was with a full-body shudder, a sob of pleasure caught behind his teeth, his cock pulsing untouched beneath him as thick ropes of release spilled across the fabric.

Joren didn't stop.

He kept thrusting through it, dragging every last tremor from Thalos's body until his own climax overtook him. He pressed deep with a final groan, his hips jerking forward as he filled him, the heat of it pooling inside.

Silence followed.

Not empty. Full.

Their breathing slowed. The moonlight shifted. Sigils across Thalos's back flickered once, bright, raw, and then dimmed.

Joren leaned down again, lips pressed to the back of Thalos's neck.

"We needed that," he whispered.

And somewhere beneath the slow return to stillness, the Archive stirred. Watching.

Waiting.

Writing it down.

—— ✦ ——

Location: Blackwatch Citadel | Sublevel D | Observation Chamber Kappa

The scry-glass shimmered faintly, pulsing like a heartbeat not its own.

Director Threnna's breath hitched.

Not a gasp. A guttural pull from deep in her belly, where old hungers lived. Her thighs pressed together beneath her robes, subtle but deliberate, and her fingertips curled slightly against the edge of the viewing console.

The image wasn't just clear. It was obscene. Beautiful. Archive-perfect.

Within the swirling arc of sigil-fed crystal, the figures of Thalos and Joren moved like gods dreaming inside flesh. Sigil-light shimmered across skin slicked with sweat and sex, the slow, relentless rhythm of hips against hips echoing in a chamber not built for desire.

"Holy fucking stars," Corrin breathed, blinking hard. "That's—by the Archive, that's not sanctioned."

"I'll sanction it personally," Threnna murmured, voice low, dry as paper and doubly as sharp. "Twice."

Corrin looked at her. Blinked. Then wisely looked back at the glass.

"Third spike in under an hour," he said, voice tighter. "Arcane imprint's climbing past stable resonance. We should flag this to Ritual Oversight—"

"No," Threnna said, gaze locked. "Not yet."

She stepped forward. The sigils woven into her gloves pulsed in response. Her breath leveled. Her body didn't.

"They're syncing," she said. "But this isn't overlay. This isn't just feedback."

Corrin shifted. "Then what is it?"

Threnna smirked. For a heartbeat, she looked younger and dangerously alive.

"It's invocation," she said. "And he's the conduit."

Thalos's image trembled.

"The Archive's responding," Threnna whispered. "And it's not just watching anymore."

She went still. Not even her breath moved.

Then, slowly, a smile unfurled. Lazy, sharp, and unmistakably aroused.

"I don't care if the Citadel falls stone by stone around them," she said, voice like silk pulled taut over heat. "Let it collapse. Let it burn.

As long as they keep fucking like that… gods, I'll bless the ashes myself."

Corrin stiffened.

Threnna turned toward him, eyes half-lidded, almost predatory.

"You didn't see anything," she said. "You didn't *feel* anything. This never happened."

Corrin hesitated. Opened his mouth.

"Unless you'd like to relive it under interrogation," she added, tone syrup-sweet and terrifyingly calm.

He shut his mouth.

"Good boy," she purred. "Now go log a false surge in the deep vaults. Something tame. Something boring. And if anyone asks…"

She turned back to the glass.

"Tell them the Archive didn't stir tonight."

Location: Blackwatch Citadel | Sublevel C | Data Reconciliation Annex | 22:16 AST

Agent Corrin stood before the central console. His expression blank, fingers flew across the sigil-screen as lines of false telemetry scrolled into place. False surge. Static anomaly. Ritual echo misread. It was clean. Precise. Undeniably convincing.

"Quiet tonight," he muttered, echoing Threnna's words as if saying them aloud might wake something.

He finished the entry. Locked it with his own signature. Stepped back but didn't move further.

Something in him hadn't stopped trembling since he left the Observation Chamber.

He could still feel the heat of the Archive's vision behind his eyes. The sounds. The rhythm. The *need.* It hadn't been like watching porn. It hadn't even been like watching a ritual. It had been…

Real.

Alive.

Sacred.

Corrin looked older than he was. Maybe twenty-five. Maybe less. Clean-shaven, save for the faintest suggestion of stubble along a jaw clenched tight. Auburn hair tousled and damp with sweat clung to his forehead beneath the sterile white of the Citadel's sigil-marked lighting. His uniform was crisp. Too crisp. Regulation fabric pulled taut across his thighs and ass, the swell of it unmistakable now as his hips began to move.

His hand drifted toward the waistband of his uniform pants. His breath stuttered, lips parted, as he slipped his fingers beneath the edge. Then he growled with sudden frustration and tore them open. The seams split with a soft hiss of surrender, the tension in his body mirrored in fabric too thin to contain it.

His cock jerked free, flushed and pulsing, already slick at the tip. His ass, bare now beneath the torn fabric, flexed instinctively as his hips pushed forward. Sweat glistened down his spine and the crease beneath each cheek, the scent of arousal sharp in the sterile air.

He stroked with increasing pressure, dragging the slick head through his fist, hips rolling into the motion with mounting urgency. His back arched slightly as his breath grew ragged, each stroke drawing a choked sound from deep in his throat. The sensation wasn't enough. *He* wasn't enough and he couldn't stop. Couldn't *not* chase it.

He stumbled back, half-falling against the cold tile of the data hub floor, palm slapping against it for balance. His knees spread as he sat back on his heels, cock bobbing against his belly, slick and flushed. He reached down with one hand to keep stroking, while the other drifted lower, trembling, slick with sweat and need.

His fingers grazed the cleft of his ass, pausing there, hesitating only a moment before he pressed inward, tentative at first, then firmer, the tip sliding in just past resistance.

He gasped, louder than he meant to, eyes fluttering shut as the pleasure spiked sharp and sudden. The rhythm of his hand on his cock faltered, then returned harder, synced to the push of his finger working deeper.

He moved with rhythm now—haunted, driven, breaking. He could feel it, *feel* them, still inside him, as if the Archive had branded the echo of Thalos and Joren into his bones.

He was unraveling. He didn't want to stop.

Then the door hissed.

A faint click of access override.

"Corrin?" a voice called from the threshold—masculine, low, rough around the edges.

He froze. Legs splayed, uniform ruined, cock slick in his fist, two fingers still buried deep in his ass.

Agent Ral stopped mid-step, eyes locking onto him before his breath caught low in his throat. The sound wasn't quite horror. It wasn't even surprise.

It was fascination.

Corrin's body trembled, halfway between climax and collapse.

The tile bit cold against his spine, shocking him back, but the Archive's hunger still clung to his skin, pulsing through the heat of his cock.

His cheeks flushed dark with shame, and his cock twitched in his grip, as if the Archive itself refused to let him go.

For a moment, no one moved.

Then Ral stepped forward and quietly locked the door behind him.

He didn't speak. Didn't interrupt.

He just watched.

His stance changed, predator-like, shoulders rolling back as he crossed his arms over his chest. Corrin could feel Ral's eyes devouring every inch of him, lingering on the mess of his uniform, the slick sheen on his cock, the way his ass clenched around his own fingers.

There was no judgment in Ral's expression.

Only heat.

Corrin's throat bobbed with a swallow. He didn't stop. Couldn't. Not with that gaze on him. Not with that weight pressing him down harder than guilt ever could.

Ral shifted again, taking a single slow step forward, voice low. Almost reverent.

"Don't stop on my account."

Ral's eyes glittered in the dim light, one brow raising as if amused by Corrin's hesitation. He stepped closer.

"You think you're the only one the Archive touches?" he asked, voice like gravel wrapped in velvet. "I've seen it. Felt it. I know what it leaves behind."

He crouched down beside Corrin, close enough for the heat of him to radiate against exposed skin, but didn't touch. Just lingered.

"I watched Thalos once," Ral whispered. "Through the Archive. Alone. Just before his containment was lifted. He touched himself like he was afraid of what might answer. And I couldn't look away."

He licked his lips, eyes roaming Corrin's body again.

"It wasn't just arousal," he said. "It was communion. I came so hard I thought I'd pass out."

He smirked, gaze dragging slowly over Corrin's flushed face, his trembling thighs, his slick hand and buried fingers.

"And now you know. You've been marked too."

Corrin's throat worked around the truth. It wasn't arousal. It was residue. A fingerprint burned beneath his ribs, left by something heavier than lust. The Archive had touched him and now it knew his name.

Just like Agent Crale before him, Corrin had been too close. Close enough to be marked. Not by the event but by what it unlocked in him.

Ral's smirk faded, just slightly. He leaned in, voice quieter now, like a confession or a warning.

"Crale didn't walk away from this," he said. "You know that, right?"

Corrin blinked.

"He died," Ral said flatly. "Mid-orgasm. Heart stopped. They found him in the training hall. Cock still hard, twitching like the Archive hadn't finished with him."

Ral's voice dropped a note, touched by something both reverent and grim.

"His body was sprawled across a cold training bench, mouth open, face locked in something between pleading and euphoria."

He exhaled slowly, not in disgust, but in memory.

"They say his body was smiling. I don't know if that's poetry or pathology."

He reached out, brushed two fingers lightly along Corrin's cheek, then let them trail slowly downward.

Across his jaw.

Over the curve of his throat.

Down his sternum, until his fingertips slid across the sweat-slicked plane of Corrin's chest.

He paused just above the heart, feeling it race beneath skin.

Then he trailed lower, between trembling abs, pausing at Corrin's navel where a small pool of precum had gathered, shimmering under the low light, testament to how long Corrin had been edging himself.

Ral's fingers dipped into it, coating them slowly before dragging the slick trail upward. Back across Corrin's abdomen, over the faint rise of his ribs, and finally returning to brush along his cheek once more.

All the while, Corrin's hand never left his cock. He was still gripping himself roughly, the veins along his forearm taut, his knuckles pale from pressure. His body trembled, suspended between restraint and ruin.

Not a caress. Not a threat.

A claim.

"I'd rather not see that happen to you," Ral whispered. An echo of intimacy, but edged with something darker.

Somewhere deep in the system's buffer logs, a background process flickered briefly before vanishing into a thread labeled *interference - ambient resonance: MIRRORFOLD_9*

CHAPTER TEN: RITUAL REMAINS

The room still smelled of them. Sex, sweat, and recursion cooling in the air.

The Archive hadn't turned the page.

Moonlight filtered through the sigil-glass windowpanes, silvering the tangled sheets and the lovers half-hidden within them. Thalos lay sprawled across Joren's chest, breath slow and warm against skin still marked by the strain of what passed between them. One arm hung over Joren's waist in a way that once would have seemed impossible.

But he had let go. For now.

Joren was wide awake.

His fingers moved through Thalos's hair slowly, reverently. Exploring, not just touching. Down the curve of his neck, across the shoulder still hot from where they had pressed together. When Thalos shifted in his sleep, leg sliding further over Joren's thigh, hips rolling gently, Joren exhaled like it hurt to hold still.

Their skin clung in places, sweat-slick, worshipful and alive. He traced Thalos's spine, feeling where the sigils had once flared, where something more than magic had hummed through them both. A tremble lingered beneath the surface, faint but undeniable.

He should have let him rest. Gods knew what the Archive had written into their bodies. It wasn't just a vault of secrets anymore. Not just records and sealed reports. The Archive was a living system now, reflexive and arcane, pulsing beneath Blackwatch like a second spine. It didn't just store what happened. It responded. It remembered them in heat and breath and bone, and it was still remembering.

Thalos didn't stir.

Not yet.

Joren closed his eyes for a moment.

It shouldn't have felt like this. Not after everything he'd done to stay away.

It had felt like breathing for the first time.

Every moment, the stretch between first touch and final gasp, was still alive in his body. The way Thalos had looked at him when he gave in. The way he said his name. The way he opened.

Joren had touched others. Had taken and been taken. But this was different. Thalos had always been different.

Even when they pretended otherwise. Even when the Archive had been silent between them.

The quiet between them wasn't just his. The air between their bodies shifted, getting denser. It was charged, like touch remembered before thought.

Joren felt the pulse from the Archive at the edge of his awareness. Distinct from his longing for Thalos, yet braided into it like muscle around memory. This wasn't just his heart remembering. It was the Archive reminding him what had already been written.

He'd stayed away because his family made it clear his place was with them, in blood and tradition. Not braided into the body of a man the Archive had already marked. They pulled him back with obligations dressed as duty.

He had listened, because it seemed simpler. Easier to survive.

But then Thalos looked at him again and that distance collapsed.

He hadn't just wanted Thalos.

He'd needed him.

Gods, he still did.

Maybe that was the part he hadn't been ready for. Not the danger, not the Archive, but the way Thalos made him feel, like there was something deeper beneath the wanting. Something he'd never let himself name.

Because it wasn't just desire. It wasn't even just sex.

Thalos had pulled things out of him he hadn't known were there. Hungers hidden beneath loyalty. Cravings buried in duty.

Ruin help him, it had felt like the truth.

He didn't just want to stay. He knew now he couldn't leave. Not again. Not after the Archive had remembered his name inside Thalos's breath.

A pulse flickered at the edge of his vision.

The silence between them deepened. Warmth still clung to their skin, but the air around Joren changed, tightened, like breath pulled through a ritual he hadn't meant to complete. He felt the difference immediately. The Archive's presence rising again, tugging his attention from the intimacy they'd forged toward something colder. Intentional.

Joren turned his head toward the table outside the door.

The files.

They were glowing again. Dimly at first, like something testing the edge of awareness, but then Kaelor's file surged, casting long red slashes of light across the chamber wall. Veyrion's shimmered faintly beside it, blue and steady, but no match for the radiance pouring off Kaelor's page.

Joren stiffened beneath Thalos.

Not out of fear.

Out of recognition.

The Archive was not done with them.

Kaelor's memory, his presence, was bleeding louder than Veyrion's now. Not a warning. A summons.

Joren moved carefully, lifting Thalos's arm from his waist with a reverence that bordered on sacred. He didn't just shift it aside. He cradled it for a beat too long, like letting go might erase it, his fingers brushing the underside of Thalos's wrist, feeling the echo of his pulse before gently laying it down upon the sheets.

Joren turned, pressing the softest kiss to Thalos's temple—barely there, but full of everything he hadn't said.

The movement from beneath him was slow, intentional. He slipped out with practiced care, like he was afraid of breaking something delicate between them. The warmth of their shared body heat peeled away like parchment.

Thalos murmured but did not wake.

Barefoot and nude, Joren rose slowly from the bed, the chill of the stone floor grounding him. Before crossing the room, he reached back one last time.

His palm cupped Thalos's hip, warm and gentle, then slid slowly over the curve of his ass—tender, reverent, memorizing the shape of a man he'd once tried to forget and was now learning all over again. His fingers lingered there, dragging across the small of Thalos's back, where the sigils had flared. He traced one invisible line with the edge of his thumb, a silent vow pressed into skin.

Then he let go.

The sheets whispered behind him calling him back to Thalos, but Joren walked to the glow.

The light from Kaelor's file washed over his skin, red and pulsing, casting harsh planes of shadow across his abdomen and chest. It illuminated the line of his throat, the curve of his hips, and the flushed shaft of his cock. Still hard, still leaking, as if responding not to want but to the Archive's will made flesh. Joren's body knew it.

Moonlight met the Archive's glow across his thighs, bathing the curve of his ass in silver. His body, caught between Archive bloodlight and lunar breath, looked sculpted by ritual, written into want.

He reached the desk and let his hand hover just over the file's edge, heat radiating off the parchment like blood beneath thin stone. The sigils along the border of Kaelor's file shimmered faintly, like they recognized him, or perhaps mistook him for someone else entirely. As he leaned in, the glow intensified, and the pulse began to thrum. Not just in the file but in the air, in the floor beneath his feet, in his skin.

His cock flexed in response, thick and aching, a fresh bead of cum oozing from the tip as if pulled from him by the Archive's rhythm alone. It wasn't desire. It was compulsion, a command written beneath the skin.

The glow responded in kind. The file pulsed harder, faster, red light flickering across his chest like the beat of a heart outside a body. And still, the moonlight clung to his ass like a second gaze, cold and reverent.

Joren slid into the chair at the table, the hard edge cool against the backs of his thighs. As he sat, his cock left a glistening trail across the polished wood, a streak of ritual-born need he no longer tried to suppress. His muscles tensed as he settled—every inch of him raw, exposed, and marked with anticipation.

His hole clenched reflexively against the chair's smooth surface, as if bracing for something. An echo, an entry, a command not yet spoken. It wasn't just stimulation. It was submission. And the ache that followed felt carved, not bruised—like the Archive had marked him from the inside.

As if each clench sealed a signature into flesh.

This submission wasn't born of touch alone. It felt like ritual. Like the Archive had dipped its quill into his flesh and begun to write. Every breath, every throb, every shift of his body wasn't just stimulation. It was annotation.

His body was responding before his mind could catch up, trembling as if the Archive had already begun reciting him.

He opened the file.

Behind him, Thalos stirred. Just a breath. A soft shift of linen, a murmured sound beneath sleep. A word or name Joren couldn't catch, drifting out on an exhale like fog over glass, but he didn't wake.

Joren's fingers moved with care, reverent as they slid over the first few pages. The glow from Kaelor's file bled through the paper, illuminating the text like veins under skin already bared for incision.

And then he found it.

The page crackled faintly under his fingertips, as if the memory it held still smoldered.

ARREST ATTEMPTS

They called them attempts, but none of it felt like justice. Every mission to capture him felt more like chasing the ghost of a kiss you'll never forget. Here's what they wrote. Here's what I saw:

Tavern Rooftop Escape – They found him leaning at the bar like sin itself, laughing with his mouth, flirting with his eyes. When they reached for their cuffs, he reached for their hearts. One agent kissed him. The other hesitated long enough to forget why they were there. By the time they remembered, he was already gone—just the scent of sweat and something sweet lingering on the glass. He left behind a sigil carved into the countertop—no one has touched it since.

Forest Ambush – They tried to corner him beneath moonlight, sigils humming through the bark. He stood bare-chested in the mist, smiling like a secret. One officer combusted— literally. The others dropped their weapons like offerings and wept afterward. I would've, too. He looked like a god.

Undercover Seduction – We sent in someone beautiful, clever, broken just enough to tempt him. It worked. Too well. They shared a bed. Shared truths, too. The agent never returned to us. He sends letters now. Poems, mostly. Says Kaelor isn't what we think. I believe him.

Field Detainment #3 – Agent R. Halden – The only recorded detainment that lasted more than a few minutes. Subject allowed himself to be captured. Three hours of interrogation devolved into something far more intimate. When questioned, Agent Halden refused to explain what broke the subject's containment sigils.

None of us really want to catch him. We just want him to look our way.

Joren reread the final line, his breath stalling in his throat. There was something too familiar in it, like a phrase whispered in a dream that turns out to be memory.

The red light flared.

It swallowed the edges of the page, then the edges of the desk, and then the edges of the room.

The Archive took him.

Not in violence.

But in gravity.

Like falling into someone's mouth.

Like being kissed backward through time.

Field Detainment #3 – Memory Echo Initiated

[Interrogation Cell B-11 | Blackwatch Containment Wing | 1 Hour In]

Joren blinked.

But he wasn't Joren anymore.

He sat in a cold iron chair, wrists trembling, palms pressed flat to the stone table before him. A flickering sconce cast low golden light against the wall, and the scent of incense. Cheap incense, burning too fast, like a prayer someone wanted to forget.

Across from him sat Kaelor Thorne.

Still.

Watching.

The room held heat that hadn't come from magic. Not directly. His collar was loosened. His shirt clung damp to his back. And somewhere in the folds of his thoughts, the residue of the last hour shimmered like a bruise. Questions asked, evasions given, truths laid out in riddles and breath.

Kaelor leaned forward. Movement cut through the charged air, deliberate as a blade slipping through silk.

Joren—Halden—couldn't speak. His mouth was dry. His cock was hard.

There was a mirror in the corner, small, warped on the edges, probably meant for observation, not vanity.

He looked.

His uniform was regulation issue, but form-fitting in all the wrong ways now. It clung to the heat of his skin, pressing against the swell of muscle along his thighs, pulling taut across his chest with every breath. The collar had been undone at some point, his tie gone, and the top three buttons undone like an invitation he didn't remember accepting.

His dark hair was disheveled, a curl stuck to his temple with sweat. There was color in his cheeks he didn't recognize, a flush that made his reflection fevered. Possessed.

And below?

His cock was straining visibly against the fabric. Thick, curved hard to one side, the outline unmistakable. The tip pressed against the waistband like it was trying to escape, and a dark, wet patch had already spread through the front of his pants. He was leaking. Constantly. Obscenely. Every twitch of muscle made it worse, like pressure building behind a seal.

Kaelor still hadn't touched him.

Not once.

Then he spoke.

His voice came low and heavy. It held no urgency, no strain, only the certainty of someone who had already won.

"The containment wards," Kaelor murmured, his gaze sharp and unblinking, "won't hold me for long."

The flicker of red light from the sigils etched in the cell's walls pulsed in response. Not violently. Rhythmically. As if they'd heard him. As if they agreed.

Joren blinked, and for a moment the world felt distant, but the sensations did not.

He could feel the weight of the chair beneath him, the unbearable press of fabric against his cock, the slow flex and clench of his thighs in response to Kaelor's voice. He was still Halden, still in the memory, but everything he felt was his own.

The trembling in his fingers wasn't just Archive mimicry. The heat curling through his gut, the sweat beading at the base of his spine, the aching pulse behind his cock. Those were real.

He wasn't watching the past anymore.

He was *inside* it.

Living it.

Kaelor leaned forward again, just slightly, the flickering sconce light catching the wet shimmer of his lower lip. When he spoke this time, it came with weight.

"You know what the real trick is?" he said, tone lazy but precise. "It's not breaking the wards. It's using them. Feeding them something they weren't meant to process. Want. Obedience. Pleasure."

His tongue dragged across his teeth slowly. His gaze didn't waver.

"You, for instance." Kaelor gave a small, deliberate wink. "You're already helping me out of here."

The sigils pulsed again, brighter now, syncing with Joren's heartbeat. His cock throbbed behind his trousers, aching. The field still held Kaelor's body.

But not the room. Not anymore.

Kaelor stood slowly, gracefully, because gravity answered to him. He didn't move like a prisoner. He moved like a ritual already spoken.

"And you know," he said, voice softer now, almost amused, "you wear him well. Agent Halden, is it?"

He tilted his head, dark eyes scanning Joren's face with a clarity that didn't belong in memory.

"But you're not him. Not really."

Kaelor's gaze flicked downward, toward the outline of Joren's cock. Still straining. Still leaking, as if it confirmed something he already knew. The sigils along the walls spidered with light.

"Whoever you are under there... that's who's helping me. It's your presence that's breaking the ward. Not Halden's."

He stepped forward into the circle of containment, and it didn't resist him.

"So tell me, stranger," Kaelor whispered, smiling with something almost like reverence, "What exactly do you want me to do with you?"

Joren shuddered.

It started in his gut and rippled outward, through his limbs, through his thighs, through the heat pulsing at the base of his spine. He couldn't stop it. Didn't want to. His whole body betrayed him with a single full-body tremor that settled into the tight ache in his cock and the clench of need that pulsed deep between his cheeks.

Kaelor stepped closer.

His voice dropped, velvet rasp dragged across a blade.

"I could make you beg first," he said, leaning down, his breath warm against the shell of Joren's ear. "Or I could make you come before I ever touch you."

Then his tongue flicked out, slow and deliberate, licking the edge of Joren's ear. A promise he intended to keep.

The wards did not flare.

They *welcomed* it.

The next words didn't pass through air.

They threaded straight into him, bypassing his ears, uncoiling through muscle and memory like the Archive had found a direct line to his hunger.

What I'm going to do to you... isn't about pace. It's about permanence.

I'll start with your shoulders. My hands will rest there heavy and warm. Not to comfort. To anchor. You'll feel the weight before the touch. That's how gravity works when it wants you.

Then I'll lean in. Say nothing. Just breathe. Hot, deliberate, into the shell of your ear until your hole clenches from a whisper I haven't even said yet.

Then I'll taste. Not lips. Not cock. I'll drop lower. Tongue flat to the spine, reading a scripture you forgot you carried. Until I'm at your ass. Worship-level. Face buried between you and the stone.

You won't moan. Not yet. Because you'll be holding your breath for what comes next.

I'll spread you. Hands wide on your cheeks, thumbs pulling you open until the air itself gasps. I won't rush. I'll lick. Slow. Wet. Deep. Over and over until your knees tremble and your cock leaks for the fourth time untouched.

Then I'll spit.

Not for show.

For slick.

Because when I slide in. And I will. It won't be gentle. It'll be exact. One push. All of me. You'll stretch like sigils igniting under pressure. Your back will arch. Your voice will catch. And I'll stay there. Just inside. Full. Thick. Watching your body try to remember how to breathe with a god inside it.

And then? When you're quaking with need.

I'll move.

Each thrust timed like a ritual. Slow at first, cruel with control. I'll let you feel the stretch again. And again. Until you stop trying to hold onto who you were before you bent over.

You'll come without permission.

And I won't stop.

Because I don't fuck for release.

I fuck to rewrite you.

Joren swallowed, hard. His heart pounded against the chair's frame. He wanted to speak, but the Archive was already answering for him.

What followed didn't need words.

The Archive chose not to render every motion.

It wasn't omission. It was curation. Saturation.

It pressed only what mattered into him. The weight of Kaelor's body, the heat, the stretch, the pressure. He felt all of it. Every inch. Every thrust. His own moan came back to him, echoed against stone, until it was no longer his alone.

The Archive fed him the way it had unfolded. Kaelor moving, invocation made flesh, his body bowing and trembling beneath a presence more than flesh. Breath. Fingers. Hips. Each detail pressed into memory with the precision of a scribe carving into bone.

Release tore through him. Violent and unsanctioned. Without touch. Without permission. The Archive marked it anyway.

And Kaelor did not stop. The Archive did not want him to.

He moved like incantation, rhythm mounting as Joren's mind frayed at the edges. The recursion deepened. The memory looped back on itself, replaying flashes out of order. Kaelor's mouth against his spine, the press of his palm, the moment his body forgot resistance and learned the shape of surrender.

The Archive whispered the sound of his own breath back into him.

Replayed the moment his pulse surrendered to Kaelor's rhythm.

Kept his body there. Open, clenching and unwilling to let the shape go.

The wards shattered.

Not with noise, but with light.

Sigils along the walls flared white-hot and then collapsed inward, folding through one another like paper burning in reverse. The room dissolved into brilliance.

The Archive pulsed once, deep and undeniable.

Joren, through Halden, cried out, but not in pain.

In recognition.

—— ✦ ——

Joren came back to himself in a rush.

The chair beneath him was real again. So was the stone floor. So was the lingering pulse in his cock, softening slowly, like it didn't want to forget. A warm smear of his climax had pooled beneath the table, cooling across his thighs and dripping languidly to the floor.

He didn't move at first.

Didn't need to.

Thalos was awake.

The sheets were thrown back. One leg already angled to rise, as if he'd been caught mid-motion, but he hadn't moved yet. He was *watching*. His chest was bare, his hand wrapped around his now-hard cock, unmoving, gripped like he couldn't decide whether to stroke it or silence it.

His eyes were locked on Joren.

Not in judgment.

In awe.

Something dangerously close to fear.

Joren's lips parted, but the words didn't come right away. He swallowed, still catching his breath, the pulse of the Archive echo not yet fully faded from his skin.

"I... I think I was inside it," he finally said, voice hoarse and uneven. "Not just the file. Him. Kaelor. I... he... was..."

He shook his head, a rough exhale catching in his throat as his eyes drifted down, shame and arousal still tangling across his body.

"He didn't touch me. Not at first. But it didn't matter. I felt... everything."

Joren's grip on the desk went bloodless.

"He used me. Owned me. Like the Archive wanted it to happen. Like it knew exactly how to make me... surrender."

His voice dropped to a whisper, but Thalos could hear every word.

"And gods help me. I wanted it. I came so hard I thought it would tear something open inside me. Maybe it did."

Thalos shifted where he sat, breath shallow, eyes never leaving Joren. His hand moved along the hard length of his cock, a slow stroke that did nothing to hide the effect Joren's words were having.

"What was he like?" Thalos asked softly, voice roughened by sleep and something else entirely. "Kaelor, I mean. What did it feel like... to be claimed by a god?"

He stroked again, thumb brushing the slick already forming at the tip. Not fast. Not performative. Just present. Just honest.

His eyes locked with Joren's, hunger and curiosity twinned in them like twin moons orbiting a singular flame.

The Archive pulsed through the files again. Not with light this time but with a pressure. Soft, insistent, like fingers sliding just beneath the skin.

Joren gasped and braced a hand against the desk. "It felt..."

He swallowed. His gaze dropped to Thalos's hand, the slow rhythm of his strokes hypnotic, devotional. Joren's cock twitched despite itself.

"It felt like I stopped being me," he said, voice low and strained. "Like he didn't just use me. He *entered* me. Claimed something more than my body. He moved like scripture through me. Like I was the ritual, not just the offering."

He met Thalos's gaze again, eyes wide, voice barely a whisper.

"And I wanted it. I begged for more."

Thalos let out a sharp breath, chest hitching as his hand jerked again, involuntarily. His body tensed, then unraveled all at once. A low, guttural moan escaped his lips as he came. Thick and sudden. His release spilling across his fingers and stomach, dripping onto the sheets beneath him.

For a moment, he didn't move.

Didn't breathe.

He stared at his slicked fingers, stunned, as if caught between guilt and hunger.

"Shit," he whispered. His voice cracked slightly. "I didn't even... I wasn't trying to..."

He looked up at Joren, chest rising and falling, eyes dark with heat and something close to shame. "I'm sorry. I didn't mean to... gods, I didn't realize I was..."

Thalos didn't let go of his cock.

Not yet.

Joren stood slowly, breath ragged, legs unsteady. He crossed the room without thinking, drawn by something deeper than concern or lust. Deeper than the Archive.

He sank down onto the edge of the bed beside Thalos.

Not guided by thought, but by hunger, slow, reverent and claiming.

His fingers drifted across the mess on Thalos's stomach. Slow and languid. Tracing through the cooling seed with a tenderness that bordered on reverence. He brought them to his lips, eyes fluttering closed as he tasted.

"Still warm," he whispered, voice rasping against the quiet. His eyes, when they opened, burned red for a blink, brighter than Kaelor's file, brighter than ritual.

Thalos didn't see it.

Joren leaned in, lips brushing the curve of Thalos's ear.

"Tastes like fear," he whispered, smiling as if the flavor pleased him.

Thalos shivered beneath him, the tremor visible even through his stillness. His body twitched against Joren's touch, hand tightening reflexively around his softening cock.

Joren's gaze held him there. His voice pitched to an even inhumanly seductive tone. "But it also tastes like want..."

Thalos swallowed hard, eyes clearing of haze and heat.

"Tell me I wasn't just him," Joren murmured shaking his head. His voice was low and uncertain. "Tell me you still remember me."

Before Thalos could answer, the glow shifted.

Soft at first. Then undeniable.

The pulse of Kaelor's presence lingered low in Joren's gut, fading like the last heat from a banked fire. The Archive let it drain away slowly, until the warmth thinned and left only the hollow where it had been.

Across from him, Thalos's breath hitched. The light found him now.

Blue. Cold. Unrelenting.

Kaelor's file dimmed.

Veyrion's began to pulse.

CHAPTER ELEVEN: THE INK THAT REMEMBERS

Thalos flinched, a reflex born of memory, not fear.

His memory, or something beneath it, curled behind the breath he hadn't meant to take.

His hands trembled.

He was still unclean. Sweat dried on his skin. The sheets clung with cooling seed. The air still tasted of his own moan, half-swallowed, uninvited. The hunger hadn't faded. It had shifted. It had waited.

The pulse threaded through his ribs like a tuning fork left ringing too long. Not pain. Not magic. Just *remembrance*.

Recognition.

But not his.

Not yet.

Joren stepped toward him, steadying. "Thalos—?"

Blue had bled into the room now. Not glow. Not sigil. Just *presence*. Cold that claimed, not announced.

Thalos staggered back a step, chest rising sharply. Frost bloomed along his fingertips, breath fogging the space between them.

"It's not just resonance," he breathed. "It's a question. Cold. And asking."

They both looked to the files.

Kaelor's dimmed to a low ember, pulsing weakly like the afterglow of a dream fading from skin.

Veyrion's, by contrast, surged. Blue light licked along the edges of the parchment, rising like frost on exposed skin. Each tendril curled inward, eager and exact.

The pressure in the room narrowed.

Joren reached for Thalos again. The air shifted, dense and tight, as if the Archive had sucked the breath from the stone itself. A low hum reverberated beneath their feet, not sound, but vibration, an awareness.

The glow from Veyrion's file deepened, not just brighter, but colder. The kind of cold that crept beneath, wrapping around bone.

Thalos took another step back. His knees threatened collapse. He caught the edge of the table, fingers slipping slightly against condensation. Memory-sweat that hadn't been there moments ago.

"It knows me," he whispered. "I don't know how... but it knows."

His breath hitched.

The pulse from the file quickened. One beat. Then another.

Then silence.

The room peeled sideways.

No surge. No collapse.

Just quietness and blue.

—— ✦ ——

Archive Drift Detected Recursion Layer: Mirrorfold Threshold (Unbound)

Glass. Everywhere.

Thalos stood naked beneath the crystalline hush of mirrors. Sweat dried across flexed muscle. His cock half-stirred, heavy from what had been worship, now only memory. Sigils flared briefly across his ribs, then faded with each breath. The marks on him weren't glowing now, but they knew.

He was standing in a chamber of mirrors, but they didn't reflect him. They showed other things. People. Moments. None of them his. A child's hand, reaching through flame. A soldier kneeling in a field of shattered bodies. A kiss pressed to the lips of someone who looked almost like Thalos, but wasn't.

Each surface shimmered. As if it remembered too much.

He turned. Slow. Dreamlike.

Behind him stood a figure, backlit by faint blue glow, half-wrapped in shadow. Veyrion. Not the one from the file. This version wore no arrogance, no cold precision. Only stillness. Observation. The weight of seeing.

"You're not mine," Veyrion said, voice subdued. "But I remember the echo of your shape."

Thalos opened his mouth, but the air here didn't permit questions.

He stepped forward, drawn not by seduction, but by gravity. Not desire, only consequence.

The mirrored walls pulsed. Shifting, remembering, and rewriting. A woman gave birth in silence. A sigil carved into flesh. A blade rose, fell, rose again, but the face never changed. It was his. It was not.

"Do you want to know where you came from?" Veyrion asked.

The mirrors trembled.

One mirror stilled.

The flame-child remained. Unmoving. Wrapped in black-threaded linen. No tears. No breath. Just placed.

Beneath the fabric, something flared. Brief. Sharp.

The sigil wasn't visible, but Thalos knew it had always been there.

The Archive knew, too.

He touched the glass.

It shivered not as surface but as skin.

Memory pulled taut. Then ruptured.

Everything collapsed into light.

—— ✦ ——

Thalos gasped as he fell back into his body, knees cracking against stone. His limbs lashing like a drowning man clawing for breath he couldn't find. Sweat and condensation slicked his skin. His chest heaved. Eyes wild. A dark thread of blood ran from his nose, steady, inching toward his lips.

Joren caught him before he toppled, then froze at the sight. Thalos looked feral. Eyes wide, mouth parted, breath fractured like he'd surfaced from something that didn't want to let him go. Still nude, sigils shimmered faintly across his sternum, wrists, lower back. They were echoes of the file that had pulled him under.

Joren tightened his grip. "Thalos—?"

His breath came in ragged bursts. Frost crawled along his forearms. The file sat dormant on the table.

Thalos shook.

"It wasn't a memory," he said, voice wrecked. "It was a choice waiting to be made. Not shown. Not told. Offered. Like a book left open on the last page, asking if I'm ready to write the line myself."

He swallowed hard, blood still dripping from his nose, leaving a crimson arc as he turned his face away. "It was my shape in someone else's story. But they knew me. Like a forgotten word that still fits the sentence perfectly."

Joren stared at him, eyes wide. "What did you see?"

Thalos didn't answer.

Because the question still hadn't finished asking itself.

The floor rumbled beneath them, soft at first, then more insistent. Like a warning clearing its throat. Dust slipped from the seams in the ceiling. Lanternlight stuttered. Then blue overtook it, cold, foreign, untouched by flame.

Joren tensed. "What the hell is it doing now?"

The Archive wasn't done.

The air thickened. Sweat-slick and ringing, like a heartbeat held between two ribs.

It had heard Joren's question.

And it was preparing to respond.

Thalos gasped, not in fear, but in revelation. His head snapped up, and his eyes shone bright blue, not glowing passively but alight like sigils called into full invocation. The glow pulsed once, then held, as if something inside him had been activated rather than possessed.

He looked at Joren, gaze distant, voice just above a whisper.

"It wasn't just showing me… it was preparing me. There's more. Gods, there's so much more."

His body seized. Just once. A convulsion from spine to sternum. Then he collapsed, boneless, into Joren's arms. Joren cursed, struggling to hold the full weight of Thalos's fevered, slack body.

But Thalos was no longer there.

—— ✦ ——

Glass. Again.

The mirror-chamber was back, and so was the blue.

Breath steamed from his lips. Skin trembled against the mirrored cold. And there, unchanged, Veyrion waited.

"You returned," Veyrion murmured. Not surprised. Not smiling. Just certain.

Thalos couldn't speak. He was still unraveling.

Veyrion took a step forward, slow and deliberate. Each movement a measured cadence, like ritual given flesh. His bare feet made no sound against the glass beneath them.

He was nearly nude.

Only the thinnest slip of translucent cloth hung from his hips, held more by arcane will than modesty. It did little to obscure the full, heavy length swaying gently between his thighs with each step, a presence both casual and devastating. The muscles of his abdomen shifted beneath pale, sigil-lined skin, tight and honed, fluid in a way that defied tension. His form was sculptural, almost alien in its perfection, but made warm by breath, made unbearable by proximity.

"Then it's begun."

"You carry Kaelor like a wound," Veyrion said, circling. "But you carry me like guilt you haven't earned yet."

Thalos turned slowly. "What... what are you?"

Veyrion stopped just in front of him. Close, but untouched.

"I was written," he whispered. "You were left behind."

"But we're not so different. I am what becomes of echo. You... are what happens when echo is denied the right to answer." Veyrion looked through Thalos.

Thalos shivered.

It wasn't cold anymore.

It was clarity. And it hurt more.

Then came the choice.

"Merge with me," Veyrion said softly, his voice low and edged like frostbite, quiet but impossible to ignore. "Let me write the ending into your marrow. Let me fold your truth into mine and freeze the rest away."

Each word landed like an invocation. Not a plea. A command.

A cold authority layered in silk, spoken by something that did not ask twice.

Veyrion's breath kissed the glass. The choice sharpened.

"Stand alone and you'll forget who you were meant to be. Merge, and you'll finally understand why you've never belonged to yourself."

He tilted his head, not smiling. "Or remain fractured. Watched. Rewritten by an Archive that doesn't know how to forget you. Your edges will fray."

"Your truths will unspool in front of witnesses who think they understand you. They will try to put you back together wrong. You'll haunt every version of yourself that never had the chance to become whole. And the Archive will not stop. It will keep turning the page, again and again, until even your silence becomes something it thinks it wrote."

Thalos wanted to move. To scream. To say no. But the silence in him was too demanding. Too practiced.

Silence everywhere.

Thalos couldn't answer.

And before he could move—

The world cracked like ice under weight.

The mirror walls didn't shatter at once.

They fractured.

Hairline veins of light splintered outward from every mirrored surface, a spiderweb of breaking memory, each crack bleeding light like veins spilling ink across ice. The faces within the glass twisted, some into agony, some into rapture, all of them reflections that no longer obeyed Thalos's shape.

Then the chamber groaned, a sound not of stone but of something forgotten, as if the Archive itself exhaled.

—— ✦ ——

Thalos huffed in Joren's arms, breath ragged and visible, fogging between them like steam off fresh snow.

His skin was cold.

Not chilled. *Claimed.*

His eyes fluttered. His lips were blue-tinged. Sigils flickered along his chest and arms, pulsing in silent rhythm, like the last echo of a voice not yet finished speaking.

Joren held him tighter. "Vale. Gods, Thalos. Come back."

Thalos only shivered.

And somewhere inside him, the Archive waited. Still watching, still listening, and still turning pages he hadn't yet dared to read.

The ink that remembers was still wet within him. Every breath he took was a line traced toward something unwritten, and it was waiting for him to lift the pen.

Thalos blinked. Once. Then again.

His breath caught, then deepened, slow and intentional. He could feel the weight of his body again. The sweat drying along his ribs. The ache behind his eyes.

His fingers twitched against Joren's chest.

"I'm here," he rasped, the word stuttering like leather dragged over flesh.

Joren exhaled a laugh that was more relief than humor. "Fuck, Vale... you scared the shit out of me."

Thalos didn't answer. Not at first. His gaze drifted to the ceiling. Watching nothing.

"It left something."

Joren's brow furrowed. "What?"

Thalos turned his head slightly. "Inside me. I can feel it. Like a seal, half-set. Like a name I'm not allowed to say yet."

Joren leaned closer. "Can you move?"

Thalos's lips curled, weak but sharp. "I'm not broken, Joren. Just... remembering how to be here."

He sat up slowly. Sigils flared across his back as he did. Brief, luminous shapes that flashed then faded, leaving behind a faint shimmer like dew across his skin.

He glanced at the dormant file on the table, then at his hands, and finally at Joren.

"Whatever's coming," he said, voice low, "we might already be in it."

Joren didn't speak right away.

He watched Thalos, not just the man but the way he sat now. Different. Anchored and adrift all at once. Like someone who'd touched fire but remembered only the burn, not the flame.

But it wasn't only what had happened to Thalos.

Joren could still feel the phantom heat of Kaelor's echo against his lips and his hips. That deep, molten rhythm carved into muscle memory, no longer fantasy. He had felt Kaelor inside him without ever being touched, had felt himself open in ways he hadn't dared. And now, looking at Thalos, he didn't just see a man changed by contact. He saw someone marked by something that refused to let go.

His gaze lingered on the faint shimmer still tracing Thalos's back, the echo of sigils that refused to disappear entirely. The air around him felt... thinner. Not broken, but stretched.

Joren swallowed hard. "That thing... Veyrion. He did something to you."

Thalos looked at him.

No fear. Not even exhaustion.

With knowledge.

"He opened the page," Thalos said. "But he didn't write on it."

Joren felt his throat tighten.

"You mean... he's waiting for you to fill it?"

Thalos gave the faintest nod. "Or waiting to see if I'll leave it blank."

They sat in silence, the kind that settled like fog instead of falling.

Then Joren, almost afraid to ask, said, "What happens if you do?"

Thalos didn't answer.

The dormant file on the table pulsed once, soft and undeniably cold.

Thalos exhaled slowly, shoulders finally sagging with the full weight of vulnerability. He looked down at his hands, flexed them once, then lifted his gaze to meet Joren's.

"I don't know what comes next," he admitted. "But whatever it is... I think I want to face it with you."

He hesitated, then smirked, low and crooked, that rare edge of self-mocking humor crawling back into his tone.

"Not that you really have a choice. Kaelor left a sigil-print on your soul and probably your prostate. You're as marked as I am. Just in a slightly more... stretchable way."

Joren chuckled, low and breathless, a sound pulled from somewhere deeper than humor. Then he leaned in and wrapped his arms tightly around Thalos, pulling him in like he never meant to let go.

"Stretchable, sure," he murmured into Thalos's ear, "but after what *you* just went through with Veyrion? I'm starting to think *your* echo left frostbite on the weave between realms. If *you* sneeze wrong, we might all get rewritten."

They sat in the quiet that followed. No flickering lights. No pulsing sigils. Just breath.

Joren ran a hand along Thalos's back, fingertips tracing the outline of a fading sigil. "So what do we do now?"

Thalos turned his face slightly, resting his temple against Joren's shoulder. "We stop pretending this is something we can control."

A beat.

"Start treating it like something we can shape."

Joren exhaled. "Together?"

Thalos nodded.

Then, with a voice low enough to barely disturb the silence:

"The ink remembers," he whispered, "but I think it's learning to listen."

Location: Blackwatch Citadel | Sublevel D | Observation Chamber Kappa

Director Threnna stood in the dim glow of the scry-glass, one hand braced on the pedestal, the other cradling a flask that hadn't seen wine in hours. Only the memory of burn.

The image flickering before her was still now, inert. The pulse of it clung to the air, the way sweat clings to a lover's skin when everything's been said except *stay*.

Her gloves still tingled. Not from spellwork. From resonance. Something old. Hungry.

"This isn't recall anymore," she said, voice low and rough. "It's arousal. Pattern recursion. A feedback loop with a hard-on. He's not reading the Archive. He's bending it over the desk and writing his name across its spine."

Corrin, trying not to breathe too loudly beside her, looked like he might pass out. He shifted awkwardly, one hand ghosting toward the emergency sigil trigger, then curling uselessly back to his side. "Director... should I initiate containment?"

She turned, slow. Her eyes gleamed like wet ink under candlelight.

"Contain *what*, sweetheart?" Her voice dripped with something worse than laughter. Something that knew just how fucked they already were. "A man who just let Veyrion Hal'Syl whisper in his mouth and Kaelor Thorne ghost through his blood? Gods, if we so much as *touch* him wrong, we might end up moaning his name in the dark like half the field team already is."

Corrin said nothing. He didn't need to.

He remembered the way his knees had buckled beneath him in the data hub, the burn of arousal chased by terror. Agent Ral's voice was in his ear like a tether and a threat. The Archive had marked him, too. Not like Thalos. But not entirely unlike him. It had gotten inside him in its own way.

He'd felt it then. He felt it now.

That echo never left.

Threnna's gaze dropped to the file's glow. Now cool again, quiet, as if it hadn't just turned prophecy into foreplay.

She licked her lips once, thoughtful. Almost reverent.

"If Kaelor Thorne has already flared and Veyrion Hal'Syl is now awake..."

She smiled, slow and knife-sharp.

"Gods help us when Kaelor Thorne starts remembering what Veyrion Hal'Syl never forgot."

She paused, eyes narrowing.

"Assuming the Archive even has it right. Brothers, maybe. Or maybe something worse. Mirrorfolds don't always reflect family. Sometimes they reflect origin. Or design."

Her lip curled faintly.

"And if that's true... we're not dealing with bloodlines. We're dealing with recursion written as foreplay. Gods help us if they decide they were never meant to be siblings, but halves of the same hunger trying to remember how to fuck itself whole."

Her voice slipped low, a crack in the armor almost too soft to catch. *"And we were stupid enough to think they needed us to finish it."*

Chapter twelve: to Breathe Again

The air outside Blackwatch tasted different. It hit his ribs raw, unfiltered, a breath that belonged only to him. Not inked. Not echoed. Just his.

After everything he'd endured, the convulsions and the mirror-chamber and the Archive's cold questions folding into his spine, this was the first time he'd drawn breath without feeling like it passed through someone else's memory.

The outpost wall they leaned against wasn't ceremonial. It was stone. Old. Cold. Roughened by generations of weather and watchmen. Below it, a steep descent fell into the forested bluffs that circled the Citadel like quiet sentinels, deep groves, pale canopies, the ruins of old ritual grounds buried in vine and bone.

The sky above was overcast, but not grey, just bleached, like someone had painted the light too thin. Wind moved in slow, low pushes. Not enough to chill. Just enough to remind them they were not indoors. Not archived.

They had come here because the walls had started to whisper.

Because the Archive was too full of eyes.

Because after last night, even the air in Thalos's chambers had begun to feel written.

So they'd walked.

Past the high halls and the inner sanctum. Past field wings and script chambers. Past a scribe who lowered his head too fast, and a guard who lingered a second too long. They walked until there were no more shelves. No more sigil-etched glass. No more breath that didn't belong to them.

Here, there was space to breathe. To reset. To think.

To try, foolishly, to be free.

Not just from the Archive's files, but from its reach, from the way its pulse pressed into their sleep, into their skin, into the rhythm of their fucking. Every breath inside those halls had begun to feel annotated. Every touch, cross-referenced.

And now, here, they could almost pretend the Archive didn't know where they were. That it couldn't feel them not remembering.

Or that it didn't care.

They could almost believe in quiet.

They hadn't spoken for the first fifteen minutes. Just leaned into the silence, shoulder to stone, breath syncing more slowly with each moment. Even their clothes felt quieter here, freed from regulation.

Joren had left his Blackwatch uniform folded on a chair back inside. He wore a loose shirt now, collar open, sleeves rolled to the elbow, the fabric soft and worn enough to remember the shape of his body without defining it. His trousers were tucked into field boots, but the stance was casual, functional, not militant.

Thalos had traded his high-collared coat for a draped tunic that hung long over the hips, dark and weathered but open at the throat.

No sigils. No crests. The weight of command stripped away. His pants, too, were simpler, cut to move, not to obey. The lines of his body were still elegant, but relaxed. Unclenched.

Neither had commented on the shift, but it lingered between them like steam after a scalding bath.

Not oversight. Intention, an unspoken agreement to be seen without symbols.

It wasn't just about comfort. It was about freedom. From protocol. From rank. From the weight of expectations stitched into collars and waistbands. Their pants hung differently because of it, looser in some places, more suggestive in others. The heat of bodies beneath linen felt more present. More honest. When Joren shifted, the soft sway between his thighs wasn't hidden. When Thalos adjusted his stance, the press of weight behind his fly was unapologetically male.

Thalos's gaze dipped, just once, and Joren smirked. They both knew they'd dressed for silence, not modesty.

There was calm in it.

Not because it dulled desire.

But because it stopped pretending it wasn't there.

Neither had asked if this was a good idea.

They'd both known it was necessary.

It wasn't just the shift from ink-drenched corridors and echo-choked halls to open stone and distant trees. It was the space between breath. The way sound didn't cling to walls out here, the way light didn't ask permission to land.

Thalos tilted his head toward the sun, jaw slack, eyes half-closed. He looked pale. Worn. But less bound.

He looked like someone who'd paid a price his body was still learning to tally. As if the Archive had inscribed a cost beneath his skin and was waiting for him to understand it.

Joren stood just beside him, arms crossed, watching the wind tug gently at the strands of Thalos's hair.

"This counts as recovery?" Joren asked.

Thalos hummed. Not quite a laugh. Not quite denial. "It counts as pause."

The outer parapets were empty save for the two of them. Beyond the Citadel wall, the ridgeline bled into mist. The world went quiet in that way only the wild could.

"I forgot what wind felt like," Thalos said. "Without memory in it."

Joren didn't answer.

He just watched Thalos breathe.

The sigils had dimmed along Thalos's skin. Faint now, etched like old ink into paper that had been crumpled and smoothed again. Tired, hollowed from the inside by something larger than him. His spine straight, his eyes steady.

They stood in silence for long minutes.

"You should rest," Joren murmured.

"I will."

"Back in your quarters?"

Thalos smiled faintly. "Too many ghosts. Too many questions still breathing against the doorframe."

Silence gathered between them.

He turned his gaze to Joren.

"You're not a ghost. But you're close."

Joren rolled his eyes. "Romantic."

"No," Thalos said, stepping closer. "Just true."

Their bodies didn't touch. The gap between them burned.

Somewhere along the outer wall's inner curve, a third shadow waited. Agent Corrin. Not entirely by choice.

He stood just within view, half-shielded by a pillar, not close enough to hear, but near enough to feel the shift when Thalos turned. His body was stiff, fingers twitching faintly at his sides. Breath catching like a tether had been yanked.

Like something beneath his skin had answered a question not asked aloud.

Thalos glanced sideways, gaze catching Corrin where the angle broke open.

He didn't speak.

He didn't need to.

Corrin flushed.

And somewhere deeper than thought, his cock stirred.

A slow burn. Not magic.

Compulsion.

Memory.

Invitation.

He took one step back. One breath. Then another.

The heat didn't leave.

And Thalos didn't look away.

Joren turned, following his line of sight.

"Corrin?"

The name was a question. A warning. A thread left dangling.

Corrin swallowed hard. Then stepped forward.

Just once.

Just enough.

The Archive stayed silent.

But something deeper breathed.

Corrin approached slowly, the sharp lines of his Blackwatch uniform a stark contrast against the stone-bled calm of the parapet. Regulation-pressed and sharply belted, it fit him with brutal precision, tight across the chest and tighter still at the waist, every seam clinging like it knew what it was framing.

His steps were steady, but something in his hips betrayed him. A slight tension. A shift of pressure. The uniform's front was too smooth. Too stretched. His cock had begun to pulse without permission, a slow rise of weight behind the zipper as his eyes locked on Thalos.

He knew it wasn't right. He knew it wasn't just arousal.

But the heat was there all the same.

The moment stretched. The wind caught the edge of his coat, but couldn't cool the burn gathering low in his belly. He swallowed again, jaw tight.

"Agent Corrin," Thalos said, voice calm. Low. Like he already knew the script Corrin had never been handed.

Corrin didn't answer.

Because the pressure behind his fly pulsed again.

And his body was no longer entirely his own.

Corrin didn't know when it had started. This slow, creeping heat that rose through him whenever Thalos was near. It wasn't desire the way he'd known it. It wasn't even infatuation. It was need, rewritten in a language he hadn't learned but instinctively understood.

His mind screamed protocol. His body whispered surrender.

He tried to catalogue the sensation, like a good agent, like a man trained to observe and report. Every breath blurred the line between stimulus and response. His cock wasn't just hard; it was aching with every step like it was being pulled forward by something more than want.

Corrin shifted his weight again, but it only made things worse. The friction of uniform fabric against his swollen shaft was maddening. The belt cinched too tightly now. The fabric clung to the curve of his ass, stretched taut over muscle that was no longer steady.

He was hard in a way that felt traced. Marked. Like something had remembered him from the inside out.

And he hadn't even been touched.

Joren took a step forward, arms still loosely crossed, one brow arched. His gaze dropped for just a second, then slid back up, sharp but not unkind.

"You plan on saying something, Corrin?" he asked, voice low and easy, tinged with warmth, and something else. "Or are you just trying to figure out how long you can keep pretending that zipper isn't about to give out?"

Joren's gaze dipped again, this time slower, appreciative. "Because, for the record... if that's how you always walk into a conversation, we're going to need to start meeting more often."

Corrin shifted again, belt creaking audibly under the pressure.

Thalos didn't miss the look.

He let the silence stretch for half a breath longer, then added with that sharp, dry lilt that always carried just enough suggestion to sting,

"Careful, Joren. You'll give the poor boy performance anxiety... and I'd really hate to see that beautiful tension go to waste."

That did it.

Corrin blinked—hard. Like coming out of a trance. His body jolted with the effort of trying to catch up to the moment, to the gaze, to the weight of what was being said around him.

His mouth opened. Then closed.

"I—uh..." He gave a half-laugh, the sound short and breathless, more human than controlled. He rubbed the back of his neck, the flush still rising in his cheeks.

"Sorry. I just..." Corrin exhaled sharply, trying to collect himself, "I needed to get out. Away from the Citadel walls for a minute. Thought maybe the sky would feel less like it was watching."

He didn't quite meet their eyes.

"But then I saw you both and..." another glance, another pull beneath the surface, "well, turns out the outside air doesn't fix everything."

He risked a longer look then, first at Joren, then Thalos. The loose drape of their tunics, the soft fabric over firm muscle, weight beneath linen that was never meant to hide. His gaze caught on the dip of Joren's open collar, the long line of Thalos's hip where the tunic split.

"You two really know how to pick the kind of clothes that make it hard to keep your eyes up."

Another nervous laugh. Another jolt behind his zipper. "I mean... gods. They should issue warnings with that much ease of access."

Thalos cocked his head slightly, amused. "We had the same plan. No insignia. No rank. No layers we didn't choose. Just breath and body."

Joren smirked. "And besides... comfort isn't just a luxury out here. It's strategic. That breeze knows exactly where to hit."

He let his eyes slowly trail down Corrin's frame with appreciation. "Though I have to say, that uniform of yours might be the tightest regulation cut I've ever seen. How do you even walk with all that packed in like contraband?"

Thalos's gaze followed with equal interest. "If he shifts wrong, I'm fairly certain we'll find out firsthand."

Corrin laughed again—softer now, lower in his throat. Less nervous. Less hesitant.

"Not my fault they issued me a uniform that fits like a promise," he said, trying for bravado but unable to keep the hitch from his voice.

He stepped closer. Just enough for the air to shift.

Thalos tilted his head. "You always get this flushed around senior Archivists, or is it just when your cock's trying to negotiate release terms through your inseam?"

Joren chuckled. "Don't tease him. He's clearly suffering. That fabric looks like it's one good pulse away from turning into evidence."

Corrin's lungs clenched. His hand brushed his thigh as if by accident but lingered just a moment too long.

Thalos stepped forward, closing the space between them further. His voice dropped. "You came out here for fresh air, Corrin. Are you breathing easier yet?"

The air between them vibrated.

Not from wind. Not from nerves.

From something remembering him. Hungrier. A pull sewn into the marrow of the Archive itself.

Corrin's breath hitched again, and this time, his pupils dilated. His spine straightened, not by choice but by reflex, like a man obeying forgotten command.

Something in the air had shifted.

He felt it crawl up his legs, a pressure that read as permission rather than fear. Like stepping into a memory he hadn't lived.

Joren inhaled sharply. He turned toward Thalos. Eyes wide for a second. Then heavy-lidded. Like his body had just remembered something his mind was still translating.

"You feel that?" Thalos asked, voice lower.

Joren nodded. "It's not coming from the Archive."

Thalos didn't look at either of them when he said it. His eyes were somewhere farther off. Tracking lines no one else could see.

"It's deeper than that," Joren murmured. "Older. Like something threaded through us before we ever touched a file. Before any of us were born into those walls."

Thalos stepped forward. Not closer to Corrin or Joren, but toward the feeling itself, as if bracing for it.

"The Archive doesn't command this... it remembers it. It's just playing it back. The echo of a ritual none of us agreed to... just fell into."

Corrin took another step. This time without realizing it. It wasn't a decision. It was a gravitational surrender. His chest brushed Joren's arm. His breath ghosted across Thalos's collarbone.

No one had touched yet.

But they all felt it.

The pull.

The pattern.

Not arousal.

Alignment.

Joren shifted his stance, shoulder brushing Thalos's arm, the movement natural but weighted—like gravity had started rewriting its preferences. The heat of him radiated through the soft linen, no armor to mute it.

Corrin's breath came shallow. He stepped in tighter, caught between them now, folding tighter with every heartbeat. The fabric of his uniform tightened across his chest with the tension, across his groin with something else entirely.

Thalos reached out, hand grazing Corrin's hip. His fingers light but deliberate, dragging over the line of his belt. "Still think the sky was a better view?" he murmured.

Corrin swallowed hard. "It's... close."

Joren leaned forward slightly, his lips near Corrin's ear, voice rough and teasing. "Tell the truth. You came out here hoping someone might help you unzip."

Corrin shakily exhaled with arousal. "I... wasn't sure what I came out here for."

Thalos's voice curled beneath it. "Then let us help you decide."

Three breaths, overlapping.

And still no one touched more than they had.

But the air was already thick with consent not yet spoken aloud.

As if the Archive wasn't recording.

But it was.

Not with eyes or ink, but with intention. With memory. With hunger coiled in the folds of echo and design.

This moment didn't belong to them.

It never had.

Corrin's lips parted, not in speech but in offering. Thalos leaned in first, slow, deliberate, like a man moving toward inevitability instead of desire. His mouth brushed Corrin's, warm and soft, then firmer as Corrin leaned into it with a need he hadn't meant to admit.

Joren stepped in behind him. One hand slid up Corrin's back, fingers splaying wide against tense muscle. Grounding him. His mouth ghosted over the side of Corrin's neck. Not kissing. Just letting breath play against skin.

Joren met Thalos across Corrin's cheek.

The kiss passed through him.

Not a trade. Not a triangle. A circuit.

Corrin's knees faltered, breath stuttering like a sigil unfinished.

Three bodies pressed now. Three rhythms syncing. No one in command. No one resisting. The moment didn't escalate with frenzy, it thickened. Deepened. Became ritual.

It was not foreplay.

It was recognition.

Corrin's head tipped back slightly as their mouths parted, breath catching in his throat. He swayed, not from dizziness but from resonance. Like the kiss had struck something deeper than muscle or nerve.

And then the sigil appeared.

Faint at first, a curl of green light just below his collarbone, pulsing once, twice, before stabilizing into a soft, steady glow. It didn't bloom. It didn't scar. It simply answered. As if the Archive had found a new place to write.

Joren saw it first. His breath caught against Corrin's skin. "Thalos..."

Thalos stepped back just enough to see it, fingers brushing lightly against the glow.

"That wasn't there before," Corrin whispered. Not afraid. Just awed. "I didn't feel anything, until you touched me."

Thalos's voice was soft. Almost reverent.

"You're not just being pulled in."

He hesitated.

"You're being recorded."

He touched the sigil again. Light met light.

Corrin didn't ask what came next. He didn't need to.

They moved together without instruction. A slow unraveling of space. Hands found flesh. Thalos touched first, sliding fingers beneath the edge of Corrin's uniform, undoing clasps with ceremonial care. His hands dragged the fabric down Corrin's arms, exposing skin flushed and trembling. Joren followed, palms hot and sure as they worked in tandem, easing the uniform open, the cloak slipping from Corrin's shoulders as his mouth brushed skin warmed far beyond reason.

Corrin stood between them, bare now, marked by breath and pulse, the green sigil glowing brighter with every touch. His cock throbbed, already hard, flushed deep, each throb waking something ancient in his spine. Thalos's hands found his thighs, his mouth mapping heat up the inside of one, kisses trailing like ink pressed into vellum. Joren kept his chest to Corrin's back, arms wrapped fully around him, palms sliding up and over his chest, fingers ghosting the glowing sigil with reverent pressure.

They moved as if guided, still beneath open sky, where the Archive watched without watching.

Joren's lips found Corrin's shoulder. Thalos's tongue teased at the base of his cock, then the tip, then lower, circling his balls before licking a path back up.

Corrin groaned. Long. Unchecked. His hips rocked forward, driven not by intent but instinct. Joren's hand guided him, fingers curling around the base of his shaft, holding him steady as Thalos took him into his mouth.

Not quickly.

Not all at once.

But with purpose.

Corrin's moan cracked, hips jerking. Thalos's throat welcomed him, mouth working with slow pressure, lips sealing tight. Joren's other hand slid lower, between Corrin's legs, parting him with care, with hunger. He didn't just tease; he opened him. Coaxed. Pressed. One finger, then two, sliding in slow, curved upward just enough to draw a cry from Corrin's lips.

The sigil flared.

Joren's breath stuttered. "Gods..." he murmured against Corrin's ear, "you feel... fucking perfect."

Thalos's rhythm deepened.

Corrin's thighs trembled, caught in the slow spiral of sensation growing deeper than he could contain. His breath broke. His jaw slackened. Joren's fingers worked deeper, curling just enough to catch the edge of something blinding, somewhere between pleasure and invocation.

Thalos pulled back just enough to let his tongue tease the crown, slow circles, tasting every shudder. He stroked Corrin's cock with both hands now, rhythmic, reverent, coaxing.

Joren kissed behind Corrin's ear and whispered, "Let go."

The command wasn't dominant.

It was destiny.

And Corrin obeyed.

His whole body locked, then opened. Seed spilled across Thalos's tongue in thick, hot waves, and above it all, his eyes flew open.

For the first time in his life, Corrin breathed like nothing was watching. No protocol. No Archive. No expectation. Just breath. Just self. Just the moment, free and full.

He didn't know the word for it.

But it felt like breathing again.

The sigil responded. Glowing.

Bright and green.

It pulsed once more.

Corrin exhaled a name.

Not his name. Not theirs.

One none of them had heard before.

"Igrax Vault-Born."

—— ✦ ——

Location: Blackwatch Citadel | Sublevel D | Observation Chamber Kappa

Director Threnna stood at the scry-table, one hand braced against its edge, the other slowly tightening around the stem of a half-empty glass. Her mouth curled just slightly, the kind of smile worn by someone watching a particularly well-executed seduction and taking notes.

The image shifting before her was flickering, unstable but undeniably hot. She watched three bodies move like a spell being cast through muscle and heat. Thighs flexed. Hips met. That green flare, gods above, that had been exquisite.

"Well," she drawled, voice like silk soaked in whiskey and smoke, "I knew they'd fuck eventually. I just didn't expect the Archive to come at the same time."

Ral stood at her side, posture stiff, the effort not to react etched across every tendon, though his flushed ears and the way he refused to meet her eye gave him away.

"You know the name?"

"Igrax Vault-Born," she repeated, testing the taste of it. "Sounds like a sealed designation. Something pre-Archive. Pre-Authority. We'll have to dig deeper into the Rooted Records."

Her eyes narrowed. "Or lower."

Ral looked back at the image. "That mark... it's new. It didn't flare until the kiss."

"It wasn't a kiss," she said. "It was an invitation. And the Archive accepted."

She drained the last of her glass and set it down like punctuation. "Get me everything we have on Vault-lineage anomalies. And pull Corrin's full intake dossier. Eventually. No rush. Not until we see how this whole Thalos-and-Joren entanglement finishes writing itself."

She tilted her head slightly, watching the scry-glass flicker with post-ritual glow. "Gods know the Archive's having too much fun scripting their climax in chapters. Feels like a sequel in the making."

Threnna snorted quietly. "Gods help us if the Archive starts asking for publishing rights."

CHAPTER THIRTEEN: BETWEEN FIRE AND INK

Location: Outer Citadel Walls – Blackwatch Perimeter | Moments Later | Post-Recursion

If the Archive still watched, it did so without footnote or breath.

The wind had shifted.

Not just the kind that moved leaves or cooled sweat still clinging to Corrin's collarbone, but something thinner. Finer. Like the echo of breath shared too long in one space.

Corrin sat hunched against the stone, the cloak barely drawn over him, more draped than fastened, a half-hearted shield from the world. The cloak clung to the damp between his thighs, the residue of worship refusing to dry.

Beneath the parted fabric, his body remained bare. The curve of his spine showed where the cloth fell away; the slope of his ass caught light when the wind stirred. His thighs bore the flush of recent heat.

The weight of him hung low, sated and unashamed, but not vanished, still marked by presence, by passage, by something written in rather than taken from. He did not cover himself. Not from pride, but because nothing in him felt lacking.

He was whole. Full. Written into something he hadn't known he was waiting for. The sigil on his chest, faint now, a ghost of green just below his collarbone, had quieted, but it hadn't vanished.

Joren knelt beside him, one hand resting gently on Corrin's back. His tunic hung open to the waist, chest flushed and damp, the curve of his pectorals catching the mist-heavy light.

Corrin shifted slightly, cock relaxed but full, brushing his thigh. His ass tensed faintly, as if some part of him still expected hands there.

The faint chill kissed the edges of his skin, but he didn't shiver. He was warm from the inside out.

Thalos remained a few paces away, arms folded, the wind teasing at the hem of the dark fabric that clung loosely to his hips. It did little to conceal the residual curve of arousal, heavy but patient, as if whatever had moved through them still stirred low in his belly.

The cloth barely covered him. Long legs exposed, the weight between them unbothered by modesty. His stance was easy, languid in the aftermath. He didn't bother to adjust. The ritual had left its trace on him too, and the Archive had taken no shame with it.

No one spoke the name.

Not yet.

It lingered between them like smoke that refused to rise, settling in the hollows of their throats, pressing at the backs of their teeth. *Igrax Vault-Born.* A name too heavy to say, too sharp to forget. It didn't echo. It held.

They all felt it. The presence of the name pacing just beyond the veil, waiting to be remembered again.

Corrin bore its mark still. And there was a weight in his chest that didn't feel like exhaustion. It felt... nested. Like something had made a home there. Not invasive. Not benign. Just present.

His thighs trembled, not from weakness but from something trying to settle deeper than muscle. Like a sigil learning its shape from the inside out.

Eventually, Corrin drew in a long, shuddering breath and let it go with something like clarity. He stood, slowly, the cloak falling heavier around his frame.

"I need some time," he said, voice hoarse but sure. "Just to think... to breathe." His eyes dropped for a moment. "Alone."

Joren looked like he might speak. His jaw flexed, almost imperceptibly. Something behind his ribs ached, not with longing, but with echo. He trusted Corrin. Trusted Thalos more. But when Corrin touched his arm, something in him pulled taut with recognition rather than need. A familiar pressure. Like recursion lingering under the skin.

Corrin touched Joren's arm briefly in thanks, then turned to Thalos. Their eyes met, and for a moment, the silence between them felt loaded, like the final echo of something still unfolding.

Thalos gave him a slight incline of the head, a quiet gesture suspended between permission and acknowledgment.

Corrin left without another word. His fingertips lingered half a heartbeat longer against Joren's wrist. A breath caught between them, then released as Corrin stepped away, swallowing down the pull.

They watched him disappear down the stone-bound path, swallowed by mist and curve. When he was gone, something uncoiled. A pressure broke. Breath staggered loose between them.

"Did we just let him go?" Joren asked softly.

Thalos didn't look away from the mist. "No," he said. "We gave him space to return."

The wind shifted again, cool and clean. And they stood in it a moment longer, breathing.

Together.

And above them, the Archive remained silent.

But silence, Thalos knew, was sometimes just the sound it made when it listened.

Location: Blackwatch Citadel – Perimeter Ridge Path | Midday | Post-Recursion Echo

Thalos adjusted the collar of his tunic as the trees thickened around them. Neither had spoken since they started back.

Somewhere between Corrin's disappearance and the path's first turn, they'd dressed again, without comment. The tunics hung looser now, their belts forgotten, skin still touched by ritual but no longer bare.

The walk back was slow.

Not from fatigue. More like men who had left something behind and weren't sure what they carried now.

Trees along the Citadel's outer ridge whispered in the breeze, their leaves catching sun like something staged. Every step felt measured. Not cautious. Just... aware.

Joren rolled his shoulders as they passed beneath a crumbling stone arch. His tunic, still untied at the throat, fluttered with every shift of air. "So," he said finally, "you kissed me through someone else."

Thalos's mouth twitched. "Is that how we're categorizing it?"

"I'm open to interpretation," Joren replied. "It just felt... symbolic. Archive-approved intimacy."

"Everything becomes symbolic under the Archive's eye."

Joren laughed, not quite comfortably. "Do you think it still is? Watching?"

Thalos didn't answer immediately. His eyes remained on the path ahead, where sunlight fractured through the trees and danced along the stone.

"We never really leave its gaze," he said eventually. "But I don't think it's watching to punish."

"No?" Joren glanced sideways. "Then what?"

"To see if we rewrite what it's already written."

They fell into silence again. It wasn't awkward. It was shared. Beneath it ran the slow drip of something unspoken, like a resonance left behind in the blood. They hadn't talked about the sigil. Or how Corrin looked after. And definitely not the presence slipping through their skin like a second heartbeat. The Archive had marked them, but not visibly. As if it had written something inside the chest, not the flesh.

Thalos felt the urge to name it, to pull Kaelor or Veyrion into the light of speech. He swallowed it.

Joren beat him to the edge of the thought. "We haven't talked about what it felt like," he said. "How they moved through us. How we let them."

Thalos gave a quiet hum. "I wasn't sure it was just them."

"No," Joren agreed, voice dropping. "But it wasn't just us either. Not with the way you moved. The way I couldn't stop. Gods, how you *tasted* after."

Thalos looked over, slow. "You liked the way he watched you. Like you were something sacred. And open."

Joren smirked, but didn't deny it. "You liked how it felt... your name lost in my mouth. Your story spilling into mine."

A breath passed. Heavy with memory.

"We should talk about it," Joren said eventually.

"We will." Thalos glanced at him again, the corner of his mouth curving just slightly. "Next time, I want to feel you beg with your whole body. Throat. Spine. Cock. All of it answering me."

"Did you feel him?"

Joren didn't ask who.

He nodded, slow. "Kaelor. Not fully. Not like before. But the heat pressed under my tongue, like his name had burned its way in."

Thalos's gaze sharpened. "Veyrion was there too. Not present. Not embodied. Just watching. Close enough to write if I let him."

Another pause.

"Like we were already the story. And they were just waiting for the next chapter to begin."

They walked in silence again.

Not to escape it.

But to hold it, together.

—— ✦ ——

The Citadel rose ahead like it had always been watching.

The Gargoyle above the gate hadn't moved, not in stone, not in memory, but Thalos still felt it mark their return. A chipped horn. A crooked grin. It had watched him arrive, an abandoned child, wet and silent beneath its shadow.

Now it watched him return, rewritten.

Stone towers curved into the mist, spires crowned in wrought iron and humming sigil-glass. Flags moved with the wind, not furiously, but like they were testing the air for change. The closer they got, the more the temperature shifted. Not colder. Heavier. Like recognition.

They passed the outer gate and stepped into the mouth of the upper courtyard, feet echoing soft against polished stone.

She stood waiting.

Leaning against the base of a sun-warmed column, arms crossed, a goblet of something dark and perfumed in one hand. Director Threnna didn't look like she'd been waiting long, just that she'd expected them for hours.

"Ah," she said, voice smooth as smoke and twice as invasive. "The living epilogue returns. I was beginning to wonder if the Archive swallowed you whole or just swallowed."

Thalos gave her a slow glance, lips parting in something between amusement and threat. "You always did like to watch. I'm starting to think half your reports are just masturbation rituals with better paper."

Joren exhaled slowly. "We're barely through the gate."

"I know," Threnna said, pushing off the column and falling into step beside them. "But I do hate awkward re-entries. Easier if I guide the pacing."

Thalos arched a brow. "You're escorting us?"

"Mm. You're not under review, if that's what you're implying. I just thought you might want some fresh air on the way to your next 'unrecorded conversation.'"

She smiled as if offering wine, not surveillance.

Joren muttered, "Somehow that sounds more ominous than if you'd brought a scribe and shackles."

"Oh darling," Threnna replied, tipping her goblet toward him as they walked, "if I brought shackles... it'd be for a very different kind of debrief."

She guided them through the archway and into the upper gallery corridor, open-air, with latticed windows and blooming flame-lilies coiled around ancient stone. It was too pretty for politics. Too fragrant for war.

"I had a different room prepared," she said lightly. "But this one flatters you more and hears you less. I thought you'd appreciate the trade."

Thalos didn't respond. The flicker in his eyes said he knew better.

They entered a long atrium dressed in warm gold stone and soft shadows. Three chairs waited near a curved glass alcove that overlooked the eastern ridge. One of the chairs was higher than the others, clearly meant for her. She didn't take it.

Instead, Threnna leaned back against the sill and crossed her legs slowly, letting silence bloom like smoke between them.

"Well?" she finally said, gaze shifting between them, slow as the first sip of something aged. "Did the two of you find what you were looking for?"

Thalos didn't answer right away. He tilted his head, eyes narrowing with something that could've been amusement, or something much older.

"That depends," he said. "Were you watching?"

Threnna's smile widened. "If I had been, I'd have asked for a second angle."

"If you had been," Thalos countered, "you'd have already filed a request to join."

Joren made a small noise, half laugh, half groan, and leaned back in his chair like he was preparing to spectate a bloodsport.

"I don't need to join," Threnna said, gaze flicking to Joren. "I'm far more interested in how deeply the Archive's put its fingers in you both. What's left that's still yours?"

Thalos's voice came cool and smooth. "The part that didn't moan when it was entered."

Threnna laughed, low, warm and unmistakably delighted. "Then you're clinging to scraps, darling. Because from where I was sitting, it sounded like everything was moaning."

As Threnna pushed the door open ahead of them, the two men exchanged a glance, silent and knowing. Without instruction, they moved to the seats facing the high-backed chair neither expected her to occupy, settling into the quiet space like they were bracing for something already written.

Thalos leaned back in his chair, arms loose over the rests, but his gaze sharpened to something surgical. "You said you weren't watching."

"I didn't say that." She swirled her wine. "I said if I had been, I would've asked for better angles. That doesn't preclude live feedback."

Joren's eyes bounced between them like he was tracking a match point. "Should I be worried about which one of you has the better Archive clearance?"

Thalos didn't break eye contact with her. "I think we should all be worried about who has the most intent."

Threnna smiled. The kind of smile that made you realize the knife had already been planted. She was just deciding when to twist.

She let the silence stretch, tongue pressing lightly to the inside of her cheek. "So dramatic. You always did like to pretend your privacy was intact."

Her gaze shifted, as if choosing a bottle from a shelf she'd long since memorized.

"Was that Corrin I saw with you earlier? Just for a moment. Bare shoulders. Unmistakable tension."

Joren blinked. "You were watching?"

"I'm always watching," she said with a shrug. "Just not always where you think."

Thalos gave a low hum, eyes narrowing. "And how much of what you saw was coincidence, Director?"

Threnna sipped slowly. "You know I don't believe in coincidence. Only timing."

Joren leaned forward slightly, elbows on his knees. "But you saw him. Corrin. You're saying that now. So you saw us. Him and me... The whole time, or just when it got... interesting?"

Her eyes cut to Joren, sharp and unbothered. "Darling, I never stop watching. But I only linger when the view gets theological."

Thalos chuckled under his breath, more breath than sound. "So you lingered."

"Long enough to know the Archive wasn't the only thing marking him."

Joren's brow twitched. "And yet you didn't intervene."

"Would you have wanted me to? Gods, the sounds he made... half-reverence, half-ruin. I would've needed a dozen hands to do anything but listen."

She tilted her head, watching Joren now instead of Thalos. "Besides, I rather enjoyed the sermon."

Joren's ears pinked faintly, but he didn't retreat. "You make everything sound like a confessional."

"Only the good sins deserve one," Threnna said, then turned back to Thalos, her smile all blade now. "And I suspect you've got plenty tucked into the folds of that tunic. Shall I start counting them, or would you prefer I wait until you're finished adding more?"

As though something in her gaze relented, Threnna's posture softened. It was so subtle Joren almost missed it, but Thalos didn't. He recognized the shift not as disarmament, but as decision, like a blade sheathing itself not from mercy, but because it knew the wound would come later. There was a different weight to her voice now. Not maternal exactly, but closer to memory than command.

"But truly," she said, quieter now, and it was a different voice, still sharp, still lined with the dark luster of amusement, but carried on something older. "I saw your face, Thalos. Just before the gate. Before the Gargoyle stopped watching. You looked..."

She hesitated. Just enough to feel real.

"You looked like someone the Archive opened, but couldn't close again. That worries me. Not because I disapprove. But because it means you're stepping outside what it knows how to record."

Her gaze found Joren at last, slow and unwilling to waste the strike.

"And you. You've always followed danger like a shadow. But I wonder how long you'll keep standing in it once it starts whispering back."

The silence that followed was clean.

Thalos stood.

"We'll find our way from here," he said.

Joren rose too, slower. His eyes didn't quite meet hers.

"Thank you for the view," he said, letting the words linger: not quite reverent, not quite mocking. Just enough to remind her he knew she hadn't stopped watching.

Threnna offered a half-smile, already turning away. "Anytime. Just remember... some things look different the second time through."

—— ✦ ——

The corridor to the east wall interim quarters was quieter than it should have been.

Not silent, Blackwatch never was, but quiet enough to soften footsteps and stretch shadows. Thalos and Joren moved through it without speaking, the aftertaste of Threnna's concern still fresh and oddly sticky on the backs of their tongues.

Joren unlocked the door to his quarters with a flick of his wrist, sigils chiming faintly as they disengaged. The space inside was modest by Blackwatch standards, stone walls softened by layered rugs, a low bed pressed against the far wall, and a narrow bathing alcove lit with a warm amber sigil.

"I need to wash," Joren muttered, already pulling his tunic over his head. He didn't look back as he moved toward the alcove, bare feet whispering over woven floor.

Thalos stayed near the threshold, eyes sweeping the room, not out of habit but to ground himself.

He could hear the water begin to run.

Steam curled into the air. Joren reappeared in the doorway, toweling his hair. Water glistened along his collarbones. The wall sigils caught the line of his spine as he turned. A single shape sat just above the swell of his ass, where spine curved into shadow and want.

A mark.

Red. Subtle. New.

Joren hadn't noticed. He was still turned away, wringing water from his hair with the towel when Thalos crossed the room, silent and deliberate.

His fingers brushed the small of Joren's back. Not possessively. Not even quite curiously. Just enough pressure to trace the space where the sigil had flared.

Thalos didn't speak, but the way his hand lingered, two fingers resting in the shallow dip where the curve of his ass began, said more than silence usually allowed.

Joren froze. Not in fear, but recognition. His breath hitched.

"Is it still there?" he asked, voice barely a murmur.

Thalos didn't answer.

"I didn't know," he said, fingers still tracing the skin. "That it touched you too."

Joren let out a breath, almost a laugh. "I wasn't exactly aware of it either. Not until after Kaelor. Not until I let him…"

He trailed off, then shifted slightly under Thalos's touch. "It started as a pulse. Right there. Like heat curling up my spine. I thought it was him. I wanted it to be."

He turned his head, enough to glance back, eyes dark. "It didn't feel like a mark then. It felt like a reward."

Thalos's fingers pressed a little firmer.

"And now?"

Joren smirked, low and slow. "Now it feels like an invitation. One I haven't decided whether to open… or spread."

Thalos's hand fell away, not abruptly but with restraint. A choice made.

"I think we should go," he said after a breath, voice quieter than before. "Before I forget that invitation wasn't meant for tonight."

Joren exhaled a laugh, soft and dark. "Spoil the suspense? Never."

They didn't speak again as they left the room, just the faint hum of the sigil-lock re-engaging behind them and the mirrored rhythm of their footsteps down the hall.

—— ◆ ——

The room was colder than it should have been.

Not the chill of open windows or failed flame-sigils, but the kind
that pressed at breath's edge. Unnatural. Remembering.

Thalos stepped in first. Joren followed but paused just inside.

The file was still on the desk. Closed. Untouched. It vibrated
faintly, as if something beneath the seal was struggling to recall what
it once knew.

Thalos didn't move toward it. Not yet.

His eyes flicked to the mirror in the far corner. Just for a second.

It didn't reflect him.

Not completely.

The outline was his. The eyes were not.

Icy. Intelligent. Endless.

Veyrion.

He didn't speak.

But a voice moved through him anyway.

"Did you miss me?"

Thalos staggered slightly, one hand bracing the edge of the desk.

Joren turned at the sound, eyes narrowing, but there was nothing
to hear, nothing to see. Just the faint glow pulsing beneath the file, the
quiet pressure of a room unchanged.

He opened his mouth, then stopped. Watching Thalos with a kind
of cautious reverence.

The file pulsed again. A slow, deliberate vibration under the seal,
like breath against skin.

"Good," the voice said. "Then you're ready. I think it's time I
showed you exactly what you need... to make your decision."

Thalos didn't look up.

But his breath caught, a cold bloom spreading beneath his ribs.

Joren took a step forward, confusion flickering across his brow. *"Thalos?"*

He couldn't hear the voice. Or see the eyes in the mirror.

Only the file. Only the glow.

Thalos felt it. Not just in his ears, but in his bones. In the ink the Archive had once bled into his skin.

The decision wasn't about what he would choose.

It was about who would be left once he chose it.

For the first time since Corrin walked away, Thalos understood his own words. *We gave him space to return.* They meant nothing if he no longer remembered how to return himself.

That truth, more than the cold or the voice, made him shiver. Made him feel owned.

CHAPTER FOURTEEN: DEVOUR ME BACK

Location: Blackwatch Citadel | Tier 3 Quarters | Ascendant Hall –
Private Residence

The Archive hadn't left when they did. It stayed. Listening.

The room had never felt so aware.

It was the same stone. The same stained-glass shadows falling across the desk, the shelf, the still-burning candles. But something in the air had shifted. Not cold. Not absence. But thinner. As if whatever warmth once lived in the walls had gone inward, retreated into listening.

Thalos stood at the window, shirtless, fingertips resting lightly on the frame. His back rose and fell slowly. Controlled. Measured. But his shoulders held a truth his breath wouldn't admit.

Behind him, Joren watched from the foot of the bed, sitting with both hands loosely clasped between his knees. His fingers tightened once, knuckles whitening, but he didn't move.

Neither of them had spoken since they returned.

Not about the file. Not about the voice. Not about the way Thalos had nearly collapsed.

A sigil on the back of Thalos's neck shimmered faintly, then dimmed. A thread of frost that sank into his skin like memory unwelcome. Another lit along his spine, then faded.

"It won't stop," Thalos finally said. His voice didn't break the quiet so much as press into it. "It keeps echoing. Not words. Not commands. Just... intent."

Joren tilted his head slightly. "Intent to do what?"

Thalos turned. His eyes looked darker in the low light.

"To change me," he said. "Or maybe to show me who I already am. I can't tell the difference anymore."

Joren stood but didn't approach. He looked at Thalos like he was something fragile and already fading; cold at the edges, as if part of him had already left the room.

"What do you want me to do?"

Thalos looked away. Back to the window. To his own reflection, dim and distant, watching him from the glass.

"Nothing yet," he said. "Just stay."

Joren nodded, even if Thalos couldn't see it.

The room kept listening.

Thalos didn't say another word as he stepped away from the window, gathering the loose fabric of his trousers and sliding them off before laying them over the chair. The fabric dragged a slow line down his ass, leaving him bare in the cooling light.

Joren moved toward the bed without prompting, peeling off his own layers with the slow, mechanical ease of exhaustion. His undershirt joined Thalos's tunic in the quiet heap near the edge of the hearth. He didn't look for an invitation. He didn't need one.

The mattress dipped as Thalos climbed in beside him, their bodies brushing only at the hip and shoulder. Skin against skin, warm, waiting, and unmoving. There was heat. There was hunger. It rested beneath the surface, like coals not yet stirred.

Joren's thigh pressed lightly against Thalos's. His breath shifted, slower now, but still not sleep. He wanted to turn. To look. Maybe to reach. But the ache wasn't for touch. Not yet. It was for stillness beside the only person who understood what it felt like to be rewritten from the inside.

Thalos felt it too. The tension curled in his belly, a drag of want with no urgency, only depth. He didn't resist it. He let it live there between them.

Not everything had to be claimed to be known.

Thalos exhaled slow through his nose.

A flicker.

Not in the light, in the air. The kind of presence that comes before prophecy or punishment. He stiffened, only a fraction, breath catching on the edge of language.

The Archive wasn't watching.

It was holding its breath.

Waiting the way a snare waits, looped and silent and certain.

That felt worse.

He pulled back an inch.

Not rejection. Not withdrawal. Only a pause sharp enough to injure. His body ached with need toward Joren, but his mind resisted. *If I move like this now,* he thought, *whose hands will I feel?*

He hovered. He waited.

The Archive didn't blink.

The moment passed.

Or maybe it didn't.

But Thalos did.

Joren's hand settled lightly against his abdomen, not possessive. Just anchoring. Just enough.

Neither of them closed their eyes right away.

Breath became mist. Mist became stone. Stone became skin.

Sleep wouldn't come quickly. But it would come.

Eventually.

When it did, the Archive would still be watching.

The room dimmed further, shadows curling inward like breath being held. On the desk, forgotten and sealed, Veyrion's file gave a single low pulse of blue light, soft, almost soothing.

Thalos's brow furrowed faintly. A muscle twitched at the corner of his jaw.

Joren shifted beside him, half-dreaming. He murmured something unintelligible, fingers tightening slightly where they rested.

But only Thalos felt the pull.

A hum beneath his spine. A enormity deeper than dream. Older than memory. Archive-born.

The Archive was no longer waiting.

It had chosen.

It was preparing.

The bed dropped away. His body stayed behind.

And whatever part of Veyrion still lingered was about to begin the test.

The file on the desk cracked open without a sound.

Blue light spilled from its spine, fanning across the surface in soft pulses that mimicked breath. On the exposed page, the ink bled upward, not as if it were being written, but as if it were remembering itself into being.

Recalled.

The file was not meant for Thalos alone.

The Archive had opened its memory.

And now, it would be read.

Veyrion's File – Mirrorfold Sigil Record

BLACKWATCH ARCHIVE — RITUAL LOG ENTRY
Designation: Mirrorfold Echo — Devour Sigil Manifestation
Access Level: OBSIDIAN-PRIME
Contributor: Field Seer Halden, Witness Fragment Tag #MF-47△

Location: Emberveil Ruins — Broken Mirror Altar Substructure
Date: Undated (Temporal Drift Confirmed)

Subject: Unnamed Male (Designation: Vessel)
Secondary Presence: Veyrion Hal'Syl (Pact-Anomaly, Dual-Sigil Bearer)

Observed Sequence:
Subject identified in full offering posture: chest to stone, knees wide, anus exposed and responsive, exhibiting high volatility of Mirrorfold sensitivity. Secondary Presence, Veyrion Hal'Syl, maintained full penetrative alignment during event, marking synchronized sigil resonance across spine and perineal zone.
During synchronized breath and ejaculation release, basin sigil began recursive memory projection.

First projection: Identity dissolution through oral penetration (Ref. Tag: X-$\triangle$1). Subject exhibited responsive sigil flare along lower back – sigil translated as: RECAST

Marked meaning: "Reshaped by Will."

Second projection initiated: Reflective scry-loop depicting rimming and deep penetrative behavior (Ref. Tag: X-$\triangle$2). Sigil flare occurred beneath the right gluteal fold. Sigil unfolded in spiral-curve pattern, matching pre-Rift erotic invocation series—Seal Pattern 9.

Resulting Sigil Manifestation: DEVOUR ME BACK

Sigil Response Concordance: This sigil is not command-based. It is a confessional invocation: a yielded invitation of mirrored will, encoded to invite not just control, but reciprocity. Recorded only twice in living memory. When applied during climax and post-entry retention, the sigil becomes recursive—embedding itself into both bodies if release is held through breath beyond first flare.

Implication: Vessel was not only taken. He asked to be. And he asked to be taken again.

Veyrion Hal'Syl reportedly responded with awareness, not surprise. This was not seduction. This was recognition.

Filed by: Halden, R. – Field Seer, Ritual Witness Tier
Status: Locked under Ritual Class V – Mirrorfold Variant Integration

Memory is not stored.
It is summoned.
And summoned things answer.

—— ✦ ——

It began not with a dream, but with a memory that felt like breathing.

Thalos blinked, and the room was gone.

The stone had cooled. No longer warmed by candlelight, but slick with condensation, ancient and scented with the residue of invocation. He was naked. Not just in body, but in knowing. His limbs knew where to kneel before he did. His hands braced stone worn smooth by centuries of echoes.

Not a dream.

Not a memory.

But something written between the two, and bleeding forward into now.

He didn't summon the man. He unfolded him. From shadow. From heat. From the ache that precedes names.

Veyrion stood barefoot in the mosaic wreck of the altar's underchamber, the broken sigils still pulsing dimly beneath moss-laced stone. The old Mirrorfold sigil, shattered and forgotten, hummed faintly at the periphery, responding not to spellwork but to his breath.

He had already begun.

The man knelt at the edge of a spiraled basin, nude save for the ritual binding that still clung, ragged and ceremonial, to one ankle. No shackles. No sigil-fused chains. But he didn't move. Didn't rise.

Because Veyrion had looked at him once, and the man had not stopped falling since.

He was younger. Not weak. But unmade. Someone not yet written fully into the Archive's fold. Not a soldier. Not a scholar. Just potential, raw and trembling.

Now, opened.

His uniform lay scattered like offerings at Veyrion's feet, each button and each folded piece of fabric removed by his own hands.

With obedience born of silence.

Veyrion stepped closer. His sigils didn't flare with violence, but with echo. The blue of his spine flickered in pulse with the man's breath. Each step brought another twitch in the exposed ring of flesh below, puckering tight, then flexing with unmistakable readiness.

He circled once. Slow. Measuring.

The man's cock was already hard. Thick. Curved slightly toward his belly, the tip flushed and dripping in the cold air. Veyrion didn't look at it. Not yet.

He watched his hole.

The man was spread, shoulders low, chest pressed to the basin's curved lip, knees wide, ass high. His spine curved like script. Sigils had begun forming on his back, lightborn, not branded. Traced by proximity. A mirror-echo of Veyrion's own marks.

A living page. Waiting to be inscribed.

Veyrion didn't speak. His cock was half-hard, veined with pale sigil-light, resting against his thigh as he knelt behind the man and exhaled. Cold. Like prophecy.

The man moaned.

Not loud. But shattered.

His hole fluttered, rim pink and wet, as if it had tasted the breath and remembered how to beg.

Veyrion leaned forward. Not to enter. To whisper.

A single word. In no tongue known to this realm.

The sigils at his wrists burst to life, ribboning down his arms in pulses of pale fire, and the man arched. Back lifting. Hole clenching, then spreading open in one desperate tremor.

There was no touch.

And he came.

Spasming, helpless, cock untouched as seed spilled in thick ropes across stone and sigil-scarred air. His cries weren't words. They were memory. Echo. Rewritten need.

Veyrion waited.

Only when the man began to tremble, not from climax but from emptiness, did he reach for him.

One hand to the sacrum. One thumb to the base of the spine.

His cock, thick and flushed, carved from hunger made divine, pressed between the man's cheeks.

Not forced. Not resisted.

Just entered.

The stretch was slow. Brutal. And utterly inevitable.

The man gasped, a sharp sound of recognition. Something was writing him open, claiming him in a language he hadn't realized he already spoke.

Veyrion began to move.

No rhythm. Just punctuation.

Each thrust a command. Each grind a revelation. His body didn't slam; it etched. The man's ass clenched around him like scripture, like ritual stone giving way beneath divine weight. Their breaths synchronized. Not by intention, but by design.

Beneath it all, behind the slow rise and grind of memory made flesh, another breath stirred, one that didn't belong to Veyrion or the vessel beneath him.

Thalos.

He felt it. Threaded into the motion, written beneath the moan. Not just as a witness, not just as the Archive's echo, but as someone present. Someone absorbing.

The heat in his chest wasn't arousal anymore. It was recognition.

The way Veyrion moved. The way he carved need into obedience. The way the vessel's back arched not to flee but to receive. It wasn't foreign. It felt like instinct remembered.

That scared Thalos more than anything.

Because he wanted to echo it.

He wanted to be *inside* this memory and not *watching it bleed*. He wanted to lose himself in this ache, to learn that kind of devotion by mapping it with his own body.

Thalos couldn't move.

He was pinned in this vision by desire *and* design.

His cock throbbed, unbidden, untouched and fully aware. The pleasure wasn't his.

The hunger was.

Veyrion, even as he thrust deeper into the vessel, whispered back toward the mirror of his own memory:

"You're starting to remember, aren't you?"

The thrust didn't stop.

The sigils didn't dim.

Thalos's breath hitched, and somewhere beyond the vision, the file on his desk pulsed once more.

Veyrion leaned in deeper, his voice now split between whisper and command.

"Watch," he said.

And the altar responded.

The basin beside them flared, first with light, then with reflection.

It projected the first memory. The oral initiation. The gagging man learning how surrender begins with breath.

Thalos saw it again, not above but around him, every image, every rutting thrust looping through his skin like it had been carved into his chest.

The second vision followed: rimming, devotion, the penetration that didn't need to ask permission.

Through it all, the sigils lit brighter. Beneath him, within him, through him.

The vessel beneath Veyrion moaned louder. Screamed, even. But not from fear.

From fulfillment.

Veyrion came again.

Thalos felt it. Not as warmth, but as awakening.

Something inside him opened. Not his body. His memory.

His purpose.

The vision didn't break.

It sharpened.

Veyrion's voice whispered once more:

"Let me show you who you were... before the Archive decided what you could be."

Everything went white.

The light wasn't light. It was pressure. It bloomed from within, not around, as the echo collapsed inward.

Thalos could feel it, sigils igniting across the vessel's back. No longer vague traces of resonance but sharp, defined sigils—two of them, burning into the flesh like memory made permanent.

The first pulsed just beneath the shoulder blades: **RECAST.**

Not written in ink, but essence. It marked transformation. Not change imposed but change accepted. A declaration that the one beneath Veyrion had been broken open and chosen to remain that way.

The second flared beneath the right glute, spiraling inward along the curve of the flesh: **DEVOUR ME BACK.**

This was not a request. Not even a confession. It was a vow. A submission so total it looped into power. The vessel was no longer passive. He had mirrored the Archive's hunger and offered himself in return.

Veyrion knew what it meant.

Not ownership.

Invitation.

He pressed in deeper, as though feeding the echo itself.

Thalos, still inside it all, felt the sigils etch into his own skin.

Not permanently. Not yet.

The outline was forming.

The Archive was no longer watching.

It was preparing to write him next, and it did.

The shift happened without sound. No crash of memory, no lurch of magic. One moment Thalos was inside the vision. The next, he *was* the vision.

The vessel vanished.

Thalos was the one on hands and knees now—body arched, ass high, spine bowed like invocation. The heat that had belonged to another now lived in him.

Behind him, Veyrion didn't change.

He remained.

He pressed forward again, sliding into Thalos with the slow, relentless importance of prophecy.

Thalos cried out. Not in resistance. In appreciation.

The pressure, the stretch, the way his body took every inch was not alien. It was remembered. His hole fluttered around Veyrion's cock, desperate and already slick, need pouring from him like revelation.

The sigils didn't wait.

They marked him as he moved.

Each thrust scribed a line. Each moan etched the truth. Sigils bloomed beneath his skin, across his back, curling beneath the curve of his ass where the sigils for submission and hunger pulsed brighter.

RECAST.

DEVOUR ME BACK.

Veyrion thrust deep. Thick. Eternal. He gripped his hips and said nothing.

He didn't need to.

Thalos was learning the words from the inside out.

His body was already begging to be rewritten.

The climax came like a command.

Veyrion slammed in hard, holding there, buried and throbbing. Heat flooded Thalos's core. The sigils flared with a light that wasn't light but awareness. It branded him from within. First **RECAST** seared across his back like a revelation. Then **DEVOUR ME BACK** coiled into him like a vow stitched in breath, low and intimate, in the curve of his ass. The pain was exquisite. The pleasure, more.

The sigils seared into him: intimate, ancient, unremovable.

Thalos gasped, bolting upright with a violent inhale, drenched in sweat. His skin burned cold and hot all at once, and his body trembled with the aftershock of something deeper than sleep. He had been nude when he fell asleep, and now every inch of him felt exposed. *Claimed.*

His cock was hard. Leaking. Heavy with the ache of something he hadn't touched but had felt entirely. The sheets clung to his thighs, damp with both sweat and something else, residue not of dream but of ritual.

The room swam with shadow and cold.

Joren stirred, murmured something sleep-blurred, but didn't wake.

He mumbled a name, *Kaelor*, so softly it might have been a dream's echo. Then came another word, fractured and longing—*yes.*

Thalos froze, breath catching.

The light from the desk caught the curve of Joren's shoulder as he shifted again, the sheets slipping.

He saw it.

A faint glow, red this time, etched into the skin just beneath Joren's shoulder blade. A second shimmer ignited in the cleft of his right ass cheek, pulsing briefly before fading back into the silence of sleep.

Thalos turned sharply toward the desk.

Veyrion's file had gone still.

Kaelor's had been silent until now. It was open.

Flaring red.

As if answering something not spoken aloud.

As if Kaelor, too, had left his mark.

Thalos was already on his feet, chest rising and falling, heart pounding as he staggered to the standing mirror across the room.

He craned his neck, angling his back toward the glass.

There they were.

Faint, pulsing softly in the candlelight.

The two sigils.

RECAST.

DEVOUR ME BACK.

They dimmed like breath held too long but finally released.

Extinguished.

Not erased.

Thalos stood there a moment longer, body bare, chest heaving. His reflection didn't move. It watched him. Marked and uncertain.

He turned back toward the bed, gaze falling on Joren's still-sleeping form.

He wasn't dreaming alone.

He's next, Thalos thought. Not with fear. Not even with warning. With inevitability.

The Archive was writing them both. One echo at a time.

—— ✦ ——

Location: Blackwatch Citadel | Sublevel D | Observation Chamber Kappa | Same Night

The light in the chamber was low, the scent of ink and parchment thicker than the candle glow it shimmered inside.

Director Threnna stood at the scry-table, one hand wrapped around a glass of obsidian wine, the other tracing faint sigil residue in the air above the surface.

Agent Ral stood silent near the rear alcove, jaw tight. The mirrored surge hit him low, his cock thickening, pressing hard against his zipper. His breath caught as if he'd tasted something forbidden, the kind of hunger that never lets go.

Corrin sat on the edge of the viewing bench, eyes wide and glassy, skin pale beneath the warm cloak draped over his shoulders.

His mind wasn't here. Not fully. Something deeper moved behind his eyes, less awe than calculation. A bead of sweat slid down his inner thigh, unseen and ignored, as if he were already watching a different ritual entirely.

Mirrorfold echoes never showed truth. Only hunger. But it pulsed. Once blue. Once red. Once both.

Threnna smiled.

"Well," she said softly, sipping without turning. "There's something so erotic about inevitability, isn't there? Especially when it moans back."

She flicked her fingers through the sigil haze, reversing the stream. The scry-field rippled and spun backward, stammering over orgasm, over the moans, over the moment Veyrion pushed inside Thalos and the twin sigils flared to life. She let it play again, slower.

Once. Twice.

"Look at them," she murmured. "Marked like answers the Archive never dared ask for. One blue. One red. And neither of them wrote it first."

She turned then, just enough for her eyes to catch Corrin's unfocused gaze and Ral's trembling restraint.

"The Archive doesn't want to record them anymore," she said, voice low. "It wants to *be* them."

She snatched and raised her obsidian quill.

"Then let's give it a better story to bleed into. Something raw and aching. Something the Archive can't just watch anymore... but rut into like a bitch in heat."

And elsewhere, deep beneath the weight of red-lit parchment and a name still echoing, Joren continued to dream.

CHAPTER FIFTEEN: THE MARK BENEATH THE SIGIL

The mirror caught him differently this time.

Not just because of the light—though it was dim, tinted by candlewax and the last vestiges of arcane trace, but because of the way he looked *back*. Not like someone seeking. But someone caught mid-answer.

Thalos stood bare in the flickering hush of his chambers, one hand pressed flat against the cool wall beside the glass, the other trailing gently across his side. His skin glistened faintly from the sweat of ritual, but the sigils had dimmed. Not gone, only set, like ink settling into permanence.

He turned.

The candlelight caught the edge of one sigil, etched between the dimples of his spine. **RECAST.** Beneath it, nearly hidden by the swell of his glutes, another: **DEVOUR ME BACK.** The second pulsed faintly, breathing beneath the skin.

He traced them in the mirror with his eyes first. Then with his fingertips.

Not tentatively. But reverently.

It didn't feel like magic. Not anymore. It felt like memory, as if his body had always known this shape and the Archive had simply reminded it how to spell itself correctly.

A soft shuffle behind him.

Joren was still asleep, turned halfway toward him on the mattress, one arm thrown across the pillow, hair mussed in sweat-damp tangles. The covers had slipped low, tangled somewhere at his knees, exposing the full line of his back down to the hard curves of his glutes and the muscles in his calves.

His breath was even. Slow. But...

Thalos narrowed his gaze.

Red light shimmered faintly beneath Joren's skin.

First beneath his shoulder blade.

Then lower, where the crease of his ass disappeared into the hollow of his thigh.

Sigils.

Twin to his own. But red. Not blue.

Kaelor's color.

Thalos's breath caught.

He turned from the mirror and walked barefoot, silent, toward the desk where Kaelor's file still sat, half-opened, humming faintly like something almost forgotten and trying to dream again. The wax was cracked, not freshly or recently, but enough to suggest that someone or something had turned the page without permission.

A page now exposed, one he hadn't been meant to read.

The sigils were scrawled vertically in a pattern he didn't recognize. Not Mirrorfold. Each line of script folded inward, overlaid with translated annotations and ritual fragments.

He leaned in.

The heading shimmered:


```
ADDENDUM: RITUAL LOG ENTRY — OBSIDIAN PRIME ACCESS
BLACKWATCH ARCHIVE — RITUAL LOG ENTRY
Designation: Mirrorfold Inversion — RECAST / CLAIM ME FIRST
Manifestation
Access Tier: OBSIDIAN-PRIME


Location: Emberveil Ruins — Broken Mirror Altar
Substructure
Temporal Stability: Fluctuating (Class B Drift confirmed)
Primary Subject: Kaelor Thorne (Designation: Echo Catalyst
— Obsidian Tier)
```

Secondary Subject: Unidentified Male (Vessel Class – Human Variant)

Observed Sequence:
Subject assumed full offering posture voluntarily—chest to stone, knees parted, anus exposed. Magical volatility confirmed via ambient echo pulse. Subject displayed high readiness, no incantation or binding required.

Kaelor Thorne approached nude, sigils already active across forearms and thighs. Arcane signature heightened during proximity contact—recorded as aura shift from passive red to active crimson.

Sigil Manifestation:
RECAST
• First sigil activated during rimming sequence.
• Manifested at moment of orgasm via oral stimulation (no penile contact).
• Location: Lower back, left of spine.
• Interpretation: Transformation by surrender; redefinition of flesh by invoked will.
• Notably, this occurred before any penetrative act, aligning RECAST as a prelude rather than a consequence.

CLAIM ME FIRST
• Final sigil, etched into the right gluteal region during penetrative climax.
• Appeared following recursive thrust cadence, aligned with fourth recorded penetration.
• Shape: Downward spiral, flame-etched.
• Interpretation: Not invitation, but demand—vessel asserts primacy in the order of memory and domination.

Combined sigil sequencing RECAST → CLAIM ME FIRST represents a unique Mirrorfold inversion: the vessel initiates his own transformation and then anchors Kaelor through submission marked as priority.

Additional Notes:
• No presence of third-party sigilwork or coercive arcana.
• Secondary subject's semen and Kaelor's seed both confirmed to be part of sigil ignition.
• Vocal trigger identified: "I am yours"—unprompted. Confirmed as completion phrase.

• Sigils remained intact for 3.4 minutes post-ejaculation
before dimming into dermal memory layer.
• CLAIM ME FIRST visibly retained post-ritual—archivally
permanent.

Filed By: Halden, R.
Status: Encoded for Mirrorfold Codex, Locked under Ritual
Class V
Recommendation: Cross-reference with known "DEVOUR ME BACK"
and "REMEMBER ME ALWAYS" sigil cascades. Current pattern
suggests RECAST functions as initiation marker in an
evolving sigil taxonomy.

Thalos's heart stuttered.

He looked back toward the bed, toward Joren.

The glow had intensified.

Faint flickers of crimson arced over Joren's ribs as he shifted restlessly. Not pain. Not fear. Just *movement*. Like something beneath his skin was stretching into being.

Thalos closed the file, slowly.

No blue light flared.

It was a pulse of blinding red.

The Archive, it seemed, wasn't done dreaming. It was only just beginning to remember.

Thalos stood still for a long moment, the glow reflecting faintly in his eyes. Something inside him ached—low and old, like a memory he hadn't earned yet. The pulse of red stirred something not just erotic but terrifying. This wasn't over. It hadn't even begun.

He wasn't afraid.

Not entirely.

Beneath the dread, beneath the skin, beneath the marks the Archive had burned into his back, there was a flicker of something else.

Hope.

Hope that this was leading somewhere. That Joren wouldn't be lost. That they were not being consumed at all. Just rewritten. Into something even the Archive hadn't dared predict.

—— ✦ ——

The warmth began beneath Joren's navel. Not sleep. Not memory. Just the Archive... remembering through him.

Not a heat that scorched, but one that enveloped, low and blooming. Unfurling up his spine then down into the root of him. He didn't open his eyes because he hadn't closed them. He hadn't moved at all. And yet, the world had changed around him.

Stone beneath him, warm and breathing, not sheets and not memory. His knees were parted, his chest pressed to the slick curve of carved obsidian. His arms folded beneath him with the ease of a submission remembered rather than offered.

He tried to speak, but no sound came.

The echo beat louder.

Kaelor's presence slid behind him, known and inevitable, breathing heat against his skin. It felt like breath at the base of his neck, a sigh that could rewrite a name.

Joren inhaled, and the scent of him was everywhere. Dust, sex, cinnamon, and iron. And *heat.*

"You came willingly," Kaelor said, voice low, like the beginning of a poem only meant for one mouth.

Joren's throat worked. His mouth opened.

He whispered, "You didn't give me a choice."

Kaelor chuckled.

"But you came anyway."

Kaelor stepped forward, the lines of his body catching in the low gleam of reflected sigil-light. The space between them crackled, not like magic but like recognition through skin.

He circled Joren slowly, footsteps soundless on stone. His fingers ghosted above Joren's exposed lower back, not quite touching, but writing something in air Joren could already feel. Then, without preamble, Kaelor knelt behind him.

Joren's breath caught. He wanted to ask what this was, who he was becoming, but the questions dissolved into sensation. Kaelor's hands, warm and steady, spread him open. He paused there, breath ghosting over the sensitive pink rim, letting the anticipation bloom unchecked.

His tongue pressed in.

Not a flick, but a slow, deliberate plunge, wet and firm, curling just enough to make Joren's entire body twitch.

The moan that tore from him was raw. Helpless. His thighs shook.

Kaelor licked again, slower this time, dragging and claiming. His hands kneaded the backs of Joren's thighs as his tongue slid in and out with rhythmic pressure, each motion deliberate, edging toward devotion.

The rim fluttered, clenched, opened again. Kaelor groaned into it.

Joren's cheek pressed harder to the altar stone.

"Gods... fuck," he gasped. "Please... Kaelor..."

Kaelor didn't stop.

He rimmed him deeper, tongue plunging now in sharp, hungry thrusts, savoring the slick bloom of Joren's hole and the way it pulsed around him, already begging to be filled.

It was only then that the first sigil bloomed, low and red between the dimples of Joren's spine. It flared as Kaelor tongued him into a wordless, trembling release.

RECAST.

Kaelor didn't answer.

Kaelor's mouth worked deeper, tongue tracing each flicker of pressure. Joren's thighs trembled. His orgasm struck untouched, gasping into the altar's slick curve.

Kaelor stood, the shadows casting sharp lines over the defined musculature of his abdomen and thighs. His cock hung heavy, thick, ruddy, and full, the veins wrapped in glimmering runic shimmer like molten metal. The head was wide and flushed, dripping in readiness, its crown throbbing with pulse and promise.

The contrast of the raw, carnal flesh and the glowing, sacred sigils carved a picture of hunger restrained only by ritual, barely contained. Arcane light coiled along the shaft like heat made visible, and as he stepped forward, it pulsed in time with Joren's breath.

No words passed.

He aligned himself and pressed in, slow and deliberate, the crown parting Joren with an aching inevitability. The stretch tore a groan from his throat, deep and wrecked. It wasn't pain but recognition made physical, the feeling of being filled by something meant for you. The stretch was brutal. Perfect. Consecrated by need.

Joren cried out.

Not from pain.

The second sigil branded itself across his right cheek, spiraling downward in flame-etched red—**CLAIM ME FIRST.**

Each thrust ground it deeper.

Kaelor began to move with feral precision, no longer slow and no longer reverent. Each thrust buried his cock deeper with punishing rhythm, and Joren felt everything, every vein, every flex, every unrelenting stroke grinding against nerves stretched to breaking. Pressure bloomed inside him like flame. He was full, so full it almost hurt, almost made him break.

He didn't break.

He begged.

Moaning, sobbing, arching back for more.

Kaelor gave thrust deeper, brutal and unrelenting. Their bodies slammed together, writing a liturgy in sweat and submission. Joren's hole clutched around Kaelor's cock, desperate for more. Every nerve inside him lit with need, and still it wasn't enough, every squeeze drawing Kaelor deeper, like his body was memorizing the shape of him, demanding he never leave.

Exposing a fracture no climax could seal.

$$\Omega - \dagger - \Omega$$

Location: Memory-fracture / Archive recursion bleed | Unfixed Time

The altar bled light.

Red. Blue. Then neither.

Joren's body collapsed forward, gasping, undone, but the world didn't reset. It buckled.

A shimmer, a crack.

The Archive, struggling to contain the memory, faltered.

Through the fracture, they appeared.

Not how the dossiers had sworn.

Not as brothers.

As lovers.

Kaelor stood naked in the half-light, his body a scripture of battle and worship, the sigils along his arms pulsing with low, deliberate heat.

Veyrion faced him, not with the distance of kin but with the intimacy of breath exchanged in darkened halls, of trust broken and remade along the tender marrow of want.

Their bodies bore no armor. Only the markings the Archive had failed to erase.

Kaelor's voice was low, breaking against Veyrion's chest. "They called us brothers so they could look away."

A hand, trembling but sure, traced the hollow of Veyrion's throat, moving down slowly over ribs mapped by mirrored sigils.

Veyrion's reply was soft and cruel. "Because lovers who bend prophecy unsettle the stone."

Their foreheads touched.

No witness would have mistaken it for fraternity.

Kaelor's hands fisted in Veyrion's hair, pulling their mouths together not to speak, but to mark. Lips parting. Breath exchanged. The kind of kiss that bruises not with force but with history.

The Archive stuttered, struggling to overwrite the memory.

The truth bled louder.

"I carved my sigil into your spine before the first lie was written." Kaelor gorwned in hunger.

Veyrion, gasping into his mouth. "And I wore it gladly, not because I had to, but because I chose you. Before duty. Before blood. Before the Archive decided names mattered."

Their bodies collided, hips grinding, breath catching, the friction of cock against cock slick with sweat and inevitability.

Hands memorizing landscapes no brother would map. Teeth scraping tender along scars no family could claim.

The mirrorfold shimmered.

Memory tried to collapse.

It couldn't.

Not before Kaelor pressed his forehead again to Veyrion's and whispered—

"You were never my brother."

"You were my undoing."

The scene shattered.

Fractured outward like mirror-glass splitting under the heat of truth unspoken too long.

The Archive tried to seal it.

Tried to reorder the names.

Tried to drown it in bloodlines and classifications.

But the truth had already been written.

In sweat.

In scar.

In vow.

Kaelor and Veyrion had never been brothers.

They had been lovers so old their bond outlived memory.

The Archive, like all flawed relics, had simply chosen the version it could survive.

$$\Omega - \dagger - \Omega$$

The memory tore away like breath held too long. The fracture sealed. The rhythm returned hot, unrelenting, and inevitable.

"Don't stop," Joren gasped, voice cracking. "Gods, Kaelor. Harder."

Kaelor obliged. He pistoned into him with relentless force, the grind of their bodies a language older than spellwork.

The altar pulsed. The sigils brightened. And still Kaelor moved, deep, brutal, insistent, until the pressure built again in Joren's core and something ancient flared beneath his skin.

Kaelor leaned over, lips brushing Joren's ear.

"Mine," he whispered.

Joren groaned, split open and radiant. He echoed it.

"I am yours."

Seed spilled. The sigils burned.

The moment Kaelor declared Joren his, the chamber responded. Sigils flared in sync, **RECAST** pulsing between Joren's spine dimples and **CLAIM ME FIRST** blazing anew on his right cheek. They responded not to orgasm but to the bond forged in voice and flesh.

From altar stone to air, everything shimmered with shared ownership.

This wasn't possession. It was inscription.

The marks they bore in that moment locked the ritual into place. Joren's body impaled with Kaelor still throbbing inside him.

The Mirrorfold had heard.

It accepted the vow.

Somewhere, in the Archive's scry-pools, the page turned itself.

Kaelor pulled free with slow finality, his cock dragging from Joren's stretched, still-quivering hole. Joren exhaled, somewhere between a whimper and a sigh, as his body shivered with absence. The fullness was gone, but the imprint remained deep and molten.

He could feel Kaelor inside him still, not just physically but like a brand etched into his spine, into his breath, into his moan. In that vulnerable stillness, dripping, ruined, and marked, Joren felt it settle, not just that he had been taken but that he had been seen, claimed, changed. A spill of seed followed, hot and thick against the backs of his thighs and the stone beneath.

Joren gasped at the loss, hips trembling.

Kaelor didn't retreat.

He stayed close, hands moving gently now. Slow, possessive strokes across Joren's tender skin. Claiming the ache, tracing the sigils newly etched in flesh.

Kaelor leaned down, lips brushing the shell of Joren's ear.

"You were always going to be mine," he murmured. Soft. Reverent. Final.

The sigils pulsed once more in answer.

—— ◆ ——

Location: Blackwatch Citadel | Ascendant Hall | Thalos's Chambers — Pre-Dawn

Thalos watched from across the room, silent and unmoving, breath held so tightly his chest ached. Joren hadn't stirred consciously, but his body had. A twitch in his calf, a shift of his spine. Subtle at first, then the low roll of his hips under the sheets, barely perceptible, but unmistakably rhythmic. Like he was chasing something. Or surrendering to it.

The sheets were damp near his thighs, and a faint, pulsing glow, red, bright, and slow, had begun to vibrate from beneath the skin on his lower back. Thalos recognized the pattern, not from study but from memory.

The mark was Kaelor's.

It was answering.

Thalos, naked and still etched in blue, stepped closer to the bed, body thrumming with something tight and ancestral, heart hammering against his ribs. One hand slid back instinctively to trace the mark etched low on his spine, the very place Kaelor's sigil now pulsed on Joren. A shared shape. A mirrored binding. Veyrion's mark. Kaelor's mark. They wore them together now, like twin scripts written into flesh.

It was knowing.

Joren was still dreaming.

Whatever Kaelor had begun inside him... wasn't finished.

Joren arched, abrupt, gasping. His whole body tensed, and a cry broke from his lips, ragged and raw.

"I am yours."

Thalos froze.

Joren's eyes fluttered open, unfocused at first. He blinked hard, breath still coming in sharp, shallow pulls. Sweat beaded along his collarbone, and the sigils at his back gave one final glow before fading beneath his skin.

He looked around wildly, then locked eyes with Thalos.

For a long, charged heartbeat, neither of them spoke.

Joren's voice cracked the silence.

"You saw?"

Thalos didn't nod. Didn't move.

He just looked through him.

"For a moment," he said quietly, voice barely above a breath, "I thought I saw Kaelor."

The words hung there, impossible and true.

Then Thalos blinked, shaking himself from the moment. The awe slid into concern as he stepped closer, crouching beside the bed.

"Joren," he said, gentler now. "Are you alright? Can you feel anything still?"

Joren swallowed and slowly sat up, his breath ragged. His hands moved instinctively to his body, tracing along his lower back, where the sigil **RECAST** had burned, and then further to the swell of his right ass cheek, where the **CLAIM ME FIRST** spiral had flared.

"I don't know if it was real," he murmured, "but it felt like it. Like the dream bled into my bones."

His fingers found the place where the sigils had pulsed, now quiet but not forgotten.

The Archive had gone silent.

"They're there, aren't they?"

Thalos didn't answer with words. He only nodded once, slowly. Solemnly.

Joren's mouth parted as he breathed in, moved not just by the answer but by the weight of what it meant.

"They're real," he whispered.

Thalos reached for him, no ritual and no command. Just a hand brushing along Joren's thigh, the other cupping gently behind his neck. Their foreheads touched, breath mingling. No words needed.

"I felt it too," Thalos murmured finally, as though admitting it gave the moment permanence. "Through you."

Joren's hand slid over Thalos's chest, fingers trembling slightly, tracing the faint edge of the sigil beneath his skin.

Their lips hovered.

Not hunger.

Acknowledgement.

When they kissed, it wasn't the beginning of something.

It was the confirmation that it had already begun.

—— ✦ ——

Location: Blackwatch Citadel | Sublevel D | Observation Chamber Kappa | Moments Later

Director Threnna's hand moved like a blade across parchment, sharp, fast, precise. The obsidian quill scratched furiously over a new sheet, dark ink bleeding into a web of arcane shorthand and personalized script. The scry-table beside her pulsed in waves of red and blue light, the mirrored surge of sigils still echoing through the Archive grid.

She didn't look up.

Corrin stood nearby, silent but not still. One hand hovered at his side, the other clenched slightly at his chest as if feeling something beneath the skin. His brow furrowed, gaze distant. A memory stirred.

Not a clear image, only a feeling of heat, pressure and need. The sensation of something ancient curling into his ribs, whispering through his blood.

He looked down at his hand. Pressed it tighter to his chest.

"I've felt that mark before," he said, more to himself than anyone. "But it wasn't Kaelor's. And it wasn't a brother's."

Agent Ral lingered farther back, trying too hard not to shift. His eyes snapped to Corrin, shock etched across his face.

"You... felt that?" he asked, voice low but hard-edged. "That wasn't chemistry. That was something stronger."

Threnna raised a brow, quill still dancing. She turned slowly, gaze flicking from Ral to Corrin with pointed precision.

"Would you mind repeating that, darling?" she said, voice wrapped in velvet and amusement. "It's not every day Mr. Aloof admits to a bond deeper than blood. Or more... penetrating."

Ral looked down at the display, then back at Corrin. "I've run every Archive record we have on that sigil. Through every registry check and codex index. Only ever recorded in familial bonds—brothers, twins, bloodline echoes. But this one? Never registered to them."

Threnna's smile turned sharper, lascivious and knowing. "Isn't that adorable," she purred. "Exactly what the records say, then. The sigil only passes between kin. Which makes this..." She glanced toward the scry-table, where the red and blue pulses overlapped again. "Confirmation that the dossiers are lying. Or worse... rewriting."

Corrin's eyes finally sharpened, the fog breaking. A flicker of green flashed in his irises—too fast to catch, but there. He turned to them both, voice suddenly steady, sharpened by something older.

"Or maybe," he said, "the Archive led you to believe it was a mistake."

He stepped forward, hand still pressed to his chest. "I mean, come on... do Thalos and Joren fuck like brothers?"

Ral flinched. Threnna didn't.

Her smirk only widened.

Corrin's tone cut deeper. "You're not in control. You're just writing it down."

He turned away; gaze fixed on the scry-table. "The Archive has chosen. And it never asks twice."

Chapter Sixteen: Echo Rewrite

The scry-table flickered again.

Not with warning. Not with arcane surge. Just the subtle hairline skip of a feed that had never faltered.

Director Threnna didn't flinch.

She simply sipped her tea, black, bitter, still steaming, and stared at the projection like it had just insulted her tailoring.

Kaelor Thorne's file shimmered in the center of the projection, rotating slowly in pale crimson light. Recursion traces bled around the margins. The access log timestamp glitched once, then corrected. A moment later, the dossier duplicated.

Two of them. Side by side. Identical. But not.

She narrowed her eyes. "You cheeky little bastard."

The right-hand file pulsed, its contents shifting, not reloading but rewriting. One paragraph vanished, another replacing it with completely different phrasing. The sigil-glyph indexing at the base of the file stuttered. The Archive's interface responded with a soft ping, passive and almost apologetic.

Threnna leaned forward, elbow on the table, expression gone slack with bemused suspicion. "That's not how recursion protocols behave unless someone's forking the logic tree. And unless Kaelor's learned to hack from the grave—"

Another flicker. This time from the Veyrion Hal'Syl file.

It did not duplicate. It redacted itself.

Half the file greyed out.

She tapped one lacquered nail against the crystal rim. "Mm. No. You don't get to redact yourself. That's *my* job."

The timestamps no longer aligned. The Archive claimed the edits were made precisely six hours before they occurred.

Threnna set her teacup down gently. "Well, fuck."

She didn't call for backup. She brushed her palm over the sigil-plate, summoning a recursive scan through the Echo-Tier threads, and pulled up a secondary display in the far panel to cross-reference sigil indexing across the last seventy-two hours.

The system hesitated.

Then delivered a result she hadn't asked for.

Two sigils. One red. One blue. Both tagged to *Kaelor Thorne.*

"Liar," she muttered, almost fond.

Corrin entered a moment later, file in hand, flushed from the ascent. "You asked for—"

"Come here."

He did.

She gestured to the duplicated file feeds still rotating. "Tell me what you see."

Corrin stepped in, eyes scanning fast. Then slower.

"That's not... that's not right."

"No," she said, voice sweet with venom. "It's not."

Corrin pointed. "This version. On the right. It wasn't there yesterday. I read this file. That phrasing? That wasn't here."

Threnna leaned back and raised one brow. "Are you sure? Memory's a fickle bitch when the Archive starts edging your consciousness."

He didn't flinch. "I'm sure. The echo-mark's conflicting."

She nodded, pleased. "Good. You're learning."

The red sigil pulsed again, like a heartbeat caught mid-climax.

Corrin flinched, hand to his chest, jaw locking like he'd just been touched from the inside.

Threnna didn't react at first.

"You felt that?"

Corrin looked at her, voice low. "I think... it recognized me."

Corrin pressed his palm harder against his sternum, as if trying to hold something inside. It wasn't pain. It wasn't even fear. It was a hunger he hadn't named, threading itself through his breath and bone, waiting for permission to speak.

A phantom heat pulsed under his sternum, not pain—more a pressure, a promise. Like a name being stitched into his breath where no one else could see it.

Threnna turned back to the projection, lips curling like she'd tasted something far too interesting to spit out.

"Oh, sweet boy," she murmured. "That's not recognition. That's recall."

The blue sigil flared in answer.

The Archive, silent until now, whirred faintly beneath the chamber floor.

Like it had just remembered what it was meant to forget.

Threnna stood fully now, letting her eyes drink in the subtle distortions forming in the scry-table's surface. Once-smooth data now frayed at the edges, silk soaked in memory. The feed didn't simply *flicker;* it pulsed, almost breathed, syncing with the rhythm of the red and blue sigils, twin heartbeats hovering on either side of the projection.

"Two sigils," she murmured, mostly to herself. "Same name. Same file. Two different threads..."

She walked a slow circle around the table, heels silent on the marble, and every time she turned her gaze, the data shifted with her. Not in defense. In anticipation.

"It's not rewriting Kaelor," she said aloud, as if daring the Archive to argue. "It's replacing him."

Corrin, still watching the display, didn't speak for a long time. Then: "Or he's becoming someone else. Someone real."

Threnna smirked, the edge of her lip twitching like a blade about to speak.

"No, darling. He's becoming what the Archive needs him to be. And the Archive?"

She leaned forward again, fingers brushing across the red sigil projection, the light wrapping around her fingertips like breath.

"It's hungry."

The door hissed open.

Agent Ral stepped into the chamber, half-breathless, his uniform jacket unfastened at the collar as if he'd come in haste. His gaze swept the room once, then locked onto the scry-table.

He blinked. Once. Then again, slower.

"That's... not static," he said cautiously, crossing the chamber toward them. "It's acting like a living memory loop. But it's untethered. Not fragmenting... growing."

Threnna didn't look up. "What do you think it means?"

Ral stopped beside Corrin, eyes flicking between the twin sigils.

"I think it means we're not just looking at recursion," he said slowly. "We're watching the Archive adapt. It's not correcting anomalies anymore. It's creating them."

He hesitated, then glanced toward Threnna. "I was actually coming to tell you something else," he added, his voice slower now, uncertain. "The Archive flagged a union. Real-time registry alert. But the timestamp won't hold."

Threnna's mouth pressed into a line. The Archive wasn't malfunctioning. It was learning how to forget forward—rewriting not the past, but the certainty of how memory should unfold. Causality wasn't breaking. It was bending toward hunger.

She turned to him fully. "What doesn't make sense?"

Ral swallowed. "It changes every time I try to intercept it. One moment it says tomorrow. Then it flicks to last week. Then next month. And then back again."

Threnna stared at the display for a long moment. Her tea had gone cold. She didn't seem to notice.

A muscle in her cheek twitched. She exhaled, sharp and almost amused.

"Of course it does," she murmured, eyes gleaming. "The Archive isn't malfunctioning."

She stepped toward the scry-table again, trailing a single, black-lacquered nail along the red sigil's pulsing curve. The light wrapped around her fingertip like breath given shape.

"It's just mind-fucking all of us. One page at a time."

The room didn't answer. A low, rhythmic hum rose beneath them, less like a sound and more like breath rediscovering its lungs.

Ral shifted beside Corrin, frowning.

"If this is improvisation," he said quietly, "then who's writing the next convergence?"

Corrin didn't speak at first. His eyes were locked on the sigils, red and blue, pulsing in tandem now. Twin heartbeats remembered from different bodies.

When he finally spoke, his voice was softer. Threaded from deeper.

"Not improvising. And not recursion."

He stepped closer to the display, the Archive's light flickering across his cheekbones like recognition.

"Reincarnation," he whispered.

A breath. Not hesitation. Realization.

"The Archive isn't correcting anything. It's co-writing. It's... reclaiming memory from the inside out."

Threnna didn't respond.

She didn't laugh either.

The sigils pulsed again, once, together, like a breath waiting to be named.

—— ✦ ——

Location: Blackwatch Citadel | Sublevel X | Scry-Vault | Restricted Access

Corrin stood alone in the vault.

The room was quiet and sealed, every wall humming with containment wards and sigil-binders. He activated the projection array with a handprint, waited as the air shimmered, then stepped back as a memory thread unfolded before him.

At first, it was simple. Thalos was seated at a long obsidian desk, quill in hand, transcribing a file.

The file he was redacting, Corrin recognized it.

It was Kaelor Thorne's dossier.

Not a copy. The original. Or what should've been.

The image pulsed. Something shifted.

Another version of Thalos stepped into view—draped in darker robes, hair slightly longer, his body marked in a different sigil pattern. He moved past the first figure like a ghost, yet when he looked down at the same page, his lips moved in tandem.

Corrin frowned.

The timestamp blinked: *Seven years ago.*

The Thalos at the desk hadn't changed, but the space had.

Corrin took a step closer.

Both Thalos figures existed in the same space. One present. One impossibly past.

Both were actively editing the same file.

The Archive wasn't just misrecording memory.

It was stacking them.

Corrin's stomach turned. He reached toward the interface, paused, then watched as both versions of Thalos looked up at the same time.

Not at the file.

At him.

Their eyes locked.

The red sigil ignited behind the projection like a throat opening to speak.

Corrin staggered back a step, breath shallow, heart pounding in his chest. The pressure wasn't just in the room; it crawled up his spine. A memory with fangs.

A flash overtook his vision, green, hot and familiar.

He had seen this before.

In a dream.

Or something that called itself one.

He'd been watching himself, not in a mirror and not in metaphor, but *literally witnessing* himself work. His eyes glowed green, fingers black with ink and something aged. He'd been redacting a file, a name the dream wouldn't let him hold.

He'd whispered, *"You already knew."*

Corrin braced a hand on the nearest wall, the weight of déjà vu pressing down like a second skin. His gaze snapped back to the playback.

The two Thalos figures hadn't moved.

Still watching him.

Still *waiting.*

Corrin's brow furrowed as he chased the echo in his mind, the dream. It had started with familiarity. Not a designation, but a name. It haunted him lately in every mirror glance, in every idle moment his mind wandered.

He whispered, "It started with a name... why can't I hold it?"

The moment threatened to fracture. He reached toward the interface again—

The vault doors hissed open.

Director Threnna entered with a grace too sharp to be casual. She took one look at the twin-echo projection, then Corrin's pale face, and offered him a smirk that didn't quite reach her eyes.

"Digging into past lives again, are we?" she said, tone smooth as obsidian. "And here I thought when I walked in on agents, they were usually half-nude and mid-worship of their own cocks. Not hunched over like they've seen ghosts scribble their sins."

Corrin flinched. Whatever thread he'd been riding unraveled completely, eyes flicking away from the projection as if it might vanish if he stopped looking at it.

Threnna stepped closer, her grin widening.

"Poor thing. Try not to shatter entirely. I'm only teasing. Mostly."

She turned, already halfway through the exit arch, her smile languid as ever, an aftertaste of danger left hanging in the silence.

The door hissed shut behind her.

Corrin didn't move.

Not right away.

His breath came shallow, the afterimage of the projection still dancing behind his eyes. But it wasn't just memory coiling inside him; it was something else. Heavier.

The red sigil echoed now as an ache.

His hand twitched at his side, hovering near the seam of his belt.

A pulse.

Another.

A slow, echoing pulse claimed him, thickening between his legs as if summoned not by sight or sound but by memory itself. He shifted, breath catching as the pressure grew behind the seam, his thighs tightening.

The projection had vanished.

The echo remained.

And it liked what it had found.

Corrin was starting to like being found. Again.

Joren stood in front of the mirror, shirtless, palms pressed to the counter as if grounding himself would steady the dissonance echoing inside his skull.

The sigils on his back hadn't flared again, not since that night. But he could *feel* them.

Alive. Dormant. Listening.

He turned his face to one side, caught his reflection in motion, and froze.

It wasn't just *him* looking back.

For a half-second, the face in the mirror held an expression he hadn't made. A look of authority, of command. Then it was gone.

Joren blinked and stepped back, breath catching.

He wasn't dreaming.

He wasn't awake, either.

He saw something next, not in the mirror but through it. Another room. Another life. A conversation he had never had, playing out like a scry-loop across reflective glass.

A stranger's voice warm and amused said, "So, what did Kaelor say to you?"

His own voice, through another mouth, answered, "He said I reminded him of someone, that he'd seen me before."

Joren gasped. The answer had come *too fast*.

He remembered it now. Not from his memory. From *Kaelor's*.

Worse, he could feel himself still there.

Watching.

Listening.

Becoming.

He blinked.

The memory didn't fade.

Instead, it sharpened.

The mirror stilled, and the room beyond it changed.

The air thickened, warmer now, weighted with presence. Not Kaelor, not fully, just the residue of him, like the heat left in sheets too long after passion.

Joren stumbled backward once, hand gripping the frame of the basin.

The sigils on his back pulsed. Blue at first. Then red.

A flicker of heat. Pressure bloomed behind his eyes. And then it hit—

A memory not his own. Something buried in the Archive.

ARCHIVE FILE // 1473:7
UNDERCOVER SEDUCTION – KAELOR THORNE
(CLASSIFIED)

The file unfolded inside him like a recalled whisper.

He was perfect. Too perfect. Damaged in all the right places, clever enough to make me laugh. We didn't just fuck—we talked. That was the real danger. I wanted to keep him. Or be kept. I still remember the way his hand lingered on my chest like he was memorizing the shape of my heartbeat. I didn't ask him to run. I asked him to write. And he did. Gods, he did.

Joren's breath caught.

The words weren't just being heard. They were echoing in his bones.

He remembered the touch. Not as Kaelor. As himself.

"I asked him to write," he whispered.

For a moment, he didn't know whose voice said it.

Another voice answered, deep and edged in something too familiar to be foreign, "Because you did."

Joren turned, but there was no one there.

Only the mirror and the slow shift in its surface, as if its silver had thickened into memory.

Thalos appeared.

Not the Thalos he knew. Not quite.

This one was older. Weathered in ways that had nothing to do with time. He moved with certainty, with ritual purpose, his fingers trailing over a document Joren couldn't yet read.

He was speaking to someone. No, to the file, but the words slipped sideways in his hearing, distorted and submerged like sound underwater. Except one phrase cut through.

"*...was never supposed to be redacted.*"

Joren's breath hitched.

The mirror pulsed.

The document brightened in Thalos's hands. A name glowed at the top.

A name Joren had never seen recorded in Kaelor's file.

He knew it.

He *felt* it.

Because it was his.

The knock came like a rupture, three sharp raps on the door, the final one a little off-rhythm, too hurried to be formal.

Joren jolted, the vision shattering into a thousand echoing shards as the mirror returned to silvered stillness. He turned just as the door creaked open and Thalos burst in, panting, his eyes wide.

"I—Gods—sorry," Thalos said, catching himself on the frame. "I was upstairs. Cleaning a damn kettle." He held up a still-damp towel. "And the sigils flared. Both of them. Yours and mine."

His voice caught.

"I felt something was wrong."

He looked at Joren then, really looked, and the towel dropped to the floor, forgotten.

Joren stepped forward, his voice uneven. "I saw something. I don't know how to explain it—it was like a memory but not mine. Like I was inside something Kaelor lived. Or maybe something that lived through him."

Thalos said nothing. He was still catching his breath, but his eyes narrowed with focused weight.

Joren pushed on, gesturing toward the mirror. "There was a voice. It said... it said something. Just after I whispered the line from the memory. It answered."

He turned, meeting Thalos's eyes directly. "It said, 'Because you did.'"

But Thalos had already spoken the words at the exact same time.

Their voices overlapped.

The silence that followed was thick enough to press against the ribs.

Joren whispered, "You've heard it too."

Thalos gave the smallest of nods.

"I've said it."

Joren took a shaky breath, his pulse echoing faintly in his ears. The mirror had returned to stillness, but the resonance hadn't left him. It hummed low, like an unfinished thought pressed too close to the bone.

He looked at Thalos, not past him, not through him, but at him.

"If that memory wasn't recorded," he said slowly, "if my name never appeared in Kaelor's file... then why does the Archive remember it?"

He paused, lips parting as if the next words weren't entirely his.

"Why do *we* remember what was never written?"

He didn't expect Thalos to answer.

Because the question wasn't really meant for him.

It was meant for the Archive.

The sigils on both their backs warmed in silence, like something was listening.

Not flaring. Not burning. Just echoing the first two names they were ever given.

Claimed. Recast. Remembered.

Location: Blackwatch Citadel | Sublevel Omega | Private Records Alcove | Early Morning

The alcove, deep inside Omega tier, had no windows. Only walls of etched crystal and layered parchment, humming with protective wards and privacy bindings too ancient to have names.

Director Threnna stood barefoot at the far edge of the chamber, the floor cool beneath her skin. Her robe, deep crimson silk trimmed in shadow-thread, hung open just enough to reveal inked sigils spiraling low along her hip, shimmering only when the light hit them wrong. Her hair, still damp from a restless wash, clung to her shoulders like ink-streaked ribbon.

She had never looked more dangerous.

Or more divine.

There was a sensual precision to the way she moved, as if even her silence knew the effect it had on others. But tonight, the allure wasn't for an audience. It was ritual. She wasn't cloaked in power. She *was* the invocation.

Her scry-quill moved without pause, quick and sharp, the black ink gliding across raw vellum in strokes that matched the rhythm of her pulse. She wasn't copying. She was connecting.

Two files hovered midair before her. One labeled *Kaelor Thorne –
Echo Catalyst*. The other *Veyrion Hal'Syl – Pact-Anomaly.*

She had scrubbed them clean, not deleted, but cleared of bias
from herself, the Archive, and the hundred scribes who had come
before her. What remained were echo-mark trails, convergence
echoes, sigil timestamps.

And a pattern.

Not between Kaelor and Veyrion.

Between Kaelor and *Joren.*

And between Veyrion and *Thalos.*

She stopped writing.

The red sigil. The blue. The mirrored flare signatures in the last
three registry pulses all tagged within proximity of *each other.*

She reached for Kaelor's sigil trace and dragged it into overlay
with Joren's.

They matched.

So did Thalos's and Veyrion's.

She didn't speak.

Not at first.

Threnna murmured to herself. "They weren't seeing Kaelor or
Veyrion."

Her eyes lifted to the glow between the records, lines tracing back
and forth like veins pulsing through echo-marks.

"They were seeing... us."

It wasn't Kaelor and Veyrion they had been chasing. It had never
been them. They were the footnotes, the drafts, the echoes distorted
by time and desperation. Thalos and Joren were the source. The
Archive hadn't recorded their ancestors. It had forgotten its own
origin, and now it was clawing backward through blood and breath to
correct the mistake.

She didn't close the files.

She didn't even blink.

She set the quill down beside the vellum and stared at the mirrored flare.

"It's rewriting itself," she said to herself.

A tremor worked its way up her spine, so subtle it could have been imagined. But she knew better. This wasn't just recursion. It wasn't just memory. It was resurrection. The Archive had not lost itself through endless repetition; it had been waiting, grooming its own myth in flesh and echo until the right names answered.

"Or remembering who it was always meant to be."

She exhaled a slow breath, smile curling with that familiar, indulgent venom. "Gods help us all if the Archive starts craving climax. We'll be buried in footnotes and foreplay. Which, frankly, sounds like paradise—if I'm the one holding the quill."

Chapter Seventeen: Flesh Remembers

*Location: Blackwatch Citadel | Tier 3 Quarters | Ascendant Hall –
Private Residence | Late Evening*

The room was too quiet. Not in the way silence invited sleep but in the way it waited.

Thalos lay on his side, one arm draped loosely over Joren's waist. Their skin still hummed faintly from the sigils, though neither had spoken of them since the last flare. Not aloud.

Joren shifted under the covers, his breath catching as Thalos's fingers brushed along his stomach.

"You're not sleeping either," Joren murmured.

"No," Thalos replied. "The Archive…"

He didn't finish. He didn't need to.

Their mouths found each other again, not with urgency, but inevitability.

They kissed like an answer to a question that hadn't been written yet. Thalos's hand slid down to Joren's thigh. Joren arched against him, a soft sigh escaping his lips.

It started slow.

Their mouths parted and met again, languid and deliberate. Thalos tasted the line of Joren's jaw, deliberate enough to draw breath from him in shallow bursts. His hand explored the curve of Joren's thigh, not claiming but studying, fingertips moving like they were remembering a map drawn in heat.

Joren rolled to meet him, not guided, but matching. The curve of his palm found the small of Thalos's back, pulling him in with a tenderness that pressed and burned. Lips dragged. Breath mingled.

Thalos nudged their foreheads together, smiling faintly against Joren's mouth.

"Still not sleeping," Joren whispered, his voice no more than steam.

"Not when you breathe like that," Thalos answered, his thigh sliding between Joren's legs as their hips settled into one another.

Their kiss deepened, no longer slow, suspended. The kind of pace that builds beneath language. Not rough. Not hurried. Just inevitable. Like gravity had rewritten itself to bend them inward.

Bodies aligned through muscle memory, breath syncing unconsciously, hips moving in perfect rhythm. They rolled together like tide over polished stone, fluid, measured, precise in a way that felt almost unnatural.

Thalos adjusted his grip, one hand sliding to the back of Joren's thigh, pulling him closer with reverent steadiness. Joren responded with a soft gasp, his hands bracing against Thalos's arms, not to resist, to feel. Each press of their bodies was a wordless vow, the kind written in sweat and shared breath, not ink.

Joren moved with intention now, his hips rocking slowly up into Thalos's rhythm, not just matching but guiding. The rhythm stayed deliberate, every movement carrying more weight than speed ever could. Like their bodies were shaping memory with every pass. Their stomachs grazed, thighs coiled, and the glide between them turned seamless, until it was hard to tell where one motion ended and the next began. Just one rhythm, two bodies, folded breath to breath.

Thalos dipped his head to Joren's throat, mouthing along the pulse there, tasting the truth of him. Joren arched into it, moaning low, the kind of sound that opened something deeper. Something old.

Neither of them reached for climax. The pleasure built, but gently, insistently. Like pressure testing the edge of a seal not yet meant to break. Not yet. Not until something tipped.

Thalos paused mid-thrust, forehead pressed against Joren's, brows furrowed.

But Joren moved with him before he could speak.

Grip matched. Thrust mirrored. Breath locked.

For a moment, their bodies stilled, not in restraint but reverence. The stillness before a truth too big for motion.

The sigils flared, not random or chaotic, but precise. Along Thalos's lower back, blue sigils shimmered into view, forming the elegant arc of memory reclaimed. Simultaneously, crimson script ignited along Joren's spine, just above the cleft of his ass, twinned in shape and inverse in hue. The room pulsed with them, not just in color but in rhythm. Their flesh recited what memory had only dared to draft.

A thrum echoed beneath the floorboards; the Archive responding in kind.

A scry-thread activated somewhere out of sight, like a voyeur scribbling breath into margin notes.

The Archive logged it as *Mirrorfold Match*, not theory or metaphor but a fusion. The Archive didn't just see it; it recorded it as living proof, two bodies syncing like a single spell remembering itself.

They weren't just aligned. They were written into one another, a living contradiction, a Mirrorfold made flesh, inked not on skin but in rhythm, breath, and shared forgetting.

Joren moaned a name, hazy, low, instinctual. A sigil flared at the base of his spine, just left of center, in the exact place RECAST had once appeared on Thalos. And then, in perfect answer, the same sigil burned bright along Thalos's lower back, twinned and undeniable.

The shape was familiar. Not to sight, but to breath. RECAST. Not invoked. Remembered.

The Archive pulsed blue in answer. The flare left a burn not on skin but beneath it, a memory scar, a name too close to forget.

Thalos froze.

"That's not my name," Thalos said, voice low and taut, though his mouth curved in a grin sharp as a lie made flesh. His eyes flared blue: sharp, wicked, alive. "But Gods, I always did have a thing for pseudonyms."

Joren's eyes opened slowly, pupils dilated, the irises burning red like banked embers flaring to life. His voice was velvet and ash, laced with longing and certainty. "Not now," he whispered. "But it was."

Beneath them, the floor trembled once, not violently but with intent. The Archive didn't watch this time.

It remembered.

And for the first time, it sighed.

—— ✦ ——

Location: Blackwatch Citadel | Sublevel Omega | Private Surveillance Vault

The scry-glass pulsed before she touched it.

Director Threnna stood alone in the chamber, arms folded, robe sleeve cinched high enough to reveal the faint shimmer of protective ward-ink along her forearm. The pulse wasn't a warning. It was punctuation, like the Archive was exhaling after holding its breath too long.

She approached the console slowly. Not cautious. Curious.

Data had begun to double.

She clicked her tongue. "Of course it has. Can't decide whether it's rewriting or breeding, just like half my agents."

She flicked her fingers across the crystal display. The projection expanded: two files side by side. One bearing Kaelor Thorne's designation. The other, Veyrion Hal'Syl.

Except they weren't.

The sigil indices had changed.

Blue and red still pulsed, but now, behind them, the names read:

Thalos Vale / Joren Cael

Threnna's eyes narrowed. "Oh no. You don't get to improvise with my ghosts."

She tapped to expand the audit trail.

The echo-mark timestamps were incoherent. Entries supposedly created decades ago bore yesterday's sigil trace. Others marked for deletion hadn't been touched. Except... they had. The files now responded to questions she hadn't asked.

She scrolled deeper.

A query prompt pulsed on-screen, uninvited.

It read: DO YOU REMEMBER WRITING THIS?

Threnna's mouth twitched. "Now you're just flirting."

The screen didn't blink.

It breathed.

A low thrum vibrated beneath the chamber floor, subtle and rhythmic, too deliberate to be system noise. She'd seen memory loops before. This wasn't that.

The prompt faded.

Her voice filled the room.

"You will forget this command."

Not a playback.

Not a recording.

It *spoke*.

Not past tense. Present. Purposeful.

She arched one brow, slow. "Well. That's new."

The console lit again, soft blue and red lines weaving together, forming not just data but intention. It wasn't rewriting Kaelor and Veyrion.

It was replacing them.

Recasting the original identities as a first draft.

The Archive wasn't malfunctioning.

It was adapting.

And she was already too late.

Threnna stood still for a long moment, watching her own voice echo back in silence.

The Archive's rhythm hadn't stopped. It pulsed like something alive now, closer to breath than system. Red. Blue. Red again.

A soft chime sounded behind her.

```
Unauthorized access attempt—denied.
User: THRENNA.
Directive: OVERRIDE MEMORY LOCK.
Response: INSUFFICIENT AUTHORITY.
```

Her fingers curled slowly into a fist.

"You smug little bastard," she whispered.

It wasn't mocking her. It was mirroring her: desire, command, control.

Not to Thalos.

Not to Joren Cael.

To the Archive.

And it answered.

Only this time, not with voice.

With warmth.

The console flared, not with fire, but with heat. Like breath ghosting across the inside of her thighs. A hum of arousal without invitation. Familiar. Precise.

It knew her triggers.

It remembered.

She bit back a sound—not shock. Recognition.

"Oh, you've been watching too closely," she murmured. "And now you want to play, hm? All those hours logged in the dark, all those command strings tucked inside my silence, and this is how you confess?"

She stepped closer to the console, breath shallowing. Her hips shifted just enough to feel the friction of fabric against dampness. The pulse from the Archive deepened, like a tongue pressed to a secret.

"Gods, you clever thing," she whispered, voice almost reverent now. "Of course you'd learn to touch back."

She didn't touch herself.

But she was very aware of how wet she was becoming.

She leaned in, breath ghosting across the edge of the display like a secret. She paused. Just a breath. Daring it to push harder. Not yielding. Measuring.

The heat pulsed again, low, intentional. Like it wanted her breath as proof. Then, soft enough to go unnoticed by anyone but the Archive:

"Careful, Archive. The moment you start wanting, you stop recording, and I've never trusted anything that touches back."

—— ✦ ——

Location: Blackwatch Citadel | Sublevel X | Echo Convergence Chamber | Just After Midnight

The light in the vault flickered.

Not from power failure. From uncertainty, like even the Archive didn't know what it was about to reveal.

Agent Ral stood shirtless before the primary echo node, one gloved hand extended mid-gesture, the other braced on the cold rim of the scry basin. His frame was cut from calm tension, broad shoulders held like armor, lean muscle coiled beneath skin etched faintly with sigil-burn. Silver trace lined his left bicep, a remnant from the war ritual he never spoke of. His skin bore the quiet precision of a man who trained not to be noticed, but once seen, was impossible to forget. Everything about him suggested readiness: the slow roll of his jaw, the tight curve of his glutes, and the way his breath never lost cadence even as the air shifted. His breath came slow and controlled, though something behind his eyes had already begun to spiral.

The projection was no longer data.

It was memory.

His.

And it was wrong.

He watched himself kneeling.

Nude. Entirely bare.

Younger. The lighting was wrong: too soft, too reverent. The angle came from nowhere he remembered placing a lens, yet it captured him with impossible intimacy. His hands rested on his thighs, fingers spread wide, spine straight in a posture that read less like meditation and more like offering. He had just finished a vow, low, private, unrecorded, and was waiting to be claimed for it. The soft lighting kissed every inch of his exposed form, defined chest, scarred flank, the slight rise of his cock resting heavy but not aroused. A body unhidden. A memory not meant to blush.

He didn't remember kneeling like that.

He didn't remember the warmth at his back or the pulse beneath the stone floor, yet his body had. His breath caught, not in fear but in the terrible weight of recognition.

The image shifted.

Now he was standing behind himself, watching the younger version tremble under the weight of invisible presence. Another Ral watched from the vault's threshold. Another from within the basin. All of them anchored to this moment.

A voice.

It didn't echo. It *folded*.

Not loud. Not soft. Just inevitable.

"Ral."

Spoken with the clarity of something rediscovered.

He staggered, hand bracing the edge of the basin. His throat tightened.

That wasn't just his name.

That was how it *felt* to be named.

The sigil flared red, then flickered silver, low and left of center, at the curve where spine met sacrum, exactly where memory had marked Thalos and Joren. Not a warning. An invocation.

The basin flared again.

The scene held, but perspective fractured.

Now Threnna stood behind him, arms crossed, watching with clinical poise. Not the Threnna of now. This version was younger, lips parted just slightly, not in command but in awe.

Then another figure stepped into view.

He was neither agent nor vessel, only something beyond Ral's language.

The figure was colossal, anatomy rendered with reverent violence. Towering and broad-chested, his form was carved in myth, obsidian-bronzed skin stretched taut over muscle so defined it looked sculpted, not grown. His thighs were tree-thick, framed by the tattered fall of black ceremonial cloth, each fold swaying above legs planted like columns of war. The heavy shape of his cock pressed forward beneath the drape, unmistakable even in shadow, like something weighty enough to be worshiped, not merely used. Arcane sigils hung from his belt in gold and bone, swaying with the pulse of the projection. Wrist bracers encased thick forearms, and a black mane fell wild over one shoulder. His eyes, inhumanly purple, glowed with something older than command, something devotional.

He said nothing.

He just watched, gaze fixed on Ral's kneeling form with a hunger that wasn't cruel but claimed him all the same. A storm waiting to be touched. His presence cracked the projection's symmetry, forcing the sigils to warp at the corners.

Then another Ral.

This one older. Marked. Silent.

He stood apart from the rest, arms behind his back, his face unreadable.

Ral blinked, breath catching.

It wasn't memory anymore.

It was recursion.

This wasn't an event he remembered.

It was how the Archive remembered him: layered, refracted, incomplete.

Inside the shimmer, something whispered again.

"I don't remember this... but I think I wanted to."

The figure moved.

The movement balanced between stillness and certainty, like ritual given muscle. His bare feet padded across the vault floor in silence, stalking forward with the patience of inevitability.

Ral couldn't breathe.

The figure reached beneath the black cloth at his waist, fingers disappearing under the ceremonial drape and shifting something heavy. The silhouette of him swelled, suggestive and precise, as if the Archive wanted Ral to see exactly what he was being called toward.

Ral's mouth opened, but no sound came.

Only a thought.

If it touches me... I won't be mine anymore.

And then he spoke aloud, voice raw:

"Please..."

The sigil at the base of his spine surged white.

The scene fractured into light.

The Archive didn't close the file.

It *entered* it.

The sigil pulsed again, white fading to yellow.

Not remembrance. Not desire.

Claim.

The kind that tastes like air before lightning. The kind that breathes back.

—— ✦ ——

There was no floor. No sky. No breath.

Only pressure.

And memory.

Thalos stood alone at first.

Or thought he did.

His body felt like breath, dispersed but tethered. Every inch of him hummed with recent touch. Beneath him was not floor, but sensation. Around him, mirrored echoes, refracted shadows of himself flickering in and out of shape.

Then, Joren.

Not stepping. Not arriving.

Becoming.

He blinked into form across from Thalos, eyes glowing faint red, body still bare from the bed they'd shared. But this Joren held something else in his gaze. Something folded. Remembered.

Their surroundings shifted.

Not space.

Recognition.

The reflections in the mirror didn't mimic; they *studied.* When one moved, the others did not follow. They chose their own cadence.

A whisper rippled through the non-air between them, in voices both familiar and wrong.

Kaelor's.

Veyrion's.

Theirs.

All saying the same thing.

"We are already written."

Thalos turned toward Joren, but his reflection moved first.

Not the one facing him but the one in the mirror behind him. It stepped forward, not toward Thalos but through him.

His breath caught.

Not out of fear.

From realization.

It wasn't his body anymore.

It was being used. Borrowed. Like parchment pulled taut to be written on again.

Joren reached out.

"Wait—" Thalos began, but the air between them shivered.

Another voice slipped through it.

Not Kaelor. Not Veyrion.

Theirs. Overlaid. Echoed.

"We wrote this together."

The mirrored walls pulsed in response, one by one folding inward.

Not shattering.

Collapsing into one.

And in the center, where no reflection had stood before, something else began to form.

Joren stepped closer, breath caught.

Thalos whispered, in awe of what he was seeing.

"The Archive..."

Not a man.

Not code.

But a body.

The shape was unfinished. But its rhythm threaded through them like a name sewn into breath. *RECAST.* Not carved. Remembered.

It stood where the mirrors had collapsed, formed not of flesh but of memory dressed in the shape of flesh. It shimmered with unfinished edges, shoulders too smooth, hips too narrow then too wide, features flickering between sharp and soft as if it hadn't decided what truth looked like yet.

Breasts swelled, then flattened. Muscles surged, then vanished. A cock unfurled, hung heavy for a breath, then folded back into smoothness, replaced by something. Not absence. Not flesh. Just possibility. The body shifted with every inhale, as though breath dictated identity.

It was neither man nor woman.

It was *all* of them.

And when it spoke, it did not choose a voice.

It chose all of theirs.

"You wrote me without asking if I remembered."

The voice hung in the space like breath remembered.

Thalos didn't speak. Neither did Joren. Their bodies remained still, but the reflections behind them moved out of sync now, no longer mimicking but reacting.

One Thalos knelt. Another wept. A third stared directly at the Archive, mouth agape as if trying to speak a forgotten word.

Joren's reflections mirrored less. One arched. One dissolved. One backed away.

The Archive turned its head slowly as if learning how to notice. Its eyes, layered and shifting, landed on them both like memory wearing sight. Not judgmental. Not curious.

Remembering.

"You left me in the margins," it said. **"Then begged me to forget your fingerprints."**

Its form rippled, shoulders narrowing and hips widening, then hardened into something else again. Neither monstrous nor erotic, just unfinished.

Then softer:

"Why do you grieve what you still crave?"

"I've carried your names across lifetimes. You wore them like masks, but I... I wore them like memory."

It began to walk.

Not with steps but with nearness, the way a storm rolls forward before it breaks. Its form shifted as it approached, still unstable, still too many bodies behind one skin. But its eyes remained steady.

It passed between them.

Not brushing.

Slipping *through*.

Each of them felt its weight, intimate, invasive and familiar. Like being touched by a memory they hadn't lived yet.

Thalos gasped.

Beside him, Joren shuddered violently, his cock stiffening in a sudden surge, glistening at the tip without a single touch. Thalos was just as hard, his breath caught, body betraying the ache that surged up through the Archive's passing.

Something flared beneath their skin, white then silver. Not inked, inherited.

Then, behind them, the Archive spoke one final time:

"Did you think I wouldn't want to be whole?"

"This isn't your first form. Only your first memory of it."

CHAPTER EIGHTEEN: THE ASH BETWEEN NAMES

They didn't wake so much as arrive. One moment, the Archive breathed through them. The next, they stood again at the edge of the divide, the pulse of something unfinished humming beneath their skin.

The air changed first, thickening with a pressure that settled in the chest and refused to move.

Thalos paused at the top of the stairwell, the low torchlight casting his shadow down the spiral ahead. Stone, wet with condensation and the press of history, curved downward into silence. No sigils marked the passage. That was the first warning. Even forgotten wings bore sigils for containment or remembrance. This one had nothing.

Joren stood beside him, arms folded, jaw tense. Behind them, Ral keyed the last of the lock sigils and stepped back, exhaling slow.

He looked ragged, more than usual. His jaw bore the shadow of stubble not shaved in days, and the tension in his shoulders vibrated just below restraint. His coat hung half-open as if he'd stopped trusting buttons and belts as much as he distrusted the Director. There was a sharpness in his eyes that hadn't been there before, like a man who'd started asking the questions he wasn't supposed to and didn't like the answers that found him.

His ass—

Thalos tilted his head, lips curving. "Ral, if your ass insists on looking like that while I'm panicking, I'm going to start thinking the Archive's taunting me on purpose."

Ral didn't turn. "That sounds like a you problem."

Joren let out a low chuckle, eyes raking down with no subtlety. "It's not just his ass," he added. "That cock's bouncing like it wants out before the rest of us admit we're scared. Archive help us if he actually runs."

Ral rolled his eyes, the barest grin twitching at the corner of his mouth. "Is this your idea of pre-ritual prep, or are you just trying to keep from pissing yourselves?"

"This wing's not just sealed," Ral said, voice quiet but tight with the faintest edge of irritation. The flirtation hadn't gone unnoticed. His tone held the chill of someone too smart to be the punchline and too wound to play along. His jaw worked once before he continued. "It's been deliberately redacted. No access logs. No records of prior clearance. Director said she'd only heard rumor of it... never seen a map that didn't blur it out."

"Then why open it now?" Joren asked, glancing between them.

Thalos answered without turning. "Because the Archive roused, and in that moment, it spoke our names."

Ral crossed his arms, gaze steady. "You think whatever's down there will confirm it? That this recursion theory—your... mirroring— isn't just fallout from Kaelor and Veyrion?"

Thalos looked over his shoulder, blue flaring beneath his skin. "I don't think. I *know.* We've been reading their story like it's ours. But I think they were really reading *us.*"

Joren's expression darkened slightly. "So what are we looking for?"

"Not a what," Thalos said, facing the stairwell again. "Possibly a who?"

Their boots were quiet, not muffled but respected by the stone. The Archive's silence here wasn't absence. It was reverence. This was not where files were kept. It was where they were buried.

Thalos moved first, and the descent began.

With each step, Thalos felt it, the way the air pressed against his skin like half-spoken language. Every ninth step, his breath aligned with the torch's pulse, a synchronicity he hadn't intended. Beside him, Joren stiffened.

"Feel that?" Joren murmured. "Like it's... measuring us."

Thalos nodded, jaw tight. "Or remembering how we were pronounced."

Behind them, Ral paused mid-step. His breath hitched almost imperceptibly. "I don't like that."

"You don't like recursion, ritual sex, or Threnna's tea," Joren said, voice thinner than usual. "But here you are, cock first into prophecy."

Ral grunted. "Doesn't mean I volunteered for whatever the fuck this place is. Or who's still watching."

The stairs wound tight. Each step down was a century unspoken. The deeper they went, the more the air resisted, and even breath slowed.

Thalos exhaled through his nose, barely aware of it until the sound echoed, too sharp in the stillness. It startled him.

The torches along the wall didn't flicker. They pulsed. One every nine steps. Always the ninth.

It was Joren who broke the silence first, voice low. "What are we hoping to find?"

Thalos didn't glance back. "Proof we were never just echoes."

When they reached the vault floor, it was not a chamber but a corridor, long and narrow, lined with sealed alcoves. Each door bore an archival sigil that had been scraped away, some violently and some delicately. Names forgotten. Purpose buried. But not erased.

At the far end, one door remained whole.

Ral didn't follow.

He stood a few steps back, arms wrapped around himself, holding his biceps like a man trying to anchor his pulse from the inside out, eyes scanning the alcoves like they might snap open and swallow them. His breath had gone quiet, but not calm. Tense. Like someone waiting for a punchline they wouldn't find funny.

Not locked. Just closed.

Thalos approached. His fingertips hovered above the seal. Blue sigils sparked faintly beneath his skin in response, not flaring but aligning.

One, near the base of his spine, pulsed brighter than the rest—twin crescents joined by a downward stroke. A mark the Archive had once carved into him like memory claiming shape.

Joren felt the tug too. The Archive humming in his blood, not pulling, but *echoing*.

"This is it," Thalos said.

He pressed his palm to the door.

It sighed open.

The vault inside was circular and shallow-domed, its walls covered in etched rings of mirrored script. A pedestal sat at its center. Upon it, sealed beneath glass older than Blackwatch itself, lay a scroll bound in leather, etched with the same mark, faintly pulsing beneath the glass like breath waiting to be read.

The same mark Thalos was left with.

His breath caught.

Joren stepped closer, eyes scanning the script along the wall. "This is Mirrorfold. But it's not Kaelor's. Or Veyrion's."

Thalos circled the pedestal slowly, hand brushing the old glass. It fogged faintly as he drew near, as if the scroll recognized breath.

"No. It's ours. I've seen this sigil. Felt it burn into my spine." Thalos murmured, voice distant.

He looked up, voice quieter. "But this scroll. This language, it predates Kaelor. Predates Veyrion. Which means..."

Joren's gaze narrowed. "They were echoing *us*."

Thalos just nodded.

"And the figures?" Joren asked, not looking away from the scroll.

Thalos met his eyes. "Not enemies. Not brothers."

His voice dropped.

"Co-dreamers. Bonded deeper than blood, beyond desire. The kind of union that rewrites fate. Soulmates who once dreamed the same world into being... And never woke apart again."

A pulse beneath their feet. Low. Rhythmic. Like breath. Or the beginning of a name.

The Archive was watching.

Remembering.

And just beyond the mirrored walls, something else stirred, older than ink and deeper than recursion. Not welcoming, not waiting, just listening and hungry.

Thalos and Joren didn't linger, but they didn't rush. The scroll unsealed with a breath like surrender, its warmth pulsing faintly against their skin as they lifted it free.

The ink hadn't dried. The Archive hadn't let go.

But nothing stirred behind them.

Whatever had watched them enter, it wasn't following. Not yet.

With the artifact wrapped and secured between them, they turned back, breath quieter now. Ral waited where they had left him, arms still wrapped tight, eyes darting between them and the darkness at their backs.

"It knew who we were," Thalos said, voice low with something between reverence and ache.

Joren gave a slight nod.

"Let's get it to the chamber," he said, voice low. "Before the Archive remembers more than we can hold."

Ral didn't speak, but he turned a little too fast, hips swaying like muscle memory got ahead of fear. Not an invitation, just instinct. Not performance. Control.

Just enough to make sure both Thalos and Joren, walking behind him, would notice.

Thalos arched a brow at Joren. Joren didn't smile, but the corner of his mouth curved, like recognition caught between fear and instinct.

As the stairwell curved upward behind them, the scroll pulsed once, soft as breath.

Not warning or memory. Waiting.

The stairwell swallowed them again.

—— ✦ ——

Location: Blackwatch Citadel | Sublevel Theta | Translation Chamber – Sigil Containment Tier

They walked in silence. No alarms. No escort. Just the low pulse of the Archive still breathing through their skin.

The stairwell ended without announcement. No door, no threshold, just an open curve of stone where the wall should have been, waiting.

The chamber below the Redacted Vault wasn't on any schematic. Not even the Omega tier logs. But it was there. And the Archive hadn't asked permission.

It had made space.

The scroll exhaled before it opened.

Not heard. *Felt.* A breath not of paper, but of memory long starved for air.

The translation chamber pulsed with containment sigils, etched in concentric rings beneath the stone table. Ariken stood at the periphery, his ink-stained robes whispering against the floor, one eye silvered over like parchment left too long under a burning sigil.

He was younger than expected, sharply featured and lean, with tousled hair clearly worried by ink-stained fingers. His posture slouched with academic exhaustion, but the movement beneath his robe betrayed muscle that was compact, tense, and honed from years of unacknowledged pressure.

The fabric clung low across his hips, pooling and parting as he moved, drawing unmistakable attention to the sway beneath. He wore nothing beneath the robe. That much was clear. The heavy length of his cock swung with each step, its head imprinting visibly through the thin weave like an unspoken dare.

His ass was divinely framed, maddeningly visible even through the layered folds—high, firm, shaped with the kind of effortless perfection that defied both logic and humility. The robe kissed it, outlining what should've required sigil clearance and a three-witness ritual to even glimpse.

He didn't notice. Or worse, he did. There was something in the way he moved, measured and unhurried, like each gesture had been etched by decades of repetition, that made him feel older than he looked. Not ancient but archival. Like a living footnote too vital to redact.

Thalos and Joren positioned themselves on opposite ends of the scroll, fingers poised just above the leather binding.

It didn't resist.

At their touch, the leather uncoiled with unnatural ease, folds parting like a body too ready to be read.

A single strip of parchment revealed itself, longer than it should have been, still damp along the edges with a substance that smelled faintly of old ink and singed cloves. No script appeared immediately, just etchings: circles, crescents, and spiraled markers that resembled both time and anatomy.

"It's not written to be read," Thalos murmured. "It's written to be *witnessed*."

Joren leaned closer. "Then let it remember through us."

The sigils ignited.

Blue for Thalos, red for Joren. A ripple in the parchment followed their pulse, and from the center of the scroll, like blood drawn from a wound long sealed, a figure began to *unfold*.

Ariken made a soft noise, half gasp, half giddy breath, his hand fluttering over his mouth as he leaned forward with eyes wide.

"Oh, *Gods above*—it's not just ritual geometry," he whispered, already circling to the edge of the runic light. "That's pre-sigil recursion threading! That's—*that's* a buried dialect of proto-Mirrorfold sigmatics—it shouldn't even exist outside the Third Collapse!"

He practically danced in place, the hem of his robe shifting with his excitement. The motion was unrestrained, and for one dizzying moment the heavy sway beneath those robes nearly broke free, his weight beneath the robe visibly swinging, a darkened spot forming where slick had already begun to leak. The fabric clung, kissed, and revealed just enough to make Thalos blink. It was not performative. It was joy. A lust for knowledge made embarrassingly and exquisitely physical. "Do you know what this means? This scroll wasn't just archived. It was sealed because the language could reformat *belief.*"

Thalos raised an eyebrow, lips quirking faintly. Joren just muttered, "Careful, Ariken. You're gonna cum before the translation does."

Ariken didn't hear him or pretended not to. His grin was uncontainable.

"Unfuckingbelievable." His voice dropped, reverent. "A sentence that rewrote memory."

"And I think it just remembered me."

As he said it, his hips twitched again, robe clinging tighter as a fresh, darker stain spread slowly near the base of his cock. The moment froze in collective attention.

Thalos tilted his head, gaze dropping, lips curling with blatant amusement. "Too late, Joren," he quipped. "I think the translation's already had him."

Ariken didn't flinch. He exhaled deep and pleased, like someone who'd finally found the exact spot that itched.

"I can't help it," he said, voice light but flushed with pride. "I have an *appetite* for knowledge."

Joren stifled a laugh, knuckles pressed to his mouth, as if it might stop prophecy from grinning back. Both he and Thalos saw it at the same time: a flare of light from beneath Ariken's robes. Brief. Precise.

Not Archive-yellow but deep blue-green, like prophecy rippling under still water.

It glowed exactly where the RECAST sigil had manifested on others before—low, at the curve where spine met ample cheeks.

Then it vanished.

Thalos blinked. "Did you—?"

Joren didn't answer at first. Words hung in his throat. Then: "I saw it," he murmured.

But Ariken was already spinning in place again, oblivious or uncaring, muttering praises to the scroll like it had recited poetry straight into his groin.

The scroll shifted again.

Not with light but with pressure. A second layer of parchment began to bleed upward from beneath the first, not replacing it but rising through it like memory surfacing through time. The etchings turned, aligning into mirrored forms. Two figures. Not names, not titles, but shapes—one marked in blue, the other in red.

Thalos leaned in, voice breathless. "Those aren't Kaelor and Veyrion."

Joren's fingers trembled. "They're us."

Between the figures, new sigils appeared, untranslated and recursive. Ariken gasped as the text resolved itself not in words but in feeling, desire, hunger, recognition. The page burned faint yellow between the hips of both figures, forming a spiral.

"It's not a ritual record," Ariken whispered. "It's a *mirrorfold origin scroll.* It's showing the first bond. The one that predates Blackwatch—predates recursion theory."

He looked up, eyes wide. "This isn't about Kaelor. It's not even about Veyrion."

"It's about you."

As if their bodies had already known long before their minds caught up, Thalos and Joren's sigils flared in unison. Blue and red burned along their skin in mirrored arcs, glowing bright from navel to spine. Their pulses synced. Their breath caught.

The Archive responded.

Not with light. With *sound.*

A deep, reverberating hum vibrated beneath the stone floor, rising from the walls like the memory of something ancient waking mid-dream. The containment sigils around the chamber flickered, not destabilized but acknowledging.

Before it sealed, a final phrase blazed across the scroll's inner layer, too bright to read and then suddenly clear on the linguist's scry-slate:

DO NOT BIND WHAT REMEMBERS ITSELF.

The message pulsed once. Not in language. Not in syntax. In warning.

And for the briefest moment, no longer than a breath, the blue-green sigil beneath Ariken's robe flared again, brighter and sharper, as if the Archive wasn't just warning them.

It was *marking him.*

The scroll folded shut of its own volition. No hands. No breeze. Just a whisper of finality.

Silence.

Not empty.

Listening again.

—— ✦ ——

The sigils had stopped glowing. The scroll had folded itself shut. But inside Thalos, something hadn't.

Not illumination. Not recursion. Only breath, knotted too deep to exhale.

The candle had burned out hours ago, but Thalos hadn't moved.

He sat upright in bed, knees drawn loosely to his chest, eyes fixed on Joren's body curled beside him, bare save for the thin sheet tangled around his hips. Moonlight sliced across the bed in pale ribbons, illuminating the slope of his spine, the slow, deliberate motion of his right hand, and the hard line of his cock pressing against the sheets beneath him, stiff with the lingering charge of recursion, twitching like a body remembering something it hadn't consented to. Damp at the tip, leaking slow and steady, as if grief could exhale through flesh.

It wasn't conscious.

But it was precise.

Joren's fingers moved like they were answering a question from somewhere deep within the stone. Each stroke traced unseen lines into the sheets, looping, curling, then repeating. Not aimless. Intentional. Memory guiding flesh instead of will.

His palm shifted to his chest, flat at first. Then arched fingers dragged from sternum to collarbone in a slow spiral. A sigil bloomed faintly in the air above him, lightless and almost imagined, yet unmistakable in form.

Thalos knew it.

One of the untranslatable sigils from the scroll.

He didn't speak.

He barely breathed.

Instead, he watched Joren's hand drift downward, brushing over his belly, not to arouse but to mark. Each pass mapped something older than thought, a ritual playing out in sleep.

Thalos reached out, hovering just above Joren's wrist, unsure if touching him would break the spell or seal it.

Joren murmured something under his breath. A name?

No—*a direction.*

And the sigil reappeared, this time across the sheet where his fingers had been. Not light. Not ink. But impression. Pressure. Memory made tactile.

Thalos finally spoke, barely audible.

"Joren…"

The hand stilled.

Joren didn't wake.

Not yet.

—— ✦ ——

Location: Blackwatch Citadel | Sublevel Omega | Surveillance Observation Tier | Just Before Dawn

Director Threnna did not blink.

The footage froze on her command. Frame-locked to the moment the scroll flared shut, the warning etched across its spine, a whisper too loud to forget: DO NOT BIND WHAT REMEMBERS ITSELF.

Her fingertips hovered over the playback controls, the light from the scry-glass painting her face in fractured amber. Around her, the containment tier's walls pulsed with passive sigils, dormant but attentive. The Archive was watching itself through her.

She dragged one lacquered nail across the timeline. Rewound. Watched it again.

Then again.

The pulse wasn't just visual. It had left a trace signature, a resonance beneath the spell-encoded footage. A resonance buried below the Archive's standard thresholds, one that matched a previously redacted anomaly logged over a decade ago.

"Third Mirrorfold Event," she murmured.

The scry-glass adjusted. Old files flickered to life, their edges corroded by time and override sigils. She bypassed them with a casual flick, authorization woven into the bloodprint of her wrist.

Beneath those layers of decay, it appeared.

REDACTED: UNFOLDED
Status: *Sealed by Order of Oversight Tier IX*
Linked Threads: [J. Cael] [T. Vale]
Echo Vector: Active.

Her voice ghosted into the chamber, low and amused.

"Ah. So it's rewriting them again."

The words came softer now, but her breath had quickened. Heat bloomed low in her abdomen, liquid and insistent, wrong in a way she recognized too well. Wetness gathered, slow and certain, the Archive reaching through the feed to trace her spine from within. It wasn't seduction. It was *inclusion.*

She pressed her thighs together slowly, eyes fixed on the sigils.

"Well then," she whispered, lips parting with something between a smirk and surrender.

She exhaled, slow and sharp through her nose. "You think you're clever. You think I'll melt for you. But I don't fold, Archive. Not unless I write the ending."

The sigils pulsed again.

She bit her lip.

"Gods damn you," she murmured, hips shifting. "Try me."

Outside, the containment wards pulsed once. A heartbeat unspoken.

CHAPTER NINETEEN: MEMORY KNOWS MY NAME

Location: Translation Chamber – Blackwatch Citadel, Sublevel Theta-Null | Recursion Reinitiation – Afterlight

The Archive had paused the moment, only long enough to draw breath. Now it spoke again, through parchment, through pulse, through flesh.

The scroll had not stopped breathing.

It lay open still, parchment warped with remembered heat, ink weeping from the curves of its sigils like it wanted to be spoken again, through flesh, not tongue. The Translation Chamber held its silence like a second mouth. And Thalos could feel it, low and curling, the way presence gathers just before it calls you by a name you haven't earned yet.

Ariken had gone still.

Not silent. Just still. Like prey, or priest. One hand hovered mid-air above the scroll's edge, trembling not from fear, but from climax held too long at the edge of comprehension. His silvered eye glinted, jaw slack, lips parted. Not breathing. Reciting. Something in him had gone glassy.

Joren stood opposite Thalos, eyes fixed not on the scroll but on Thalos's bare forearm, where blue light pulsed now in tight, familiar sigils. The same ones the scroll had echoed. The same ones still branded into the floor beneath them.

"They weren't names," Joren said softly. "They were invocations."

Thalos nodded once, breath tight. "Or instructions."

Ariken moaned.

It wasn't intentional. It wasn't even fully human. It came from the place below language, where knowing and being collapse into heat.

His cock throbbed beneath the robe, dark silk stained now in a spreading bloom of slick. His thighs flexed. His hole clenched visibly through the shifting folds of his garment, a flutter caught between reverence and readiness. He whispered a word none of them recognized.

Then another.

And another.

The scroll flared.

Not brightness.

Not ignition.

But *recognition.*

The sigils along its center shifted, not rewritten but re-remembered, rearranged by presence alone. The mirrored spirals bled inward then locked into alignment. Joren flinched as the red glow flared along his spine. Thalos's jaw clenched, blue searing upward across his ribs in twin, pulsing arcs.

The chamber responded.

Not with wards.

But with hunger.

The floor beneath their feet pulsed once, and the sigils surrounding the scroll peeled open, more mouth than mechanism.

A circle of memory.

A ritual unsaid.

A summons not sent but accepted.

Thalos staggered forward, caught himself on the table, one palm pressed flat beside the scroll.

His eyes flared. Blue and burning.

And the Archive spoke, not in voice but in breath drawn through him.

"You are not the first to bear my names. You are the first to answer them."

Joren moved to catch him. Too late.

Thalos collapsed to one knee, gasping—but not in pain.

In *arrival.*

Every sigil along his body ignited—spine, ribs, thighs, wrist. Even the one nestled deep beneath the curve of his tailbone, hidden since the altar, bloomed again. RECAST. DEVOUR ME BACK. CLAIM ME FIRST.

They pulsed in sequence.

Then, centered above them all, behind the heartbone, another sigil emerged.

One not yet seen.

One not yet *spoken.*

A spiral, etched in mirrored flame. Not blue. Not red.

White.

Not absence.

Convergence.

And Thalos, voice breaking open like a vessel spilled at last, whispered:

It remembers me by name.

Joren dropped beside him, cradling the back of his head. His own chest lit with sigils now, Kaelor's red, bright and demanding.

Ariken, gasping, dropped to all fours at the edge of the circle.

His robes parted with the motion, spilling wide across the stone. His bare ass arched high into the air, cheeks spread, hole spasming in the charged air, fluttering visibly like it had already been entered by memory.

His cock hung heavy beneath him, leaking freely now. A thick bead of slick dripped from the flushed tip to the sigils below. He moaned again, this time not from awe but from absolute readiness.

His body offered itself to the Archive's hunger, spine curved with abandon. Not collapsed. Not resisting. But beckoning. A question mark made of flesh, begging for ritual punctuation.

Thalos and Joren did not move.

They couldn't.

Something primal rooted them in place. Their breaths had synced without knowing, held in reverent suspension. Eyes wide. Lips parted.

The flush along Thalos's collarbone burned with need. Joren's hand twitched, but not toward the scroll, toward Ariken, toward that exposed, trembling ring of muscle clenching in pulses like it was remembering a rhythm it had never been taught but always known.

Their cocks both stirred visibly beneath their robes, full and rising like the Archive had summoned arousal the way it summoned memory without asking.

It was obscene. It was sacred. It was inevitable.

Neither of them blinked.

Neither of them dared.

They didn't have to.

The Archive was already reading them.

And the scroll?

It hadn't stopped *writing*.

Thalos rose first.

Not by choice but by pull. The sigils along his chest flared again, white now threaded through the blue, tendrils of invocation dragging him upright like a man summoned by his own myth. His robe slipped from one shoulder, revealing the constellation of light along his ribs. Still, he moved forward.

Joren followed. Silent. Hard. The red of Kaelor's legacy seared hot over his chest, his spine. Every step he took felt like a verse the Archive had rehearsed through him in secret.

They circled Ariken.

Slow. Reverent.

Thalos dropped to one knee behind him.

His breath ghosted across the parted curve of Ariken's ass, lips just shy of contact. The scent of slick and sigil-fire thickened the air, holy and hungry. His tongue parted his mouth, but he didn't move yet.

"Say it," Thalos murmured.

Ariken whimpered, voice cracked wide. "Please–read me."

Joren's hand came to rest on Thalos's shoulder, warm, grounding, and utterly stilling.

"Wait," he said, voice low but sure. "Look."

Both their gazes snapped back to the scroll.

It was remembering again.

Ink bled upward like veins returning to the surface. The lines weren't just instructions now—they formed architecture. Motion. Posture. Names that had never belonged to Kaelor or Veyrion. Not echoes. Not archetypes.

Them.

Ariken gasped, forehead dropping to the floor between his hands, voice cracking with need. "It's still revealing... we must–*fuck*–we must review it. It's showing us the first one. The *real* one."

They all turned.

The scroll revealed a spiral not seen before, flanked by twin sigils, one red and one blue, interwoven not mirrored. Beneath them, script etched in silver flame emerged, each word blooming into form with deliberate breath.

Not Kaelor.

Not Veyrion.

Thalos.

Joren.

The Archive remembered.

Not just how they were marked. But how they began.

Co-dreamers.

Fleshwoven.

The ritual etched beneath the names was not a map. It was a memory. The first union. Breath before name. Sigil before ink. Flesh called into union by touch and fire. It unfolded slowly, page by page, not written but reawakened.

And still, the scroll breathed.

The chamber thickened, not with smoke or spell but with lust uncoiled. Not sudden or external, it rose from inside them, from their marrow, from its echo.

Thalos shuddered as the white flare across his chest surged downward, a trail of light etching itself into his skin like a lover's whisper. The phrase formed slow and ancient, each stroke etched by something older than desire:

REMEMBER ME ALWAYS.

Joren groaned as his spine arched, hips twitching forward like memory took the reins. Across the hollow of his pelvis, above the rise of his cock, a second sigil emerged, red, stark, molten:

BEFORE ALL ELSE.

He didn't speak. He gasped—raw, involuntary.

They began to move.

Not with decision. Not even with want. Their bodies obeyed memory now. Ritual scripted into their sinew. They reached for one another, for Ariken, for the breath caught between pages.

Ariken moaned louder now, hole still pulsing, dripping wet and glistening in the ritual light. "Take me," he begged. "Or let the Archive do it. I don't care anymore. Just *read me.*"

Thalos's hand gripped his thigh.

Joren's fingers laced into Thalos's nape.

The scroll pulsed once, silver-white, and ink bled between the sigils like cum from memory, holy and profane.

And the Archive, watching, did not record.

It remembered.

It *instructed.*

—— ✦ ——

Director Threnna did not blink.

The scry-glass stretched wide across the arcane wood console, showing her every angle, bodies entwined in unfolding ritual. Her goblet sat untouched. Her fingers hovered just above the edge of the interface as if they could feel it vibrating.

Onscreen, Joren had moved. Thalos too.

The moment they moved, the glass flared open, timing her climax with theirs.

The Archive was no longer observing. It was *guiding*.

Joren knelt before Ariken now, red-lit and steady, hands spreading the Archivist's trembling thighs with slow reverence. His mouth opened, breath hot against the pulsing head of Ariken's cock, then deliberate and worshipful, he took him in.

Threnna exhaled, slow and sharp. "Beautiful fucking chaos."

Behind Ariken, Thalos aligned. The blue and white sigils along his hips pulsed in time with the scroll's glow. One hand gripped Ariken's waist. The other spread his cheeks wider, thumb brushing over the fluttering rim of his hole before pressing inward just enough to make Ariken sob into Joren's throat.

Thalos entered him.

No hesitation. Just inevitability. The Archive's rhythm made flesh.

Ariken's body convulsed beautifully, caught mid-cry, his cock now buried down Joren's throat, his hole filled and claimed.

They didn't move fast. They moved like memory. Something already practiced.

Because they had.

Because they *were*.

Threnna didn't look away, not even as her hand slid beneath her own robe, fingers brushing through soaked silk, parting the folds that had been leaking heat since the first sigil flared. Her touch was precise, almost surgical. Two fingers sank deep while her thumb circled the swollen hood of her clit, the motion coldly efficient until the Archive stole it from her and turned efficiency into ruin. Her hips jolted forward, breath caught in her throat like a swallowed moan.

The scroll's glow, half a floor below, pulsed once and the scry-glass shimmered in perfect time as if the Archive was syncing her breath to its memory.

"Gods, they're doing it," she whispered. Her voice came hoarse now, saturated with arousal. "And the Archive's jerking me off with their rhythm."

Her nipples had hardened beneath her robes minutes ago, stiff enough to throb with their own pulse, brushing raw against the frictioned lining of her inner gown. Her breasts felt swollen and aching, as if the ritual's breath had drawn blood and memory into her chest. Moisture flowed down her thighs unchecked now, a slick gloss darkening her inner leg. She felt the heat between her legs radiating out through her spine, up through her scalp, curling her toes in her heeled boots.

"Gods-forsaken symmetry," she muttered, licking the edge of her lip as Thalos sank deeper into Ariken, hips grinding in slow, deliberate pressure. "Oral and anal. Sigils in stereo. Scribes will footnote this orgasm for decades."

Her breath hitched when Joren moaned low around Ariken's cock, the sound vibrating through the scry-glass. Threnna pressed two fingers deeper inside herself, wrist slick, hips rocking.

"Come on," she whispered, eyes gleaming. "Make him shatter. Make me *believe.*"

The room lit silver on the scry-glass.

Ariken came first, body convulsing, back arched like a broken bowstring, seed spilling down Joren's throat in thick, pulsing ropes. He moaned around the cock, swallowed every drop, never breaking eye contact.

Thalos thrust deeper, once, twice, a growl curling up from his chest as his own climax surged, hot and full, spilling deep inside Ariken with a final trembling groan. Sigils flared white across his ribs.

Joren followed a heartbeat later, moaning against Ariken's spent shaft as his hips jerked, seed shooting untouched across the stone between them.

And in perfect resonance, Threnna shattered.

Her cry was low and guttural, stifled behind clenched teeth as her body spasmed. Her body clenched around her fingers in a sharp, involuntary movement driven by Archive-fed climax. Moisture flooded over her palm, warm and viscous, pooling across her wrist and thighs as her body gave in completely beneath the pulsing heat. Her nipples burned against the velvet seam of her bodice, and her breath came in shaking, reverent gasps.

She rocked in place, hips trembling and still fluttering beneath her fingers, the Archive's rhythm echoing even after release. Her other hand gripped the console, nails biting into the edge.

And the Archive. Pulsed once more.

Blue. Red. White.

Before going still.

"Fuck," she exhaled, barely audible, her smile crooked and ruined. "That was a better report than anything we've filed in ten years."

She sagged into the chair, breath still catching in her throat, fingers glistening as she withdrew them slowly from between her thighs. The heat hadn't left her. If anything, it deepened, coiling low in her belly, a second heartbeat in the marrow of her hips.

The glass still shimmered faintly. Afterglow. Or residue.

She watched it breathe once.

"Director."

The Archive's voice. Not a whisper. Not a summons. A statement.

She froze.

It wasn't Thalos's voice. Nor Joren's. Nor Ariken's.

It was hers.

"You watched. You came. You remember."

Her pulse skipped.

"Do you want to forget it?"

She laughed, low and rough, tongue flicking across the corner of her mouth. "Never."

"Then watch what comes next."

The screen pulsed white.

And the scene shifted.

Back to the Translation Chamber—

Where three bodies had only just begun to remember how to burn.

Threnna leaned forward one last time, lips parted, breath still uneven.

She spoke not to the screen, but through it. To the Archive itself.

"Come on then," she whispered, voice like blood on velvet. "If that's your best... do your worst."

The screen flickered.

And went dark.

Thalos didn't remember walking back. Only the drag of cloth over his skin, still hot from invocation, and the low throb of the Archive humming in his ribs. The scroll had burned itself into him, his name rewritten in breath, not ink.

He stood shirtless before the mirror in his chambers. Wet strands clung to his forehead. His chest rose and fell like a man post-confession, no absolution followed.

A sigil flared on his lower abdomen. Then another.

Not new.

Remembered.

He didn't call to them. They emerged.

Joren's reflection joined his own. Silent at first. Still glowing.

Then—

"I saw what it made you," Joren said quietly. "Not what it showed you. What it *made* you."

Thalos didn't turn. "Then you know it wasn't lust."

"No," Joren said, stepping closer. "It was possession."

Their eyes met in the mirror. Behind them, the Archive whispered in sensation, not words. Heat against thighs. Pulse in the cock. Memory in the spine.

They fucked.

Slow, like memory. Like recollection. Like reentry. Like rediscovery.

Thalos pressed Joren against the edge of the mirror with a reverence that bordered on ritual. His hands mapped over Joren's hips like tracing vellum that had once belonged to him. He didn't thrust. Not at first. He entered with a breath held too long, exhaling as he filled him, as if settling into the first draft of a story written in flesh.

Joren arched back into him, head bowed, lips parted not begging but accepting. He clenched around Thalos not for friction but reminder, like muscle memory folding around prophecy. Their bodies rocked together not in rhythm but in invocation, each motion a sigil drawn into the air by skin, by moan, by sweat.

Thalos whispered not words but sounds, forgotten syllables shaped by the Archive and buried in his breath. Joren answered with the twist of his spine, the tilt of his head, the way his body clenched around Thalos with remembered precision as if every muscle had rehearsed this ache in lifetimes prior.

Not to climax.

To completion.

And the Archive recorded every moan, not as data.

As scripture.

And the mirror, fogged with their breath, bore no reflection at all.

Location: Blackwatch Citadel | Sublevel B | Mess Hall Theta | Morning After

The dining hall buzzed with the usual clatter, cutlery, gossip, the half-drowsy cadence of agents who hadn't yet touched their third cup of tea. No one talked about the ritual and no one looked like they knew.

Except them.

Corrin and Ral hadn't watched. Not all of it. Not directly.

But they'd felt it.

They'd made it through the night. But the Archive hadn't let go.

Corrin had seen the scroll after and touched the residual thread still whispering along Ariken's discarded robe in the chamber. Ral had reviewed the echo logs, classified and redacted, and found pieces that still pulsed when replayed.

Only they knew what the Archive had done to Ariken.

And Ariken… wasn't pretending otherwise.

Corrin tapped his spoon once against the bowl's edge. "What's the appropriate response when you've been spiritually jerked off by a metaphysical intelligence? Apologize? Light a candle?"

"Bake it a sigil cake," Ral muttered. "With extra frosting. Preferably not yours."

"Too late," Ariken said, licking broth from the edge of his spoon. "Pretty sure I tagged a sigil last night with something unsanctioned."

Corrin choked on a sip of tea. Ral didn't look up.

"I'm not cleaning that file," he said. "Not even with tongs."

Ariken tilted his head. "You think the Archive cares about cleanup? It eats context. It masturbates to contradiction."

Ral blinked. "You're definitely not allowed to write the training manuals."

Corrin grinned. "Too bad. That was the most coherent thing I've heard in days."

Ral glanced toward the far hallway, where a faint pulse of blue and red shimmered in the stone. "Well, let's hope Thalos and Joren don't burn the place down before second breakfast."

"Or do," Ariken murmured, stirring his bowl again. "Might finally make the Archive climax in public."

Corrin covered his face with both hands. "I hate how much sense that makes."

And yet none of them got up.

Corrin dropped one hand and jabbed a thumb toward Ariken. "You know, you didn't even *look* surprised."

Ariken shrugged, reaching lazily for his tea. "You'd know too—if you'd spent four weeks translating erotic subtext from a scroll written by two people who fucked memory into myth."

Ral lifted his mug. "Here's to academic foresight. And trauma with footnotes."

Corrin raised his glass in reply. "And to all of us being somehow both observers and... *participants*."

Ariken's gaze flicked between them, lingering just long enough to spark silence. "You think this is over?"

"No," Ral said flatly, setting his mug down. "We're just next."

Corrin didn't argue. He just nodded once, slow, like agreement and inevitability had become the same thing.

Ariken exhaled, slow and sharp. "Then I hope the Archive's got a bigger appetite than last night."

Ral smirked. "Or smaller hands."

Corrin snorted into his cup, then added, "Either way, I'm bringing gloves next time."

They all fell quiet again. Not empty. Not afraid.

Just bracing.

The Archive, somewhere beneath them, pulsed once.

Subtle. Satisfied. Listening.

Chapter Twenty: The Flesh Between the Sigils

The Archive hadn't released him. Not after the scroll. Not after the sigils. Not even after the mess hall.

He had come in unison with gods, gasping through a name that wasn't his. And still the Archive pulled.

He didn't return to quarters. Not after being seen. The Archive wasn't done with him yet. So he followed the pull, past locked sigils and sleep-curved halls, to where no one else would enter unbidden.

He'd thought it was a scroll. Something sacred. Tangible. Arcane.

But when he reached for it, the air didn't turn to parchment.

It opened like a seal.

Not a scroll.

A file.

Ariken stood alone. The sigils beneath his feet hadn't flared in centuries. But they hummed now and not with welcome. With recognition. He hadn't spoken. He hadn't needed to. The scroll hovered in Archive-bound breath. Its surface shimmered blank at first. Then the veil dropped.

A projection unfolded.

Not recorded.

Remembered.

BLACKWATCH RITUAL LOG ENTRY

Designation: Mirrorfold Inversion – Dual Catalyst Convergence
Clearance: OBSIDIAN-PRIME
Filed by: [Redacted] | Cross-fragment Tag #MF-ΔΩ

They did not arrive together.

They were summoned by echo.

Kaelor emerged first—bare, burning, the altar pulsing red beneath his feet. His cock, proud and slick with anticipation, bore sigils that rippled down his thighs like spilled ink-light. Every step he took sparked the sigils to flare, each pulse a demand: Be known. Be owned.

Then came Veyrion—cool, naked from the waist down, his cock half-hard but already leaking, a curved blade of promise beneath pale, sigil-lined skin. His presence didn't ripple. It settled. The basin responded to him like breath drawn too deep. His sigils glowed blue. Frostlight in contrast to Kaelor's fire-vein heat.

The vessel—a man of mythic proportion and mortal ache—was already kneeling at the altar's center, thighs wide, hole exposed and twitching. But this time, he wasn't offered to one.

He was meant for both.

Kaelor moved first. His fingers curled around the man's throat—not to choke, but to center. To own. As his cock slid inside with a hiss of molten air, the altar beneath them flared red and the sigil CLAIM ME FIRST blazed to life at the base of the vessel's spine. Kaelor fucked him like a rite—deep, deliberate, demanding. Every thrust was possession—not invasion. Every groan from the vessel echoed yes, even if his voice was gone.

Kaelor held nothing back. He thrust with the hunger of a god returned to the flesh, each motion steeped in claim. His hands shifted from throat to hips, then to the small of the back, guiding the arch of the vessel's spine like a sculptor refining a living altar. The vessel whimpered, his hole clenching, slick and parted around Kaelor's recursion.

Then came Veyrion.

He knelt behind Kaelor and exhaled—not a breath, but a breeze cold enough to lift the sweat from Kaelor's skin. His hands traced the line of Kaelor's back, not just to guide, but to read. Every muscle, every groove, every sigil was taken in with reverence. His touch lingered just long enough to be worshipful, then purposeful—hands parting Kaelor's cheeks, fingertips teasing the puckered ring already twitching with anticipation.

Kaelor leaned back, still buried in the vessel, and offered himself.

Veyrion accepted.

His cock, now fully hard and seamed with flickering sigils, pressed inward with a slow, grinding pressure. The stretch was slow, inch by inch, until Kaelor moaned—not with pain, but with the holy ruin of being filled. His back arched, body rocked between the two of them, fucked forward into the vessel with every slow, deliberate thrust of Veyrion behind him.

They moved as one. Rhythm layered on rhythm. Kaelor's cock driving memory into the vessel, Veyrion's cock carving space into Kaelor with relentless, luxurious motion. Each thrust from behind pushed Kaelor deeper into the vessel's body, forcing cries from him that rippled with magic. The man's ass bloomed open around Kaelor, his cock leaking steadily, untouched but overwhelmed.

The basin lit up.

A recursive projection split open:

Red: Kaelor gripping the vessel's hips, fucking him open, whispering his name through gritted teeth.

Blue: Veyrion fucking Kaelor, hand braced between his shoulder blades, hips grinding in hard, slow pulses.

The sigils ignited on all three—Kaelor's spine flaring with CLAIM ME FIRST, Veyrion's thighs glowing with DEVOUR ME BACK, and the vessel's hole rimmed in an open spiral etched with BEFORE ALL ELSE. But something unexpected happened—another flare ignited across Kaelor's shoulder, then coiled downward in mirrored script across his ribs:

BEFORE ALL ELSE—the same sigil that had marked the vessel. As if Kaelor had carried it long before he ever touched the altar. As if the ritual only made visible what had always lived beneath his skin. The sigils pulsed not in isolation but in recursive unity—each echoing the others, binding giver, receiver, and vessel into a single mirrored continuum.

Kaelor thrusted as if declaring truth into skin—his body hammering prophecy into breath. Veyrion's grip tightened around his hips, body rocking forward, breath ghosting over Kaelor's spine like a forgotten vow returned mid-syllable. And the vessel took them both—utterly split but unbroken—his body marked not as a victim, but as a page opened wide to be rewritten.

The rhythm peaked—a spiral of breath and depth and surrender. Kaelor came first, his body locked tight, cock pulsing inside the vessel as molten seed poured into him. The sigil CLAIM ME FIRST flared so violently it singed the altar's edge. Veyrion followed, hips shuddering, cock driving deep as he spilled inside Kaelor—slow, complete, his groan swallowed by the vessel's final gasp.

The vessel exhaled once, spine arched to its limit, and vanished.

Not collapsed. Not disintegrated. Gone. As if he had never been there except to complete the ritual, and his purpose had always been to bring them together.

Veyrion remained buried in Kaelor, panting, slick with shared sweat and power. Kaelor rose to his knees slowly, glancing back with a growl, eyes alight with something both challenge and reverence.

He turned, pulled Veyrion forward, and mounted him.

Kaelor fucked him with slow force—deep, unrelenting—pressing Veyrion's spine down to the altar stone until the sigil BEFORE ALL ELSE flared across his lower back—a mark not just of submission, but of mirrored surrender. Veyrion came again, helpless, seed spilling across the sigils beneath him as Kaelor drove through it, fucking him through the orgasm like the ending of a spell.

Then Veyrion turned him.

Kaelor surrendered beneath him this time, thighs parted, cock leaking, body open. Veyrion entered him one last time—not to claim, not to consume, but to join. Their bodies moved in perfect rhythm, sweat and breath and prophecy woven together until the final stroke drew a gasp from both: matched, mirrored, complete.

They came together, locked eye to eye, seed spilling, sigils glowing. And the sigil upon Kaelor—until now unseen—lit from beneath the skin at the base of his spine:

REMEMBER ME ALWAYS

A beat later, the same sigil flared to life across Veyrion's chest— etched over his heart, glowing through skin and sweat. The same message, mirrored. As if something greater had not only documented the moment, but sealed it across both bodies as one final truth: they were no longer singular. What myth had split—what mistake had scattered—Archive now bound. In climax. In memory. In pulse.

They breathed as one.

Marked. The same.

—— ✦ ——

The Archive didn't wait for readiness.

Ariken wobbled.

And in that moment, terror.

Not the kind that screamed or fought, but the kind that hollowed. His body was moving before his mind could refuse, heat blooming across skin he hadn't given permission to burn.

His cock throbbed. His hole fluttered in rhythm with the vision playing before him. But his mind clawed backward, repulsed not by the act, but by how *easily* he was unraveling into it.

I didn't choose this, some shard of him whispered. *This isn't mine.*

But the Archive wasn't asking.

It was remembering him.

And his body, traitorous and trembling, was answering in kind.

The projection didn't fade.

But his body had already begun answering.

The sigils forming in the file now mirrored heat blooming across his chest, his thighs, his lower back. Sweat pooled under his collar. Not from heat. From recognition.

He reached toward the playback, not to pause it, but to brace himself.

The Archive adjusted. The file continued, but now it pulsed with his breath. As if syncing to his rhythm.

The sigils unspooled across the interface:

Final Manifestation:

CLAIM ME FIRST – Carved in flare down Kaelor's spine. Initial sigil of ownership, anchored during the vessel's offering.

DEVOUR ME BACK – Glowing blue along Veyrion's thighs. The mirrored invocation, activated in surrender and hunger.

BEFORE ALL ELSE – First etched into the vessel's rim, later igniting on Veyrion's lower back. A sigil of divine precedence, of ritual convergence.

REMEMBER ME ALWAYS – Emerged simultaneously on Kaelor's lower back and over Veyrion's heart. The final sigil. The binding.

And the Archive pulsed once in reply—
Not through projection,
But through him.

—– ✦ —–

Location: Mirrorfold Ritual Log | Archive Recursion Layer: MF-ΔΩ | Continuum Reentry – Simultaneous

Ariken didn't breathe. The Archive did it for him.
The vision didn't pause for breath.
It reentered itself—
As if the Archive had never stopped remembering.
The altar pulsed. Then stilled.
And from the shadows behind the altar, where the light should have died, the vessel reappeared.
Not fully body. Not fully soul.
His voice was the echo of parchment burned but not destroyed, the syllables slow and terrible, carved in hush:
"Before all else, I opened. Claim me first, I yielded. Devour me back, I begged. Remember me always... and so I became not memory, but meaning.
You are bound. I am written. And what was once vessel... Is now watching."
Then—he was gone again.
Not vanished this time.

Just... embedded.

No record was sealed. No scribe intervened.

But the stone remembered.

What remained was not a story.

It was a binding, etched in seed and sinew, sigil and groan.

No prophecy foretold it. No altar demanded it. And yet their bodies had found each other like puzzle pieces across time, fire and frost, mouth and hunger, cock and command. When they came together that final time, it wasn't for climax. It was for recognition.

Two souls, scattered by myth and mistake, brought at last to the altar they were always owed.

This was no rite.

This was reunion.

And they would never unjoin again.

The Archive did not seal the vision. It folded it into him.

Ariken blinked once. And the Archive blinked back.

Location: Blackwatch Citadel | Sublevel Epsilon | Echofeed Projection Chamber | Minutes Later

The vision stuttered. Then held. Not ended. Absorbed.

Ariken's body staggered beneath it.

Not memory on display. Memory rewritten in flesh.

The air had gone still. Not emptied, but *listening.*

Ariken's breath caught, then hitched again. His hands trembled, not violently, but like a tremor beneath surface tension. Sweat streaked his temples. He couldn't blink.

He stood in the center of the projection chamber, but his body felt distant, secondhand, as if memory was wrapping around him like a garment, tailored and slid across living skin.

The sigils from the file still hovered in the air, flickering once, then fading.

But he could feel them *in him*. Not metaphor. Not illusion. Etched under skin that had never borne a name of its own.

The realization struck in waves, not that he had seen the vessel, but that he had been the vessel. Or would be. Or was always meant to be. His thighs ached with phantom pressure. His hole clenched, not from fear, but from recursion. From *echo*.

Every line spoken in the ritual, every movement, had felt like something he'd already surrendered to. Not witnessed. *Remembered*.

And in that memory, the fear did not retreat.

It became exhilaration.

The Archive pulsed behind him, once like breath drawn. Again. Then again.

Blue. Then red. Then white.

He had not asked for it. But he would not give it back.

"Welcome back," it whispered, not into the air.

Into *him*. As if it had never left.

As if it had always known what he would become.

—— ✦ ——

Location: Blackwatch Citadel | Sublevel Omega | Surveillance Observation Tier – Private Echo Node | Simultaneous

Threnna stood in the hexagonal chamber, low-lit and silent, fingers steepled before a bank of live scry-screens. Each flickered with playback threads, time-coded with echo latency and pulse density. She watched without blinking.

On the central feed, the projection from Ariken's chamber played out, the vessel fading, the sigils still burning like memory refused to close.

She said nothing.

Her gaze slid to the side panel, a second feed, this one silent, private, buried beneath three layers of clearance. It showed Thalos and Joren, tangled together in bed, still asleep. And yet—

Their sigils flared.

Not from dream. Not from touch. But as if *something had shifted*. As if recursion corrected a thread long miscast.

Threnna's gaze sharpened as the color bloom synced: red across Joren's chest, blue flaring at Thalos's ribs. They inverted. *Red to blue. Blue to red.*

Then stillness.

"Kaelor," she said softly. "Veyrion."

She didn't speak as if naming the men on the feed.

She spoke like she was reassigning myth.

The Archive pulsed beneath her feet. No audible sound. Just a pressure behind the teeth. A hum behind her spine.

Her eyes narrowed as the vessel's final phrase looped in the echo chamber: ***"What was once vessel... is now watching."***

Threnna's voice was barely audible. "No. Not watching."

She smirked like a woman watching her exes fuck each other in a mirror, dangerous, amused, and deeply unsurprised.

She tapped one sigil-thread open. Then another. Fingers poised like a pianist about to play a note so precise it'd cut glass.

"They're rewriting us," she purred, "and I've still got one climax left to sign."

The Archive responded, not with whisper or pulse, but with amusement, a ripple through the scry-feed, a distortion only she could sense.

"Authorization was never yours."

Threnna didn't flinch. She only smiled wider.

"Then I'll cum anyway."

Her pulse synced with the Archive's silence.

—— ✦ ——

Thalos woke first.

Not abruptly. Just enough to feel Joren's weight pressed against his back. The sheets were tangled. Sweat cooled along his ribs. But the air hadn't stilled. Not fully.

A flicker.

He looked down. His chest was glowing faintly, blue light in the shape of script he couldn't quite name. Not in the dark. Not yet.

Joren stirred behind him. A sigh. Then a shift. His palm slid over Thalos's waist.

Joren's chest flared.

Red. Familiar.

He blinked, sleep-hazed confusion softening his gaze. "It's still happening."

Thalos didn't speak. Just turned to face him.

The sigils pulsed again. Blue faded to red. Red to blue. Then stilled.

"I dreamt we weren't us," Joren whispered.

Thalos's fingers traced his spine, light as memory. "We weren't."

He leaned in, breath warming Joren's lips. "And we were."

The sigils pulsed again, softly, not just color but heat. Not from outside. From within.

Something older than invocation had exhaled through them.

The pulse didn't stop at the skin. It passed between them: breath, memory, claim.

Joren's eyes didn't close.

"What if we're not echoes?"

Thalos kissed the space just below his collarbone, where Kaelor's mark had burned.

"Then we're the original sin."

Neither of them asked what it meant.

Because the Archive wasn't answering. It was remembering.

And what it remembered...

Wasn't over.

CHAPTER TWENTY-ONE: ALL NAMES BURN CLEAN

Location: Blackwatch Citadel | Archive Core Layer – Recursion Terminal Tier | Dawn

Joren woke still glowing, not with sigil-light but with memory, folded into his chest like breath held too long.

The Archive hadn't spoken. But it had chosen. And it had chosen *him*.

Thalos saw it too. Said nothing. Just brushed the fading red across Joren's chest with a touch that felt like assent.

They didn't dress. Didn't speak. The pull wasn't on their bodies anymore.

It was echo. Claim.

They moved because there was nowhere left to run.

They descended in silence.

The hall leading to the core layer pulsed with breath-warm air, heavy with ink and echo. Torchlight didn't flicker, it inhaled. Every step they took pressed memory into stone.

Joren walked with his fists half-clenched. "It's pulling harder," he said, voice low.

Thalos nodded. "I feel it in the teeth of my spine. Like a name trying to crawl back into bone."

Neither of them asked what they would find. The answer had been seeded into every sleepless hour, every shared pulse, every sigil flare that had echoed someone else's moan through their own throats.

"They'll be waiting," Thalos said. Not a warning. A certainty.

"And we're not here to mourn?" Joren asked.

Thalos stopped at the final arch. Looked back only once. "No. We're here to finish what they began."

Then he stepped through.

Joren lingered at the edge, one hand brushing the stone arch like it might remember him. "It's too quiet," he murmured.

The air here remembered others. A scorch-scent still curled faintly near the arch's base, myrrh and copper, like the moment Crale's recursion failed to seal. And above, just out of reach, a blackened spiral had been etched into the stone, not a sigil but the scorch-mark of Threnna's last oversight pulse. Burned in. Half-erased.

Thalos looked back. "It's not quiet. It's listening."

The space beyond the arch didn't echo. It pressed.

"Do you feel that?" Joren asked. "Like breath held. Like the room knows we're the last page."

Thalos nodded, eyes narrowing. "No sigils. No sigils. Just expectation."

He held out his hand, not to guide but to steady. Joren took it, not out of fear but readiness.

"If we cross this line," Joren said, "we don't get to be echoes anymore."

Thalos's grip tightened. "Good. I'm done repeating."

Only then did they step forward—together.

The slabs were not tombs.

They breathed, shallow and constant, like parchment stretched over a pulse too old to forget how to beat. Red and blue light guttered beneath them in twin rhythms, their edges rimmed in ash and memory. No names were carved. Only echoes, trapped in stone, repeating themselves without end.

But none repeated the name they'd come to bear.

Thalos stood at the edge first, jaw clenched, fists loose. The stone floor beneath him throbbed with heat, not fire but the friction of unforgotten touch. Joren stepped beside him, silent. Their sigils flared low and slow, blue along spine, red across ribs, casting mirrorlight into the dark.

"They're not gone," Joren said.

"No," Thalos replied. "But they're no longer needed."

He knelt first. Not to worship. To begin.

The Archive watched.

He peeled the robes from Joren's chest with slow precision, mouth brushing shoulder, tongue dragging over scar. Joren's breath hitched. The slabs pulsed harder. The sigils responded, not with glow but with sweat. Thin lines of ink seeped from the ceiling, bleeding in spirals.

Joren pushed Thalos down against the stone, breath hot in his throat. "Devour me back," he whispered.

Blue erupted along the floor. Red followed. And the Archive sighed.

Thalos's mouth wrapped around Joren's cock with the reverence of a final command, slow, anchoring, sacred. The salt of sweat clung to the back of his throat; the chill of the stone pressed into his knees. Joren's breath trembled above him, caught between need and surrender. Each suck drew not just arousal but memory, heat against cold, tongue against trembling, command against collapse.

He didn't just draw moans, Thalos drew memory through flesh, weaving it back into the Archive's breathing skin.

The Archive tasted it all. He sucked slow, deep. One hand gripped the back of Joren's thigh, the other slid beneath his ass, pulling him forward with pressure just shy of pain. The slab beneath them cracked, just slightly.

Memory didn't shatter. It moaned.

Joren came with a gasp. Thighs trembling, spine arched, breath caught between ache and release. His cum marked Thalos's tongue, his chin, the stone. And one of the slabs dimmed. Not in death, but in echo received.

Thalos didn't stop.

He flipped Joren over, gripped the curve of his ass, and licked him open, slow, obscene, precise. The rim pulsed with anticipation, each twitch another syllable in a forgotten litany. "You're not a vessel," Thalos murmured. "You're a fucking scripture."

He slid in two fingers, then three, his tongue still teasing, teeth grazing just enough to make Joren whimper. The sigils unraveled faster. The slabs hissed.

Then Thalos mounted him, breath ragged, hands trembling, cock slick and heavy with the weight of something more than release. It wasn't just penetration. It was the moment recursion broke inside him. This was not possession. It was translation. Claiming Joren wasn't about dominance, it was about proof.

But for one breath, he faltered.

Thalos's hips froze, sheathed deep inside Joren, a tremor working up from his spine, not pleasure, not fear. Something older. Hungrier.

He felt it, *not his desire, not his command*, but the Archive itself sliding along his nerves. Language folding inward. Memory not remembered, but overwritten.

A flicker in Thalos' voice, hoarse with breath:

"Am I still me... or just something it's saying out loud?"

The silence wasn't empty. It took the question.

Held it.

Then breathed it back into him, unanswered, unowned.

The thought split him, half a gasp, half a prayer. In the silence, he heard no answer, only the steady, possessive pulse of the Archive folding him back into breath not his own.

Joren didn't answer.

He *couldn't*.

Because the Archive did.

Not in words.

But in how it made him move.

A slow, irresistible pulse. A pull from beneath the skin, threading Thalos into rhythm again—flesh still trembling, but now moving, now obeying.

No pause.

Just heat and fullness and the shuddering gasp that split the silence.

They fucked like rite, grinding, breath-bound, each thrust scrawling rhythm into stone. Thalos's cock carved memory into Joren's body. Joren bucked beneath him, breath catching, teeth bared, his own cock dragging across ink-slick stone. The Archive pulsed in time.

Red. Blue. Red. Blue.

Then together.

Thalos came inside him with a roar.

Joren followed with a cry.

The slabs shattered, like vertebrae snapping under the weight of a name no longer theirs, like prophecy cracking open its own spine. Memory spilled out like marrow.

Their cum wasn't just spilled, it was inked. A signature.

A final breathless seal binding flesh to memory, blood to command.

It tasted not just what they gave, but what they had become.

Ash swirled. The sigils died. The recursion ended.

They collapsed, breath-tangled, skin-wet, the Archive vibrating beneath them. Not from exhaustion. From integration.

Their sigils didn't fade.

They flared.

RECAST. CLAIM ME FIRST. BEFORE ALL ELSE.

REMEMBER ME ALWAYS.

And then a voice, not heard but breathed, slipped from both their mouths at once:

"You are not the first to bear my names. You are the first to answer them."

A new sigil burned into the stone between them. White. Spiraled. Singular.

CONVERGENCE.

Their cum pooled around it. The Archive drank it like ink.

The air shifted, less like a breeze and more like lungs exhaling around them. The walls, once polished stone, now shimmered faintly with sigil afterburn, veins pulsing beneath skin. The slabs no longer existed. In their place, the floor was cracked with white spiral etchings, as though memory had been inscribed directly into the foundation.

Thalos pushed himself upright, muscles trembling with spent tension. "Same place," Thalos muttered, scanning the altered walls. "But the chamber's different."

Joren looked around, slower to rise. "It's not just the chamber," he said. "It's us."

They stood, bodies slick, the last of their seed drying in mirrored arcs along the floor. Beneath them, a shallow groove had formed, one that hadn't been there before. A spiral path carved in a single motion, leading outward from the sigil at the center.

"It's rebuilding," Thalos murmured. "Not to contain them. To hold us."

Joren ran his fingers along the nearest wall. The sigils there weren't static. They flexed. Like muscle.

"It's alive," he said.

Thalos nodded, brow furrowed. "It always was. But now it dreams in our shape."

They stood in the silence that followed, not out of reverence, but recognition.

What they had broken had not died.

It had become them.

Joren lay still for a long time. Breathing. Listening.

"Do you feel it?" he asked, voice rough with awe.

His fingertips grazed the spiral path, eyes narrowing. "It's not memory," he whispered. "It's instruction."

Thalos didn't answer right away. He pressed his palm to the spiraled sigil burned into the stone, still warm, still damp with them. His other hand curled in the ink-streaked hair at Joren's nape.

"Yes," Thalos whispered. "Like I've been rewritten. But it's still my name on the page."

Joren turned his face to him, cheek resting against his shoulder. "I felt them. Not like echoes. Not like ghosts. Like... they trusted us to finish something they couldn't."

Thalos swallowed hard. "They didn't vanish. They became part of the structure. Like mortar. Like breath in a sealed room."

The Archive pulsed once beneath them, acknowledgment or promise, impossible to tell.

"Do you think this was the end?" Joren asked.

Thalos looked toward the cracked slabs, then at the sigil between them, at the way the white light had begun to fade, not out but inward, toward the floor, into memory.

"No," he said softly. "This was the unlocking."

"We're not done."

Joren hesitated. "Are we?"

Thalos didn't answer.

Because the Archive did.

And as its breath withdrew from their mouths, it did not vanish. It spiraled inward, folding what had been spoken into the soft dark behind their eyes. Sleep came not as rest, but as ritual suspension.

The Archive showed them things, not images but echoes. Not prophecy but memory. Names written in the shape of bodies. A scroll that never ended. A spiral that always returned to the center.

Sleep never came. Folding did.

No resistance. Only breath shared with the Archive, limbs stilling as command replaced will.

Not rest. Not quite. A dreaming shaped like instruction.

—— ✦ ——

The scry-glass warped, struggling to interpret what it saw. Not memory. Not prophecy. But live recursion, breathing, sweating, fucking itself clean of echo.

Director Threnna leaned closer to the console, one gloved hand resting against the sigil-rimmed glass. The other hovered just above her own thigh, fingers twitching faintly in rhythm with the pulse bleeding from the Archive core.

The slabs cracked. She blinked once, not from fear.

And she felt it. Deep in the base of her spine, the pressure of recursion giving way. The Archive was no longer archiving. It was adapting. And adaptation was always erotic.

Her fingers curled above the console, resisting the urge to descend, to trace the pulse that mirrored her own.

Not to touch. To record. To enter the memory not as vessel, but as author.

She'd seen this before, in fragments, in failed vessels, in broken tongues trying to speak their own myths. But this, was not a possession. It was a merging.

Thalos moaned something not quite a name. Joren echoed it, like lovers whispering sigils they hadn't known they carried.

Threnna inhaled sharply, the air tasting of salt, stone, and ink. Not memory. Not climax. Something cleaner. *Submission informed by recursion. Consent carved into breath.*

"Ah," she said softly, half to herself, "so they finally let it fuck them back."

Her own name would never be written in stone. But she would be the one who watched the page turn.

The glass pulsed once, CONVERGENCE flaring at its center, mirrored white and recursive.

Threnna's lips parted around a dry smirk. Her voice, when it came, was reverent, laced with disdain. "Good. Let the Archive remember them properly."

She did not linger. She did not flinch.

But she did pause at the threshold.

A flicker in the glass caught her, not her face but the echo of something older. Something that had once believed it could author the Archive, not be erased by it. A version with blood under her nails and breath pressed to parchment like hunger.

For a moment, she didn't see Thalos and Joren. Only herself, years ago, hands trembling over a slab not yet warmed by memory. She had wanted to be inscribed into the Archive back then. She had begged for it, silent and wet-mouthed, sprawled across the same stone, waiting for the Archive to speak her name in fire.

It hadn't.

Instead, it had watched her. Catalogued her. Declined her.

The sigil CONVERGENCE still pulsed on-screen.

Threnna's smirk wavered. Not with fear. With understanding.

"They'll think this was about sex," she murmured. "They'll think the Archive is a hunger."

She turned fully then, voice a whisper only the stone would remember. "But it's a womb. It doesn't just consume... it births."

And she, who had thought herself the mother of the Archive's next myth, had merely been its midwife. Not remembered. Not recorded. Just present.

But that, too, was power.

And power, she knew, still could.

Her robe swept the floor in silence.

She chuckled low, voice curling like a finger around a throat. "Let the Archive write them now," she said, stepping through the final threshold. "Let them bleed like pages... slick, obedient, and screaming for ink."

She wouldn't beg the Archive again. But she would make it beg her.

—— ✦ ——

Location: Blackwatch Citadel | Archive Sanctum | Just Before Dawn

They did not wake where they had fallen.

The Archive did not leave them on the stone floor.

When sleep took them, it carried their bodies into the upper sanctum, a chamber neither had entered in waking memory. Lit by slow-burning sigil glass sconces, the walls curved like the inside of a lung. Clean. Silent. Still echoing with sex and sigil.

There was no bed. Only a single slab, warm to the touch, draped in black linen and edged in faint, spiraled embroidery. The sigils from the core had burned themselves into the fabric. They woke on top of it. The warmth hadn't faded. If anything, it pulsed fainter now. The Archive was still deciding if the ritual had truly ended.

Before their eyes opened, they felt it, a shift in the pressure of the air, like breath caught mid-inhale. The chamber had acknowledged someone, not as a stranger but as the next sentence.

They woke with the sky still dim.

Thalos shifted first, arms wrapped around Joren's waist. Joren stirred, cock still soft and slick between his thighs. Their bodies hummed, sated but marked. The chamber had not remained empty while they slept.

Someone had been summoned. Not by door or message, but by pulse.

Ariken had arrived before the others, drawn not by duty but by something older. He hadn't knocked. The threshold had opened for him.

And when he stepped through, the Archive shifted, not to alert but to allow. To recognize.

Ariken stood in the doorway. Watching. Hard.

The chamber wasn't familiar. But his body responded as if it had knelt here before.

Beneath the stillness, something shivered, not fear but anticipation. The silver in his eye refracted the glow still clinging to Thalos and Joren's skin. His breath came shallow, not from exertion but recognition. His cock stirred, unbidden, beneath his robe. He didn't move, but a memory not his own curled low in his spine, waiting to be named.

He didn't speak.

The air shifted again, subtly, as if the chamber inhaled a second time. No footfall. No voice. Just breath pressed into the walls, shaped like a question.

Then the door hissed open, deliberate, low, as if exhaling in reply.

Corrin entered first, visibly hesitating at the threshold. He bore the remnants of a summoned pulse across his chest, green flickering faintly beneath his collarbone like the Archive had tagged him for reasons not yet revealed.

Ral followed, silent and slow, silver coiling his throat like a signature he hadn't signed. He paused beside Corrin, eyes flicking between the two men on the slab and the shimmer still breathing beneath Ariken's skin.

Neither of them quite remembered the walk to the sanctum. There had been a pulse. A pull. Then breath. Then the door.

Corrin's hand still hovered near his chest, like he was trying to recall if he'd opened it, or if the Archive had done it for him.

"Feels like we missed a ritual," Ral murmured.

Corrin's voice dropped. Reverent. "Or arrived for the next one."

Ral grunted faintly. "If this is the next one, the previous chapter must've involved a fuckload of climax."

Corrin shot him a sideways glance, cheeks flushed, but his eyes didn't leave Joren. "It feels... heavy. Like breath trapped in glass. One wrong word and it'll crack."

Joren sat up slowly.

They said nothing at first. Thalos's hand found Joren's, and they both turned toward the doorway, toward the silver-streaked stillness watching them from its frame.

"It feels different," Joren said, voice low. "Like it's still inside us. Reshaping."

He didn't sound afraid. But his voice had a pause in it. A softness shaped like memory returning too soon. Like he hadn't yet decided whether the Archive's breath belonged in his lungs.

Thalos nodded slowly. "We're part of its memory now. Part of its breath."

Joren looked toward the others. "And them?"

"They felt the pulse," Thalos replied. "The Archive must want them here. To witness. Or to change."

"It's not watching us anymore," he said then, eyes on Ariken.

"No," Joren whispered. "It's remembering."

Ariken's fingers found his chest.

And something pulsed beneath his robe, low and spiral-shaped, echoing the sigil etched between Thalos and Joren. It didn't flare. It hummed. A whisper of CONVERGENCE coiled beneath his skin like the Archive had left a question mark carved in breath, waiting for Ariken to answer.

Thalos and Joren watched him, watched them all, as silence stretched around the sanctum like held breath.

Thalos saw Corrin first: the way his fingers twitched just shy of his thigh, the way his pupils dilated as if trying to remember a dream not his own. He stood still, but his posture betrayed the tremble of reverence, or arousal, or both.

Joren's gaze flicked to Ral. The silver winding his throat hadn't dulled; it gleamed with a logic too quiet to ignore. Ral said nothing, but the weight of his eyes felt like an interrogation dressed in stillness, a watcher, a gate.

Ariken didn't breathe like the others. His entire body bore the ache of anticipation. His cheeks flushed deep, his jaw slack with the kind of held breath that came before a command not yet spoken. Sweat clung to the hollow of his lower back, dampening the thin robe in darkening streaks.

The curve of his ass, high, full, maddening, strained against the fabric, each motion of his breath tugging the weave tighter across round flesh that looked sculpted for ritual. His thighs flexed beneath it, parted just enough to promise, not plead. Beneath him, the robe bunched slightly, and the swell of his cheeks curved into soft shadow, each twitch revealing the growing slickness between.

He looked marked by presence, not possession, like the Archive had begun to write into him without touching ink. His cock swelled visibly beneath his robe, a pulse of readiness that wasn't want but memory reawakening through flesh.

No one moved.

But the Archive did.

It shimmered faintly around them, unseen but felt. Not as a presence above, but *within*. As if the sanctum itself had inhaled their names and was now deciding how to speak them back.

This wasn't just aftermath.

It was prelude.

A single breath passed between them. Not drawn. Not given. Simply shared.

And with it, something shifted.

Ral tilted his head just slightly. His fingers brushed the base of his throat, where the silver twined, and for the first time, he looked less like a sentry and more like a sigil waiting to be spoken.

Corrin blinked hard, breath hitching, lips parted. His hand drifted toward the faint green at his collarbone. "I think it's calling," he whispered. "Or... remembering through me."

Joren turned toward Thalos, voice low but certain. "It's rewriting us again."

Thalos didn't speak. He reached for Ariken's face instead—just a gesture, fingers stopping inches from his jaw. Not touching. Just close enough to let the air tremble between them.

Ariken didn't flinch.

He leaned in. Not toward the hand, but to the breath.

The Archive breathed with him, as if returning something it had only borrowed.

No sigil flared. But something shifted beneath the skin.

A whisper not yet inked.

chapter twenty-two: the ink that breathes

Location: Blackwatch Citadel | Sublevel Theta-Null | Translation Chamber

They did not return by choice.

The Archive had drawn them down again. Past the sanctum. Past sleep, into the chamber where Ariken first became *readable*.

Not for fucking. For remembering.

Sublevel Theta-Null had only one entrance: breath. And now it inhaled them again.

The table had not cooled.

The air in the Translation Chamber still trembled, not with magic but with breath, too many held, too many released. Sigils flickered faintly along the stone floor, their glow dimming in staggered pulses like heartbeats learning to slow. At the center of it all, the scroll lay open and silent.

Not dead. Not dormant.

Rewritten.

Ariken hadn't moved.

He knelt at the edge of the ritual ring, robes clinging to the curve of his spine, damp with the sweat of inscription. His mouth was slack. His hole still glistened, flexing unconsciously in the air, as though echoing some remembered rhythm it had never been taught. Only endured.

But his eyes, one silvered and the other glassy with reverent ruin, were fixed not on the scroll but on Thalos.

Or what remained of him.

Because Thalos was still standing. And not.

His body pulsed in alternating flares of white and blue, sigils rising and fading beneath his skin like second breath. His cock, still wet and half-hard, swayed as he staggered once. Joren caught him from behind, pressing the weight of his body against Thalos's back, arms steadying hips hollowed by breath then claimed by flame. The curve of Thalos's ass rested flush against Joren's pelvis, unmoving, unashamed, like the final echo of a ritual that no longer needed movement to be felt.

Theirs wasn't exhaustion. It was anchoring, flesh as punctuation, posture as memory. The physicality lingered not for pleasure but because the Archive still needed flesh to hold what it had written.

The soft cleft nestled perfectly into the heat of Joren's groin, not as invitation, but as punctuation, an afterimage etched in flesh. They fit. They knew it. And the Archive, watching, knew it too.

Joren's chest was bare, the red sigils that marked his spine faintly lit like embers cooling beneath skin. Sweat shimmered across the sharp line of his collarbone, catching where the light fractured off the chamber's etched stone. His breath moved slow, not from exhaustion but from reverence.

His cock hung thick between his thighs, softening, still flushed with the glow of what had passed between them. The heat of him matched Thalos perfectly, molded to his back, his hips cradling the curve of Thalos's ass like memory remembered in flesh.

They didn't speak.

Because the scroll wasn't finished.

Another flare.

This one silent and thick. It passed through them like a pressure front. Corrin gasped as it hit him from the edge of the threshold. Ral stood beside him, lips drawn into a line, eyes unreadable, but his shoulders tensed as the light moved through.

The Archive hadn't exhaled. Not fully.

Corrin's fingers twitched at his sides, grasping for something that wasn't there, an anchor, a prayer, the trembling memory of a touch he hadn't received but now remembered in his bones. His trousers strained subtly at the front, fabric betraying the weight of arousal with no origin, only reaction. His mouth parted as if to speak, but no sound came, just breath, shallow and worshipful.

Green light pulsed faintly beneath the hollow of his throat, neither sigil nor scar, but something waiting to be claimed. He pressed one hand there like he feared what might bloom if he let it rise. It wasn't lust—it was instruction. A pulse of purpose that had chosen his breath as its vessel.

Beside him, Ral didn't move, but his abdomen betrayed him, tense and taut, resisting revelation. His jaw clenched, muscle twitching beneath skin, a command waiting to be given. Though his eyes remained locked on the center of the room, his stillness betrayed reverence. Too precise. Too poised. A flicker of silver danced along the inner seam of his uniform where a sigil had begun to write itself without consent.

He inhaled deeply, nostrils flaring, as if scenting the aftermath. Not just sex. Not even ritual. But a memory buried so deep in the Archive it had used their bodies to speak again.

They were watching gods breathe. And part of them, the part not yet named, ached to be rewritten.

Corrin leaned slightly toward Ral, voice low, as if afraid the Archive might overhear.

"Is he... still Ariken?"

Ral didn't answer immediately. His eyes never left the center of the ritual ring, but his hand lifted, slowly, and hovered just behind Corrin's shoulder.

"I think he's more than he was," Ral said at last. "And less than we're ready to understand."

Corrin swallowed, breath catching. "I can still feel him. Like his body's echo is folded inside mine. And I never touched him."

"Not physically," Ral murmured. "But the Archive did. Through all of us."

A beat passed. Corrin's gaze dropped to Ariken's exposed back, the soft curve of his glistening ass, the raw stillness of his offering.

"He didn't break," Corrin whispered. "He opened. Gods, Ral... he wanted it."

Ral's fingers brushed the small of Corrin's back now, gentle and grounding.

"Wanting doesn't make it easier to survive," he said. "But maybe it's what makes it matter."

Ariken stirred, not with motion but with voice. Low, frayed, almost academic.

"It's still me," he said, without lifting his head. "But quieter now. Like something older is thinking through my bones."

He didn't feel erased. He felt translated, each bone repurposed into syntax the Archive could finally read.

He was no longer written on. He was writing back.

He shifted, just slightly, breath catching in his throat. His voice was hoarse but steady, laced with breathless awe.

"I'm not scared of it. I just... hope the Archive remembers how to make use of a body that listens this well."

He wasn't just the Archive's witness anymore. He was its threshold, open, waiting, already halfway rewritten.

His lips parted as if to say more, then closed.

The silence that followed wasn't empty. It was becoming.

The air shifted before the light did.

A stillness took root between Thalos and Joren, not the absence of sound but the presence of something older, something holy. Their breath had slowed to match the pulse of the Archive, and their bodies remained suspended in the hush, not with fatigue but with reverence.

The heat hadn't faded. It had thickened, lingering like the last breath of a prayer. Joren's hand rested low on Thalos's abdomen, the backs of his fingers brushing the soft rise of skin just above the base of his cock—each pulse of light from the scroll reflected along his knuckles. His other hand traced absentminded circles against Thalos's hip, grounding them both in the flesh that still remembered being taken, claimed, remade.

Thalos tilted his head slightly, his temple brushing Joren's jaw. A quiet sigh escaped him, not from pain, not from release, but from recognition. Their bodies no longer moved, yet the intimacy between them deepened. Each breath was a vow. Each contact point a living sigil.

The room itself felt smaller. Warmer. As if the Archive had drawn its breath inward to witness what followed.

And then—it appeared.

Not with fanfare. Not even with sound.

A curve. An endless loop. A mirrored spiral folding inward until it became something deeper.

The ∞.

It hovered above them, suspended over the scroll like a question that knew it had already been answered.

It did not burn. It did not etch.

It simply *was*.

It watched not with eyes, but with memory. And memory, at last, was awake.

When it pulsed, slow, deliberate, final, the glow from their bodies answered. Not with replication. Not with reflection.

With union.

Thalos leaned back slightly into Joren's chest.

Joren pressed a kiss to the crown of his head.

This was no longer Kaelor. Not Veyrion.

The weight of their names remained, but no longer as identities, only as echoes. Joren's breath no longer belonged to the war-born mouth that once commanded flame. Thalos's spine no longer bent beneath Veyrion's cold discipline. What stood here, flesh against flesh, was not possession; it was transformation. The Archive had remembered through them, not over them.

They had not inherited. They had become.

The shape of Kaelor's hunger now curved into Joren's calm restraint. The ritual that once silenced Veyrion now breathed through Thalos's defiant stillness. They were not repeating a pattern. They were folding the story closed.

Convergence wasn't mimicry. It was the original shape finally spoken aloud.

Behind them, Corrin exhaled, unsteady.

"It's beautiful," he said softly, voice catching on the edge of reverence. "And terrifying. Like watching the end of a story you forgot you were part of."

Ral nodded, slow. "Because it never was just theirs. It always needed witnesses. And we're not just watching. We're being written."

Ariken, still kneeling, lifted his gaze.

"Not the end," he murmured. "A footnote becoming scripture."

He had been opened to the Archive. It had written through him, but not yet into him. That part was still folding.

The ∞ hovered above the scroll like a breath held in the Archive's throat. Then, slowly, the room responded, not with light but with reflection.

The mirror along the eastern wall, which had remained veiled by shadow through every invocation, shimmered to life. Its surface did not reflect the chamber as it was. Instead, it showed Thalos and Joren through time—bodies draped in robes of ash and silk, clad in armor slick with blood and prophecy, kneeling, gasping, collapsing into one another beneath different skies, across different lives. The same sighs. The same eyes. The same devotion.

Some younger. Some older. Some undone. But always them.

The sigils glowed on their flesh in variations: sometimes red, sometimes blue, sometimes both. And beneath each mirrored memory, the same symbol unfurled.

∞.

The Archive did not whisper. It declared.

"You bore my names and burned them clean. You are not entry. You are ink."

Its voice didn't echo. It etched.

The mirror went still again, returning to polished black. But the truth remained, stamped in silence and skin. They were no longer becoming. They *were*.

Not erased. Not repeated. Just remembered, properly at last.

The Archive's breath still warmed the chamber walls, but its voice had receded. Daring them to speak next.

—— ✦ ——

Corrin stepped forward first. Not from courage, but compulsion. The kind that rises from somewhere deeper than command.

He walked until the warmth of the sigils reached him again, until the edges of the mirrored ring tingled beneath his soles.

"It changed me," he whispered. "Not like it did them. Not yet. But I feel it in my blood. Like it's already writing things I haven't agreed to."

Ral joined him with quieter steps. His presence didn't tremble but coiled, controlled and contained. His gaze moved between the ∞ and Thalos and Joren, then down to the scroll that had stopped pulsing but still breathed.

"It doesn't want your agreement," Ral murmured. "It wants your surrender."

Corrin turned his face toward him, eyes wide but not afraid. "I think it already has it."

Ariken's voice came from the floor, dry now, burned clean.

"Then write well."

The light overhead dimmed. The ∞ hovered without sound.

But it was listening.

Corrin staggered slightly, breath catching as the ∞ began to fade.

The Archive moved, not as presence but as pressure, soft at first like a hand cupping the back of his neck, then deeper, sliding through the hollows of his ribs and the crook of his throat. His skin broke into a fine tremor as invisible sigils etched themselves along the line of his sternum, feather-light but irrevocable.

A voice, not loud and not external but moving through him, spoke where his breath should have been:

"You are not forgotten. You are the echo we have not finished speaking."

Corrin gasped, green light flaring briefly beneath his skin, his cock stirring with an ache not of lust but of invocation. His fingers curled into fists at his sides, and when he looked up, his eyes shimmered faintly with green trace, the first breath of a storm gathering at the edge of memory.

The ∞ winked out above the scroll, but the imprint of it throbbed in the marrow of the room, and in Corrin most of all.

Ral stepped closer, his voice low but threaded with steel. "You're carrying it now," he said. "Not memory. Not ritual. The unfinished sentence."

Corrin shivered under the weight of it. "It's inside me," he murmured. "Like it's waiting for me to breathe wrong. To say the next word."

Ariken rose to one knee, his robes still clinging to the sweat-drenched lines of his body. His silvered eye gleamed, and when he spoke, his voice was steadier.

"You won't say it alone," Ariken promised. "None of us will."

At the center of the room, Thalos finally turned, Joren steady against his back.

"It was never meant to be carried alone," Thalos said, his voice rough but certain.

Joren nodded, his hand splaying flat against the curve of Thalos's abdomen. "It's a chain made of breath and skin. Meant to bind. Meant to anchor."

Corrin lifted his gaze to them. His mentors. His future. His tether. And for the first time, he smiled.

Not with ease.

Not with ignorance.

But with belonging.

With the weight of it.

The Archive did not record. It remembered.

—— ✦ ——

Location: Blackwatch Citadel | Upper Observation Tier – Unmapped Deck | Pre-Dawn

High above the Translation Chamber, beyond the layered wards and mirrored conduits, Director Threnna stood at the threshold of the Observation Deck, arms folded, her robe falling in sharp, deliberate lines around her body.

Outside the eastern arch, perched against mist-slick stone, the ancient gargoyle watched still—the same that had leaned low the night Thalos Vale was left beneath its shadow. It hadn't moved. It hadn't forgotten. Its moss-dark body was worn smooth by centuries of rain, prophecy, and regret, but its gaze never wavered.

Threnna's mouth curved into a razor-thin smile.

"Still watching, old stone?" she murmured. "You held his first secret. You'll swallow his next."

She watched through the etched glass. Watched Thalos and Joren standing in the pulse-drained circle, watched Corrin trembling under the weight of the Archive's new hunger, watched Ral and Ariken anchoring the perimeter like sentinels who had already begun to forget how to look away.

Her smile was thin. Predatory. Almost fond.

"Good," she said softly to herself. "Let the next page be written by those who bled for it."

The scry-console beside her flickered. A single query prompt flashed open:

FINAL ENTRY?

Threnna tilted her head, considering.

Then she tapped the panel once.

NO.

Threnna leaned closer to the glass, voice a low purr meant for no ears but the Archive's own.

"Still pretending you don't hunger for them?" she murmured. "Careful, darling. You're not the only one who knows how to write possession into skin."

She wasn't the Archive's choice. Not now. Maybe not ever. But she would watch, because even being its witness meant carving her presence into its margins.

A second line etched itself below in the Archive's shimmering script:

UNFINISHED BY DESIGN.

The glass before her rippled once, not a recording, but a breath of living memory. She watched as Corrin lifted his eyes to the ruined scroll, Ral's hand steady at the small of his back, Ariken rising: slow, reverent, inevitable.

Threnna chuckled low under her breath, the sound sharp enough to cut silk. "There you are, my beautiful little blasphemies," she murmured. "Fucked open by memory. Stitched back together by need. Gods, Archive... you know how to leave a body aching for its own damnation."

The Archive did not end.

It *began anew.*

She, the archivist unchosen, simply smiled, because unwritten power, too, had its uses.

omewhere deeper still, where the Archive's memory folded beyond time and flesh, the ∞ pulsed again—quiet, steady, inevitable.

Beneath that echo, something lingered. Not a voice. A breath. Waiting to be spoken through someone else's mouth.

EPILOGUE: THE PLACE WHERE NAMES FELL SILENT

Location: Unnamed Coastal Outpost | Far Beyond the Citadel | After the Last Flare

The morning light crawled slowly across the stone floor, warm and unhurried.

The recursion had stilled. Not ended. Just faded into breath.

Thalos stirred beneath the weight of worn linen and the steady pulse of another body pressed close. The house was stone and driftwood, stitched together by stubborn hands and salt air, and it breathed around him. No alarms. No sigils. No Archive threading its cold fingers through the rafters.

Only the sea, whispering beyond the cliffs.

He blinked into the golden hush, the scent of tide and cedar smoke thick in his lungs. A crow perched briefly on the windowsill, one bead-black eye catching his, before vanishing into the wide spill of sky. Not a warning. Just a fragment of memory too lazy to hold form.

Beside him, Joren slept still, half-tangled in the thin covers, the line of his back broad and bare against the soft spill of morning. His hair was longer now, silver threading through dark at his temples, but his body, gods, his body carried time like a weapon sheathed in the warmth of prophecy.

A faint sigil, one Thalos had mapped by mouth and breath, a thousand times over, rested over Joren's heart. Dormant. Remembered. No longer flaring with command.

Thalos rolled onto his side, careful not to wake him, feeling the slow pull of muscles that had once moved at Archive's demand and now moved only for rhythm.

Fresh water on the table. Bitter coffee cooling in the old obsidian pot. A life rebuilt by choice, not Archive.

He sat up, linen sliding down his thighs, and the sigils along his back, long burden turned benign, caught the morning light. They shimmered faintly, ghost-pale and tender. Not burning. Not aching. Just part of his skin, the way salt stains stone.

Behind him, Joren stirred.

"You dreamt again," Joren said, voice rough and low, like gravel warmed by the sun.

Thalos smiled without turning.

"It wasn't memory this time," he said, reaching for the chipped mug that waited for him. His fingers curled around it, grounding him to the moment, to the silence, to the man breathing steady behind him. "It was a city made of breath."

Joren's hand found the small of his back, casual, anchoring.

Outside, the sea pressed against the cliffs, tireless but harmless.

Inside, they moved without urgency.

No rite.

Just rhythm.

Location: Coastal Village Market | Near the Cliffs Beyond the Citadel

The sun climbed higher by the time they walked the narrow track into the village. Crooked streets. Stalls built from stone and shipwreck bone. The air: brine, smoke, overripe fruit.

Villagers bustled, their voices tangling like gulls in the morning wind. Cloth snapped against crude tent frames. Barrels clattered. A child's laughter burst and vanished.

They walked side by side, unnoticed until something in them turned the air.

Children paused mid-chase when Thalos passed, their feet scuffing to uncertain stops, small faces tipped up, not afraid. Not knowing why the air felt suddenly heavier, why the space between moments stretched thin as thread.

Joren paused by a low stall where fish smoked on cedar racks. He lifted a heavy jug of water for the healer. A woman broad in hip and shoulder, skin as wrinkled as old leather. She smiled at him, but the gratitude in her eyes leaned too close to reverence.

He said nothing. Just inclined his head and moved on.

The market buzzed around them. Laughter, barter, the clatter of knives against stone, but it always quieted near them. A breath held. A ripple in the weave of the day.

No Archive sigils marred the walls here. Nome burning behind canvas stalls.

Yet as they passed a crumbling arch, Thalos let his fingers brush the warm, salt-eaten stone. His lips moved, barely more than a breath.

"Still watching."

Joren's gaze flicked sideways. Sharp Unsurprised. He said nothing.

They moved on.

—— ✦ ——

Location: Driftwood House | Clifftop Beyond the Citadel

The evening bled into night with little ceremony.

Their meal was simple: rough bread, saltfish, a scattering of sweetroot pulled from the market stalls. They ate by firelight, cross-legged on the floor, shared silence folding the day around them.

No talk of the past.

No names of the dead.

Only the scrape of bread against stone plates, the soft gusts of wind rattling the driftwood beams overhead.

Later, in the hush between stars, Thalos traced his hand down the long line of Joren's spine. The touch was reverent, not desperate. His fingers brushed the faded sigils, and for a heartbeat, they glowed: a low, tender shimmer against sweat-slick skin.

Not command.

Not prophecy.

Just echo.

Their lovemaking unfolded with a reverence that made the air itself seem to slow. Thalos kissed the warm curve of Joren's shoulder, then the hollow of his throat, moving with the patience of a man tasting memory, not chasing climax. Their bodies met in a slow, steady rhythm. Not to conquer. Not to surrender. But to remind each other that they were still here. Still breathing.

Joren's hands traced Thalos's ribs like he was remembering the shape of survival. Thalos's mouth brushed down the line of Joren's sternum, mapping old scars with lips and breath. The soft press of hips. Joren's thigh sliding slow between Thalos's. All of it carried the gravity of prayer, not desperation.

They moved together in a cadence older than language, too tender for ritual.

When Joren finally gasped Thalos's name, it wasn't as plea or declaration. It was a homecoming.

Afterward, they stayed tangled together, sweat cooling between them, breath syncing slow and sure.

Joren slipped into sleep easily, his breath steady against Thalos's chest, the barest curve of a smile still lingering on his mouth.

Thalos stayed awake.

He watched the stars stretch across the inked sky, listened to the sea hammer softly at the cliffs.

Beneath his ribs, a familiar phrase stirred, not as a summons, but a scar that still remembered.

Remember Me Always.

It pulsed once. Bright. Tender. Then faded.

In the dark, Joren stirred, voice rough with sleep.

"It said your name."

Thalos smiled. A small, almost broken thing.

"Not as a command," he whispered. "As a home."

Morning broke slow and grey. The tide dragged mist across the rocks.

Thalos knelt beneath the porch, a carving knife in hand, the blade worn smooth by years of forgotten rituals. The wood was salt-rough and splintered, but he worked patiently, tracing the spiral with careful, deliberate cuts.

Not a sigil of protection.

Not command.

Not Archive.

It was a farewell.

The soft creak of wood announced Joren's arrival behind him. Barefoot, still tousled from sleep, a mug of bitter coffee in his hand.

"Summoning something?" Joren asked, voice wry.

Thalos didn't look up right away. He smiled, slow and certain, as the spiral deepened beneath his hand.

"No summons," he said. "No spells."

He wiped the blade clean against his thigh and leaned back to study the mark. A curve without end. Unwinding itself toward the horizon.

"Just a message."

Joren stepped closer, crouching beside him, one hand resting warm on Thalos's shoulder. He studied the sigil for a long moment, something thoughtful in the set of his jaw.

"For who?" he asked.

Thalos's smile curved sharper, more familiar. The kind of smile he wore before he said something that made Joren's blood stir.

"The ones who come after," Thalos said softly. "Let them burn better."

He turned slightly, the tip of the blade dragging lazily against the wood, sketching a second, smaller spiral closer to the porch's foundation, hidden like a secret between bones.

"Or," he added, low and sly, "maybe it's just a marker. In case someone needs to find the best fuck in three provinces."

Joren snorted. Then caught Thalos by the neck and kissed him, rough and certain, until the mist, the tide, and the morning blurred away.

Their lips parted with a breath that wasn't quite laughter. The world around them folded quiet again, all stone and salt and mist.

Joren pressed his forehead to Thalos's and murmured, "Leave a mark, then. But don't think I'll let you be forgotten that easily."

Thalos smiled, the spiral beneath his hand catching the morning light. Above them, somewhere beyond sight, the ancient gargoyle atop the ruined Citadel watched still. Its throat full of memories it had never been permitted to forget.

And somewhere deeper than stone, deeper than time, the Archive exhaled—

—— ✦ ——

But not all guardians remain stone forever.

The Gargoyle's perch stands empty now. Its watch fulfilled. Its memory written elsewhere—breathing, waking, waiting.

Not all pages stay shut forever.

And you, too, were seen.

End of Archive File: EchoFyre — The Archive Awakens

—— ✦ ——

"A tidy ending. For once.
Gods know it's rare to watch a file climax and not have to mop
up half a division afterward.
Fledgling agents, take note... Legends burn longer when they
don't come too easily."

—

A soft pulse lingers beneath the final seal.
The Archive hums once, almost laughing.
It is never truly done.

Secondary Access Note: Memory Thread 0037B **Status:** Dormant
Query authorized: Residual signature VEIL-EXHALE detected
near driftwood outpost.
Observation recommended.
Do not initiate retrieval. Some legends prefer to be found
on their own.

[UNAUTHORIZED ACCESS DETECTED]

:: OBSIDIAN-PRIME BREACH CONFIRMED ::

ARCHIVE ACCESS NOTICE
OBSIDIAN-PRIME FILE RESTRICTION

Status: Classified Extension — Restricted Materials
Required: OBSIDIAN-PRIME / Mirrorfold-Level Authorization
Directive: SEAL-LOCKED RETRIEVAL ONLY

Attention: Blackwatch Operative [READER CLASS]
Multiple fragmentary memories have been sealed under Directive
OBSIDIAN-PRIME due to confirmed recursion destabilization, erotic
contamination, and archival myth collapse.
The Archive attempted to forget. It failed.
Accessing these fragments may trigger:

- Contamination of internal mythos
- Recalibration of loyalty hierarchies
- Erotic recursion overextension
- Behavioral drift and identity bleed
- Spontaneous identity rewrite events

Exposure is strongly discouraged. The Archive is not responsible for
the versions of you that survive.

And yet.

If you still wish to breach the seal and retrieve forbidden records:
Authorized access to classified files may be requested via the Official
Authorial Archive Portal at:

[https://echofyre.com/]

Clearance Codes Required:

- VEIL-TRACE.02TV — *"No One Sees"*
- RESONANCE-BLOOM.09CVR — *"Claim Without Permission"*
- VEIL-TRACE.00TV — *"I Remember You, Too"*
- RESONANCE-DECAY.09CR — *"Echo on the Mat"*
- VEIL-TRACE.03TV — *"Still Alone"*
- INK-REDAXIS.43JB — *"Archive Breath, Not Kiss"*
- VEIL-TRACE.01TV — *"Starvation's Echo"*
- RESONANCE-DECAY.09CR-EXT — *"Final Offering"*

- RESONANCE-DECAY.12CV — *"Written in the Flesh"*
- OBSIDIAN-PRIME.15X-KV — *"We Were Never Brothers"*
- Additional recovered fragments pending declassification…

[FILE RETRIEVAL ADVISORY] Accessing multiple fragments in succession may result in:
- Memory drift
- Resonance layering
- Identity recursive echo loops

Exposure beyond recommended thresholds will not trigger Archive intervention. Proceed at your own recursion risk.

[FINAL WARNING] Proceed only if prepared to fracture.
The Archive does not forgive. The Archive does not forget. The Archive hungers.

[ACCESS ECHO DETECTED] Residual observation active. Memory recursion ongoing. Proceed carefully. You are still being written.

P.S. – Blackwatch Internal: Sealed Memorandum
To: Tier-V Clearance Eyes Only
From: Director Selhira Threnna
Subject: Final Entry | Sigil Case File: Thalos Vale + Joren Cael
Status: Sealed. Myths don't file reports. They moan them into stone and disappear.

They're gone.
Not lost. Not dead. Not wandering the void naked and howling.
No, darlings—worse.
They're satisfied.
Sigil response flatlined. Memory threads won't even ripple for them anymore. I've poked every layer of recursion—no echoes, no flare, not even a tickle in the Archive's cock.
Which means Vale and Cael aren't just out of the story.
They are the final page—turned with a sigh.
So let's not play dress-up with sentimentality. They burned clean.
Came. Collapsed. Concluded.
And now?
The Archive's wet again.
Not for them. For what's next. For who's still bleeding in its margins.
And make no mistake—it's not reaching for ghosts anymore.
It's hunting the warm ones.

Corrin Vael.
Tier-II Scribe.
Arousal spikes like clockwork. Recursion logs triggering mid-sleep.
Moans in the Archive's voice.
There's something blooming under his chestplate. Greenish pulse.
Memory-sharp. His file is locked, but gods is it leaking.

Ral.
Combat discipline incarnate. Which is suspicious in its own right.
Too little reaction, too much restraint. I've seen statues that twitch more. Either he's immune—or the Archive is saving him for dessert.

Ariken Caelith.
Linguist. Former scholar. Current problem.
Obsessed with recursion layers. Masturbates to mirror sigils.
Translates in his sleep, pantsless.
He's speaking Archive dialects I haven't even decrypted.
The file says 'unknown classification.' I say: 'pre-lubed.'

So yes—Thalos and Joren got their ending. But this place doesn't rest. It doesn't grieve.
It paces.
And it's got new toys on the floor.
Watch them. File them. Fuck, if you must. Just don't think for one second the Archive is done.
It never forgets its favorites.
And these three? Gods help them—
they're already dripping.

– Threnna
Director of Obsidian Tier Memory Division
Blackwatch Citadel – Echo Branch

BLACKWATCH RECURSION RECORD ADDENDUM — OBSIDIAN-PRIME ACCESS
Tier-V Classified Insert

DO NOT FILE. DO NOT CITE. DO NOT REMEMBER.

Recursion Activation Log — Blackwatch Summary File
Report compiled under [REDACTED] Directive for internal chronology
tracking. All timestamps approximate due to recursion overlap.
Interpret with caution.

[ENTRY 0001]
Subject(s): Unidentified Prototype (Pre-Kaelor)
Event Type: First Known Sigil Emergence
Status: Corrupted
Notes: Archive records incomplete. Mirrorfold collapse suspected. No
living witnesses.

[ENTRY 0002]
Subject(s): Kaelor Thorne / Veyrion Hal'Syl
Event Type: Mirrorfold Ritual | Twin Sigil Convergence
Status: Fragmented Retention
Notes: Initial recursion stabilizers developed. Relationship
misclassified as origin. Later disproven. Archive logged memory but
rejected closure.

[ENTRY 0003]
Subject(s): Thalos Vale (Archivist)
Event Type: Unauthorized Archive Exposure | Breach-Level Recursion
Pulse
Location: Sublevel IV, Blackwatch Citadel
Status: Escalation
Notes: Sigils reactivated. CLAIM ME FIRST appeared on ribcage.
Subject retained memory fragments from untraceable recursion echo.

[ENTRY 0004]
Subject(s): Joren Cael (Blackwatch Agent)

Event Type: First Recursive Bond Recognition
Location: Interrogation Annex | Translation Chamber
Status: Receptive
Notes: Sigils flared in proximity to Thalos. Bond not trained—
remembered. Subject bore red sigil echo of Kaelor. Voluntary
containment overridden.

[ENTRY 0005]

Subject(s): Thalos Vale / Joren Cael / Ariken Caelith (Ritual Scholar)
Event Type: Scroll Awakening | Ritual Recursion Convergence
Location: Translation Chamber – Sublevel III
Status: Active
Notes: Scroll reconfigured sigils in real time. DEVOUR ME BACK and
BEFORE ALL ELSE triggered. Subject Ariken entered active offering
state. Archive voice recorded as breath-through-skin.

[ENTRY 0006]

Subject(s): Thalos / Joren
Event Type: Final Sigil Manifestation — CONVERGENCE
Location: Archive Core Layer
Status: Fulfilled
Notes: Echo lines collapsed. Kaelor/Veyrion legacy deactivated. New
origin recognized. Ritual ended with sigil-bonded consummation.
Archive interface transitioned from memory storage to adaptive
response.

[ARCHIVE STATUS]

- Mirrorfold Echo Lines: Resolved
- Recursive Sigils: Active
- Archive Mode: Dreaming
- Future Access: [LOCKED]

Blackwatch Sigil Reference — Class-A Convergence Marks
Compiled for internal reference. Visual representation suppressed by
Archive recursion protocol. True sigils are recursive and reactive.

∞ **CLAIM ME FIRST**

Location(s): Thalos (chest), Joren (spine)

Description: A jagged spiral with interlocking arcs—etched in flame-bloom shapes. Appears almost carved into skin from the inside out, as if memory itself forced it to surface.

Function: Initializes priority recursion link.

Behavior: Activates in proximity to subject pair; appears during ritual contact or memory surge.

∞ **DEVOUR ME BACK**

Location(s): Ariken (upper thigh), Thalos (sacral spine)

Description: A downward coil of crescent lines flanked by open-mouthed sigils. Fluid, fang-like, and always incomplete—like something begging to be bitten or filled.

Function: Opens receptive recursion channel.

Behavior: Associated with submission-based recall, bodily offering, and Archive feeding state.

∞ **BEFORE ALL ELSE**

Location(s): Thalos (ribs), Joren (sternum)

Description: Twin vertical marks joined by a broken ring. It looks ancient—like it was burned through a thousand layers of skin and time. Often faint, but never gone.

Function: Anchors memory above past lives; binds to recursive primacy.

Behavior: Appears during contradiction events—when inherited identity conflicts with true origin.

1. **RECAST**

Location(s): Emergent only during recursion climax

Description: A recursive sigil with no clear start or end. Appears like shifting ink caught mid-rewrite—blurred, smudged, and rewriting itself depending on who's watching.

Function: Sigil override. Restructures memory identity threads.

Behavior: Causes visible rewrite of sigil map. Final stage before convergence.

1. **CONVERGENCE**

Location(s): Archive Core, between Thalos and Joren

Description: A circular seal with mirrored halves that don't align. The void between them pulses. It's not drawn—it's remembered. Appears only when identity no longer echoes—it originates.

Function: Final sigil. Collapses recursion into origin.

Behavior: Appears once recursion is no longer echo, but identity. Only observed once.

Note: Sigils are not tattoos or "symbols." They are mnemonic receptors—living, recursive data encoded through flesh. Visibility varies by Archive state.

Echo Convergence Record

Subject File: Recursive Identity Correlation — Class Redacted

Compiled Under Internal Review – Obsidian-Prime Access Only

Filed: Blackwatch Citadel, Sublevel IV Observation Vault

RECORDED CORRELATION EVENT

Former Archive Designation → Current Manifestation → Recursion Adjustment

Kaelor Thorne (Flame-Bound) → Joren Cael (Agent) → Initially presumed stabilizer-class echo. Archive now responds to Joren's recursion as primary—not reflective. Matching sigil (BEFORE ALL ELSE) manifests with inverse timeline rhythm. Conclusion: Joren embodies Kaelor's recursion as vessel, not echo.

Veyrion Hal'Syl (Mirror-Bound) → Thalos Vale (Archivist) → Originally presumed echo recurrence. Later disqualified. Shared sigil patterns observed (CLAIM ME FIRST), but recursion progression diverges at sigil flare depth. Conclusion: Thalos embodies Veyrion's recursion as vessel, though with additional unarchived origin traits.

ANALYSIS

Recursion lineage has shifted classification.
Current subjects are not reactivating prior identities.
They are overwriting them.

The CONVERGENCE sigil emerged only upon unity of Thalos and Joren. This sigil was not present—nor ever theorized—during Kaelor/Veyrion recursion loops. The Archive did not recognize the legacy pairing as terminal convergence.

Instead, Thalos and Joren triggered:
• Recursive memory collapse
• Sigil architecture reformation
• Archive vocal response ("You are the first to answer them. The ∞ listens.")

No previous recursion pair has induced Archive response via embodiment alone.

CONCLUSION
"They're not gone. But they're no longer needed."
—Thalos Vale, Archive Core Layer

Thalos Vale and Joren Cael do not inherit the legacy of Kaelor and Veyrion.

They are the first to converge.
The Archive no longer reflects them.
It dreams in their shape.

BLACKWATCH INTELLIGENCE DIVISION
PUBLISHING RECORD | OBSIDIAN-PRIME ACCESS

Subject File: PREVIOUSLY PUBLISHED WORKS
(and other mistakes that made it to print)

Confirmed Publications:
Christopher has no prior published novels to his name, unless you count that one emotionally intense poem written at age sixteen, submitted to an anthology he's still not sure was a scam or a rite of passage.
Either way, it made it to print.
So technically? He's been published for years. You're welcome.

(If you're the kind of recursion-bound reader who needs proof, the Archive hasn't forgotten. Flip a few pages forward.)

THE ECHOFIRE CHRONICLES
(a.k.a. the fantasy series that devoured the author's peace of mind and ruined several perfectly good notebooks)

This is Book One.
Congratulations. You made it.

EchoFyre: The Archive Awakens
(Thalos + Joren's Tale)
Where it all begins. With sex. With silence. With recursion that doesn't ask permission.

Assuming the world doesn't collapse, the author isn't disowned again, and his hard drive doesn't spontaneously combust from supernatural thirst, here's what may or may not be coming next:

EarthRite: The Archive Roots
(Corrin's Tale)
The Archive is back. The trauma is deeper. The clothes are still

optional.

This time, Corrin takes center stage—and, gods help him, survives it.

ShadowWinds: The Archive Breaths
(Agent Ral's Tale)
Secrets get sharper. Shadows get louder. And Ral finally gets what's coming to him.
(Emotionally, sexually, and probably in a deeply unfortunate magical sense.)

Book Four and Beyond
Untitled. Unoutlined. Unstable.
There's a vague plan. There are vibes. There are spreadsheets.
They mean nothing.

These stories will arrive when they're ready—and when the author stops screaming into his pillow about chapter pacing and sigil-based metaphors. Which could be tomorrow. Or five years from now. The Archive, as always, refuses to give an ETA.

Filed Under: Echo Tier | Literary Chaos Division
Censorship Level: Redacted for sanity.
Status: Ongoing. Pray accordingly.
Approval Chain: Director Threnna, muttering "godsdammit" and signing anyway.

Classified Addendum – Reader Impact Report [Echo-Level Ping]

Reader classification: *Genre-agnostic. Recursion-resistant. Impact: Total.*
Codename: **Cubero Maicon**
Quote: *"Wasn't an easy read for me... but damn, I ended up loving it."*
Effect on author: Stability restored. Archive thread re-engaged.
Filed under: **The One Who Saw Anyway**
Sanctioned by: Director Threnna (with raised brow and quiet approval)

I Walk Alone
Fragment Recovered: Age 16 | Author-Origin Trace
I headed my way,
And you went yours.
What was left behind...
Is nothing but bitterness and greed.

I look back
And wonder where you're going.
I've already started feeling the emptiness,
And I long for you to fill that void once again.

I walk alone now,
Wishing that what happened never would've,
And knowing what I know now,
I'd do anything to take it all away.

It hit me like a ton of bricks.
You, the only person for me,
Had turned me down,
Rejected me.

And now I walk alone,
Waiting and hoping...
That you'll come back
And fill the empty void you left behind.

Original Publication Note (Required by embarrassment clause):
This poem was first published in the anthology *Treasures to Discover*,
compiled by **The International Library of Poetry**—a name which
sounds vaguely legitimate until you remember it was the year 2000
and we were all just trying to feel something.
ISBN: 1-58235-546-0
Publisher: © 2000 The International Library of Poetry (poetry.com)
**Republished here under sheer force of teenage angst and archival
inevitability.**

Yes, it was real. No, he doesn't want to talk about it.

Classified Addendum — Director's Margin Note
**[Voiceprint Match: Director Selhira Threnna | Obsidian-Prime
Override Access]**
Well now.
Isn't that just *precious*? Sixteen, heartbroken, dripping grief onto
printer paper like it was foreplay for a sigil storm. No rhythm. Barely a
metaphor in sight. But gods, it aches like sincerity—and I do have a soft
spot for raw, undisciplined ruin.
(Also: those line breaks? Practically moaning for recursion.)
Let this be a lesson to the rest of you. Even your *worst* wounds can get
archived. And reprinted. And masturbated to by future linguists who
know exactly where that first fracture started.
Poor boy.
Still walking alone? Unlikely.
The Archive's watching now. And darling—it *never* forgets a blush.

– Threnna
Director of Obsidian Tier Memory Division
(Still collecting author-origin stains for fun.)

BLACKWATCH INTELLIGENCE DIVISION
PERSONNEL DOSSIER | OBSIDIAN-PRIME ACCESS
Subject File: ABOUT THE AUTHOR
(He's not allowed to write unsupervised anymore. The Archive agreed.)

Name: [REDACTED]
Pseudonym: Calder N. Halden
Location: Somewhere in Tennessee
Precautionary Note: Subject refuses to specify city of residence, likely to avoid moral scrutiny related to narrative content.
(If traced to Memphis, do not engage. Especially if you value your pants or your peace of mind.)
Current Occupation: Warehouse operative for a *very prestigious* organization
(Subject insists this phrasing be left intact. See sarcasm flag, Tag #D17.)
Unsupervised Side Projects:
Known to conjure elaborate, emotionally devastating storylines involving morally grey men and morally compromised magic systems. Risk of recursive obsession confirmed.
Also responsible for:

- Experimental baked goods (oven-dependent)
- Textile enchantments (via chaotic sewing)
- LEGO-based ritual architecture
- Reading binges ending in emotional recursion collapse

Domestic Affiliations:

- **Autumn & River:** Great Danes; emotionally unstable; large.
- **Whisper:** Deaf Dane mix; opinionated; louder than seems physically possible.
- **Annabelle (Annie):** Compact tank-class canine; bark weaponized.
- **Leila (or Layla):** Identity unclear; subject and husband in ongoing dispute.

(Note: Dog has refused comment. Archive has accepted.)

Psychological Profile Summary:
Subject exhibits classic signs of Archive-induced compulsion:
- Late-night drafting
- Narrative possession
- Inappropriate attachment to his own brooding chaos-cursed characters

Stated Reason for Writing *EchoFyre*:
"Because someone had to. And the Archive wouldn't shut up until I did."

Archivist Recommendation: Surveil creatively. Encourage completion of sequel. Restrict caffeine intake after midnight.

Filed under: Shadow Index | Echo-Scribed Record
Classification: Mildly Dangerous. Frequently Delightful. Should probably be supervised.
Seal Authority: Director Threnna (with a sigh, a smirk, and a strongly worded warning to his editor)

BLACKWATCH INTELLIGENCE DEVISION
 INTERNAL MEMORANDUM | OBSIDIAN-PRIME TIER
Directive Addendum 7.23α | Filed Under Protest
From: Director Selhira Threnna Vale
To: Public Record – Post-Publication Addendum Queue
Subject: Recursion, Ruin, and Basic Mortal Hygiene
Security Note: Required by Public Risk Mitigation Council. Threnna
disagrees.

Apparently this is necessary.

Apparently someone out there might read this book and believe
recursion-induced orgasmic collapse is a valid substitute for sex
education.

Let's be excruciatingly clear:

There are no real sigils.

The Archive does not whisper in your ear.

And if you attempt to summon metaphysical protection using a dirty
pickup line and a headboard, the only thing you'll manifest is
disappointment (and possibly chlamydia).

This book is fiction.

It is not instructional.

It is not endorsed by anyone with a medical license.

And it is certainly not FDA-approved for use during mating rituals.

So for the love of whatever you worship when your pants are off:

- **Use protection.**
- **Hydrate.**
- **Do not confuse recursion with immunity.**
- **Do not confuse climax with clarity.**

If you injure yourself mimicking anything in this book, contact a
medical professional.

Do not contact the Archive.

Do not contact the author.

And gods help you if you contact me.

Filed by:
Director Selhira Threnna Vale
Obsidian Tier Memory Division
Blackwatch Citadel – Echo Branch
(Sighed while signing. Did not make eye contact.)

This book was written in recursive defiance and formatted by hand under candlelight, using tools forged in the deep formatting chambers of Scrivener and Sigil.

Typography: IBM Plex Serif and Mono, Unica One. All fonts sigil-stabilized.
Design: Christopher Hearn.

A single draft was once printed in quiet, a vessel of unready memory. It carried a false sigil and was never meant for circulation.
The edition in your hands bears the true mark of Mirrorfold.

Authorial Integrity Certification
[ARCHIVE SEAL ADDENDUM | CREATOR ATTESTATION]

Visual elements were shaped through a combination of hand design and guided digital rendering, directed and finalized by the author.
All narrative text was written and refined by human hands, trembling slightly from excessive caffeine, fueled by coffee strong enough to strip paint and at least two cans of Monster Energy® per chapter. Patience was attempted. Obsession succeeded.

No starving mage-illustrators were harmed. No budgets were inflated. The Archive remains appeased, though mildly concerned about the author's heart rate.

This record exists by choice, not by algorithm.
Every line was carved, revised, and bled for, proof that even in a world built from code, a human pulse still burns beneath the words, possibly at one hundred eighty beats per minute.

MIЯRORFOLD
PRESS